FRAGRANT HARBOUR

by the same author

THE DEBT TO PLEASURE
MR PHILLIPS

JOHN LANCHESTER

Fragrant Harbour

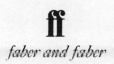

faber and faber

First published in 2002
by Faber and Faber Limited
3 Queen Square London WC1N 3AU

Typeset by Faber and Faber Ltd
Printed in England by Clays Ltd, St Ives plc

A CIP record for this book
is available from the British Library

ISBN 0–571–20176–8

2 4 6 8 10 9 7 5 3 1

In memory of my mother

This book is a work of fiction. All the characters and incidents in it are imaginary.

Conventions for rendering Chinese names changed in the course of the twentieth century. Canton is now Guangzhou, Peking is Beijing, Fukien is Fujian, and so on. Characters in this novel use the form of name appropriate to their time and place.

PROLOGUE

Tom Stewart

Longevity can be a form of spite. I am an old man myself now, and I recognise the symptoms.

This morning I met my nearest neighbour, Ming Tsin-Ho, on the path down into the village. Ming lives a hundred yards below me in a house with an ugly red-moon gate. On top of the gate is a purple dragon with green eyes and a yellow tongue. Ming bought this monstrosity in the New Territories and had it shipped here in one piece to be dragged up the hill by coolies.

The Chinese like dragons. They think of them as benign. Chinese dragons have many magical attributes, including the ability to choose whether or not they wish to be visible.

I like the fact that the South China Sea has so many moods. Sometimes the water is blue and translucent; sometimes a dirty, turbulent brown. Today it was a choppy grey-green. A faint haze blurred the view over to Hong Kong island. It was a cool morning by local standards. Ming was standing looking at his gate. He was wearing black loose-cut trousers and a white jacket and his absolutely bald head was glistening. He had an expression I had never seen before, a glassiness around the eyes which for a moment made me think he must be drunk. I looked more closely and realised the unfamiliar expression was in fact a smile, a glee he was unable to suppress. He had the air of wanting to talk. I said:

'Good morning, Mr Ming.'

'Mr Stewart – this is a sad morning. I have just heard the news of my poor brother's death,' he said, beaming, in Cantonese.

So that was it. Ming's brother was a star of Cantonese opera, an authentic celebrity in that rebarbative form. My grandson had even once taken me to see him in a film, God help me, a comedy dominated by slapstick and the broad physical humour of what in Britain would have been music hall. Ming had not been on speaking terms with his famous younger sibling for the best part of half a century. It was a great topic of conversation on Cheung

Chau island, where we both live. Once, when Ming had sued one of the local seafood restaurants after tripping over a chair on the pavement, they had retaliated by displaying posters of his brother in the window until the case was settled out of court. Now Ming was straightforwardly and unmistakably glad that his brother was dead. He held out a copy of *Today*, one of the least bad of the Chinese newspapers.

'Nothing in here yet. It will be in the evening papers,' he said, still beaming.

PART ONE
Dawn Stone

Chapter One

When I was a teenager I used to play a game called Count the Lies. The idea was pretty simple: I just made a mental note of every time I heard someone tell a porky, and kept a running total. It was a one-player game, a form of solitaire. Some days I started playing the game after some more than usually gross piece of hypocrisy or cant at school, some days it would be triggered by something I saw on TV or heard on the radio or read in a paper or magazine or book. Most of the time, though, what started me off on Count the Lies was my parents. It wasn't so much any specific thing they said as the whole family atmosphere. It was the air we – even that 'we' was a kind of lie – breathed. Some days the lies I counted began with 'Good morning' (Why? What's good about it?), carried on through 'We want you back by half past eleven' (No you don't, you don't want me back at all) and finished with 'Goodnight' (the lie here being: oh so you care, do you?).

If I had to explain in a sentence why I came to Hong Kong and why I now do what I do, that sentence would be this: money doesn't lie.

Money doesn't lie. It can't. People lie about money, but that's different.

I have no false modesty about my abilities – in case it ever seems as if I do, let me now state for the record that I think I'm shit-hot – but I nonetheless freely admit I wouldn't have done the things I have without four big breaks. The first of them was my job on the middle-market middle-England tabloid, the *Toxic*. (Not its real name.) Prior to that my life went like this: home, school, Durham University, journalism course at Cardiff, job on local paper in Blackpool. I should explain that I am just old enough to have grown up in the days when you were expected to train in journalism on regional papers before moving to London and the nationals. This was back in the Palaeolithic, before Eddie Shah took on the unions and Murdoch broke them. Mastodons roamed the banks of the Thames. Some tribes had not yet learned the secret of fire. Men were men, women were women, small furry animals lived in well-justified fear, and the only people allowed to operate the A3 photocopier in the corner of the office were members of the National Graphics Association. Say what you like about Mrs Thatcher.

Nowadays someone as bright and ambitious and sassy as I thought I was would start hawking pieces to magazines and papers while still at college, and the plan would be to bypass all that grubby cloth-cap crap about reporting and head as quickly as possible for the clean, well-lit uplands of commentary, opinion, and a column with your second most flattering photo at the top. (Second most flattering, because if you chose the best one (a) your colleagues would take the piss out of you for being vain and (b) people who met you would think, oh, she looks nice in the photo but in real life she could pass for a boxer's dog.) This, however, was the old days. So I spent eighteen months in Blackpool at the *Argus*, doing all the usual stuff from local fairs to sport to news (Granny drives Reliant Robin over cliff, survives) to gradually more interesting court cases, to features and eventually – yes – a column. Since the choice of snaps was provided by Eric the staff photographer the idea of a flattering picture was relative. It was more a question of finding one which didn't make me look like Mussolini.

The other thing which happened was I changed my name. I was christened Doris. Doris! These days I could probably sue my parents for damages. The trouble is that anyone stupid enough to call a child Doris won't have any assets worth suing for. Dawn Stone made an infinitely better byline.

There were lots of local papers. Blackpool wasn't a random choice. It was, is, regularly the site of party conferences, and I reckoned that if I couldn't make useful contacts with the nationals during party conferences I might as well give up and train as a solicitor (which was Plan B). I hope I sound as obsessed as I actually was with this issue of breaking out into the nationals. I daresay if I'd gone to Oxbridge I would have had at least half a dozen chums who fell out of bed and into useful, networkable positions on the kind of paper I wanted to work for. But I didn't, and I didn't, and I knew that I would have to make any contacts I would use. It was a comfort to tell myself that I wouldn't have had it any other way.

I had my first brushes with the nationals about two months before my first party conference season, during a missing-child case which turned into a search for a body and then, about six months later, into a murder case. (It was the stepfather. Imagine everybody's surprise.) The story would normally have been out of my league at the paper, as a new arrival, but I had written the initial 'Where's Little Jimmy?' item and so I stayed with it, on and off, until I left. The London hacks were all over it from the start, richer and pushier and yobbier than I had expected, though the man I met and became friends with, Bob Berkowitz, was none of those things. He turned up at the office one day looking for Ken, an old mate from the *Brighton Courier*, now the *Argus*'s chief reporter. I looked up from my manual typewriter – there's a Flintstones-era detail – and saw a short shy man with dark curly hair and glasses, carrying a coat and looking tactically bewildered; bewildered in that way people look when they want you to notice and to offer help.

'Can I help you?' I asked, almost certainly in a not very helpful way, a twenty-four-year-old girl scowling over a desk.

'Is Ken around?'

'Out on a story.'

He looked at his watch, frowning. 'But the pubs are shut,' he said. I gave him one of those laughs you do to show you appreciate the effort someone's made in making a joke, and we got talking.

Berkowitz was a cut above the usual reptile – that was part of the signal he sent. He wrote longish reportage for the *Toxic* and was out-of-the-closet-except-to-his-mother-who-probably-knew-but-it-was-never-spoken-about gay. One evening at his flat near Tower Bridge he told me he was 'an intellectual', thus becoming the only working journalist I ever heard use the word about himself. We hit it off right from the start.

'It's not so much a piece about the kid's disappearance *per se*,' Berkowitz explained to me later, across the road, in the pub we called The Dead Brian. (Real name, The Red Lion.) 'I'm interested

5

in the effect of these crimes on people and on communities. The aftershocks. What happens at the time when the story isn't on the front pages any more? How do people get on with their lives?'

I was able to help him out with some contacts and background stuff, and he was nicer about asking for it than people from the nationals usually were; they tended to come over all smarmy and 'we're all in this together' when they needed a favour, and the rest of the time acted like they had it on good authority that their own shit didn't smell. This was something I got a good look at during that conference, Kinnock's second as party leader, the one after the one when he fell on his bum in the water while trying to walk along the beach looking dignified and visionary. That conference has happy memories for me, because it was the occasion of my first break. I went out for a few drinks on the last but one evening with Berkowitz and a couple of his London friends. One of them was a broadsheet hack, another was a Tory apparatchik, a back-room boy for one of the big shots, in town for a bit of spying and to write a think-piece for one of the right-wing papers. Berkowitz left early to file some copy, and the rest of us ended up at my flat, where we got exceptionally drunk. I don't remember how the evening finished, other than being sick and going to bed at some point around five, having somehow called a cab for the apparatchik before passing out. The hack was on the sofa, having conked out a while before.

Gosh, how I don't miss so many things about my twenties. I had to work the next day. The morning was heavy going. I kept sneaking off to the loo and dry-retching. At lunchtime there was a buzz from reception saying someone had come to see me. It was the Tory back-room boy. He was wearing dark glasses and looked as hung over as any human being I had ever seen. At close range I noticed he was trembling slightly. He had changed his suit but still smelt of drink.

'Can we go somewhere?'

For a split second I wondered if we had had sex at some point in the depths of the night before. No – I might be blurry on the details, but I was confident I'd remember that.

There was a crappy hotel with a crappy bar not far away. We went there and he ordered two Bloody Marys. By this time I found I could remember his name: Trevor.

'Feeling a bit rough,' he said, playing with the swizzle stick. When he took the shades off, his eyes were bloodshot. We took his-and-hers swigs of our drinks.

'Bit out of line last night,' he said. 'Thing is, I told you a couple of things I shouldn't have. You know. Real D-notice stuff. I'll have to ask you to keep it, er, them, under your, er, hat. I could lose my job.'

He was having trouble with his tone. That last remark wasn't sure whether it wanted to be a plea or a threat. I put my hand on his wrist for a second.

'I won't breathe a word.'

'Really?'

'Really.'

'I can't tell you how grateful I am.'

'Think nothing of it.'

'I won't forget this.'

He finished his drink. He looked at his watch.

'Well –'

'Don't let me keep you. Thanks for the drink.'

'No, thank *you*.'

He scuttled off.

I had then, and have still, no idea what secret he was talking about, but six weeks later I had a call from the diary editor of the *Toxic*, who had been at university with our Trev. He asked if I could send some clippings and 'pop down to London for a chat'. That was my first break.

Robin Robbins, diary editor of the *Toxic*, was the first posh person I ever got to know well. He had a posh person's affectation of using language that either exaggerated or minimised the amount of effort involved in doing something. In his world people 'strolled' over to the East End to cover a gangster's funeral, and 'hurtled' to the stationery cupboard to get a new typewriter ribbon. To 'pop' meant to take a six-hour round trip to London by train, and to 'chat' meant to undergo a job interview.

He took me to lunch. The restaurant was airy, light, noisy, and metropolitan. The waiters wore blue-and-white striped aprons cut open across the back to show their bums. One of them flirted with me, which helped me to feel, albeit very faintly, as if I knew what was going on. Robin did a certain amount of Durham/ Cardiff/Blackpool small talk, and asked me how I knew Berkowitz, who he said had 'something terribly New York about him'. (This meant that Berkowitz was Jewish.) Robin asked me what I thought about Princess Diana's dress sense. I called her Lady Diana and he corrected me by using the right locution without any emphasis. Something about him made me aware that for the first time in my life I was meeting someone who would genuinely, literally, given the right circumstances, sell his grandmother. It was an exciting feeling.

'What's the most important thing for any diary journalist?' Robin asked.

I thought: self-hate. I said:

'Contacts!'

By the time we got to coffee he was talking about the job.

'The diary is where new talent gets its first try on the paper. It's our nursery, our colts team, our apprentices' workshop. It's where most people started, present company included. As I said when I rang you, this is not a permanent job, as such. Three months, with the prospect of more work after if we get along, from your point of view as well as ours. By the end of that time you'll probably be my boss, or editing one of our rival papers.'

And if it doesn't work out, tough shit. For my leaving do in Blackpool, we went to the Dead Brian and then drunk-drove dodgem cars.

The diary was a gossip column, and the page – Dexter Williams's Diary, after its notional founder – was the usual mix of anonymous innuendo and spite and half-truth, concentrating on the worlds of media, showbiz, politics, and the explosively burgeoning field of the famous-for-being-famous. Nothing wrong with that, you might well say, given that it's what the customers are known to want – and *Toxic* market research showed that Dexter was one of the first things the punters turned to in the morning. The trouble was, I hated everything about it. To get stories you needed contacts, and I didn't have any; plus, not having done anything like it before, I found that I couldn't bear the whole business of picking up fag ends, working stories up out of nothing, and all the rest. One of the ways in which people usually

8

made a start as diarists was by shopping friends – i.e. taking things friends had told them in confidence and turning them into saleable pieces. Posh people and people with London connections had a big head start.

To make it worse, I was not the only person who had been taken on to do 'my' job. This was standard management practice at the *Toxic*, part of the culture: you would give two people the same job description and resources, see who came out on top, and then sack the other one, usually by moving them sideways and downwards to a job they couldn't possibly accept. As a management technique this was impressively horrible. The person given the same job as me was a chubby public schoolboy called Rory Waters.

On my first day I arrived a careful three minutes early to find him sitting at the next desk, already typing something (what? what?).

'Er, I'm Dawn,' I said.

'How d'ye do?' said Rory.

'This is Rory,' said Robin, arriving out of nowhere and looking, as usual, like the obvious murder suspect in a production of Agatha Christie. 'He's just joined us, and he'll be helping us out a bit here too. I'm sure' – this with a hint of menace – 'you'll hit it off famously.'

Rory was posh, pushy, and thick. He had a round white face with a pink shaving rash around the collar of his striped shirt and, like all the other boys on the diary, he wore suits all the time. Worst of all, everybody at the *Toxic* seemed to love him. I suppose that was because he didn't mind being a bit of a joke; this made him easy to tease, to laugh with instead of at, and therefore to work with too. The way in which he and the other men on the diary – it was Robin, four men and me; I was also the only one educated in the state system – slipped instantly into male-bonded mode could not have wound me up more. I was uptight, on the defensive, constantly aware of being on probation, in a new job, a new city, despising my colleagues and wanting to fit in with them at the same time, doing work which was completely unlike what I'd expected and for which I had no aptitude. Every morning I woke up feeling as if I'd swallowed something that was working its way around my stomach.

At the end of my third day at the *Toxic*, after I'd put together a world-shaking item about some D-list cokehead actor telling a paparazzo to fuck off outside San Lorenzo's, Berkowitz invited me to go for a drink in the Paranoia Factory, as the office wine bar was known. He told me that he was going to leave the *Toxic* to go and work for a broadsheet I'll call the *Sensible*.

'They want me to write explanatory narrative pieces,' he said, adding, somewhere between pride and sheepishness, 'Apparently they liked the stuff I did about little Jimmy in Blackpool.'

I felt not tearful exactly, but the possibility of tears. I only knew one person at the *Toxic*, and he was leaving.

'Great,' I said. 'Just great. I'm thrilled for you.'

There may be people who do their best work in an environment where they feel friendless, isolated, paranoid, conspired against, tokenised, objectivised, and chippy. I'm not one of them. I will spare the details of the next three months. In Blackpool I had lived in a high-ceilinged flat with a view over the sea; I could come and go without bumping into anyone, and if I had a half pint of milk in the fridge when I went to bed I could get up in the morning and be confident it would still be there. I didn't have to listen to anyone else's music, field anyone else's phone calls, console anyone else for their troubles, or remove anyone else's pubic hair from the bath plug. In London, living in a shared house in Stockwell with a solicitor friend from Durham and three of her new London chums, none of that was true. There were sex noises, London noises, bathroom noises, argument noises ('*You're* the drama queen'); when I came home from work, wanting only to crawl into my burrow and drag the door in after me, I was instead reimmersed into the ongoing, reeking sitcom of communal living. It felt like a major step backwards. And although I was better off in notional terms, everything in London was so much more expensive that in practice I had less money. That stank too.

To make things worse, my love life – one of those phrases where you can use inverted commas in any configuration: my 'love life', my 'love' life, my love 'life' – had not thrived. In Blackpool I had been going out with a photographer called Michael Middleton. Or rather, a 'photographer' is what he would have called himself if he'd been American; being English, he would tell people that he worked in a bookshop, and let them only gradually realise that photography was his chief interest, his main talent, and the whole of what he wanted to do for the rest of his life. (The British see this kind of thing as a form of modesty. Americans – foreigners in general – see it as an especially invidious form of boasting and superiority complex. Nowadays I agree with them.) He used his wages from the bookshop to subsidise the time he spent taking trendily desolate pictures of Blackpool 'holidaymakers', the piers and the arcades, condoms washed up on the beach, discarded bags of chips, boarded-up shops, dead seagulls, etc.

It was in his place of work, the town's only half-decent bookshop, that I met Michael. I was standing at a shelf of staff recommendations, fingering a copy of Angela Carter's *Nights at the Circus* with a label on the shelf below it that said 'Her best yet!', signed 'MM'. The other two books on the shelf were the 1985 *Good Food Guide* with a label reading, 'It'll make you hungry: Kevin' and Martin Amis's novel *Money* with the label, 'Amy says: fabulous prose stylist'. I was standing there thinking, I'll read this eventually, why not take the plunge now. On the other hand I was also thinking, £8.95 for a book? And I suppose another part of me was liking the idea of being the kind of twenty-four-year-old *femme sérieuse* who bought new fiction in hardback.

'It's dead good,' said a voice behind me with an educated Geordie accent. I turned: a boy my age, skinny, good-looking, black jeans and T-shirt, slightly floppy but the accent worked against that. 'I'm the one who put it on the recommended shelf,' he added, with a nicely friendly, 'we-Angela-Carter-fans-are-in-this-together' air.

'You're MM?'

'Michael.'

'So it's better than *The Bloody Chamber*?'

'If you don't like it,' he said, 'and as long as you don't tell the boss, bring it here and I'll give you your money back.'

I bought it, read it, liked it, came back a week or so later, got chatting, went out for a drink, and so on. We started seeing each other.

Michael-and-me went brilliantly at the start, as these things do when they go at all, then we had the usual getting-to-know-you rows, and then settled into a basically pretty good relationship.

The trouble was that I made no secret of wanting to move to the nationals in London, whereas Michael, determined to stick to his policy of 'It's better oop North', had a big thing about not doing that; so we had no implied future. In fact, those very words used to pop into my head at times, when I thought about Michael and how much I liked him: no implied future.

Few relationships benefit from the people involved living two hundred and fifty miles apart. When I moved to London everything began to work less well, including, for the first time, the sex, with me keen to see Michael roughly every other weekend but less keen to spend the entire two days in bed, which is what he wanted to do. I was glad that he wanted it so badly, while at the same time not wanting it quite as much myself. And I must admit that I wondered what he got up to when I wasn't there, since Michael was a good-looking boy, and Blackpool a holiday kind of town. There were also complicated amounts of feeling invested in the fact that if I failed in London one of the big obstacles to our living together would disappear: I would be free to move back to Blackpool, or wherever, and Michael would be free to move in with me, which is what he said he wanted. So I at some level suspected him of wanting me to fail. I felt I had to soft-pedal my doubts and general downness about the *Toxic*, because he was enjoying or taking comfort from hearing them. Not good, in short.

The day before I moved to London, Michael told me that the business with the staff recommendations shelf had been a scam. He and Amy had switched books so that they could accidentally-on-purpose approach customers they fancied, with their chat-up line already scripted. Amy hated Martin Amis, and Michael had never read a single word Angela Carter had written. Kevin, an asexual fattie, had made the only heartfelt choice.

Chapter Two

I had a week to go – four working days, to be precise – of my probationary three months when I had my second break. It was pretty clear by this point that I wasn't going to be kept on at the paper. Chubby Rory was getting on so well with everyone at the *Toxic* that the editor himself (nickname: Headcase) had even once been seen to smile at him in the corridor, the equivalent for another man of inviting him home to be sucked off by his wife. But the waters were closing over my head, and I could tell from people's polite but disengaged manner of dealing with me, shared by everyone from oily Robin to Davina the diary secretary, that no one thought I was going to be around for much longer. It was partly as a symptom of this state that I was working a Sunday-for-Monday shift in what was going to be my last week. Sundays have an odd feel on a daily paper and tend to attract a high percentage of the unhappy-at-home; people who find it easier to get their stuff into the paper when there's less competition; people who can't (or couldn't, since it's changed so much) stand the English Sunday; and people like me, who saw it as one less day with all their colleagues present. It's also a hard day to generate diary stories, and I was working on two particular duds: a story in anticipation of a Monday-night book party at which two biographers who had once thrown glasses of wine over each other would be likely to meet again, and some dreck about a toff's son who had landed a job at the BBC despite a definitive lack of qualifications. I was not feeling at my most Martha Gellhorn-like.

The phone rang. A male voice with a respectable working-class South London accent said:

'Is that Dexter Williams?'

Eleven weeks before, that would have made me smile.

'Yes, it is, Dawn Stone speaking, how can I help you?'

There was a longish pause, during which I could hear street noise in the background. He was calling from a payphone.

'I've got something for you.'

This wasn't unusual. In addition to the regular contacts and suppliers of titbits – or 'tasty nibbles', as Robin used to call them – the diary would be approached by people who wanted to get something off their chests and earn a few quid in the process. We got some good stuff this way but these irregular informants also had the potential to be a pain in the arse.

'May I ask what it's about?'

'Yeah, you may. But I'm not going to tell you.'

Six out of seven unsolicited calls are unusable, and of those about half are from the clinically insane. Most of them are men, though there's a gender distinction in that female nutters tend to witter on, whereas male ones tend to be paranoid (that's paranoid in the non-colloquial sense).

'You have to give me a clue,' I said, thinking: he'll refuse, I'll say I can't help him, he'll say something offensive, I'll hang up, he'll call Nigel Dempster at the *Mail*, and I'll go back to my nice quiet Sunday-for-Monday biographer's wine throwing. But what he said to me next made me think different.

'It's about Fancy Nancy,' said my new friend. This got me listening. Fancy Nancy was a not-all-that-junior member of the Royal Family with theatrical pretensions (one reason for the nickname) who was rumoured to be a closet homosexual (the other reason) and who had become engaged to be married six months before to a hospital registrar, a Duke's daughter. The couple had met on a country-house weekend: 'half the time banging away at pheasants, the other half at each other', according to Robin, who sounded as if he knew the formula well.

'You have my attention,' I said, sinking slightly in my chair and swivelling it around to look out over the largely empty newsroom. Across the office a columnist was watering a plant on her desk while holding a phone receiver to her ear with her shoulder. 'Where and when would you like to meet?'

A coffee bar on Gloucester Road about three quarters of an hour later. I said he'd be able to recognise me by my yellow coat and the copy of the Sunday *Toxic* under my arm.

Duncan – as he turned out to be called; Saint Duncan, as I prefer to think of him – was a very tall, short-haired, fit, neat man of about twenty-five with an air that wasn't military but also wasn't the opposite of military. He'd done three years in the Household

Cavalry and been invalided out with pneumothorax trouble, having nearly died of a collapsed lung during exercises in Canada. He wasn't insane, but he was angry. He'd just lost the job he had had since leaving the army, and that job – at this point in the story the soundtrack swelled with hosannas of praise – was as a footman at 'The Palace': that's Buckingham Palace. There had been a row, he had been sacked, and now it was pay-back time.

St Duncan had overheard a screaming match between Fancy Nancy and his fiancée, the upshot of which was that she was now his ex-fiancée. He had overheard another reference to this later in the day from another, more senior Royal, whose name he rather sweetly wouldn't give.

'It's 100 per cent kosher,' he said. I said that I would talk to my boss, check the story out, and if it stood up and we ran it we would pay him £10,000 in cash. And then I did – though I say so myself – a clever thing. I went back to the office, took off my coat, put my bag down, put a piece of paper in my crappy typewriter, and didn't say a word about what had happened. This was part-ly the rat-like cunning all journalists need, partly the need to make sure how I felt before I mentioned anything to Robin or Derek the Pink Pig (his deputy, on duty that Sunday). So I wrote my wine-throwing story and my BBC dimwit story and went home.

The big event in the daily life of any newspaper is called con-ference. This is when section editors – News, Features, Foreign, Sport, Diary, Editorial, Op-Ed, and so on – sit around a table with the editor and deputy editor and discuss what's going to be in the paper the next day. It's a big deal for all concerned. There are lots of opportunities to squash and be squashed, especially for those with a rich variety of techniques for weeing on other people's ideas.

At the *Toxic*, conference was at 11 o'clock. At ten-thirty, Robin used to have a diary conference before conference, so that he did not have 'to go naked into the conference chamber'. (Robin, inci-dentally, was one of those Englishmen who it is hard to imagine ever being naked.) For the Monday I had dressed up very care-fully in a dark-red Chanel suit, my most expensive ever clothes purchase by about 300 per cent, and much too eighties and power-dressy for me now (though it still fits). I was in full face paint and armour, and when Robin asked, 'Any tasty nibbles?' I was, for the first time, the first to speak. The Dexter house style was to seem as understated and bored as possible, the more so the hotter the story seemed.

'Teensy something about Fancy Nancy,' I said. 'X-th in line to the throne. Apparently the wedding is off.'

There was a certain amount of shifting in seats and eyebrow raising. Robin naturally looked as if he was about to fall asleep.

'Source?'

'Sorry – can't.'

'Cash?'

'Ten.'

'Quality?'

I shrugged and looked modest. This meant somewhere between good and very good.

'Details?'

'Screaming rows. She threw a wobbly on Thursday and said it's all over. By Friday the other members of the Firm had been told.'

'Hmmm. Anything else?'

I shook my head. We moved on to other business but I could see Robin was convulsed with curiosity about where I'd got my story and whether he could trust me enough to raise it himself in conference. My isolation from my colleagues, their lack of interest in me and my life, worked to my advantage: they had no way of knowing where on earth this might have come from, so finally had no choice other than chalking it up to my journalistic skills.

An hour and a half later, Robin came over to my desk on the way back from conference.

'Mentioned your story to David and Peter,' he said. David was the editor; Robin never used the nickname Headcase. Peter was Peter Stow, the paper's royal correspondent, by general consent the most humanly repellent in the business, and a considerable power at the *Toxic*. 'Peter said it was total bollocks. Don't worry – all that means is he hadn't already heard it.' And with that he swanned back to his office. No one breathed a word to me for the rest of the day. I went home early, took Tuesday off – as I was scheduled to do, since I'd worked Sunday for Monday – and

16

spent it seeing my friend Jenny, having a massage at the health centre, buying a dress from Joseph that I took back three days later, and, intermittently but with conviction, crying. On Wednesday on my way in to the office I saw the front page of the *Toxic* screaming out from news-stands:

IT'S OFF

in seventy-two-point type. Underneath was written:

'By Peter Stow, Royal Correspondent'.

The name was accompanied by a naff little crest, as if to suggest to the unalert reader that Peter himself was royal too. When I got to the office I went straight to the loo and cried for fifteen minutes. I managed to get to my desk without making eye contact with any of my colleagues. As I sat down, a presence loomed behind me. I turned. It was Headcase.

'You're late,' he said. He stood with his hands in his pockets and flexed up and down on his feet. Then he said, as if addressing a larger audience, but without looking up,

'It's Peter's byline, but it's your story, and it's your job.'

That was my second big break.

Two days later I got home from work to find Michael sitting on my doorstep in the rain with a huge duffel bag beside him and his box of camera equipment under his bum. He said, 'Apparently they have bookshops in London too.'

The joke was that when I did eventually get the sack it turned out to be my third big break. This was ten years later.

Some things had changed in the intervening decade. Headcase had 'a nervous'; he spent six months in a bin and left journalism. Peter Stow dropped dead. Robin got his job only to be sacked when the *Toxic* decided to hire his disaffected opposite number from the *Express*. Berkowitz was briefly editor of the *Sensible* before falling victim to its famously toxic office politics and taking a job editing a magazine called *Asia* in Hong Kong. Chubby Rory now edits *Dexter*; when we meet at a party, we fall into each other's arms with cries of 'Babycakes!'

As for me: I moved from Dexter to the news desk, won an award for pieces about the *Herald of Free Enterprise*, moved to Features, was poached by *The Times*, then left after three months to be features editor of the *Sensible*; did that for two years, then moved to the same job on its sister Sunday (more pay, more status, less work – don't you love Sunday journalism?), then took on a job as features editor of the *Sentinel* when my former immediate boss was refused a sabbatical to write a book and so quit instead. This new job was an 'executive' one, meaning more money and perks in the form of a car, and putting up with management bullshit about budgets, conferences, strategies, market research, and the rest. Then our editor moved to edit the *Guardian*, and a man called William Pinker arrived, and two days later I was fired. Then Berkowitz called up and offered me a job in Hong Kong at twice my old salary.

At thirty-four you know a few things about yourself that you don't in your twenties. I am, I discovered to my own surprise, a man's woman. To me this doesn't feel like it's my fault: men like and trust me, whereas women don't, or not quite in the same way. These things tend to be mutual. I have only one real girlfriend, Jenny. She was a contemporary at Durham. She looks the same as she did then – short, dark, clever-looking – and is now a theatrical agent. I once looked in her fridge and found nothing but a single portion of Lean Cuisine lemon chicken, a month past its sell-by, a smelly pint of milk, and a half-empty, corkless bottle of Rosemount Chardonnay that had long since turned to vinegar. I told her about Berkowitz's offer the day after he made it, over lunch in a Thai restaurant.

'But what about Michael?' she said.

I had given her the reasons for being interested in Berkowitz's job offer, which were, in order, a complete change of scene, the inherent interest of the job itself, money, and the effect on my future – specifically, the idea that whatever happened, I could get a book out of it. I would go to Hong Kong a features hack who'd been around for a while, a known quantity, and come back eighteen months later a thirty-something *femme sérieuse* with an important book about Asia under her frock. In fact, the book would be so easy to write it was almost a pity I'd have to go out there to do it. *Tiger Pit: A Young Woman's Look at Asia. Time of the Tigers. When*

Tigers Awake. View from the Tiger. That's Enough Fucking Tigers. How many photogenic young female Asia experts can there be?

'But what about Michael?' Jenny said again. I said:

'I know, I know.'

But the truth was, I didn't know. Michael and I had fallen into that limbo which overtakes young(ish) couples when they don't marry at a reasonably early point and instead drift into the condition of being with each other open-endedly, with no plans for children.

'Maybe it'll give him a kick up the bum,' I said. 'It's not as if there won't be plenty of things to take pictures of in Hong Kong. He'll have to choose. We can't just potter along indefinitely. We can't stay together out of inertia. He either wants to stay with me or he doesn't.'

In another mood I would have marked that 'inertia' comment down for Count the Lies. Of course you can stay together out of inertia; staying together out of inertia is exactly what most couples do.

'Do you want him to come? If you imagine him coming or not, which makes you feel better?'

'I don't know, Jen.'

She did a long exhale after drawing on what must have been about her twentieth cigarette of the lunch. It was by now after three, and the single member of staff left on the premises was beginning to give off disconsolate-waiter vibrations. Jenny made a waggling wristy gesture at him and he happily scuttled off to get the bill.

'What you're saying is, it's more interesting, it's more challenging, it's much better money, it's a chance to live abroad, which is something you've always wanted to do, failure has no real consequences, and it gives Mike a much-needed reality check.' Jenny stubbed the cigarette out in a back-to-work gesture. 'I'd say go for it.'

So I did.

Heathrow airport when you're leaving the country and don't know when and on what basis you'll be coming back is a different place from Heathrow when you're going to Ibiza for two weeks.

Michael gave me a lift. He had taken my decision well, with just enough upset so that I wasn't upset by his lack of upset. The official plan was that he would come out between three and six months later, when it was clear what the fallout from his big exhibition was like, and he'd sorted out his backlog of outstanding commissions, and so on. It was apparent to both of us that we were waiting to see how we felt. I think he may have thought that Berkowitz and/or the place would wear me down, and I would come back home keen to resume things on their former basis – which would naturally be a significant moral victory for him. I was determined that wasn't going to happen. I sent a boxed crate of things off to Hong Kong by sea – projected journey time six weeks – and was travelling, if not light, then not heavy: clothes, survival essentials, Premier League frocks, laptop, a few books and CDs. My plan was to restock my wardrobe in the Shopping Capital of the World. Berkowitz had fixed me up somewhere to live in Mid-Levels, wherever or whatever that was.

Michael and I said goodbye at the kerb, by prior arrangement, rather than have a *Brief Encounter* moment in the terminal.

Chapter Three

I lost my virginity that day. It was my first time in business class.

'You'll be turning left, of course,' Berkowitz – who had a case of Harrods champagne delivered to my flat when I told him I was accepting his offer – said.

'Of course,' I said, not having a clue what was meant, until the actual moment when, as I clutched my business-class Cathay Pacific boarding card, the Chinese stewardess beamed at me and gestured to her right, my left, towards the front of the 747. Of course: turning left. This was not something I had done before. A Chinese man in a suit nodded politely at me as I sat on the arm-chair beside him after jamming my scruffy carry-on bag into the overhead locker. Another stewardess presented me with a valise of variably useful gifts (socks, goggles, distilled-water face spray, comb, tiny toothpaste and toothbrush, compact mirror, miniature parachute – though perhaps my memory errs on this last point) and followed it up with a glass of champagne. There is no other way to fly. I had not realised before that this was no more than the literal truth. Only a few feet away were the unimaginable splendours of First Class. What could be going on in there? Colleagues who had been upgraded by the random benifices of airline press departments spoke tearfully of the experience, which spoiled them permanently for terrorist class in the back.

'You'd don't understand,' tubby Rory said, after BA had upgraded him to and from the Oscars. (He had filed a borderline anti-Semitic piece about the backstage workings of The Industry. Headcase loved it.) 'It's ruined me.' And I had thought he was joking.

Once we were in the air, the Chinese man, who had kept his eyes closed during take-off, opened them, looked across at me, and smiled.

'That is my favourite part,' he said in impeccable English. He went back to his copy of *Business Week*. I settled down to watch *Legends of the Fall*. It was a crock. Then I had a meal and some wine and tried to sleep. The thing about sleeping on planes, I find, is that you get only one crack at it. Unconsciousness visits just once. It's always a nerve-racking moment when you come round and sneak a peek at your watch: is it six hours later, or fifteen minutes? On this occasion, I didn't do too badly. We were about halfway through the flight. The Chinese guy was playing a computer game on his laptop. When he saw me watching, he turned it off.

'I hope I did not wake you.'

'Absolutely not.'

We chatted for a bit – not, I now know, something one often does in business class. I've since flown many thousands of miles without speaking to the man in the seat next to me. This guy had a pleasant, mobile face, and perfect English. His name was Matthew Ho and he ran a company which made air conditioners in Hong Kong and Guangzhou, with plans to expand into China and generally take over the world. The parent company was German, but the subsidiary company with which he mainly dealt was based near Luton.

'You must spend a lot of time on aeroplanes.'

'It's called astronaut syndrome. The idea is you spend so much time in the air it's the same as being an astronaut.' He fished a thin leather wallet out of his pocket and took out a photo of a small fat baby. 'My daughter Mei-Lin,' he said. He didn't ask me if I had children.

All babies look alike to me.

'She's lovely,' I said.

I had heard about the landing at Kai Tak airport, but I still couldn't believe my eyes. We flew in over the archipelago of small islands, 235 of which – my guidebook told me – make up the territory of Hong Kong. As we came in lower you could see the boat-wakes, looking weirdly like jet contrails, then the boats themselves.

'That's where they're building the new airport,' Matthew said as we passed over Lantau island. 'They made your Prime Minister come out for the signing ceremony, the first Western leader to visit China after Tiananmen.'

There was anger in his voice, though not in his expression.

'Don't look at me, look out there,' he said. 'That's the harbour.'

We were now at a couple of thousand feet, coming in over the busiest harbour I had ever seen. The plane banked right over the city, and we began descending lower and lower. You could see laundry on people's balconies; you could all but smell the traffic. You could more or less look into people's flats. The air was not calm. It was as if we were flying right down into the city and the pilot was planning to attempt a landing in one of the canyons between the manically crowded buildings.

'Jesus,' I said.

'It's good, isn't it?' said Matthew.

Then suddenly we were over the airport runway and bumping down on it and the engines were roaring backwards as we headed out into the harbour. By the time we had stopped and turned off towards the terminal buildings, I could speak again.

'Do planes ever end up in the harbour?'

'Of course,' smiled Matthew. 'All the time.'

I found out later that wasn't true. He gave me his business card, which, having swotted up on my Asian etiquette, I took with both hands. You never know when contacts will come in handy; as it happens, I used him for a piece I did about astronaut syndrome a few months later.

We got off the plane comfortably before the proles at the back of the 747. The air was close. It was hot, but more than that it was lethally muggy and humid. It was as if your whole body was wrapped in warm wet muslin. Kai Tak was older and scruffier than I had expected, and both more Chinese – in the fact that 98 per cent of the people all around were Chinese, the script and the language were everywhere – and also, in that odd colonial way, more English, in details like the weird khaki safari-suit uniform of the policemen. Berkowitz was supposed to meet me, and although I had been cool and if-you-insist about it over the phone, I was now feeling distinctly glad that I wouldn't have to make my own way. It wasn't so much culture shock as what-the-fuck-am-I-doing-here shock.

In those days, summer of 1995, British citizens did not need a visa to waltz into Hong Kong and stay for as long as they liked. (The reverse, needless to say, did not apply.) Within about ninety seconds of my bags coming off the carousel I was pushing into the arrivals hall, looking and being looked at by a wall of Chinese faces. It's always a self-conscious moment, getting off a plane and running the reception gauntlet. Then I saw Berkowitz, standing with his arms crossed at the far end of the throng, marginally fatter and balder but essentially the same. Beside him stood a Chinese man in a uniform and peaked cap. People were surprisingly dressed up; many more suits and ties than you'd see in an equivalent line-up at Heathrow. I was suddenly glad that I'd nipped into the ladies and combed my hair, checked my face. My shoes were, after twelve and a half hours at an altitude equivalent to 7,000 feet, too tight for my puffy hooves. My luggage trolley was pulling hard to the left.

Berkowitz came towards me and gave me, rather than the prepared line I might have expected, a hug.

'Dawn,' he said.

'I think so. At least I was when I left. It's good to see you, Bob.'

'Let Ronnie take your bags. Dawn, this is Ronnie Lee, my driver and translator and all-round Man Friday. Ronnie, this is Dawn Stone.' At close range, I could see that what I had taken to be a uniform was in fact an unusually smart high-buttoned Italian suit (or good copy thereof). Ronnie was about five foot eight and had an intelligent face framed with the invincible jet-black hair of the Cantonese. He nodded at me, swung the two bags off the cart and began walking away towards the lift.

Berkowitz kept up a running commentary all the way from Kai Tak.

'See that stone wall around the airport perimeter? That used to be the Walled City of Kowloon. During the war the Japanese tore down the walls and made POWs build the perimeter of the airport. The city stayed where it was, a total no-go area to the cops thanks to some ancient row over jurisdiction between the Chinese and the Brits. Literally swarming with Triads, junkies, sweatshops, whorehouses, you name it. More edifyingly, if you look out at the back window you can catch a glimpse of the mountains around Kowloon. They're in the New Territories, which is the last bit of mainland before China proper. The Chinese said the hills were dragons. There were eight of them. Then the last of the Sung emperors came here in the thirteenth century, fleeing the Mongols, Kubla Khan among them, he of the stately pleasure-dome where Alph the sacred river ran. I remember the first time I heard that line thinking Alf was a weird name for a river. Anyway. The boy emperor looked up at the hills, said, look, there are eight dragons. His courtiers said, but sir, you are a drag-on too – which the emperor traditionally was. He had dragon sta-tus in his own right. So he said, okay, let's call this place nine dragons – *gau lung* – which became Kowloon. Not that it did the boy-emperor any good, since the Mongols caught him and killed him and ruled the whole of China for a couple of hundred years. Notice anything odd about these neon signs?'

It was by now starting to go dark, and lights were coming on everywhere. The neon was the only colour in this part of town, and the buildings seemed aggressively drab – duns, browns, greys, no-colours. The streets were crowded and enclosed and very, very Asian. And the traffic – what I had thought, in London, was a Ph.D. experience of shitty traffic, was now being exposed as more like a GCSE all-must-have-prizes pass grade. *This* was shitty traffic.

'You mean apart from the fact they're in Chinese?'

'Very droll. No, it's the fact that none of them blink. There's no flashing neon in Hong Kong owing to restrictions about the proximity of the airport. They're worried that if too many lights wink you'll have planes taking a wrong turn and crash-landing into girlie bars in Wanchai, with all the resultant expense and negative publicity. My point is merely that although this looks like an unfettered capitalist mêlée, the "purest free-market econ-omy in the world" in the words of the Heritage Foundation in Washington – don't you love that "purest"? – in fact Hong Kong is a closely regulated and legally supervised society. Zoning laws and building restrictions are extremely strict. Although everyone here talks non-stop about the free market and gases on about the place as a capitalist success story without equal, not least thanks to the 15 per cent top-rate tax which I believe I've had occasion to mention to you, they don't point out that Hong Kong also has the largest public housing programme in the world, with over half of the population living in public housing built since the fifties, when bad publicity shamed the Brits into clearing the shanty towns. So Hong Kong can be described in the exact opposite of the usual way, as a triumph of legislation, planning, and socialistic policy – I speak as the only bona fide socialist within about five thousand kilometres of here, isn't that right, Ronnie?'

'Whatever you say, Mr B.'

We were now in the queue to pay for entry to the cross-harbour tunnel. Above the entrance, over the water, I could see Hong Kong Island, a jam-packed cityscape with a hill or mountain rising straight up behind it. Usually when you arrive at an airport you come through some emptyish country or at least a stretch of motorway through suburbs, before you arrive in the built-up big city you're headed for. There was none of that here. It was super-urban all the way.

'Don't be deceived by the appearance of the buildings, by the way – they look like blocks of flats but a lot of them will also house factories, tiny restaurants, brothels, gambling dens, you name it. Also sweatshops. Especially sweatshops.'

We started crawling through the tunnel.

'Have you learned Chinese yet?' I asked.

'Certainly not. For all practical purposes it's impossible to learn Cantonese – which, by the way, is the language spoken here. On the mainland the official language is what used to be called Mandarin and is now known as Putonghua, because that's what the Chinese government says it should be called. The Hong Kong Chinese speak Cantonese, which is the dialect of the province of Guangdong. It's easy to tell the difference because Mandarin sounds like someone chewing a brandy glass full of wasps and Cantonese sounds like people having an argument. The written language of both dialects incidentally is the same. You'll manage just fine.'

We had emerged from the tunnel on the Hong Kong side and were moving along a raised highway, past skyscrapers and office blocks, some very new-looking, others still being built. Berkowitz pointed across to a plot of newly reclaimed land jutting out into the harbour.

'That's the site of the new convention centre, where the handover to the *soi-disant* Communists will happen in 1997. The building straight across the harbour with the blank wall facing it is the new cultural centre, opened by the Prince and Princess of Wales. You'll notice that despite facing one of the ten great vistas of the world it has no windows. Some of us like to think that's a joke about the state of culture in the territory. Territory, by the way, is the mandatory euphemism – never "colony". The C-word is completely *verboten*. Calling it a territory doesn't affect the fact that our beloved Governor Patten, "Fat Pang", as the locals call him, is a legally self-sufficient entity who can do whatever the hell he likes, but it offends the Chinese less and has the supreme virtue of not meaning anything.'

We swept round a corner and began travelling uphill.

'That's the Bank of China on the right, I. M. Pei's masterpiece. He's the chap who put that pyramid over the Louvre. It's not very popular with the locals because the feng shui is said to be very aggressive. One of its corners points towards Government House, which you'll be amazed to hear is where the Governor lives. It's got a hideous little tower on top that the Japanese put there when they owned the colony. Nobody knows what they'll do to it after 1997. The smart money is on a Museum of Colonial Atrocities. We're just going past the Peak Tram, which is a tram that goes up the peak. And now we're heading round towards Robinson Road, which is where you fit in.'

My new home was a block of a couple of dozen flats called Harbour Vista with a tiny, poky, unreassuring lift. But the flat itself was lovely, with a double bedroom, a single study or spare room, and a sitting room with a dining table set up at one end. Behind the table was a large display case of blue-and-white china; at the other end was a small bookcase of art books and paperback blockbusters, a hi-fi, a TV, and two sofas. The flooring was parquet, which helped make it an unfeminine flat, with something squared off and retired-brigadier-on-the-plantation-ish about it. The view from the balcony was almost comically without any trace of the harbour, if you excluded the tiny chink of water you could glimpse between the circular skyscraper immediately in front (known locally, I was to learn, as Phallus Palace) and the blockier but equally tall building slightly beyond it, down the hill and to the left.

'This place has good feng shui,' said Berkowitz. 'You can see both water and mountain, not much of either admittedly, but then you don't need much. When you're less knackered you must get me to tell you some feng shui horror stories. They always involve a couple who split up, husband tops himself, next people move in, consult the feng shui man, he says the *chi* is spoilt, moves the fish tank two inches to the right and installs a mirror – feng shui stories always involve a strategically placed mirror – and everyone lives happily ever after. The botanical gardens are over that way. You'll like them. Hong Kong Park is over there. It's got an aviary in it. I'm in the pay of the Rotarians. Right, now I'll leave you to it.'

Chapter Four

At various moments over the next year or so some well-wisher or other would ask whether I had 'settled in yet', or how long it had taken me to 'settle in'. Even by local small-talk standards it was a stupid question. What would it mean, for an expat on the make (any expat) to have 'settled in' in Hong Kong? It's not a 'settle in' kind of place. I felt a near-continuous mixture of exhilaration, panic, culture shock, and alienation, mixed in with another, perhaps deeper feeling of being finally at home. Money was all that mattered. In the decade I worked in UK journalism there was a huge amount of talk about materialism in Britain – all that guff about Thatcher having said there was no such thing as society. Well, I have lived in Hong Kong for a few years now, and I can tell you that every single word about materialism in the UK is bullshit. The whole country is a Franciscan monastery compared to Hong Kong. It is like a fusty family firm where the paterfamilias died years ago and they have carried on doing everything in exactly the same way, except somebody installed a 1924 cash register a year or so ago, and since then everybody has been congratulating themselves on how up to date they are. Money is a typhoon, and Britain has so far felt only its first faint breath.

On a more specifically practical level, my main initial impression was to do with the fact that nobody spoke English. Okay, that's an exaggerated way of putting it, a good few people did speak English: everybody at the magazine, for instance, in its shining high-tech office in a hideous skyscraper in Admiralty, where three quarters of the staff were in any case *gwailos*; some waiters in some restaurants; policemen, if the ID number on their shoulder of their uniform was red; the staff in expensive and/or centrally located shops. (Incidentally, my ambition to stock myself out with a brand new wardrobe at eye-bulgingly, knicker-combustingly low prices – I saw myself dressed top to toe from this madly cheap Prada factory outlet I just happened to have discovered – came to grief on the fact that Hong Kong was by now one of the most expensive cities in the world. Real estate again: if the shops in Central are paying more rent than they would be on Fifth Avenue, the Champs-Elysées, or Bond Street, your frock will tend not to be such great value. Now, *fake* designer clothes – that was a different story.) But apart from that, I was amazed by how little the language had penetrated the place – given, after all, that we Brits had been running the colony for 150 years. Other groups you might well have expected to speak English were, as a rule, remarkable for being monoglot Cantonese: taxi drivers, for example, for whom, unless you were going to some no-bones-about-it landmark like the Star Ferry or the Mandarin, you needed a bit of paper with the destination written out in Chinese. It was a mark of how little we had affected the real life of the place. I suppose part of me had thought of Hong Kong as somewhere essentially British, except with a lot of Chinese people scattered about, for local colour.

But the great thing was that none of this had to matter much, if you were one of the territories' hundred-odd thousand expats. (Forty thousand Brits and Eurotrash, fifty thousand mainly Chinese–American Yanks, ten thousand odds and ends. I'm excluding the forty or fifty thousand Filipino servants who don't, for this purpose, count.) You could live in a bubble, and most of them, or most of us, did, earning lorryloads of cash, working and partying hard and concentrating purely on the pursuit of money, which was the one thing about which absolutely everybody in the territory was agreed.

Gwailo life in Hong Kong was like living in the still, protected centre of the money typhoon. For a start, most of us had servants, which is not a factor you should underestimate when it comes to how easy and protected your life feels. I had Conchita, who was much much cheaper than the flat, at a cost of a few thousand Hong Kong dollars per month. I shared her with a Brit banker who lived two floors upstairs and who I met only in the lift; he had the haggard, masturbatory pallor of a man putting in sixteen-hour working days. Conchita was a permanently cheerful Filipina of about my age (I thought it would have been indelicate to ask) whose normal uniform was a canary yellow T-shirt and blue jeans; she lived somewhere in

Mongkok, with a bunch of other maids. Berkowitz filled me in on the Filipinas.

'Most of them are educated, capable women, with degrees and training and what-not, not to mention, most of them, husbands and children,' he said. 'They come here because there's no work at home, and they're subservient to the husband's mother, who invariably lives with them and dedicates herself to making the daughter-in-law's life a total misery. They send their money home, so they get the kudos of being the main breadwinner, plus they don't have to take their mother-in-law's shit all day long.'

Conchita's presence, and her efforts, were wonderfully lulling. She cleaned, washed and ironed, cooked three nights a week, and generally provided a welcome layer of insulation between me and the dreary reality principles of dirty knickers and bedmaking. Her all-purpose, all-weather amiability made it hard to tell, but I suspected (or hoped) she preferred me to previous employers on the grounds that I didn't make her do as much work. And the best thing was that telling Jenny about Conchita made her gibber with envy.

The activity which best summed up life in the bubble was junking. Do not be deceived by the faux-Asian term: this meant going out on a big boat to spend time drinking, boasting, schmoozing, and showing off with other *gwailos* and (sometimes) a few carefully chosen locals. It was fun, and it got you off Hong Kong island, which is one of the world's great places for cabin fever. The only bad thing about junking was that every time you went out on a boat someone told you the favourite *gwailo* urban legend, about an occasion when some pissed expat had fallen off the back of one boat and been picked up by another following along a quarter of a mile behind, to be reunited with his chums off Cheung Chau island before any of them had noticed his absence.

I knew I was making it in Hong Kong when I was invited to go junking on *Tai Pan*, a boat belonging to a local heavyweight called Philip Oss. I had been in the territory about six months and, though I say it myself, had made a bit of a splash. Asia was full of plump, juicy subjects, lying there just begging for it. The best of these were set somewhere other than Hong Kong itself, because the libel situation in the territory made London seem like a Mardi Gras of free expression. One or two local heroes simply issued a lawyer's letter every single time their name was mentioned in print. So one of my first pieces was ostensibly an account of the Nick Leeson case, and of how well the chubby Essex boy was faring in his Singapore jail – but the real meat of it was about what an extraordinarily horrible place Singapore was. The cabs had alarms to limit the top speed, the streets were 100 per cent rubbish-free, the family was central, and the city was stone dead. It was a thriving necropolis. Although the local *gwailos* were a chillingly thick, amoral bunch, even by Hong Kong standards, you too would want to celebrate your free time by smashing car windscreens or drinking fifty pints of lager and mooning bystanders – at least you would if you lived in Singapore. That piece led into another, about the big earthquake due in Japan. (It was the Kobe earthquake that caused the Japanese stock market to take a dip just as Leeson had bet his bank on its going up.) I spent a weird two weeks in Japan, mainly Tokyo but with a bit of Kobe, Osaka, Kyoto thrown in, living in tiny clean hotel rooms and being fobbed off, patronised and misled by a series of Nipponese men in dark blue suits. The gist of their story was that the Japanese earthquake preparations were the best in the world. This was not very subtle code for 'We're Number One'. The gist of my piece, on the other hand, was, if that was true, then how come a six point four earthquake – which a drawling and wonderfully quotable San Francisco architect told me was 'barely enough to shake a martini' – had killed several thousand people? That went down well. Pieces about Japanese hubris usually did, in south-east Asia and in the English-speaking world both.

The invitation to go out on *Tai Pan*, Philip Oss's boat, came via a phone call from Berkowitz, who was at pains to stress what a big deal it was.

'I've only ever met him three or four times myself, for fuck's sake. He's my boss's boss. The only *gwailo* close to Wo himself. If it was a mafia movie, he'd be the *consiglieri*. Something vaguely military about his background. Doesn't talk about it. Well, you know what not to ask.'

'Yeah yeah, big event, best behaviour, don't mention the war. I'll be good.'

Berkowitz's general view about the wealthy in Hong Kong was that 'the first million or two's always a bit dodgy. Some of these guys just pop up overnight, the money's obviously from the Triads or the Communists. Then they get into property, which is where the real money is in Hong Kong, and they start to get properly rich.' The ultimate owner of our company, T. K. Wo, controlled a multilayered and super-ingeniously structured firm which in turn controlled all sorts of businesses all over the world, among them the media concern which owned *Asia*. Wo was famous for his *guanxi* – his connections, juice, and general mojo – with Beijing. He was the son of a man who had fled to Taiwan to avoid drug charges in the sixties. There were rumours about how the Wo money had been made. The subject had only ever come up once in a work context, oddly enough when I went to visit Matthew Ho, the guy who'd sat beside me on the plane out, as part of a series about young entrepreneurs. He had mentioned in passing that his grandfather refused to have any publication owned by the Wos anywhere in his house. Needless to say I left that out of the piece.

My view of the Wo rumours could be summed up as follows: so what? Compared to other local bigwigs, one of whom was the frontman for the opium-dealing Shan warlord Khun Sa, another of whom recycled Macao gambling money back through half the new building developments in Europe, the allegations were no big deal. In any case none of these guys was in the same league as the drug-dealing companies who had founded Hong Kong, like Jardines and Swire. Not for nothing was the HQ of Jardines, a skyscraper with hundreds of porthole-like windows, known as the Palace of a Thousand Arseholes. If you worked for Wo, people would occasionally try to needle you at parties, until they saw clear evidence that you simply didn't give a shit.

That Saturday, as per instructions, I went down to Queen's Pier just before eleven. Two or three boats were bobbing about in the usual scum of filthy water and floating rubbish – cans, bottles, God knows what. One of the boats, which had just cast off from the pier, was flying a Hong Kong Bank flag on the stern mast and carrying the usual flushed quota of overseas officers, wives, chums, children. The harbour smelt the same way it always did. A fit late-forties Brit in an expensive-looking, I-could-sail-round-the-world-in-this-at-a-moment's-notice windcheater was standing on shore beside a lurching yacht, on board which I could see Berkowitz and a dozen others milling about, getting stuck into the day's first hard-earned beverage.

'Miss Stone,' said the man, smiling, affable, warm–cool. 'What a pleasure. Philip Oss. Bob has told me so much about you. And, like everybody else, I've been so enjoying your things in *Asia*.'

The calm I had shown when Berkowitz relayed this invitation was phoney. I was highly curious about Oss. He was T. K. Wo's factotum and fixer and right-hand man, and as such was unusual, because the Cantonese tended to regard the British as thick, and not many Chinese tycoons had such a close British colleague. In the first instance, it was said, Oss had gone to work with Wo to help with things that required a fluent English speaker, and he was now inseparable from all parts of Wo's business. There was said to be a Mrs Oss, an elegant German woman whom nobody had ever met. I could see that he was super-easy; not just smooth but absolutely frictionless.

'It's very kind of you to invite me out on your. . .' The word that I was going to use next was 'junk', which suddenly seemed ridiculous, since anything less like a rackety old wooden junk than this opulent floating pleasure palace, its radar aerial revolving confidently in the muggy air, would have been hard to imagine. Oss helped me out.

'Dinghy,' he said in his clipped accent. He had clearly used the line before; it had got a laugh before; and it did this time too. He handed me over to one of his boat boys, a middle-aged Cantonese in a navy blue-and-white uniform, and I was gently bundled towards the back of the ship.

The only person I knew on board was – excluding my new friend Mr Philip Oss – Berkowitz. I went over and stood next to him.

'Bob,' I said. Calling him Berkowitz, which is what everyone always called him at work, would have seemed too intimate. We stood there and talked about nothing for a while as the boat gradually filled up. A couple of the new arrivals came over and schmoozed. Ricky Tang, a legislative counsellor for the lawyers'

Functional Constituency, quondam columnist for the *South China Morning Post* – another smoothy, with a lush Oxonian voice; a half-bright journalist called Mat something, 'Pacific Rim correspondent' for some Seattle magazine I'd never heard of; Susan Lee, a dressed-up Chinese woman, my age, who worked for Oss in some unspecified capacity; Sammy Wong, a Chinese–American businessman and, highly unusually for a money guy, a rabid anti-Communist, with links to the nuttier, let's-nuke-China-while-there's-still-time fringes of the Republican Party; his wife; and another woman called Lily Zhang, a not-quite-standard-issue Dragon Lady (she showed signs of having once read a book). I had already worked out that, as a general rule, Hong Kong required you to be one and a half notches more dressed up than you would be in England. This applied not just to men having to wear jackets and ties in the permanent sauna of Hong Kong's summer, but to things like drinks parties and junking. In England, on a day like today, the boat trip would be a nightmare of exposed, lard-coloured, mottled and pimply flesh – unless the weather had already been good for a few days, in which case you could throw in some lobsterish burns for good measure. Here, though, there were crisp white ducks, imperial-purple Agnès B slacks, John Smedley sea-island cotton tops – and that was just the men. I had my lightest English long trousers (Joseph, in an all-too-easily-stainable cream) and a too-cheap-not-to-be-fake Marc Jacobs dark-blue silk shirt from a new shop in a Tsim Sha Tsui arcade – and I was only just getting by. My secret weapon was a new black Gucci one-piece swimsuit. Berkowitz calmed me down with a compliment.

'You look good enough to eat,' he said.

Susan Lee and I were doing clothes-shopping getting-to-know-you chat – her Fendi bag had cost two and a half thousand Hong Kong dollars, which I was assuring her was insanely cheap by European standards – when Philip Oss came over. The boat had cast off by now and we were plunging about the harbour through the wakes of the usual heavy traffic. Three or four young women – a couple of executive secretaries, a daughter or two – were already stretched out on sunbeds at the front of the boat; this was one of Hong Kong's rare cloudless days, and they were going for it. The rest of the party were standing or sitting around in clumps, boozing and yakking.

'Bob tells me you're enjoying it here,' Oss said. Susan held her glass up and headed off for a refill, or pretended to.

'Well, it can be hard to tell, but I think so,' I said. 'Nice boat, by the way.'

'You like boats?'

'I haven't been sick yet, so I suppose the answer is yes.'

He laughed a rich hammy tycoon laugh. It was at this moment that I realised: he's hitting on me. This, in the way that it can, caused a reassessment. Trim, mid-to-late forties, energetic, fond of himself; hard to think he would be anything other than selfish in bed, though I hadn't yet seen him eat (I'm a believer in that one); in short, thinkable, but not really *possible*. Also, Oss was tanned in a way that you didn't often see since the scares about skin cancer. Still, I had never fended off advances from a millionaire before. In a kind of emotional spasm I found myself thinking of Michael and his continual shall-I-or-shan't-I male dithering about whether or not to come out to Hong Kong. On the one hand, his show had gone well, and that was an argument for staying on and getting as much work as he could while his profile was high; on the other, the fact his work was now beginning to be known made him more able to move about and go where he wanted, so he could come to Hong Kong without worrying about vanishing off the map. On the one hand, he was missing me, on the other hand he thought that in some ways the break was rejuvenating our blah blah blah.

I said: 'Is Mrs Oss here?'

Give him credit, he didn't even blink.

'Daphne, unlike you, gets seasick. The secret', he said, leaning towards me, 'is not to brace yourself. It applies to lots of things.'

Oss then subjected me to a thirty-minute interrogation about my journalistic background in the UK, including who it was I'd worked for, contacts and sources at papers and the Beeb, my view of the country's economic fortunes and the Tories' political prospects. It was charmingly done, but it was also as thorough a grilling as I'd ever had. The questions were asked in that British way that sets a test of intelligence and insiderish-ness as a precondition to taking you seriously. At the same time he did not stop being flirty – an odd mix. Finally he called it a day.

'If you'll excuse me for a brief moment, I have a work thing to get out of the way.'

He swayed backwards to the stern and joined a claque of men who looked like younger and less successful versions of himself. I wandered over to where Berkowitz was holding court.

'Well,' he said, clutching a glass of champagne, evidently his third or fourth. 'That's enough small talk. Dawn, you've been here long enough to have formed a view about this. So tell us – who's your favourite Patten daughter?'

We sailed out to a beach at the back of Cheung Chau and moored a couple of hundred yards offshore. I talked to Oss and to Berkowitz and to the wife of a man called Mitchell who herself was called either Sonia or Sonja and had plans to start an art gallery specialising in openly fake French furniture and to another woman called Katy who said that she 'wrote pieces for the London papers' and then drifted away when I began to ask questions and avoided me for the rest of the day, and to a woman called Peta who was about twenty-five and was the daughter of a friend of Oss's and was travelling around the world for three months before beginning a course as a mature student of photography at St Martin's College. Some of us swam before lunch, others did more B & Y (boozing and yakking), talking of Cathay Pacific versus British Airways club class, about the old days when a flight to Hong Kong took twenty-one hours because planes didn't overfly China or Vietnam, about the parts of London where the Chinese were buying up property and about the ads for London properties in the Hong Kong papers; we talked about a new restaurant in Macau called Lusophonia, where the designer came from Lisbon, the maître d' from Kowloon, and the chef from Mozambique via Rio; we talked about the new Peak Tram terminal, about swimming pools, about which of the London papers was going through an off patch; there was an altercation about whether a visit to South Australia was as good as a visit to Tuscany but with fourteen hours' less flying time; someone said that FILTH (Failed In London Try Hong Kong) was an acronym you only heard from tourists and newcomers who wouldn't last ten minutes in the territory; there was gossip about the new chief executive of the Jockey Club (verdict: American – but who cares?), there was a conversation about the last time anyone present had actually bought anything from Lane Crawfords, there was talk about whether it was just us but weren't people actually beginning to get a little bit tired of the China Club? We talked about David Tang, about water temperature as a predictor of typhoons, and about ways of retiring to France without paying French tax. We ate chicken à la king and cold roast beef and mozzarella-and-tomato salad and Thai peanut-and-noodle salad and chilled spicy tomato soup and air-freighted Pont L'Évêque and fruit salad and Ben and Jerry's Chunky Monkey or Häagen-Dazs Double Chocolate ice cream. We drank gin and tonic and Virgin Marys with Worcestershire sauce and celery salt and Veuve Clicquot with or without freshly squeezed orange juice and Rothbury Estate Show Reserve Chardonnay and Guigal Côtes du Rhône and Hennessey XO Cognac and Lagavulin and Ty Nant water and coffee and peppermint tea and Tsingtao beer because Oss said that San Miguel didn't taste as good as it used to when the brewery was owned by the Marcoses. We swam and a few of us waterskied and a few others sunbathed and a couple of people tried to windsurf, and a couple of other people said they would go below decks for a little lie down. My swimsuit got a couple of good reviews. At dusk the wind died and we could hear the laughter and the talking coming from other similar boat parties off the beach and the boats looked closer now because their superstructures were strewn with lights. And then as the stars were coming out we pulled up our anchor and headed back to Queen's Pier. Life in the bubble.

Chapter Five

About three months after the trip on *Tai Pan*, Michael came out to visit. I was as busy as hell and it was wildly inconvenient, but I couldn't entirely blame Michael for the timing, since it wasn't arbitrary: it was Easter. I had been home once since moving to Hong Kong, but circumstances had stopped Michael from making the return trip. The flurry of work following his exhibition hadn't subsided, but had gone on so consistently that he was now confident – not that being confident about practical things was much of a Michael trait, but you get the gist – that he could take a couple of weeks off without everybody suddenly deciding that he was a bad photographer. I had been half looking forward to and half dreading his visit. The less optimistic part of me found itself dwelling on a heavy, cross, partly angry, partly guilty, and partly irritated sense that Michael was, to use a word that comes up often when British women talk about British men, useless. Meaning, among other things, that he was in love with his own doubts and difficulties, incompetent in practical matters, vain, clueless. Hong Kong had given me a strong appetite for the feeling that things (and people) were making progress, getting somewhere, going somewhere. This is a view that has consequences for old relationships.

At first, though, it wasn't too bad. You might even say it was good. As soon as I set eyes on him, as he came blinking through into the arrivals hall at Kai Tak with his suitcase, bag of duty-free and a ludicrously out-of-place Aran sweater over his shoulders, I felt a rush of pleasure and sexual anticipation that made me realise (a) how horny I'd been and (b) how much I had been burying the feeling of missing him. Sometimes when you've spotted someone you're looking for and they haven't yet spotted you, you see them fresh, and this is what happened with Michael, as he shoved his floppy hair to one side and shifted his weight from one hip to the other scanning the hallway and looking like he was thirty-five going on fourteen in his jeans and his skinniness.

'Michael!' I called out. 'Over here!'

'Baby!' he said as he came loping towards me, his whole face smiling, perhaps as surprised at his own uncomplicated pleasure as I was. 'Darling!'

And I thought, phew, it's all going to be all right.

But it turned out to be a little harder than that. The strange thing was the severance between the physical aspect and everything else. I'd never felt so strongly before that my body was going off and doing its own thing, leaving me to fend for myself. With my body it was sex: yes; good; thank you; more please; leave me alone (this last remark addressed to my brain). The first evening and night, for instance – with Michael admittedly desynchronised by jet lag and an eight-hour time difference – we did it four times. I don't think we'd managed that since we first started going out. It was great. From my body's point of view it was shaping up to be the best two weeks of all time. But my brain seemed not to want to go along for the ride. After the first thirty-six hours or so, drugged as I was with sex and with the simple pleasure – I admit – of having company, someone around all the time, irritation and impatience started to build like magma underneath an earthquake fault-line.

I'd been completely unaware of this subterranean build-up until the Sunday after the Friday when Michael arrived. He said he wanted to go for a walk, so I obliged him. We went down the hill, towards one of Hong Kong's most amazing spectacles, the Sunday gathering of Filipina amahs around Statue Square, spilling out towards Legco, the park, the exchange. You hear it long before you see it, a high fluttering sound, a cross between a roaring and a twittering, like thousands of birds, like no other human sound you've ever heard. The noise made by ten thousand Filipinas all talking at the same time isn't like a crowd event, a march or a rally or a sporting match, since they aren't concentrating on an external entity but on each other – eating and sharing picnics, exchanging news and reading letters from home, listening to music, shopping at the impromptu market that features carefully targeted goods (like big, cheap folding suitcases, ultra-cheap towels and T-shirts), swapping photos, but all, mostly, talking, all the time. In Hong Kong you get used, without really noticing it, to the fact that everyone is always speaking Cantonese, which tends to sound like a constant argument, whereas in Statue Square on a Sunday you are suddenly in a space where everyone is speaking the exotic twittery sound of Tagalog. Michael didn't say much, but he had his silent, taking-it-in look.

Then we went up to the Peak Tram to have dinner in the Peak Café, a thirties sort of upmarket shack with views out over the back of the island towards the South China Sea. It's a nice spot and a great trip up in the groovy green tramcar with its permanently cross Chinese driver, climbing a thousand feet in a few minutes, at angles which, at one point in particular, make you feel as if you're going straight up in the air. Michael behaved as if I'd taken him to Madame Tussaud's or some other strictly-for-tourists clip joint.

'I should have brought my camera,' he said, which for half a second I thought was a comment about how spectacular the view was – and then realised was a sneer. I said:

'I suppose a picture-postcard view like this is unworthy of a serious artist like yourself.'

That just came out. I hadn't planned to say it. Back in England I probably wouldn't have – I would have bared my teeth and smiled, while inwardly biting my lip and making a mental note to be unimpressed next time Michael tried to show me something. He looked startled.

'Where did that come from?' he said. It was halfway through the first course before we were back on speaking terms.

That set the pattern for the whole of his visit. On our walking-and-eating trip to Lamma Island, our trip to see the new Ricky Lam film, a day spent on the beach at Shek-O, a day out on somebody's boat with cronies from the magazine, a day spent taking the tram from Kennedy Town to North Point and then walking back via clothes and camera shops and a dim sum joint, a day travelling around the New Territories by public transport; not to mention most the time we spent hanging around the flat when not actually having sex, which remained fine: at all these times and in all these places it was the same. Irritation jumped off me like static. I also could not help noticing the possible signs of another influence in his life. Michael was wearing slightly more expensive clothes, not to mention Calvin Klein underpants; and once, at dinner *chez* Berkowitz, when the conversation turned to Hong Kong's tax system, he did something unprecedented – he spontaneously offered a political opinion. The next day we made a disastrous expedition to the People's Republic, in the form of an overnight trip to Shenzen, where we got lost and, unable to make anyone understand our request for directions, wandered around in the beginnings of panic until we were rescued by a landmark we had seen on the way out of the hotel – a winking neon sign for Versace jeans. We slept on opposite sides of the bed.

We were, I suppose, bound to have a big fight. I held out until the second week, congratulating myself on not having bitten Michael's head off by then; instead I mixed physical demands with occasional impatience, carping and whingeing – so attractive, don't you find? I could, however, feel a major eruption coming on. So it was a good joke that the person who did finally snap was Michael; an especially good joke since for all practical purposes he never had a temper to lose.

What happened was I woke up at 4 o'clock in the morning with a cranium-splitting toothache. Well, I say I 'woke up', but it was more as if I was woken – as if the toothache built up a sufficient head of steam, decided it had become adequately painful, and then jolted my shoulder saying, wake up, time for your pain. It was at the back of my mouth on the left side, next to where my wisdom teeth would have been, if they'd come through. The pain was both immensely sharp and specific, on one precise point, and also dull, like an ache; it was two different sorts of pain wrapped around each other. I tottered to the bathroom, ran some cold water over the side of my face, gargled over the sore spot with brandy, took two Nurofen, and went back to bed to wake Michael.

'Call a dentist,' was his ultra-helpful suggestion.

'If I had a fucking dentist do you think I would be in this state in the fucking first place?'

'There must be a dental hospital or a twenty-four-hour clinic somewhere, mustn't there?'

'How do I know?'

Michael then got up and went into a Superman routine with the phone book and with a guidebook that he had brought out with him (and which, to tell the truth, I had been secretly irritated by: why did he need a guidebook when he had me?). He eventually came up with a number for the dental hospital. By this time, however, the pain had mysteriously but thoroughly subsided, going away as quickly as it had come on.

'I think I'd best leave it till morning,' I said. 'There'll be some junior doctor on, he'll probably pull all my teeth out just as soon as look at me. Best to wait for the senior chaps.'

Rather than correctly diagnosing cowardice, Michael merely got back into bed, turned the light off, and fell asleep. Five hours later, I again came awake with fire-alarm abruptness, woken by the exact same pain. I sat straight up in bed, gave Michael an elbow and said:

'It's come back.'

He made a certain number of *mmph, mmph* noises, and then went into the next room to call the hospital. About two minutes later he came back into the bedroom bringing a blushing Conchita in his wake. Monday was one of her days. The combination of six-foot-two Caucasian male in a too-small pink ruched woman's dressing gown, and a five-foot Filipino female in flip-flops, jeans, yellow T-shirt, and rubber gloves, was quite something. Michael had on his man-of-action face.

'Er, Michael,' I said. I like to think that under normal circumstances, if my teeth hadn't been hurting quite so much, I would at this point have made a joke about not being in the mood for a threesome.

'Conchita is a dentist,' said Michael.

'What?'

'Conchita is a dentist. That's what she trained to be in Manila. Tell her what's wrong.'

'It's true, Miss Stone,' said Conchita, who was smiling and looking embarrassed. She was taking off her gloves and moving towards me.

'Just describe the symptoms,' said Michael. I moved over to let Conchita sit on the edge of the bed and said to Michael with an edge, 'Could you excuse us please?' I explained about the shooting pain, the Nurofen, the sudden and welcome going-away, the equally sudden and very unwelcome coming-back.

'Is it always in the same place?' asked Conchita, who was by now peering into my mouth. Dentist Conchita had, when compared

43

with permanently smiling cleaning Conchita, a mild but immediately noticeable severity and briskness.

'Same place.'

'You still have your wisdom teeth?'

'Aargh. They haven't come through.'

Finally Conchita said:

'Okay, is one of two things. Maybe is your wisdom tooth, but I think maybe you too old for that now. More likely is another tooth somewhere else. Sometime tooth is sick here' – she pressed down on the bed by my feet, 'but pain comes here' – she pressed near my head.

'So what should I do?'

'Go to tooth hospital,' said Conchita, who by this point was putting her gloves back on. 'They do X-ray.'

'Right.'

'Sorry I can help no more.'

'No, that's great.'

'Tooth pain always worse at night-time,' she said on the way out.

I dressed slowly, like someone who had suffered a defeat, and came through to the sitting room.

'I've called a cab,' Michael said tightly. 'I'll come with you and wait.'

We had the row in the cab on the way home, ninety minutes, an X-ray, and a tentative diagnosis of an infected tooth later. Conchita had been right in that the culprit seemed to be an abscess in the right molar, with the pain showing up elsewhere.

'Okay, so what the fuck is going on?' I said to Michael. 'It's *my* head that feels like it's exploding, and it's *you* that sits there like I've done some unforgivable evil deed. The smell of burning martyred flesh is so strong that it's nearly taking my mind off this sodding tooth.'

This, by the way, was a lie. I was by now feeling no pain. I had been given some hospital-strength analgesics by the nice Chinese dentist, with more to take over the next couple of days until the antibiotics kicked in.

Michael was on a slow burn; he looked pale and quiet and it took me a few moments to take in that he was as angry as I had ever seen him.

44

'How long do you think it would have been before you realised?' he said as we crawled up Magazine Gap Road behind a number 15 bus.

'Michael, what the fuck are you talking about?'

He didn't turn to look at me.

'You've been here almost a year, and Conchita comes three times a week. She spends three hours in the flat each time. You've known her that long and yet you never once asked her a single question about her life? You're swanking around sucking up to rich shits and going out on boats, boat parties, and finding this madly cheap little place where they sell frigging Prada espadrilles and whatever it is, and no more Bollinger for me please, it's only Wednesday, and don't you like my new mobile phone it plays the "Marseillaise" as a ring tone, and who's the richest person you've ever met, all this fucking shite, this *shite*, yet you've never asked Conchita, who picks up your fucking knickers off the bedroom floor and washes them and puts them back in the drawer where they belong, and you've never asked her a single question about her life, you know fuck all about her, you hardly even see she's there?'

'Hang on a minute, Michael, I . . .'

'The truth is I don't know who you are any more. That's the kind of thing you laugh at when people say it on TV or in films, isn't it? It's the kind of line that really cracks you up. But I'm saying it and it's fucking well true. You've turned into this . . . this person I just don't recognise. You used to laugh at people obsessed with success and money and with having *stuff*. It was a real thing about you. Now you've got a Filipino maid and you won't give her the fucking time of day.'

'Well, Saint Michael rides in on his fucking chariot, kisses the leper's sores, takes a couple of arty black-and-white photographs, and goes home thinking well of himself.'

'What did you want when you came out here? What did you think you wanted?'

'To get away from you, mainly, you stuck-up useless shit,' I said. We had stopped at a traffic light by Happy Valley Road and I got out of the car, slamming the door and catching a brief glimpse of a very worried-looking driver in the front seat as I did so. I hoped his English wasn't any better than it seemed to be. I headed for the path at the top of Bowen Road, with no plan other than to walk for an hour or so, and hope that Michael died horribly in a car accident. Then I went to see *Casino* at a Wanchai cinema. It was so-so. By the time I got home, Michael had moved his return ticket from next Sunday to the preceding Wednesday, packed, and checked into a hotel.

Chapter Six

If I hadn't been so pissed off about Michael I probably wouldn't have done what I did next. Berkowitz had been nagging me, on and off, to write a series of profiles of local billionaires – the term defined as someone with a capital value of US$1,000,000,000. (We would have a little box inset in the first piece to help our readers calculate in which currency they were billionaires. Good gag. In those days, I didn't qualify even in Italian lira.) South-east Asia is where most of the world's billionaires live, so there was plenty of material, the only difficulty being presented by the fact that of all the various types of people there are, billionaires are about the least keen on publicity. It wasn't at all clear what kind of access I would get, and I very much didn't fancy the idea of spending weeks being fended off and playing phone tag with PRs and PAs.

'That's part of the interest,' said Berkowitz. 'Inaccessibility. Shiftiness. Keeping secrets. The whole point of these guys, especially in Hong Kong, is no one knows where the money comes from. Not the real mega-money but the money they started with. Focus on the early years.'

'I thought you said that the combination of British libel laws, Chinese ideas about face and a few hundred million dollars in the bank made for a cast-iron guarantee that no one ever said a truthful word about any of this,' I said.

'Not in public they don't. But,' said Berkowitz, waving his hands in front of his face like a man trying to enact the Dance of the Seven Veils without moving his body, 'you can *hint*.'

So now, in a rage, I went ahead and wrote about billionaires – except I didn't take Berkowitz's advice about hinting. Instead I went ahead and spent a month gathering, collating and writing up the unexpurgated story of the Hong Kong *über*-rich, focusing on the issue of where their money came from. In the case of several of the biggest local fortunes, the answers involved the Communists, the Triads, Khun Sa and his opium empire, and the rights to gambling in Macao. I put in all the stories which one heard told over and after drinks: about the money that had been filtered back from Macao to the socialist parties of Portugal and France, as recompense for mysterious favours; about the money which had poured into the British Conservative Party in the run-up to the 1992 General Election, a subject on which Hong Kong was pullulating with rumours; about how the appointment of Governor Patten – who as Conservative Party chairman had been in charge of spending the party's war chest in that same election – had in some local circles been seen as a discreet gesture of acknowledgement; about many other things besides. I put in, in short, as much of the secret history of Hong Kong as I had ever heard.

There was one omission from the piece: the Wos. Everybody knew about the Triad rumours in the family's past. Since there wasn't a hope in hell of printing anything about them in a magazine they owned, I deliberately left it all out, in the hope that that would be in its own way a signal about how things worked in Hong Kong. In the end, up against the deadline, I wrote all day and all night and filed the story at dawn the next morning. It was, though I say so myself, fucking great – the best piece I'd ever written. At ten, Berkowitz called me with a herogram. I ran a bubble bath and read a Mills and Boon, booked a massagé for four that afternoon, and went back to bed.

At about six I was floating around the flat in a post-massage stupor, feeling a bit knackered, a bit drifty, and very pleased with myself, when the phone rang again. I picked it up expecting more compliments.

'Miss Stone?'

'Yup, speaking.'

'Winston Tang here. Mr Oss's personal assistant. Mr Oss asked me to present his compliments and would it be possible for you to meet him at Queen's Pier in an hour.'

'Um, yeah, sure, may I ask . . . no, that's fine.'

Another herogram, I felt sure. News clearly travelled fast within the Wo organisation.

I arrived at the pier about ten minutes early, dressed for business in a pink fake-Chanel power suit, Gucci slingbacks, with a Prada handbag, and, for a touch of offhand cool, Calvin Klein sunglasses. Not bad, though I say so myself. Men always overestimate the extent to which women dress for display, and underestimate how much we use clothes as armour.

I wasn't sure who would be waiting for me. It was Oss himself, standing beside a pillar reading a copy of the *Wall Street Journal* through half-moon spectacles. He was wearing a very well cut uncrumpled linen suit and looked up as I approached. At his feet a Chinese man was crouched in a posture which, in the split second when I first saw it, looked somehow sexual – a prelude or aftermath of some self-immolating act of public fellation. Another half second's bug-eyed looking and I realised Oss was having his shoes shined. You often see Chinese men having this done; Europeans almost never. As I approached, Oss smiled.

'I was just getting some stock-market advice from my good friend Ah Loo here,' he said. 'He gives the best shoeshine and best stock tips in the whole territory.'

'Po Lam stock go up, last week I make five hundred dollar,' said Ah Loo in apparent confirmation.

'Does that mean I get my shoeshine for free?' Oss asked. To judge from the shoeshiner's reaction, this was a running gag. He paid Ah Loo, who did a big thank-you routine – it was evidently not a trivial tip. Ah Loo picked up his kit and ambled off towards the Star Ferry terminal in a rolling walk.

'We'll be popping out for a splash in *Tai Pan*; I hope that's all right?' said Oss. It's always nice, with this kind of meaningless rhetorical question, when you're never in a million years going to say no, if people exert themselves to sound as if they meant it.

'Delighted,' said the young Katharine Hepburn.

'Captain Mok should be here any m . . . – and here he is,' said Oss, who had folded his newspaper and tucked it under his arm like a baton. Many of his gestures had a faintly exaggerated or theatrical quality. He seemed younger than I had remembered, a well preserved forty-five passing for ten years less.

The boat was docking. Two Cantonese in matelots' uniforms were standing on the other side of a folded-out gangplank with what looked like velour rails. For some reason, getting off boats, which should be harder because you're never stone-cold sober when you do it, is easier than getting on. With the slapping and bucking of the water on the pier, *Tai Pan* was none too steady. Oss put one firm dry hand on mine and passed me over the gang-plank into the waiting outstretched arms of the Cantonese cast of *The Pirates of Penzance.* He himself then skipped nimbly and unfussily across, and I remembered that mention of something military in his background. He said something in Chinese to the older of the two sailors, which made the man smile.

'I told him we haven't lost one yet,' Oss said to me. 'We can go aft, which is more interesting and has the view, or below decks, which has the armchairs and is more comfortable.' I voted for below. I had decided that if Oss was too cool to tell me what this was about, I was too cool to ask.

'Good idea.' We went down into the first cabin, which was fitted out as a sitting room, and then into the one beyond, which was an office. A door into the room beyond was ajar, swinging slightly as the boat moved, and I could see it was a bedroom. The only decoration in the office was a series of framed woodcuts of Mount Fuji and, on the mantelpiece, a number of photographs of T. K. Wo standing with various luminaries. There was one of him with the Prime Minister of China and another with the Prime Minister of the UK. It made you think. Presumably it was meant to. Oss sat in an armchair in front of his desk, and I sat beside him. Soon we were nursing matching glasses of Cristal.

'He's a millionaire, you know,' he said. 'Ah Loo, the shoeshine man. Works twelve hours a day, plays the market, supports an extended family, and has a big new house built on old clan lands in the New Territories.'

'Only in Hong Kong,' I said. This was meant to be a joke, but Oss went all serious on me.

'Yes,' he said. 'Only in Hong Kong. Does it ever strike you that England is a childish place compared to here? That we're all infantilised back home? There's no real poverty in England. If there were, people would go and do what they do here – they'd shine shoes. It only costs a couple of quid to buy polish and brushes and set yourself up. But they'd rather sit on their arses and whinge about benefits. Here people go and work. And if they make money, what do they do? In England they piss it away. Spend it as if it were water. The proles spray Bollinger all over each other, and the toffs buy big houses and give themselves delusions about being lord of the manor. Here a rich man keeps going to work every single day and concentrates on looking after his family. Since the market became a big thing here, you have cab drivers, hotel doormen, lift operators who are worth millions. They all keep on doing what they do because they haven't been turned into children. But they know damn well that money is the only subject in the whole world that is completely serious.'

'Is that why you asked me out on your boat?' Oss had been leaning closer and closer towards me as he spoke; he smelt, not unpleasantly, of cologne.

'I liked your piece about local billionaires very much,' he said. 'Terribly amusing. Wonderful detail about Bob Lee's first business partner ending up in the foundations of the Cross-Harbour Tunnel.'

'Thank you.'

There was a pause; this wasn't quite the kind of congratulations I'd had in mind. Still, if your boss's boss's boss likes something you've done, you don't fuss about the form of the praise. Then Oss said:

'But I'm afraid we can't publish it.'

I didn't know what to say. I have once or twice seen people's jaws drop; it does actually happen; I suspect on this occasion it happened to me.

'What?'

'Perhaps I should have said, there's bad news and there's good news. The bad news is, as I say, we can't publish the piece. This is an extremely sensitive time for Hong Kong. The territory is about to enter a difficult period. The eyes of the world will be on us. The glare of publicity. It is a transitional phase. In thirty years' time, when China is the richest country in the world, people will be careful what they say. They will not lightly attract her wrath. At the moment there are some people who feel they can say anything, make any criticism, however intemperate. Hong Kong, or rather the future prosperity of Hong Kong, has many enemies. This story, in this form, will be a tremendous boon for them. I am sorry.'

I stood and ran upstairs. I was gasping for air, and I felt sick. We were round the corner of the island, and the water was less rough, so it wasn't that. It was a feeling from childhood. Something had been taken away from me. I started crying.

Oss left me alone for about ten minutes, and then came out to the rail beside me with a handkerchief and more champagne.

'I'm taking you to Po Lam. It's an island where Mr Wo has a house,' he said.

'Great, fabulous, whatever,' I said. He nodded. We did not speak again until we got to the island. When we did, Oss said, 'This is the good news part.'

I'd never seen anything like the house. But why would I have? It's not as if I knew lots of billionaires. If pressed, I think I would have imagined that Wo lived somewhere big and traditional. Where he did live was somewhere huge and modern, devised by a famous Chinese–American architect. It seemed to rise out of a bamboo terrace and weave around the hillside with views out over the smaller outlying islands. I was left on my own in the sitting room beside a gleaming Bang and Olufsen stereo which was playing some plinky-plink minimalist modern music. Oss had gone off 'to attend to a couple of things'. So far the only people I had seen were four silent Chinese servants dressed in white smocks and black trousers. I was feeling highly pissed off and also highly curious. The whole place had, more than anywhere else I had ever known, the aura of wealth, intense and concentrated down to an essence – and the essence was not to do with luxury or being able to have anything material that you wanted, but to do with insulation. Here, you were insulated from all consequences. Nothing that happened anywhere in the outside world could affect you. It wasn't that you were safe – because the idea of being safe admitted that you could be unsafe, implied the potential existence of its opposite. It was that the whole world could not reach you here. You could do anything you wanted to it and it could do nothing back.

A door that I hadn't noticed opened, and Oss said,

'Dawn, would you care to step in with us?'

I crossed the room, hearing my heels click, and went into what must have been Wo's office, or one of them. It was a huge bright clean room with a large fancy antique desk at which was sitting, in a shirt and tie but no jacket, behind thick glasses, Wo himself. Without smiling he stood up and extended his hand.

'Miss Stone,' he said.

'Mr Wo, it's a great honour.'

He gestured at a chair – a Mies van der Rohe, I think. Oss kept standing.

'We would like to offer you a job,' said Wo without preamble.

'What?' I said.

'A job,' he said again.

'I spoke about some of the special circumstances facing Hong Kong on the boat here,' Oss said. 'Special circumstances create special opportunities. Mr Wo's concerns will invariably attract attention. Hong Kong is going to be crawling with press. The prediction is that there will be more journalists here for the handover than were in Atlanta for the Olympics. We want our relations with the press to be handled sensibly and intelligently by someone who understands the way the western media work. The job is as a media liaison for all of Mr Wo's companies. You would be working for Mr Wo but, in the first instance, would report to me.'

'It sounds like you're buying me off.'

'This is a serious offer.'

'It sounds like glorified PR work.'

'There is obviously a PR component. But you will have much more power than that. In the future, if there were the need for a little conversation such as the one you and I had earlier, it would be you who took the decision.'

'I'm flattered but this sounds like a rather limited brief. What happens when they pack their bags and go home? Collect my P45 and get on the plane back to Heathrow?'

Oss looked at Wo, who nodded. For a moment I thought he was agreeing with what I'd just said and that, yes, I would be on the jumbo with my severance pay crammed into the top pocket of my Armani jacket.

'Mr Wo's business interests are diversified and not all of them are in Hong Kong,' Oss said. 'There are opportunities all over the world and a wise man does not neglect any of them. The wise man also seeks to diversify his interests during difficult times – times of transition. There will be many opportunities for a hardworking executive in the areas in which you show knowledge. Mr Wo's investments in the area of media already amount to many tens of millions of pounds. A not inconsiderable amount of those interests are in the English-speaking world. He's a man who has influence. The job we have to offer a successful executive in this field would be, it is safe to say, an opportunity of unparalleled range and interest and, dare I say so, power.'

Then he mentioned the salary. That was how the strangest day of my life brought me to work for Philip Oss and for T. K. Wo, and for money. And that was my fourth and biggest break.

On the boat home, Oss left me to myself for the first quarter of an hour, and then, just as I was thinking, disappointedly, that I'd be on my own for the whole return trip, he appeared on the afterdeck carrying another bottle of champagne and two glasses.

'So what do you think?' he asked.

'Of what? The place? Mr Wo? The offer?'

He shrugged in a way that meant all the above.

'It all seems a bit much. I'm not sure. I liked being a journalist. Part of me has misgivings about, well, going over to the other side.'

At that he just smiled and looked away from me, at the view of Hong Kong as we came around Lamma. Aberdeen was in front of us, its harbour as packed and frenetic as ever, as if the boats had hurtled in helter-skelter to avoid some large disaster.

'There was a waterfall over there,' he said, pointing off to one side of the Peak. 'It's what brought the British here in the first place. They came here for fresh drinking water for naval ships. The harbour on the other side was a bonus. Everything afterwards was a bonus.'

He smiled again and put the bottle, which he hadn't yet opened, back on the table. He stared hard at me as if to show me that he knew something I would never know, and then he took me by the hand and led me downstairs.

PART TWO

Tom Stewart

Chapter One

My parents ran a pub near Faversham in Kent. The Plough had already been in the Stewart family for two generations before my father came to inherit it. This was a mixed blessing, because he was a bookish and private man who wasn't suited to being landlord of a busy inn. At least that's what his mother, my grandmother, told me. I have almost no memories of him. I was born in 1913, when he was twenty-eight and my mother twenty-three. He spent the years 1916 to 1918 serving in the Kent Foresters, where his weak lungs kept him from the front. During these years my grandmother looked after me, my sister Kate, and my brother David, while my mother ran the Plough. I remember late Sunday evenings when we would go out on walks with her through hop fields which in my memory are huge and gold and fragrant. I remember the 'Welcome Home' sign that my mother hung over the doorway, just after my fifth birthday. Someone gave me a mouthful of bitter, which I swallowed despite my shock at its nasty, acrid, adult taste. I thought it was revolting. I felt sick and dizzy and over-excited.

Publicans often catch things from their customers. Nine months after my father came home from the war, he and my mother and sister were dead of influenza. David was the only member of the family not to be affected. He always was a little bruiser. I was the first in the family to come down with the illness, and went in and out of a fever for ten days before recovering. There used to be a photo, one and only one, of all six of us, my father looking peaky and nervous, my mother looking cheerful, and all three children in various states of bored distraction, all in our holiday finery for the 1919 camera. My grandmother looked like a clever pixie. She used to seem so old in that picture; a quarter of a century younger than I am now.

After that my grandmother ran the pub, as she had done when her husband was alive, and looked after me and David. Luckily, business was so good that she could hire help, and from the age of about ten, David and I would do our bit too. David liked to boast about his 'barrel-rolling muscles' and never got into a fight that he didn't win. I was better at stocktaking and doing the books. The regulars liked us and used to tease us about being so different. We had the two basic ways of working behind a bar divided between us: I was the listener, he was the talker.

One steady source of trade at the Plough was people heading to and from the Channel ports. My grandmother used to joke that people should make the most of their last chance to enjoy good English beer. Perhaps my desire to travel was something I was born with; but this steady stream of people leaving on business or pleasure or escape helped the idea to grow in me. I loved hearing stories about foreign places and would fasten on regular customers who broke their journey with us. One man called Mr Morris, a commercial traveller who often went to Paris, used to tell stories of the French who ate frogs and snails and blood pie and entrail sausage. He made Calais sound as exotic as Timbuktu.

I had inherited a globe from my father, faded and brown but beautifully detailed in the drawing. It was tilted slightly, like a man angling his head. I would spin it for hours, telling myself stories about all the places on the map. Sometimes I just recited the names. Khartoum. Vladivostok. San José. Chile. Tasmania. But the place that really caught my imagination was China. I used to like even the sound of the word.

When I could take the time away from work, I would go up to the coast and look out over the Thames estuary from Whitstable or Sheppey. David liked to go south to the sandy beaches, I liked to go north to the wildness and big views. I loved the coming and going of boats, especially the Thames barges, which seemed so sturdy and low-slung, so romantic in the matter-of-fact, practical way they set out to sea. I loved the huge skies over the estuary, the flatness and sense of space. It made me feel small and safe, and it made me want to leave.

My grandmother, who had never been outside Kent – had never been to London, forty miles away – understood this with no difficulty.

'It's all the world out there, all the things you might be able to see. You don't want to be in one place forever.'

'Nothing wrong with Faversham,' David would say if he was listening. 'There are cannibals in Africa. Boil you up in a big pot.'

I began saving money. Once we were eighteen, David and I drew allowances from the inn's profits. Not much but enough for pocket money and small treats. I didn't spend any of it. Then one day Mr Morris came with a more serious expression than usual. He said he was going away and that this was the last we would see of him for some time. I was drying glasses behind the bar and I asked him where he was going.

'Hong Kong. It's part of China.'

'Why?'

'Work. Been offered a job.' He thought for a while and added:

'The map is red. If you're British you can go anywhere in the world.'

When I turned twenty-one I did a deal with David. We owned a third of the Plough each. Our grandmother owned the other share. David would give me half of my share's worth in cash as soon as he could raise it. He would send me my sixth of the profits once a year until he raised the money to buy me out at whatever my sixth of the pub was then worth.

'Gran won't like it,' he said. We were sitting on the orchard wall about a mile from the pub. David swung his short legs.

'Ah, she won't mind really,' I said.

I thought my proposal was brilliant. The idea was to use David's cash plus the money I had saved to fund my own departure abroad. There was a grave flaw in the plan, however: it made me dependent on my brother's ability to save money. When it came to anything financial, David was all holes and no colander. I spent most of the next year close to going mad with frustration every time he left for the races or came home with a new shirt or dreamed aloud about buying a car. I forced myself not to say anything. Instead I fumed and planned. I split up with Monica Potts, the girl I was seeing, because I thought it would be cruel to drag things out until the moment of my departure, and then spent months watching her step out with another man, Eric Perks, whose father owned Faversham's first garage. I bought a suitcase and practised packing everything I owned into it. I studied expressions in the mirror – what I thought of as travellers' expressions: amused, calm, detached, experienced, enigmatic. I longed to be gone and burned with frustration as I stood behind the pub counter. It was a year-long sulk.

On my twenty-second birthday, in the summer of 1935, I decided that I couldn't bear it any more. I asked David if we could go for a walk. We went back to the orchard and hopped up on the crumbling wall.

'Look, David,' I said. He was staring at me as if trying to control an outburst of temper while he rummaged in his jacket pocket for his cigarette tin. 'The thing is . . .'

I took a breath, and as I did so, David started laughing. Now it was I who was getting angry. He laughed for some time. Then he took a fat envelope out of his jacket and gave it to me. I opened it. There were twenty ten-pound notes: two hundred pounds. The notes seemed huge, the biggest I had ever seen. It was the amount we had agreed on to buy out my one-sixth share of the Plough.

'David –' I began. He just shook his head.

'Standing there with your long fucking face all fucking year,' he said. 'I tell you, it's so easy getting up your nose, it's almost no fun.'

'How? Two hundred quid, how?'

'None of your business,' he said in a final way. I never did find out. I think he borrowed some of it and won the rest at the races.

Chapter Two

SS *Darjeeling*, a P&O ship, was leaving in September from Tilbury docks for Hong Kong via Marseilles, the Suez canal and Calcutta. I bought a ticket for £35. When I told my grandmother, she was standing in the kitchen of the Plough making a pot of tea. She showed no expression, but asked me how long I would be gone. I said I didn't know. I also realised for the first time how upset the thought of my leaving made her; it was something I had deliberately prevented myself from seeing. Later she gave me a gold necklace that had belonged to her mother.

'This is to sell if you need the money in an emergency. To get you home.' The next few weeks were difficult.

I said my goodbyes at the Plough rather than the docks.

'Good luck, Tommy son,' said David as we shook hands.

'Write,' said my grandmother. 'God bless, see all the things you want to see. Write.'

In the end I had two suitcases, not just the one. I took the train to London Bridge and then, for the first time in my life, a taxi. London was exotic, crowded and brown. The docks were the busiest thing I had ever seen. My stiff shiny passport, never used, was checked by a customs man whose uniform looked so spick he was something out of a film. Then I was sent over to the *Darjeeling*, much smaller and lower in the water than I had expected. My mind's eye was seeing something like the *Queen Mary*, a floating castle of lights. This looked only a few steps up from a tramp steamer. I asked the man in charge of allocating cabins how many passengers there were.

'Good few,' he said without looking up from his clipboard. He was Scottish.

I had heard about shipboard romances. The trip to Hong Kong would take six weeks. He had the plan for the dining room, at which the sittings were to be unchanged for the whole voyage. I said:

'Any single women at my table? Please say yes.'

'Aye, a pair of sisters. They're getting on in Marseilles.' He gave me an amused look as he handed back my ticket. I took it to be a token of male conspiracy or fellow feeling.

My cabin was tiny but because the ship was not full and I had it to myself, I had the choice of sleeping on the upper or lower tier of the bunk. There was a washbasin and a chair. The cubicle bathroom fitted a shower and a WC into the floor space the size of a doormat. The folding chair, I was to find, creaked and wobbled underneath one in rough weather.

There was no formal dinner on that first day. It was assumed that we had 'taken care of ourselves', as the purser explained it. He was a fleshy, oily man whose uniform buttons were always shiny and whose skin often had a sheen of sweat. He had a faint air of corruption which I came to think of as characteristic of his job. I had had nothing to eat since breakfast, and so stood at the rail as the ship left the dock conscious not of any large feelings about leaving England so much as of a bitter, cavernous emptiness in my stomach. Most of the other passengers and some of the crew had people at the dockside waving them off. A smart young married couple were seen off by both sets of parents, who stayed on the quay until we had gone out of sight round a wide corner into the Thames. Even the sardonic Scot who had given me my cabin, whom I now knew as the Third Officer, stood at the rail and watched the shore recede. I felt lonely and also felt for the first time the rashness of what I was doing. I stayed on the deck as we headed out to sea, with our pilot boat making visibly heavy going of the choppy water. Before long we were passing the Isle of Sheppey, looking back at all the places I'd liked to visit on Sunday afternoons. I had enjoyed watching ships head out into the world. Now I was on one of them. The Thames estuary seemed busier from the land than it now did from the deck. Out here on the water there was more space, more light, and more weather. As the light faded, the shore became a long flat line and then disappeared into the sea. I went down to my cabin to count the hours until breakfast.

Life on board the boat was more formal than I had expected. It was as if the sensation of openness and possibility brought by sea travel was feared, and so was warded off by a deliberate policy of stuffiness. I was travelling in something which once used to be called Standard, and had now been renamed Tourist Class. That word, 'tourist', was new. First-class passengers did as much as possible to pretend that they were on an entirely different ship. I took a glance into their lounge, pretending to be lost, and could not believe my eyes: it was the dining hall of a baronial lodge in Scotland, down to the fireplace, panelled roof, leather arm-chairs, crossed tapers on the wall, and mounted stag's head. A man in a tweed suit folded down the top of his newspaper to look at me. For a few seconds we stared at each other with frank class hostility and then he flicked the top of his paper back up with a harrumph.

Breakfast on that first day at sea was a crisis at which I ate two full cooked meals, and then felt so ill that I skipped lunch as we pulled down through the Bay of Biscay. I convinced myself that I was going to be a martyr to seasickness. It turned out that my queasiness was due purely to overeating. I spent all day in a chair on deck reading *Kim*, on the theory that it would prepare me for life in the East, and by the evening I had recovered, ready for the first formal meal.

The dining room was bright, a good space with heavy fixed fit-tings. Each table took twelve guests; several didn't have their full complement yet, as other passengers would be joining at Marseilles. Our table had three spare seats. Two of these belonged to the sisters who would be joining us in Marseilles. The third was to be taken by a soft-voiced captain in the Royal Artillery, who missed dinner on the first day; he seemed to need food only at irregular intervals, since he often skipped meals. Apart from myself, there were eight people present. The smart couple I had seen waving goodbye to their parents were the Scott-Duncans, heading out to Bombay for the husband to take up a post in the Indian Civil Service. He had, I gathered as much by hints and silences as by what was said, done very well in the qualifying exams. They had been married for six weeks. They were both clever and quiet and shy. They already seemed to be getting on well with a young Australian called McCague, who'd spent four years at Oxford and was now going home to his fami-ly in Adelaide, catching an onward connection from Hong Kong. He had the kind of Australian–Irish face in which the ears stick out as a young man, only to fall back into proportion as his visage fills out. There were two almost identical young men heading out to take up jobs with the Hong Kong and Shanghai Bank. They were called Cooper and Porter. Both of them looked very clean. Another young man, Tuttle, more raffish in demeanour, was taking up a post with Jardine Matheson, which he explained was one of the Hongs. I had no idea what that meant.

The last two people at our table were a married couple called the Marlers. I have lost count of the number of couples I have known in whom one partner's apparent vices exactly correspond to the other's virtues: bumptiousness to charm, noisiness to quietness, talking to listening, selfishness to grace, nastiness to kindness, meanness to generosity, closed to open, nasty to nice. I suppose people often look for a partner who can voice the parts of themselves they have difficulty in expressing. The Marlers were like that. He was a bluff Yorkshireman who spoke of himself as being 'in business', details unspecified. He was fifty or thereabouts, five and a half feet in each direction. She was an inch taller and spoke mainly to tell him to be quiet, stop bullying people, give someone else a chance to get a word in; and she smiled encouragingly at whomever Marler was trying to browbeat. She was a decade or more younger.

The atmosphere on board, and the difference between the boat's classes, came up as a topic of conversation at the very first dinner. That was thanks to Marler, who prided himself on never being in any doubt as to what was on his mind, and on never being slow to speak it. He had the kind of bluntness which is proud of itself.

'I could afford to travel first class perfectly easily. That's not a boast, it's a simple statement of fact. I've just paid a pound for a bottle of claret. It was damned good claret and I was happy to pay what it cost. It was worth it. A hundred pounds for a ticket to Hong Kong when you can take the same boat and travel through the same weather for a third of the price, that isn't luxury in my book, it's nothing more than stupid waste.'

All this was said in a tone which implied that someone had been arguing the other side of the case and it was his duty to set the record straight. If there was no one else to start an argument with, Marler would simply start one with himself.

'If people don't spend money, the whole economy grinds to a halt,' said one of the Hong Kong Bank men.

'Albert,' Mrs Marler said, with a warning note in her voice. She knew what was coming.

'And what would you know about the real economy, a lad like you just off to take up his first job? I built a business up from the ground with my own salt sweat. Forty years man and boy, getting up at dawn and going to bed after dark, and that means I know the value of money and I'm not going to sit in some over-stuffed armchair while my own lifeblood leaks away. Whatever some boy in his stiff new shoes tells me about so-called economics.'

'I've been in there,' I said. 'The first-class lounge. It's got a tiger-skin carpet.'

Everybody looked at me. Mrs Marler smiled.

'Quite right,' she said. Somebody changed the subject.

For a few days after that the weather was rough. It wasn't a full storm but it was enough to make most people ill. I found that I was what was called a 'good sailor', meaning I did not get seasick. In those days this was no trivial matter. I was often to meet expatriates who lived in dread of the journey to and from England.

The ship had a small library which was, in those seas, deserted. After finishing *Kim* in less time than it had ever taken me to read a book, I went and rummaged among the shelves. The material had a strong Eastern bias. Every magistrate who had ever sat on an Indian Bench or soldier who had put down a rebellion seemed subsequently to have written a volume of memoirs. As for most of the other writers, about the only one I had heard of was Somerset Maugham. I took *Of Human Bondage* down from the shelves, and killed time until we got to Marseilles.

We had half a day in the docks, so the Hong Kong Bank men, the Jardines man, and I were going to 'do the sights'. There was some kerfuffle about passports and transit visas and the like, which the Jardines man solved by speaking fast, confident, surprising French, and then we were let loose in the old part of town. Abroad, I could quickly tell, was different from England. The light and the smells and the people were all different.

My plan had been to keep the news about the sisters to myself. Perhaps the others would get tipsy and appear at dinner flushed and garrulous; perhaps they would gorge themselves in Marseilles and miss dinner. One way or another, my secret knowledge would give me a crucial advantage in making the all-important first impression.

In those days I had trouble keeping secrets. The two Hong Kong Bank men quickly went into a routine of saying 'Ooh la la' every time they saw an unaccompanied Frenchwoman under the age of sixty. We sat in a café where the Jardines man ordered us beers all round. The drinks were stingingly cold. A girl carrying a parasol over her shoulder walked by, sparing us a cool sidelong look as she did so.

'Ooh la la,' said both the young bankers.

'There may be some of that a little closer to home,' I said, unable to resist.

'What does that mean?'

'Oh, you know, rumours.'

'What sort of rumours?'

I made a point of observing the Marseilles streetscape at my own speed.

'You've noticed our table is missing two of its full complement.'

This had been the subject of open speculation.

'And?'

'Perhaps I happen to know that two glamorous young sisters are embarking on their own great journey eastwards.'

This news had all the effect I had hoped for. All three men sat back in their chairs. The Jardines man recovered first and said, in a note of dazed wonder, 'the fishing fleet'. This was the P&O term for single young women travelling East in search of a husband. Failures encountered on the homeward journey were known as 'returned empties'.

'How do you know?'

'I have my sources.'

My companions were not so much exhilarated, which is what I suppose I had expected, as thoughtful. I did not know then that in those days the life of a company man out East was close to that of a young army officer, in the sense that it was ordered within narrow social confines, and the opportunities to meet young women were not all that common. Both the bankers, for instance, were going to live in the 'mess' – company quarters for junior bachelor staff. The idea of young women made them feel pre-emptively wistful and sorry for themselves, with, of course, a wild romantic optimism bubbling underneath. They had all gone to single-sex boarding schools; they were almost totally ignorant of what women were actually like.

'What else do you know about them?'

By now I was beginning to feel chastened by their reaction. The giggles and high spirits had vanished; they were behaving as if this was an extremely serious development. A note of consterna-tion was present. Expectations of the journey were undergoing upheaval.

'Nothing that I haven't told you. I'm in the dark.'

I could tell that they didn't believe me. It was a muted four-some who spent the next few hours ambling about Marseilles; cries of 'Ooh la la' fell into abeyance. We went to visit the Sailors' Church at the top of the hill and the sight of the crowded bay, so dramatically curving round, and the thought of the number of sailors who'd seen this as their last ever glimpse of land, were sobering. We lunched, also soberly, in a brasserie by the old port which I remember not so much for the food, though that must also have seemed surprising, as for the wildly different nature of the restauration.

'There's no English equivalent to this,' I told my companions.

Then we simply wandered about, that skill of the young. By now we were all at the stage of pretending to be casual.

'I think I'll just have a wash and a brush-up before dinner,' said Cooper. Potter – they were sharing a cabin – agreed. The Jardines man muttered something about a quick snooze. Nobody was at ease.

At seven-thirty I went through to dinner, skipping a prelimi-nary drink in the bar on grounds of not wanting to appear disso-lute. I'd heard stories of what the East could do to a man and did not want to be seeming to get an early start. All three of my day's companions were already seated at the table. The other seats filled up over the next quarter of an hour. Our waiter brought a tureen of soup and began ladling out portions. I had my head lowered to the bowl and was taking a mouthful when I heard the dining-room door swing open and knew without having to look up that there were the sisters, making their entry. I straightened from my dish. On the one hand, the Third Officer had clearly been lying about the two women being sisters, since one was European and the other Chinese. On the other hand, he had been telling the truth, because it was apparent from their grey habits that the two of them were missionary nuns.

Chapter Three

Their names were Sister Maria and Sister Benedicta. They were Catholic missionaries from the Order of the Annunciation of the Blessed Virgin. The order was founded in the early nineteenth century. It was based in France and had an emphasis on education in Asia and Africa.

Sister Benedicta was the older of the two. She was a wiry Frenchwoman in her mid-forties, and was senior in the order's hierarchy. I found her intimidating, not least because she was alarmingly frank and – this was something I later came to expect from Catholic missionaries, though it was a shock on this first encounter – interested in and well-informed about all worldly subjects. Her special area of interest was politics and her sympathies were always and provokingly on the side of the local peoples. She made no bones about seeing all us young men setting out Eastwards to make our fortunes as a type; by no means her favourite type, either. The only time I heard her implicitly admit some sympathy for a governing power was when she spoke about French Indo-China. If I hadn't been so frightened of her I would have liked her very much.

The Chinese nun was Sister Maria. She was my age, more or less, tough and delicate at the same time; quick-witted; not so much pretty as perfect, as small-boned Chinese women can be. It was much later that I heard her story. She came from an inland part of the province of Fukien, a wild backwater famous for producing pirates. Her parents died when she was young and she was sent to live with relatives in Canton. A branch of the family had converted to Catholicism; they took her up and sent her to missionary school, where she simultaneously discovered her vocation and a talent for languages.

'It's the gift of tongues,' she told me. When she spoke of religious subjects her manner became heavy and serious, as if there were some increase in the level of gravity. Along with her lively side there was this pompous religious persona. She could switch between the two in a moment. I never got used to it.

Maria joined the Order when she was eighteen, and went to work in a mission school in Hong Kong, where she learnt her fluent English, which in those days had a faint and rather lovely Chinese–French accent. At this time she also spoke French, Mandarin, Cantonese, as well as several different varieties of Fujianese and Chiu Chow. She never made a big fuss about this, it was just something she could do.

'People are always more interested in what is impossible for them,' she once said.

The arrival of the two sisters at our table caused upheaval, though not in the way I had been expecting. The Jardines and Hong Kong Bank men – the other bachelors, if you exclude the absent Gunner – teased me about the nuns for a few days and then let the matter drop, referring to it only occasionally and affectionately in the past tense, like a favourite practical joke that somebody had played at school. ('That was a good one,' I said to the smirking Scottish Third Officer the next time I saw him.) They dealt with the nuns surprisingly easily, notwithstanding Sister Benedicta's obvious scepticism about the promising young Englishman as a genre. I suppose they had established models for dealing with women in a quasi-official capacity, formed by encounters with nannies, school matrons, and housemasters' wives. They were polite and interested when Sister Benedicta spoke about politics. Before long, the Jardines man had developed a technique for responding to her opinions – diatribes would be too strong a word – about British India, by asking innocent-sounding questions about the regime in Hanoi or Algiers.

All was not harmony and peace at our dinner table, however; on the contrary. For some reason the arrival of the two missionaries seemed to strike Marler on a psychic sore point. Right from the start, when he was introduced to them, he behaved like a man inflamed, provoked beyond all reason. His opening words to the sisters were:

'Off to save souls?'

This came out so bluntly, so much like a direct insult, that the rest of us simply laughed, as if this were a deliberate exaggeration of his usual directness, a clumsy attempt at humour. It seemed impossible that anyone would be this consciously rude, at first

meeting, to somebody he didn't know. Even his wife looked
embarrassed. But that didn't impede Marler in any way, and it
did not take long for the first proper argument. In fact, it happened during the dinner the first night after Marseilles. Sister
Benedicta had asked the army man whereabouts in India he was
headed. He said he was going to the Punjab.

'Ah, the Afghan frontier. So troubling to you British for so long
now. Subject peoples are often so ungrateful, are they not?'

Many of us may have been thinking, steady on, this is a bit
much for someone we've only just met, but everyone smiled
politely, except Marler.

'I think that those remarks are extraordinarily offensive,' he
said at considerable volume.

Sister Benedicta gave him a long cool French look.

'You are challenging the idea that the so-called North-West
frontier of your Indian Empire has been disputatious?'

'We brought order and justice to half the world. There was no
such thing as India before the British arrived there and civilised
. I simply will not accept this easy jeering from a citizen of a less
successful empire whose only real objection to British achieve-
ments, if the truth is admitted, is that they were British and not
French. As for the Catholic Church, systematically spreading
superstition, idolatry, ignorance, and wishful hocus-pocus wherever it lands, the whole institution, with its greedy corrupt priests
and credulous populace, casts a dark shadow on the earth and
the world would be better off without it.'

'Hocus-pocus is an accurate term. It is derived from "*hoc est cor-
pus meum*",' said Sister Maria.

'It is enviable to be able to speak with such confidence on subjects about which one knows so little,' said Sister Benedicta. 'I
was briefly in Peshawar, in which we have a little mission teaching medical skills to the local people as part of our mission to
spread darkness and unreason over the earth,' she said, speaking to the army man, who was listening with his eyes while continuing to eat soup. 'They have a remarkable range of
unfamiliar breads which I think you will enjoy. As for the
British bringing civilisation to India,' she went on, turning to
Marler, 'you will find, if you have the opportunity to spend
some time there, that the Indians were civilised many hundreds

71

of years before the Roman Empire first brought the light of reason to your homelands.'

It went on from there.

The next day, as we chugged across the tideless Mediterranean on our way to the Suez Canal, most of the passengers had settled down to a quoits tournament. The prize was a dinner for two at the Captain's table, with champagne. (Although meals were included in the ticket price, we had to pay for our own drinks.) I had teamed up with Cooper.

'What did you make of all that then?' I asked him.

'Bit rum,' he said. 'Not sure you should speak to a woman like that, however much you think she's talking rot. Still, bit of rough diamond, isn't he?'

'Bit of a bully,' I said.

'You have to get along with people if you work in an office,' he said, apropos, I then thought, of nothing.

We got as far as the semi-final stage of the quoits tournament before being knocked out by the eventual winners, the Purser and a young Welsh passenger. The Purser had the physical agility of a plump man and had also had lots of practice. His quoit throwing was a revelation.

I went into dinner that evening without a thought in my head beyond hoping there wouldn't be another argument. On that score I was in for a major disappointment.

It began innocuously enough. People had been talking about the next few days' sailing and the question of whether or not they were going to have a chance of spending some time ashore at Aden; it depended on our speed of progress.

'I've always wanted to see the souk,' said Mrs Scott-Duncan blushing. The young Australian made some casual remark about how much he was looking forward to going through the Suez Canal.

'A remarkable triumph of vision, perhaps even more remarkable as such than as a feat of engineering,' said Sister Benedicta. 'A victory of the imaginative and theoretical over the mere empirical. De Lesseps was convinced a canal could be built because his historical researches told him that the ancient Egyptians had managed to do it, and he was sure that anything accomplished in the past by guesswork and forced labour could be matched by the skills of French engineering. Many sceptics, not least some of your own countrymen' – Sister Benedicta appeared here to be bracketing the Australian in with the rest of us Anglo-Saxons – 'proclaimed the self-evident impossibility of the scheme. A favourite objection was that the desert winds would fill the canal with sand. De Lesseps of course paid no attention, as confident in his researches as in his calculations and his imagination. As a result the canal is a united triumph of reason and faith, so perfect as almost to resemble a parable.'

'Typical,' said Marler promptly and loudly. 'The French dressing up their imperial aspirations in a fog of claims about this and that. The simple truth is that we are a world power, you're not, and you want to be. No offence,' he then added.

'Not everything is about power,' said Sister Benedicta. This made Marler even more angry.

'Come off it, France is the most power-mad country in the world, the only one to conduct their foreign affairs without even a shred of concern for anything beyond national self-interest and self-aggrandisement. Power is precisely what French foreign policy has been all about since before the tyrant Bonaparte.'

'Reason and enlightenment are universal values and France has done what she can to spread them. Not every country can say the same.'

'It fails to make any sense to me how a member of an institution as corrupt and benighted as the Catholic Church can spout about reason. Your church spreads superstition and ignorance wherever she goes. Talk about power, that's the only thing your church has a significant interest in – the slightest real interest.'

Sister Maria responded by saying:

'When to the sessions of sweet silent thought
I summon up remembrance of things past,
I sigh the lack of many a thing I sought,
And with old woes new wail my dear time's waste.
Then can I drown an eye unused to flow
For precious friends hid in death's dateless night,
And weep afresh love's long-since-cancelled woe,
And moan th'expense of many a vanished sight;
Then can I grieve at grievances foregone,

And heavily from woe to woe tell o'er
The sad account of fore-bemoanèd moan,
Which I new pay as if not paid before.
But if the while I think on thee, dear friend,
All losses are restored, and sorrows end.'

There was a silence.

'An Irish nun, Sister Bernadette, taught me that poem,' she said to Marler. 'I suppose she was only interested in power, too.'

'Well –' he said, but she went on:

'The Church brought me out of darkness and ignorance into light. It taught me that thanks to God's grace I have a gift, and thanks also to his grace I can share some of my gift with other people through teaching.'

'And shoving a bucketload of superstitious claptrap down their throats at the same time.'

'Nobody shoves anything down my pupils' throats. Education is the opposite of ignorance.'

'I am sure you have great gifts, Sister, and I'm sure you're wasting them in such a backward institution.'

'I can reach more of the people I need to reach where I am than in any other body on this earth.'

'But they can't learn as much as they would if they were being taught in an atmosphere that didn't reek of superstition and idolatry.'

'On the contrary, our students learn quicker than in secular schools.'

'I find that difficult to believe.'

'Nonetheless it is so.'

'It's easy to make claims when there is no way of substantiating them.'

'Who said there was no way of substantiating them? I can take a person wholly ignorant of a language and raise him up to a functional standard within a matter of weeks. I could do it with any of the gentlemen around this table tonight. I could even do it with you, Mr Marler.'

'I find that also difficult to believe.'

And then, I suspect for no other reason than that she was sitting next to me, she said:

74

'I can have this gentleman able to pass muster in Cantonese by the time we get to Hong Kong.'

Marler laughed at that, and sat back in his seat.

'You should be careful what you say, young Sister, or I'll take you up on that bet.'

'About five hundred of your pounds sterling would more than keep our mission in Hong Kong running for a year,' said Sister Benedicta.

Marler became serious. For him, talk about money was always fighting talk.

'Well now,' he said, 'perhaps there is an opportunity for a meaningful wager here, if we look hard enough. Let's see. You can hardly put up an equivalent amount in cash, of course. Perhaps you have the leasehold on a property or two, which might be of interest . . . no, again that's missing the point. Somehow it would be wrong to exchange a thing for a thing. An exchange of goods for labour, perhaps that would be more like it. Yes. All right, Sister Maria, how's this: you win and I give you your five hundred pounds. I win, and you come and work for me in my Hong Kong office for a year. How's that?'

Sister Benedicta and Sister Maria looked at each other for a moment and then Sister Benedicta said:

'Agreed.'

'I think I must be missing something here,' I said. 'The part where someone asks me if I'm willing to go along with the bet? Or doesn't my view matter?'

Sister Benedicta gave me what I think is usually described as a winning smile'.

'We were merely seeking to be clear about the terms on which we were soliciting your invaluable help,' she said.

My spirits were rising and sinking at the same time. The prospect of a six-week cruise playing shovelboard and reading bad books about the mysteries of the Orient had a lot of appeal. On the other hand, I knew right from the start that I was interested in Sister Maria. Could Benedicta have already seen this? I said:

'It's a heavy responsibility. If I fail –'

'With God's grace we can have every confidence,' said Sister Benedicta.

I gave in. I left the table slightly shell-shocked and, thanks to

Marler ordering claret to toast the bet, which he clearly thought of as a sure thing, a little drunk. The two nuns had gone to bed an hour before. Sister Maria's last words to me were:

'We'll start work in the morning.'

'You must not drink so much coffee,' Sister Maria told me. 'Just one cup. It is bad for the memory. I learnt this in France.'

We were sitting in the library, which we had decided to commandeer. No one ever seemed to use it much. The Eastward-bound did not seem to be great readers. Sister Benedicta had come and fussed around us while we were arranging two armchairs on either side of a table on which Sister Maria had put an ominous pile of what looked like reference books. For a moment I thought queasily that we were going to be chaperoned all through the next weeks. But the older nun left after satisfying herself that the room had been set up correctly.

'It helps wake me up,' I said. Through the library window I could see a perfect patch of bright, clear Mediterranean blue.

'The best way to wake up is to exercise the brain. Now,' she said, opening a large spiral-bound notebook and picking up her fountain pen with a flourish, 'let's see. Do you speak any foreign languages?'

'No.'

'Not at all? Fragments of French, German, Latin studied at school?'

The truthful answer was yes, at school, where languages had been my best and favourite subject. Speaking to foreign visitors was one of my reserved occupations at The Plough. I was feeling irritated and in low spirits, so I said:

'Not a word.'

'Excellent. Of course the very best thing would be if you were a trained and gifted linguist, a scholar, ideally with experience of learning a non-Indo-European language. But to have no experience at all is second best. It means you have less to unlearn. Now. What do you know about Chinese? Nothing? Don't be embarrassed, it's only to be expected.'

I indicated by gesture that I was not embarrassed but that I did indeed know nothing about Chinese.

'Chinese is for our purposes two entirely separate sets of lan-

76

guages, one of them written and the other spoken. The written language is everywhere the same, and the spoken languages are everywhere different. The written language allows a scholar from Fukien to correspond with a scholar in Peking even though the words they pronounce when they look at the characters are entirely different, just as a mathematician in Moscow and a mathematician in Paris can read each other's equations even though they cannot understand each other's speech. But the written language is complex, allusive, and has no bearing whatsoever on spoken Cantonese, so I propose to leave it entirely apart. Except for one thing.'

She sketched a pair of crossed lines on her pad with a quick, light pen stroke.

'Can you see a man walking?'

I could, sort of. I said so.

She complicated the figure with a cross stroke and a prow-like line.

'He is kneeling?' she asked.

'Sort of.'

'No – he is a woman.' She laughed – the first time I heard her laugh, and at one of her own jokes.

'Of course.'

'The position of women in traditional Chinese society is subordinate. Now this character means son. Put the woman and the son together and you have – guess.'

'Family,' I said.

'A reasonable guess – but where is the father? No, it means "good". Or, in other senses, "to love". I'm not going to talk any more about Chinese writing, but I wanted to show you, so that you can bear it in mind over the next days, that some things are universal and belong to all languages. People everywhere share the same creator, and therefore people everywhere are essentially the same.'

This she said in what I came to call her missionary-miss manner, the same one she had used to talk about 'the gift of tongues'. Because of that I said:

'I thought "East is East and West is West, and never the twain shall meet."'

'Your Kipling is overrated,' she said. 'Now. I have some good news. English is a complicated language, with many long words.

77

The favourite example is antidish –' she made a slip, and gave a quick, girlish giggle – 'antidisestablishmentarianism. A sensible doctrine, by the way, since it opposes the separation of church and state, which is something of which Confucius would have approved. But these big words are very difficult to learn. In Chinese we have no big words. We have indeed no words of more than one syllable. Do you know how many sounds can be made that are no longer than a syllable?'

She assumed that I knew what a syllable was; I liked her for that. It turned out later that she had guessed that I was lying about my French and German. I said:

'A couple of hundred, I suppose.'

'Correct. About four hundred. That doesn't sound enough to make a whole language, does it?'

'Um – no, I wouldn't have said so.'

'That's right. In Chinese, because we have only monosyllables, we have extra ways of distinguishing between them. For this we use tones. For foreigners trying to learn Chinese this is often the most difficult thing to grasp, because they convince themselves of its strangeness. But it is not strange at all. Woman and son means good. Everyone is similar and so are languages. The greatest obstacle to learning is fear. Tones you use also in English. Consider. "Here!"' she said emphatically, 'is not the same meaning as, "here?" One is a command, the other is a question. The difference is the tone. In Chinese we use these tones in a structured way. The meaning of a word is made by the monosyllable and its tone together. Yes?'

I gestured that I understood, more or less.

'Every word has for our purposes six tones. So the language consists of four hundred monosyllables and six tones – about twenty-four hundred words. Very very easy, compared to English. We shall win our bet with no difficulties. For instance, *yau yau yau*.'

'I beg your pardon?'

'*Yau yau yau*. Can you hear the difference? *Yau yau yau*.'

I could, sort of. The first was high and level, the second flat and medium pitch, the third clenching and final.

'*Yau* means worry. *Yau* means paint. *Yau* means twin. You try it.'

And so we began.

*

Sister Maria and I did eight sessions a day: four in the morning, four in the afternoon. These sessions were forty minutes long, and after each of them I had a five-minute break, which I usually spent standing at a railing or wandering around the deck. My memories of these interludes are vivid. The open sweep of the sea and the salt air and the sun felt like a reprieve.

As news of the bet with Marler became more widely known, people began to smile at me and wish me luck. Or rather, most people did. After about a week, one of the passengers, a red-faced man who was headed all the way out to New Zealand, protested to the Purser about the way we were 'hogging' the library. The Purser attempted to calm the man down, or at least said he did, and then asked the Captain to adjudicate. Maria and I and the red-faced man were summoned to the Captain's cabin.

'So what's all this then?' said the Captain, a large slow man who was filling his pipe as he spoke. The red-faced man complained about what we were doing at some length, focusing on the impossibility of 'getting any serious reading done' in earshot of me and Maria.

'These bloody squeaking noises, they're worse than somebody learning the violin,' he said.

I explained about my crash course in Cantonese.

'Trying to learn the old Chinee-speak, eh?' said the Captain. He then fiddled with his pipe without looking at anyone for about sixty seconds. Finally he said:

'Good show.'

The subject was closed. We were allowed to use the library. Maria and I kept slogging ahead.

Every now and then Marler would try and raise the subject of the bet with me at dinner, by way of needling the two nuns.

'How you coming along there, young Stewart? Able to order dog cooked in different ways yet?'

'It is not appropriate to discuss the wager now that it has been laid,' said Sister Benedicta. Marler would go quiet, which was the closest he ever came to being tactful.

was looking forward to Aden. ('A pure creation of British fears about Napoleon's extraordinary success in Egypt,' said Sister Benedicta.) It would be a welcome break. How long we would

79

have to spend there depended on whether we made good time, so I cheered the boat on as we ploughed across the Med. I got my wish: we made reasonable progress across the sea and through the canal and had a whole day in the city. I wanted to be on my own so I made excuses to my Hong Kong Bank and Jardine companions, who were beginning, due to the pressures of the bet, to treat me solicitously. It was their first time out East too, though the fact that all of them had jobs with big companies made them behave as if they were seasoned veterans of life beyond Suez.

'Chap gets off the boat at Aden. This little Arab man comes up to him. "Go away," says the chap. "You want girl?" says the Arab. "You want boy? You want picture?" "Go away!" says the chap. "Leave me alone! I demand the British Consul!" "Ah!" says the Arab. "Very difficult! Very expensive! But I can fix!"'

There was a reality underneath our jokes and nervousness. Aden was, for the first time, the East. It was hot, especially once I got away from the docks into the city proper. I had a glass of mint tea at a roadside stall, ordered by pointing at what the other customers were drinking. The man who poured it for me was dressed in a djellaba and his teeth were stained black. He crammed sprigs of mint into the glass and poured boiling water from a kettle suspended over a brazier. The smell reminded me of summer in Kent.

All the stalls in the market were busy. People plucked at me wherever I went. I caught a glimpse, down a crowded and overhung alleyway, of the Scott-Duncans, sitting on stools surrounded by at least a dozen shouting carpet-sellers. A mountain of samples was being brandished and extolled. Mrs Scott-Duncan looked happier and less self-conscious than she ever did on board the ship.

I stopped for a late-afternoon meal in a place called Tommy's Tea Parlour, with the intention of skipping that evening's dinner on the *Darjeeling*. The premises were designed to appeal to half-genteel travellers. Its walls were decorated with hunting prints and English landscape pastels. The effect was grotesque. I ate an omelette and set off back to the ship feeling dissatisfied. As I came out of the door, a man in Arab dress burst past me, running at a speed made possible only by pure terror. A few seconds later an English voice, out of breath, called 'Stop, thief!' The Arab, by now about fifty feet away from me, turned to look back over his shoulder and as he did so ran straight into a group of four policemen who had appeared, as if by telepathy, out of a side alley. I do not mean 'ran into' as a figure of speech: he collided with the first two policemen and went over in a heap of limbs. The cacophony, as the policemen all got up, dusted themselves off, seized and shook and shouted at the prisoner, was extraordinary. Meanwhile the victim of the robbery was getting closer. He was a stout fifty-year-old Englishman in white colonial clothes, breathing hard and carrying a straw hat by the brim. When he got to the thief, now being held firmly by all four policemen, he stopped. The thief's expression was of pure animal terror. His eyes were all whites. The Englishman stood still for a moment and seemed to be waiting for something. Then he spat into the thief's face.

As we sailed through the Red Sea, the heat and, somehow, the density of the air seemed to grow daily. The sun appeared bigger and closer. First-class passengers switched from black dinner jackets to white for the evening meal.

The weather grew even warmer, the sunsets more abrupt, as we sailed south towards the tropics. The novelty of the voyage and of my Cantonese lessons had worn off. Conversations settled into predictable patterns; Marler and Benedicta got into fewer arguments. Maria two or three times gave me leave to compete in quoits tournaments which would otherwise have clashed with our lessons. Once, the Jardines man and I got to the final, where we were defeated, inevitably, by the Purser and his (I was now convinced) catamite. We had engine trouble in the Red Sea, which made the ship three days late into Calcutta – which in turn meant there was time only to load supplies and head off again eastwards. I wasn't really sorry. Even in our brief view of the docks, after the peace of the long days sailing from Aden, the city looked overwhelming. I was touched by the fact that the artillery officer came down to my cabin to say goodbye; or rather not to say anything, but to give me a very firm and prolonged handshake while looking into my eyes, as if we had braved great tribulations together. Perhaps, for him, that was what those communal dinners had been.

*

Two days after leaving Calcutta we hit genuinely bad weather for the first time. The Bay of Bengal is shallow; its storms arrive quickly and can be severe. As a good sailor I was spared sea-sickness but I was not spared fear. The dread was made worse by the fact that the storm came on at night when there was no moon, so the ship began to yaw and pitch in a dark which offered no point of reference. The sea seemed malevolent. The sense that we were bobbing loose on the waves was hard to resist, especially when a wave carried the *Darjeeling* upwards and let her fall freely on the downslope. You could feel the engines lose traction in the water as we slid forward, and it was hard not to tense one's muscles in anticipation of the bow's punching into the bottom of the next wave.

I found it difficult to sleep that night. Like a man with a fever or a bad worry, I hoped that the morning would automatically bring relief – and in a way it did, since the steep, grey, quick-moving waves were less frightening when I could see them. I also thought that daylight would somehow cause the storm to go away, a view of which I was disabused by our waiter, who had the seaman's love of frightening novice travellers.

'Two or three days of this would be normal for these parts,' he said. 'Once going around the Cape . . .'

I stopped listening. After breakfast I went down to my cabin to clean up before my lessons and found a note from Maria pushed under my door. No one else from our table had made it to breakfast.

> Dear Mr Stewart,
> I am afraid I have to cancel today's lessons as I am indisposed. I hope you will understand. Please feel free to look over your vocabulary cards.
> Yours sincerely,
> Sister Maria

My vocabulary cards had the English word on one side, the Chinese word, spelt out phonetically, on the other. They stayed safely untouched all that long day. I wandered carefully around the boat. There was something regal about my isolation. I had most of the Tourist Class parts of the *Darjeeling* to myself. I even contemplated paying a visit to the Scots baronial sitting room of the first-class passengers. But the ship was moving about so much and so violently that I decided simply to stay put, so I spent most of the day in the Tourist Class sitting room looking out of the stained windows at the unyielding storm.

That night I again couldn't sleep. After going to bed, turning off the light for an hour or two and feeling the pitch of the boat, I gave up. I put the light back on and lay there a while before finally getting dressed and going up to the public rooms. It was now about 1 o'clock in the morning. I opened one of the doors out on to the deck proper, at the back of the ship. It was disconcerting to feel the rainless warmth of the strong wind. Maria was standing at the same rail. She didn't hear me approach and startled when I arrived beside her.

'I can't sleep either,' I said. 'Are you all right?'

It was a stupid question. Even under the dim light spilling out from the back of the ship's public rooms, she was a peculiar blanched colour.

'Sick,' she said. 'I feel sick. For over a day now. It is such an unpleasant feeling to be so protracted.'

'I don't get that, but it does make me nervous. My stomach's all right but I do feel frightened. I suppose I'm the other way around from you.'

'No, I have fear also. Faith does not cancel fear.'

She was gripping the guardrail with both fists. She did not move away. After a while she said:

'N. G. O. H. Ngoh.'

'What?'

'It will help take our minds off the storm. I'll test your vocabulary. Ngoh. N. G. O. H.'

'Er . . . I, me.'

'Chín.'

'Money.'

'What is the word for thing?'

'Yéh.'

'And for weather?'

'Er . . . tinhei.'

'And for the verb to eat?'

'Sihk.'

She fell silent. The boat was still pitching as violently as ever. We stood there for the better part of an hour. Maria said:

'I'm starting to feel a little better.'

I reached out and put my right hand on top of her left. She stood there for a few seconds and then went inside. When I woke up in the morning the sun was shining and the sea was flat.

A few days before we were due to arrive in Hong Kong, a crewman I had never seen before – one of the First Class stewards – knocked on my door after the morning lessons. I was lying on my bunk, smiling at the ceiling. There had been a vocabulary test, and I had done well.

'The Captain presents his compliments and says he would like to see you in his cabin at your convenience, sir.'

'I'll follow you,' I said, my heart beginning to thump. I assumed I must be in trouble, though I couldn't imagine for what. We went forwards and upwards towards the crew's quarters. The steward knocked, was told to come in, saluted and left. The Captain was sitting at a desk in his bare, entirely unhomely quarters: no pictures, no evident comforts, apart of course from the pipe he was still sucking and fiddling with. He didn't meet my eye.

'Good voyage?' he asked.

'Yes, thank you.'

By now I was dreaming in Cantonese; or rather, since my Cantonese was still primitive, in chunks of it, bits of the language floating past me in my sleep like debris. Maria and I had spent so much time together it felt as if we could read each other's minds. At lunch we finished each other's sentences.

'Good.' There was another of his silences while he looked down and across the room. If there had been a porthole across his cabin at floor level, he would have been looking out of it.

'How's the Chinese? Coming along?'

'Difficult for me to say, sir. I'm too much in the middle of it. When I ask her how she thinks the bet will go, Sister Maria just says, "Do not despair, do not presume."'

The Captain nodded but did not speak. There was more pipe activity. Then he said:

'I've been sailing out East for thirty years. My whole sea life. Not many chaps bother with the lingo. I've noticed that. So you have something most people don't. Bear that in mind. You need a job, accommodation?'

I was so surprised that for a second I couldn't speak. Eventually I managed:

'Well . . .'

'No shame in that. With your permission, I'm going to take the liberty of mentioning your name to a chap I know. Go and see him in a couple of days' time after we arrive. He's called Masterson and he runs the Empire Hotel. Anyone will tell you where it is.'

In that act of unsolicited kindness, I catch a glimpse of how I must have seemed to other people in those days; how very young.

By the time we arrived in Hong Kong, Sister Benedicta and Marler had come to an agreement about the precise form of the bet. We would meet three days after arrival, to have lunch at the Hong Kong Club. The Captain would be present. Afterwards we would go and find a Chinese passer-by with whom to test my Cantonese in the following way: Marler would ask me a question, I would ask the Chinese passer-by the same question, I would relay the answer to Marler, and if the reply was satisfactory Maria would have won her bet. The Captain would adjudicate.

People often say that their memory of an event or an occasion is a blur. Mine never is. I remember with crystalline accuracy or not at all. My recollection of those first days in Hong Kong more than sixty years ago is still sharp enough to cut. We came into the harbour an hour after dawn. The last shreds of mist clinging to the Peak were being burnt off by the sun; they looked like smoke, as if the island was an active volcano. The harbour was, as it always has been, busy. The junks were like overgrown children's toys, or things seen in a dream. At first glance you could see they were family enterprises. Children and grandparents jostled on the decks, cooking and eating and living their lives. The sampans bucked up and down the waves like skittish young horses. A British warship, HMS *Leo*, the first we had seen since Aden, lay low in the water, its grey North Atlantic camouflage making it conspicuous in the South China Sea. I could see the limp Union Jack hanging above Government House. I felt the purest excitement as I looked at the Peak and imagined myself up there looking down.

Maria had joined me at the rail.

'So what do you think?'

'It's –'

I laughed. So did she.

'It's Hong Kong,' she said. '*Heung gong*. Fragrant harbour.'

The harbour had a distinct, dirty smell, too brackish to be mere seawater. I said: 'That's one way of describing it.'

Maria smiled. 'Chinese joke,' she said.

'I don't want you to spend a year working for Marler.'

'Nor do I. I don't believe it will happen.'

On the day of the test I woke up feeling nervous, with a fluttering stomach. The proprietor of my boarding-house brought me a plate of fried food, bacon and eggs and sausage, which I now realise was an elaborately polite nod to my Englishness. I split the yolk of my egg and found that I couldn't eat so much as a mouthful. On the front page of the *South China Morning Post* there were items about the visit of the HMS *Leo*, a reception at Government House, and an account of a jewel robbery in Wanchai. I spent the rest of the morning looking at vocabulary cards, and met Maria on a bench beside the Hong Kong Cricket Club half an hour before our lunch date.

'You look nervous,' she said. She was dressed in her full formal habit and we must have made a strange couple.

'I am nervous.'

'No need. Our Lady will look after us.'

Even if I don't believe in her? I thought.

'Where's your stuff?'

Maria laughed.

'"Stuff." What a word. We have little luggage, as you know, and what there is of it has gone ahead to the train.'

In those days, before the Communists won the civil war, you could take a direct train from Kowloon to Canton. Immediately after lunch, that's what Maria and Benedicta were going to do.

'And if I lose, you'll be back?'

'I shall.'

'I'd better not lose then, had I?'

86

I could tell as soon as I put a foot over the threshold that the Hong Kong Club was the poshest and snootiest institution I had ever been in. There was a smell of leather armchairs and, faintly, last night's cigars. This did not help me to feel any less on edge. Mr and Mrs Marler and Sister Benedicta were already sitting at a table in the only one of the dining rooms which allowed women at lunchtime. I learnt afterwards that there had been special negotiations to have Sister Maria allowed in; being Chinese, she would normally not have been permitted in the Club. All three of them were sitting behind what looked like large gin-and-tonics. Marler, beaming, got up and held out his hand as we came in.

'Ah, the teacher and her pupil, and very welcome you are. Have a pew.'

His Yorkshire accent was less noticeable; he didn't make such a big production of it in Hong Kong. We sat down and went through what, for me, was an excruciatingly laborious lunch. I could think only of the disgrace involved if I lost the bet, and of what I would be doing to Maria. She could not fail to resent me bitterly. Marler and Sister Benedicta, though, seemed to be vying with each other in affability and chumminess. By the time we got to coffee and cigarettes I had been to the bathroom four times.

'Now,' said Marler, making great play with a balloon of brandy and for some reason smiling at Sister Benedicta as he spoke, 'we come to the business of the meeting.'

'Right,' I said, feeling I needed to take charge, assert myself, stride confidently towards the gallows. 'Let's go and find a Chinese man. Or do you want to use one of the waiters? A rickshaw man from outside? Yes? But where's the Captain?'

'Well,' said Sister Benedicta, 'Mr Marler and I have been discussing this and have reached certain conclusions.'

'The thing is,' said Marler, 'I've seen Sister Maria in action with you and I fully accept her assertions about the efficacy of her teaching methods. I also see that you show no signs of converting to the Roman Church, ho ho. So I withdraw without reservation my remarks about the deliberate spreading of ignorance and superstition.'

'And I on my part unreservedly accept Mr Marler's apology, and regret my own vehemence at the time of our earlier disagreement,' said Sister Benedicta.

'The question which remains is, whether it makes sense to carry on with the bet or not. The thing is, it's a lot to ask of Sister Maria, to come and work for me for a year. I'd be turning her life upside down, and disrupting the work of her mission. I'm not saying I necessarily agree with her mission, but it's what she believes in, and I'd be subjecting her in its stead to a kind of indentured servitude.'

'For our part, even though we are eager to subsidise our mission in Hong Kong, we have no desire to bankrupt Mr Marler, or to subject him to financial strain.'

'So we have decided, in short, to waive the bet.'

'Hey just a bloody . . . excuse me Sisters, just a minute,' I said, suddenly very angry. 'So the grown-ups make the decision and the children scuttle along behind doing what they're told? What about the six weeks' work we've just put in for your bloody wager? All that time I could have spent looking out the window and wandering around the decks? What if I don't want to waive the bet? What if we want to keep you to it?'

'Now Tom,' said Maria, 'we have to be reasonable. Mr Marler has a lot to lose if we should settle this wager, and so does our mission. Words were rashly spoken on the boat and it is only sensible that as adults we should seek a mature resolution. It would be unchristian of us to force Mr Marler to build our mission at great cost to himself, against his will.'

I got up and walked out. Maria, running, caught up with me on the pavement outside the Club, where a small crowd of rickshaw men looked on with unconcealed curiosity.

'Tom, I'm sorry, I didn't want –'

'You knew.'

She sighed.

'Not until last night. You should understand, the Bishop would never have let me go and work for Marler. Benedicta explained this to me. She lost her temper, she got carried away. She's sorry. But the bet was not really in good faith, that's why she had to settle it. Marler doesn't know the real reason.'

I said: 'Goodbye, and thank you for a highly instructive six weeks,' and walked away. I didn't see her again for four years.

Chapter Four

One hundred and twenty-four Nathan Road was a three-storey, warren-like building on Kowloon side with a large number of over-decorated small rooms, a creaking lift, and a Sikh with a shotgun guarding the locked front doors. The rooms had high ceilings and ornate lacquer-framed mirrors. The overhead lights were dim and the bedside lights had red shades. The curtains were scarlet. The bedsteads were covered in dragon motifs. Dust had secreted itself into every cranny.

'So what do you think?' said Masterson. He was standing by the open window looking down into the noise and traffic of Nathan Road.

'Can't fault the location,' I said. He nodded but did not turn around.

'Quite like the fact that it's got two entrances,' he said as if to himself. Then he pushed away from the window, left the room, and, with me following, headed back to the lift. Mr Luk, the owner of 124 Nathan Road, was waiting there. He was fidgeting. With him was a caretaker who held a football-sized ring of keys.

'So sorry, Mr Luk,' said Masterson, 'but your building is too big for me. I would be expanding too quickly, and couldn't hope to fill the shoes of a great businessman like yourself.'

Mr Luk smiled, either out of embarrassment at being turned down, or at the compliment.

'Do you wish to raise the question of price?' he said. I tried not to smirk; on the ferry ride over to Kowloon, Masterson had told me that Luk would treat refusal as a bargaining tactic.

'So sorry, Mr Luk. It is not a question of price but of scale. My business is not big enough.'

We rode down in the lift together after the caretaker had locked the room. Mr Luk confided that he had three other potential buyers coming to visit the property that afternoon. Down on Nathan Road, while the caretaker struggled again with his keys, we said our goodbyes, and Masterson and I headed off for Hong Kong side, past the Peninsula Hotel. Across the road, a flurry of porters, rickshaws, and taxis outside the railway terminus made it clear that the Canton to Kowloon train would be arriving before long. The train was one reason why Masterson had been looking for a property on Kowloon side.

'Pity,' he said, looking at the expectant crowd of greeters and baggage-handlers. 'Still, it wouldn't have worked.'

I had taken the Captain's advice. The Empire Hotel, right in the middle of Victoria town on Hong Kong Island, was a lovely, cool colonial building with ceiling fans, palms in the lobby, and a Belgian cook. Masterson was its manager and half-owner. The other half belonged to an absentee German called Munster. They had met and teamed up in Singapore in the twenties.

Masterson was a thin, intent man in his forties, with the type of concentration that can make a man seem absent-minded. In a different time, in a more heroic period of the Empire, he would have ended up running something big. He had gone into the hotel business to make his fortune and come out to Hong Kong for the same reason. When I went for my interview, he was perched at the counter of the hotel's main bar, a long room off the elegant lobby. He was dressed casually, with a white jacket and a shirt open at the neck. He was smoking. In those days, when many people smoked a great deal, Masterson smoked literally all the time.

Hoteliers have few illusions about human nature; Masterson had none. He asked me a number of questions about my experience, my Cantonese lessons with Maria, and about the Plough, and then he gave me a job. The speed and decisiveness of this process was, I was to learn, characteristic. I would act as his sidekick and take responsibility for the bar, alcoholic beverages, and all non-restaurant catering at the Empire Hotel.

'Any idea what that building used to be?' Masterson asked, as we came to the Star Ferry on our way back from 124 Nathan Road.

I had been wondering about this. It couldn't have been a hotel, because that would have been obvious from the sign outside, lobby layout and so on; but it wasn't so unlike a hotel. Some kind of hostel?

'Don't know.'

We dropped our coins into the slot and went up to wait for the next ferry.

'It was a cathouse. A Chinese one, specifically. European brothels were closed in 1932. It's taken them three years to get round to closing the Chinese ones. Don't ask me why. Not that any of that will make a blind bit of difference to the actual amount of prostitution that takes place in the colony. They'll just move somewhere else.'

'Golly.'

'Typical Hong Kong,' he said. 'Cities often set themselves up as opposites. X does X so Y does Y. It's the same the world over. In Shanghai you can get girls, boys, drugs, anything you like, more or less openly. If you have an itch you can scratch it. So Hong Kong has to be different. Nothing's in the open. Of course people want to do the same things, so people do do the same things – but no one does it where you can see. It's not that Hong Kong people would mind staying in a hotel which used to be a Chinese cathouse, but they would mind people thinking that they didn't mind, because it would show that they weren't respectable. So it's no go.'

I had been taken by surprise by the ways in which I found Hong Kong a surprise. The exotic elements were what I had been expecting. Hakka women in their sombreros, which smelt of oil or lacquer; coolies dragging impossible bundles on their backs; rickshaw men, gold-toothed shoeshiners, gap-toothed Japanese businessmen, opium smokers visible through side-street windows, eagles circling wind currents on the Peak, the brake man's crisp uniform on the Peak tram and the view from the Peak towards Kowloon; the mad clattering noise of mah-jong coming from servants' quarters on a Sunday afternoon; girls in cheongsams showing more leg than I had ever seen; Europeans of no sure nationality, uncertain unemployment, and ambiguous appetite; family groups going for picnics on ancestors' graves; furious Chinese gods with green faces and red eyes; the smell of fermented fish outside Taoist temples; joss sticks, Chinese art, mung-bean cake, dragon-boat races, face and joss and feng shui and the cheapest best tailors in the world, old women with bound feet – it would be untrue to say that all this was what I was expecting in detail, but the broader gist of it, yes. It was what I had come out here for. It wasn't Faversham and it wasn't the Plough.

The other side of Hong Kong, the expatriate side, was what took me by surprise. It was the P&O all over again, but more so. The whole idea of coming East was to loosen the shackles England imposed, it seemed to me – that was self-evident. If you so liked the way things were in England why would you leave? But the sense of respectability, the need to conform and to fit, was crushing. There were codes, visible and invisible, everywhere. Each of the big concerns – the Government, the rival Hongs, the Bank – had a precise and intricate hierarchy, each with its own set of customs, mores, patterns of social life, do's and don'ts, musts and mustn'ts, rules about where one went and what one wore and whom one talked to and what one said. My Hong Kong Bank friends were eaten alive by the life of the mess, Bank boat parties, Bank weekends in Fanling, Bank social life and career aspirations. The Jardines man disappeared into the separate world of his Hong as completely as Jonah inside the whale. There was a Jockey Club, a Yacht Club, a Country Club and Golf Club and the Hong Kong Club itself. The Chinese were not invisible, since not even the expatriate community could deny reality to that extent, but they were no more than extras – walk-on parts, menials, an exotic but ignored backdrop to the important real stage. Nothing to do with the Chinese was quite real.

Masterson and I went into the compartment at the front of the ferry and both lit up cigarettes. On the row of seats in front of us a man was tackling a weeks-old edition of *The Times* crossword. We took in the view in silence. The island in those days seemed much emptier, much more rock-like than it is today; it looked like a natural phenomenon on which man had camped, rather than like one of humankind's most crowded and vivid deliriums. The buildings now crawl all over the hill as if trying to obscure it from sight. Then it wasn't like that.

'I'm going to buy somewhere over there,' said Masterson. 'It's just a question of finding the right place. When things feel uncertain, it's a good time to buy. Confidence is expensive.' That was him thinking aloud.

'Things might get worse in China,' I said, this being a popular bar topic in the Empire Hotel.

'Things are always about to get worse in China. That's China's version of staying the same.'

It was a ten-minute walk to the hotel from the Star Ferry. When we got back Masterson went to his office and I went to mine. There had been a problem with discrepancies between the invoices we were paying for spirits and the actual quantity of alcohol that was moving through the hotel, so I had resolved to check every invoice by hand and try to find at what stage things were going awry. It was tedious work with the prospect of a confrontation and sacking at the end of it, so my spirits were low as I slung my jacket on its hook behind the door and crossed to my desk. Sitting on top of the pile of invoices in my tray was a letter from Maria.

Chang Chun
5 February 1936

Dear Tom,

Thank you for your letter. It took a week to get here which seems reasonable. I too am glad to be back in touch.

Your work sounds interesting. I'm happy that you have found a good job with a congenial employer. I suppose you will have an opportunity to thank the Captain the next time he passes through Hong Kong. My memory of him is not very clear: the only time we ever met was when that gentleman tried to prevent us from having lessons in the library. I felt his judgement was as good as that of Solomon but I daresay that the other gentleman may not agree!

Our work here is progressing well, thanks be to God. The Chapel is growing day by day according to the plans given us by Father Ignatius. It turns out that he had some training as an architect before he received his vocation so he takes a keen interest in our progress. Sister Benedicta works very hard and effectively, as I'm sure you can imagine. There is less talk here of a civil war than I had expected. Events are far away and people have become so used to reports of turmoil that they tend to ignore them. I hope we continue to have this luxury.

My work in the school goes well also. The children are so receptive and eager to learn that it is humbling. One or two of them have an aptitude for Mathematics which is already beyond mine and they have to have special teaching from Father Ignatius when he is with us. In the case of one of them, the Father is trying to get him a scholarship to a special college run by the Dominicans in Shanghai.

It is on a related subject, my dear Tom, that I have a favour to ask of you. We have a boy here called Wo Ho-Yan, for whom I have a particular affection since he comes from the same part of Fukien that I was born in. He was sent here to distant relatives because there were difficulties at home. He became involved to some extent in gangs. But he is a very intelligent and energetic boy. There is however a difficulty here in that he has fallen into disagreement with some local youths. The argument has reached the stage at which some fighting has already taken place and more violence is threatened.

My fear is for the stability of our mission here and for the boy's future. I will feel I have let him down if he gets off to a bad start in life. I have not said yet that he is only fourteen years old.

This is the favour I have to ask. I have discussed his circumstances with Sister Benedicta and we have agreed that the best arrangement would be for Ho-Yan to be sent somewhere away from trouble. The place which suggested itself to us was our mission in Hong Kong, which as you know is small but growing. We have corresponded with Sister Immaculata who has agreed to take in Ho-Yan to our great happiness.

My request is this: would it be possible for you to secure a job for Ho-Yan, at least for a short time? I would not recommend him to you if I did not believe him to be able and willing. This would enable us to send him to our Hong Kong mission and away from his troubles here. If he does not succeed with you I am confident that he will find alternative employment, but even if the worst came to the worst, which DV it will not, we will take him back here, so we will not be creating a long-term difficulty for you. He speaks Cantonese and some English and I am confident that he will learn more with great rapidity.

I hope you can help but I know that this is a large favour so do not reproach yourself if it is not possible.

Sister Benedicta asks me to send her regards and to tell you to keep up your Chinese! I add my own best wishes from
Your friend,
Sister Maria

It was the third letter I had had from her since we had exchanged apologies for the 'misunderstanding'. I wrote back and said, yes of course.

Sister Benedicta would have been pleased about my Cantonese. I was making a conscious effort to keep it up. I had moved into a three-room second-floor flat halfway up the Peak and acquired a houseboy called Mun, a dapper man of about my own age whose family in Canton were weighing the pros and cons of coming to join him in the colony. We spoke Cantonese at home; or I tried to. This caused Mun to behave as if I was mad but not dangerous.

I was beginning to be deeply grateful for the work I'd put in, and to develop an affection for the language. It was immensely useful in bargaining and doing deals for the Empire. I began to accompany Masterson on negotiations and buying meetings, and was soon made responsible for this side of the business.

Something Maria had not told me was that Cantonese is one of the world's greatest languages for swearing. This was wholly in harmony with the Cantonese character, which I had come to see as being like that of cockneys back in England: blunt, direct, argumentative, money-minded, clannish, knowing, worldly, materialist. As for the rest of China, the Cantonese had an old adage: the mountains are high, the Emperor is far away.

'What's this called?' I asked. We were standing in the kitchen of the Empire on a Saturday morning, when it was closed for business.

'*Choy sum*,' said Ah Wang.

'Ah' is the term with which one addresses friends and family in Cantonese. His full name was Ming Wang-Lok. In Chinese, the surname comes first.

'What's that mean?'

'Heart of leaf,' said Ho-Yan.

'What do you think?'

'Bitter,' said Masterson. 'But it's all right.' For an incessant smoker he took a surprising amount of interest in food.

'Good!' said Ah Wang.

Today, it is perfectly obvious that Hong Kong is a society built by refugees. Most of the six million Hong Kongers fled here from somewhere else, or were born to parents who did. After the great influx of 1949, anyone could see this. But then, in the thirties, no one knew or could guess that millions of people were going to flood over the border, and that a significant proportion of China, with all its energies and difficulties, was going to decant itself into Hong Kong. I didn't suspect it at the time, but Ah Wang and Ho-Yan were the first of very many refugees I would come to know.

Not that Wo Ho-Yan was a refugee in the strict sense; he was fleeing different sorts of trouble. Indeed, the idea of him in trouble was at first hard to understand. He was a short, bright-eyed, round-faced boy, willing and energetic and friendly. There was something a little weak about him, and his manner was more sidelong than that of most Cantonese, but he always seemed keen to oblige. Or that was what I thought. If ever I'm starting to congratulate myself on an understanding of human character, I only have to remind myself of my early view of Ho-Yan. But he was very useful at the Empire.

By contrast Ming Wang-Lok – Ah Wang, as I came to call him – was a proper refugee. In China he had worked for a southern warlord called General Chang, who even by the standards of his *métier* was known for the brutishness of his behaviour and the over-refinement of his tastes. (All Ah Wang ever said on the latter subject was – in English – 'General Chang, he like bound feet very, very much.') General Chang had some kind of contretemps with his theoretical superiors in the Kuomintang, the National Government of China, and in an unfortunate misunderstanding was machine-gunned to death, along with five bodyguards, on his way home from dinner with a subordinate. Ah Wang had been due to accompany the general to cook one of his specialities at that meal, and had been prevented only at the last minute by an upset stomach. A naturally timid and pacific man, Ah Wang was extremely shaken by his employer's murder. He ran away and came to Hong Kong. His behaviour was in accordance with a sound maxim, the first part of which is: 'Trouble in China, go to Hong Kong.' I often heard proud expatriates quote this to each other over the next few years. The saying had a second part: 'Trouble in Hong Kong, go to China.' You heard less of that, then.

Masterson and I had been discussing the possibility of putting some Chinese food on the menu. The idea was to have something to offer those of our guests who were willing to give Chinese food a go but were unwilling to venture out into the white-slave maelstrom of a real Chinese restaurant. Ho-Yan, in his capacity as my general factotum at the Empire, knew our plan. When he heard about Ah Wang's arrival in Hong Kong – he was good at hearing about things – he told me.

'Master, a famous cook has arrived from Canton. He would be perfect for the hotel restaurant.'

Hence this meeting. We picked a Saturday morning when Jean-Luc, the combustible Belgian chef, was nowhere near the kitchen.

'The fish is terrific,' said Masterson, picking with chopsticks at a large steamed grouper.

'I'm not so keen on this tripe thing,' I said. I already knew that the Cantonese loved dishes with a gelatinous texture and, to a European palate, next to no taste. Now I love and can appreciate this kind of cooking. Then, I simply didn't see the point of it.

'Yes, it's a bit on the authentic side,' said Masterson. 'But we could tell people that. It would be part of the show.'

'I like the rice,' I said. Ah Wang had cooked it wrapped in a lotus leaf. Masterson and I looked at each other.

'We would like you to come and work for us,' he said, extending a hand to Ah Wang. No translation was needed. I don't think I had ever seen someone beam the way he did as he wiped his already clean palm on his apron before shaking Masterson's hand.

Chang Chun
13 November 1936

Dear Tom,

I'm glad to hear that Ho-Yan continues to do well in your employment. It was a great favour that you did me and I'm happy that he's not proving to your disadvantage. Our mission work here is going well. People are more receptive to the Church's teaching when times are difficult. It is the silver lining. That is such a Chinese image! So our grief for China's difficult time is eased by the thought of the people we are helping to discover God's peace and save their souls.

Father Ignatius's chapel is finished. It is a very bare structure with a notable spiritual quality. Father Ignatius has adapted a Chinese design for the entranceway. So the building seems both Chinese and European. I do hope you are able to see it one day.

I am glad that your studies in Cantonese have proved useful and that you are keeping up with the language. I told Sister Benedicta and she said she was pleased also. She sends you her best wishes. She works very hard here and never seems short of energy. It is a great gift.

Our mission in Hong Kong is going well. Perhaps you sometimes hear of it? Father Xavier, a Portuguese priest of great ability, is now our chaplain there. Of course, in some ways the success is a cause for regret since, if it were struggling, I might DV be sent to Hong Kong to help it, and then we would meet again! I often think of our trip back from Europe to Hong Kong. In many respects it now seems to me like a dream.

I hope the Lord in His Providence will find an occasion for us to meet before too long.

Your friend,
Sister Maria

This letter, and more so the ones I wrote to Maria, did not leave me with a clear conscience. There was something that I had not told her. One evening, a few months after Ho-Yan had begun to work for us, I went out of my office to the delivery entrance of the Empire, in order to check through a consignment of spirits which had been delivered that afternoon. I was working by a process of elimination, checking the inventory at every point from the importer's warehouse to the bar measures. Alcohol continued to go missing, though never at the stage in the supply chain that I was examining at that time. It was a version of the three-cup trick. My current scheme was to leave the supply of spirits locked in the delivery storeroom – to which I was supposed to have the only key – and go back to check the inventory a day later. Part of me knew that I would find nothing missing, but that the end of the month would bring the usual 10 per cent shortfall.

The storeroom was at the back of the hotel, beside the boiler machinery and the maintenance department. In the corridor on the way there I to my surprise heard two Chinese voices. I turned the corner and found Ho-Yan, looking immensely startled at being walked in on, and a taller, thinner young man of about twenty. He had a scar on his left cheek which at first glance looked like a laugh-line. They had been speaking a dialect of Chinese I did not recognise.

'What's going on?' I said.

Ho-Yan, smiling with embarrassment, said:

'Master, this is my brother Man-Lee. He has just arrived here from our home in Fukien. He does not speak English.'

He said something to Man-Lee, who gave a deep nod that was almost a bow. I extended my hand.

'Please tell him that I am pleased to meet him,' I said. This was not strictly speaking true. The reason Ho-Yan had gone to Maria's mission was something to do with trouble at home; the same trouble had pursued him there and eventually brought him to Hong Kong. Whatever Wo Man-Lee looked like, it was not the opposite of trouble. Once you knew the two were brothers you could see the resemblance, but the older brother was visibly tougher and less accommodating. This is not hindsight.

'My brother is staying with me until he finds work,' Ho-Yan added. He was no longer at the mission but now shared a room in Mongkok with one of our waiters. I sensed straight away that the mission was unlikely to know about his brother's arrival in Hong Kong. 'He came by on an errand. We will keep out of your way, unless we can be of any assistance.'

'No, I'm fine. Just doing the bloody inventory, as usual.'

They went away and I unlocked the storeroom, feeling uneasy. I decided that I ought to write to Maria and let her know about this development, since I had at least implicitly taken Ho-Yan into my care. His brother's arrival struck a wrong note.

In the storeroom, I counted the bottles. Needless to say they were all there. As I was finishing and locking up, George, the maître d' (a Cantonese whose un-anglicised name was Zhu), burst into the corridor looking more excited than I had ever seen him.

'Ah Tom, come quickly! Big fight! In kitchen! Ah Luc' – Jean-Luc – 'and Ah Wang!'

We ran back through the maintenance quarters, along the passage that led to the kitchen and through the swing doors. A ring of jostling and enthusiastic waiters and kitchen staff stood against the walls. Jean-Luc was carrying a meat cleaver which he had plunged halfway through a whole duck. He was now holding this bizarre object aloft in his right hand. Ah Wang was standing five feet away from him with his arms crossed.

'This is not how you cook a duck! I cannot work in this zoo!' Jean-Luc screamed at me.

I can't claim this was unexpected. Jean-Luc had, as predicted, resented Ah Wang's arrival in 'his' kitchen. A blow-up had seemed likely for some time.

'What seems to be the problem, chef?' I said.

Jean-Luc had a bad temper even by the standards of his job, the kind of bad temper which becomes worse when people react too calmly.

'Seems? *Seems*? The problem is that I cannot work in this fucking zoo!' He then switched to French for a little while, before switching back to English with the words: 'These conditions are impossible. Him or me, you must choose.' He put down the duck and cleaver and he, too, crossed his arms.

'Let's have a word in private.'

'Him or me! Here, now! Choose.'

'Very well, Jean-Luc. Ah Wang, you are now Head Chef at the Empire Hotel. Jean-Luc, please feel free to go to Mr Masterson to discuss severance terms.'

Jean-Luc did not open the swing doors, he exploded through them, in the process nearly killing a waiter who was returning from serving beef tea to a guest with bronchitis. Ah Wang looked pleased, but, it has to be said, not surprised. I knew something which Jean-Luc didn't: the late General Chang had loved European food. In all the excitement, I forgot about my letter to Maria.

Chapter Five

'This is the only interesting thing I've seen since we left London,'
announced Wilfred Austen. We were standing in the doorway of
the Kuan Ti temple in Kennedy Town. Immediately above us was
a frieze depicting a battle between Taoist gods. In the middle of
the frieze a martial-looking god with four purple arms held two
of his opponents' severed heads and brandished two large pikes.

Encouraged by Masterson, I had developed a sideline in tours
and talks. English visitors to Hong Kong often wanted to know
more about Chinese culture. I constructed a tour: I would take
people to the Kuan Ti and Tin Hau temples; to a graveyard near
Fanling (which unfortunately was also near a tanning plant, whose
smell I can still to this day recall without effort); and to the Luk Yu
tea house, where I would supervise all the ordering, and nervous
but undaunted visitors would tackle dishes like half-cooked
chicken and thousand-year-old egg. (These taste like Brie, which
did not stop people recoiling in happy dread when confronted
with them. One woman even fainted. In truth they are only about
a month old – not so very different from the pickled eggs we used
to sell back at the Plough.) The thing visitors liked most was dim
sum, which like many Chinese food names is a metaphor, meaning 'touch the heart' – a highly poetic name for dumplings.

On this day in February 1938 I was giving the tour to two English
writers, on their way to China to cover the civil war. They were
going by boat, because the Japanese, who now occupied the greater
part of China, had begun strafing the Kowloon to Canton train. The
Japanese fighters took off from an aircraft carrier stationed in extra-
territorial waters near Hong Kong. They had been known to strafe
the boat, too, but in a more desultory and occasional way.

The poet, Austen, was the taller and paler of the two men. He
had a permanent short-sighted scowl and was a smoker in the
Masterson class. He was in his early thirties, the type of
Englishman who never entirely sheds the sense that he is an overgrown schoolboy. His sidekick, the playwright Charles Ingleby,

was shorter, more tanned, friendlier, untrustworthy, and impish. They gave the feeling of being a two-man gang. They also made less secret of their homosexuality than anybody I had ever met.

Austen and Ingleby had been in the colony for a week and were due to sail for Canton the next day. As writers from England, they both exploited and mocked their semi-celebrity status. They had undergone a round of formal dinners about which they expressed, to me, open derision. Austen in particular was not impressed. 'The intellectual level here is that of a Surrey golf club,' he said. His favourite conversational modes were the monologue and the apophthegm. The two tended to overlap. Sex was a favourite topic.

'All colonial life is essentially comic.'

'Laughter is the first sign of sexual attraction.'

'The Chinese are so much more intelligent and dignified than the expatriates, it's positively embarrassing to be white.'

'If it weren't for gin and adultery, the Empire would have collapsed decades ago.' (I passed this one on to Masterson, who immediately said, 'I don't know if that's true about the British Empire, but it certainly goes for our hotel.')

'All Chinese art is quietistic.'

'Red-headed men only come to the tropics if they want to die.'

'I've never met an Englishwoman who didn't want to be fucked by a Chinese.'

Here at the temple, however, he seemed, albeit momentarily, almost subdued. He had looked at the statues and altarpieces with close attention. I have to admit that I was pleased. The penetrating, heady perfume of joss sticks was thick in the air. A woman with a bamboo broom was making a whisking noise as she swept the floor. A Chinese goddess in jade and a fat Buddha sat companionably in the same niche.

In one corner of the temple, a fortune teller was touting for business. He was swinging a circular cylinder. When he found a customer he would invert the cylinder to drop a written slip on the ground. He would then interpret what was written on it. I am not superstitious, or perhaps I am – in any case, I have never had my fortune told.

'It's a bit chaotic though, isn't it?' Ingleby said. 'Taoism sounds so pure and simple and above board, all about the Way and being

ike a stream of water and all that, but then you see their temples
nd it's all this superstitious mishmash, everything thrown in all
ogether. This god and that god and Buddhas and you name it.'

'No no, quite wrong,' Austen said. 'Much too Protestant.
There's no contradiction between mysticism and superstition. It's
ike Mediterranean Catholicism, full of local gods and beliefs and
ituals and intercessors. Doesn't at all contradict the true faith
underneath. We must not fear encrustation.'

Austen noticed the fortune teller give up swinging his cylinder
nd light a cigarette. The poet took out a packet of Sweet Afton
nd lit one without offering them to anyone else.

Austen and Ingleby were harbingers. The war between China
nd Japan meant that the stream of tourists heading to Canton
Iried up, as did a great deal of business with, and travel to,
hanghai. But the war itself began to bring people. There was a
rowing traffic of journalists, profiteers, diplomats, businessmen
f varying degrees of credibility and probity, war tourists, spies.
They tended to drink more and spend more than peacetime visi-
ors. Trade was not as good as it had been but was nonetheless, all
nings duly considered, surprisingly robust; the Depression
neant that we were working from a fairly low base. People from
ther hotels were now starting to come to the Empire for Ah
Wang's Chinese banquets. Masterson talked about dropping
rices but then decided that we didn't need to. He was now, fol-
owing the death of his German sleeping partner Munster earlier
n the year, the sole owner of the Empire.

'Nobody minds too much about the war as long as they aren't
illing white people,' he said.

The civil war showed signs of bringing me, at least, one piece of
ood news. Maria's letters had begun mentioning the possibility
f her mission having to pack up and relocate – and if they did
nat, the likeliest place to move to would be Hong Kong.
Trouble in China . . .')

'We are torn between wanting to serve the Lord in China by
elping His children here and the reality that our work is being
nade close to impossible by the war,' she wrote. 'If we are, for
ractical purposes, unable to fulfil our mission, and at the same
me are putting all of our lives in danger, we should not be here.

But the decision would be a very big one and I am glad that it is not mine to take.'

Our letters were more intimate than we had been in conversation. I often wondered what it would be like to meet again.

My conscience over Ho-Yan was now clear. Whatever I had been expecting to go wrong seemed not to have happened. He had left the Empire, saying that he wanted to work with his brother Man-Lee. He took a job first as a delivery boy and then as something more important in a food and drink distribution company. Before very long, he came to me with an offer: if we switched delivery contracts to him he could guarantee – guarantee – that our problem with missing inventory would go away. Our losses were still running at about a tenth of our purchasing. Although I remained irritated by this I was coming to see it as a fact of life, one more or less accepted by expatriates as an unofficial servants' perk. Ho-Yan's offer was to match our contractor's price; by personally supervising the inventory, whatever that meant, he said he would make good the 10 per cent shortfall. This would translate into more than 10 per cent increased profit, since we would sell the missing alcohol at hotel prices; so the offer was too good to resist. I gave his company the contract for three months, and the inventories began to tally. I was delighted.

Many more people had come to Hong Kong in the way that Wo Ho-Yan, Wo Man-Lee and Ah Wang had done. There was also an influx from Shanghai. The Shanghai arrivals tended to be in some way exotic. I was particularly keen on the occasional White Russian, a type one quickly learnt to spot. There was something elegant and conceited and desperate about them. The arrival of these people, who were not in the strict sense refugees but who also were not the opposite of refugees, brought the war closer to us. It became a constant topic.

'The war', however, meant several different things. There was the existing war in China, or rather the two wars, the civil war between the Communist and the Kuomintang – the received wisdom was that the Communists had been, for practical purposes, defeated – and the war between the Chinese and the Japanese invaders. There was also the war that everyone now seemed certain would come to Europe, a war whose name was spoken of with a physical sensation of dread in the stomach and which to many, myself included, seemed nearer than what was actually happening over the border in China. And then again there was our own war-to-be, loitering at the back of people's minds. This was only spoken of openly by men in the company of other men. The Japs are going to take us on; the Japs won't start on us till after they finish the Chinese; the Nips are jealous of Hong Kong; the Nips breed like mice, they won't be happy until they've conquered Australia. The Navy will save us; the Americans will save us; no one can save us. Hong Kong is impregnable; Hong Kong is indefensible. We'll all have to flee to Singapore; if it happens, we won't have time to get to Singapore. The Japs can't bomb. The Japs can't fly. The evacuation boats will be sunk in the harbour; the Japs will let us go and will take the harbour for themselves. It's not a well-known fact, old boy, but the simple truth is Japs can't see in the dark. The word 'war' came to be one you picked out in conversations across the room.

It was in the summer of 1939, just before war with Germany was declared, that this became real for me. My great passion by now was walking, a solitary but energetic pastime I had taken to by way of counteracting the gregarious but sedentary life of the hotel. I spent more or less every weekend out on Lantau or in the New Territories. My friends the Higginses, a couple who ran a shop selling Chinese furniture on Des Voeux Road, had a stone house on the south shore of Lantau; Cooper and Porter, my friends at the Hong Kong Bank, let me come and stay with them when they had their alloted time-share in the Bank bungalow out near Fanling. I did as much hill walking as I could; I was fitter than I had believed possible – much more so than I had been back in flat Kent. I liked the heat, and although no one could like the humidity, I seemed to mind it less than most.

That day, I had packed a bottle of beer along with my usual two canteens of water. My leather rucksack, bought from a cobbler in Wanchai, had in it some sandwiches, an orange, a compass, and a map. The plan was to catch a lift from Fanling and spend the day walking in the Tai Mo mountains.

It was the beer that undid me. The night before, I stayed with Cooper and his friends in Fanling. We had too much to drink. I woke up late and a trifle hung over. The young bankers were heading off for a lunch party. I got a lift to the foothills. It usually took the first hour's walking to begin to feel ready for the rest of the day – to get the week's crampedness out of my limbs, and to have my lungs and legs start working properly together. I stopped at the top of a small rise, looking back down and north towards the border. It was a clear day for summer, with a trace of heat haze but none of the cloud cover which could be so humid and oppressive. Although it was only about noon, and I had a fair deal of walking ahead of me, I felt I deserved a treat. I sat down on a rock and drank the beer. The warmth and exertion gave me the feeling, pleasant at the time, that the alcohol was rushing straight to my head. Not to worry, I thought, the exercise will burn it off. I started out again for the top of Tai Mo Shan, taking a path marked with more confidence on my old map than it was on the actual ground.

It was early afternoon before I began to feel sleepy. I had climbed most of the way up the three-thousand-foot mountain and could see well into China in the north, past the paddies and villages of the New Territories. (The same view today would encompass several large new towns, very many high-rise buildings, and, over the border, one entirely new skyscraper-crowded city, Shenzen.) Going higher usually made one feel cooler and helped one to catch any breezes there might be, but on that still day I was only getting more and more hot. I hadn't had a break since the beer, and decided now to have a rest. I leant against an Indian pod tree and ate my two ham sandwiches. The butter had half melted in the heat and its paper wrapper was hot and smeary. I tipped my hat down over my eyes. The stillness meant that it was eerily quiet. I thought I would rest for a moment and then take a drink of water to perk myself up.

When I woke the sun had gone far beyond the hills and Tai Mo Shan was in deep shadow. There could be very little time until sunset. I felt a jolt of apprehension at the thought of losing the track home and spending a night out on the mountain. No one would miss me until late Monday morning at the earliest. Swearing never to touch beer again, I swung my rucksack on my back and set out down the skimpy path.

Almost immediately, I was lost. I came to a fork in the track, one I had not noticed on the way up. One path seemed to curl back on itself before turning, presumably, downwards; the other was fainter and steeper but more direct. Neither looked at all familiar. After hemming and hawing, I took the steeper track. It soon became clear that was a mistake. The bushes on either side were denser than anything I had passed through on the way up, and by the time darkness fell I was badly scratched and had lost my bearings. The only idea was to keep plunging downwards. At many points I was holding onto bushes and trees and scrambling over the crumbly rock. No path was visible. There were moments when the hill was frighteningly steep.

After some time – I couldn't see the hands on my watch – the ground began to flatten and although there was still no path, the going over the scrabbly uneven ground was less difficult. If I had to guess I would have thought I was heading more or less south, in the direction of Shek Kong. I decided that I would walk for what felt like an hour or two more and then, if I hadn't come to a village, give up for the night. As I reached that conclusion, I felt the first fat drops of tropical rain fall on my face. It had clouded over without my noticing. I promised myself that I would never go for another walk and that I would make a point of remembering my vow, even when I felt safe and dry.

Then three things happened: I felt the ground give under me; I felt myself land on something soft but unyielding, unsteady, in fact alive; and I heard someone saying, loudly and at close quarters, 'Ow! Fuck! Get off!'

The instruction was unnecessary. Whomever I had landed on twisted away, causing me to roll off, fall sideways, and smack my head against the earth. The next thing I knew a torch was being shone in my face, blinding me, and a cockney voice was saying:

'Who the hell are you?'

In the background were other voices. I heard someone approach.

'What's going on, Sergeant?' someone said in tones of command.

'Some bugger's just fallen into my foxhole, sir,' said the nearby voice.

'Could someone explain what is happening, please?' I said.

'Hoick him out, lads, and let's have a shufti,' said the in-charge voice. Two pairs of arms came over the side of the foxhole and I pulled myself up on them. The men were soldiers. Then the torch was in my face again and for a moment there was silence.

'Well he doesn't look like a Nip spy, I'll say that for him,' said the man in charge. Then in a harsher tone he said: 'We're the Royal Hong Kong Regiment and we are on exercises. Who are you and what are you doing?'

'My name is Tom Stewart, I'm a civilian, and I'm on my way home from a walk up Tai Mo Shan.'

'Do you often go walking up mountains in the dark, Mr Stewart?'

'I fell asleep, it got dark, and I got lost. These things happen.'

'Do you often go walking on your own?'

'Yes.'

'Do you often get lost?'

'It's been known to happen. As you may know, civilian maps aren't very good.'

'What happens when you get lost?'

'I ask directions.'

'What happens when they don't speak English?'

'I ask again in Chinese.'

'Do you now?' said my interrogator, softer and more curious. He thought for a moment. 'Sergeant, could you show Mr Stewart the way to the truck. The rest of us will carry on with the exercise. We're due to finish at dawn, Mr Stewart. You can sit in the truck and have a brew, and then we'll give you a lift. You'll be back in town in time for work. Most of us have got our jobs to go to in the morning. We can have a little chat on the way home. I'm Major Walter Marlowe, by the way.'

'How could you not have told me?' said Maria. It wasn't quite the very first thing she said to me after four years, but it was close. Her anger made me angry in return. I wanted to tell her to calm down, or grow up. But in fact she had already done both of those things. She looked the same only more so. Her face was unlined and her eyes were deeper and browner than I had remembered. She was no longer wearing her habit but a sort of mission uniform that made her look more like a nurse than a nun. Her cap exposed more of her hair than I could remember seeing; it was inky-black Cantonese hair, almost blue-black, in a short bubble cut that looked incongruously fashionable.

The subject of discussion was Wo Ho-Yan and his brother Wo Man-Lee. Her reaction was shock: as if my news about Ho-Yan was the worst possible welcome I could have given her. She looked as if she was struggling to control herself.

'I know that you did me, us, a great service,' she eventually said. 'But . . . oh well, it is done.'

'You never told me what the problem was.'

She sighed. 'Trouble. Crime. Gangs. The brother has a – he has a reputation.'

'Well he seemed all right to me. People don't always stay the same.'

'I do not believe you know him well.'

'Then let's not discuss it any further. I've said I'm sorry.'

This was not how I had envisaged my reunion with Maria. Her mission had decided to pack up and move in the autumn of 1939. They went to Canton, but there were difficulties of lodging and resources with the nuns already there, so they had continued on to Hong Kong, arriving at the end of the year. Their train had been strafed by the Japanese fighters from the aircraft carrier. Sister Benedicta had stayed behind in Canton and either would or would not be coming to join the mission soon. The community, as Maria called it when she was in her pulpit manner, was scattered among their friends and co-religionists in the colony. Maria was staying with Father Ignatius, their Irish priest, in Happy Valley.

Over the next months I saw her at least once a week. She enlisted me to help give an English class to her pupils, who despite being dispersed in lodgings all over Hong Kong and Kowloon, met several evenings a week. I was there to be a representative English speaker and to take part in conversation practice. 'Even Sister Benedicta says that English is the language of the future,' said Maria. There was something wonderfully touching about the serious faces peering towards me as I read out passages from the *South China Morning Post*. The best thing was describing plots from films and then discussing them with the class. They often found the behaviour of characters hilarious or incomprehensible. A repeated stumbling block was the question, where were the characters' families and why had they left them?

Maria also had a class out in the New Territories, near Fanling, where she borrowed a schoolroom to instruct some of her mission who were living in the area. She made the trip once or twice a week, and a few times I went with her. I once told her pupils the plot of *Stagecoach*. A hand went up.

'But where are the people family?' someone asked. 'Why they not here?'

'They are refugees,' I said. The class all nodded and the ones who had been slouching sat up.

'You are becoming a skilled teacher,' Maria told me after that lesson. When the class was over we would go to the house of one of the students for a stew made out of fish heads. The country air in the New Territories always smelled clean, as if it had just rained – unless the wind was coming from the direction of the tannery.

The atmosphere of that time was the strangest I have known. The war in Europe, which went from being a non-event to being a disaster, was constantly discussed, and it made our own war seem like a horrible inevitability, coming towards us with the logic of a bad dream. People behaved oddly. I had never seen collective hysteria before – a quiet hysteria, which one could hear in the pitch of voices or in sudden silences, rather than in anything obviously shrill and public. Everyone knew about what the Japanese had done in Nanking, the mass rapes and mass killings. They wouldn't behave like that to Westerners, of course.

One afternoon towards the middle of 1940, my secretary Ah Wing knocked on my door to tell me that someone had come to see me. His expression was so grave and excited that I could tell this visitor was out of the ordinary. I nodded and he showed into the room a tall heavy-set man in his early fifties wearing a dark suit and tie. I knew him immediately by sight: John Wilson, one of the senior figures in the colony's government – I didn't know his exact job. (Minister of Defence, I later discovered.)

'Mr Stewart? Might I have a moment?' he said in an unexpectedly soft voice. 'I thought we could go for a stroll?'

I tried to seem calm and unsurprised. No doubt the lower half of my face was flapping like a fish. I took a packet of cigarettes and my hat and we set off for the botanical gardens. We crossed Connaught Road, went by the new Hong Kong Bank building and up the hill. He climbed without breathing any harder.

'How long have you been here now?' he asked in his gentle voice. 'A few years?'

'Almost five, sir, to my surprise.'

'Get a chance to visit home before the war broke out?'

'I'm afraid not, sir.'

'Family?'

'A grandmother and a brother. They are both fine, the last I heard, sir.'

'Hard not to worry, though, isn't it? But you're liking it here?'

'Yes sir, very much.' We arrived at the lower end of the botanical gardens, which were looking more than usually lush. As always there were fewer visitors than the place deserved, though two or three elderly Chinese men were doing t'ai chi exercises at the end of the park. Wilson looked around and slowed his pace.

'Think there will be a war?'

'Yes, sir.'

'Got any plans?' For a moment I did not understand. I thought, giddily, he was asking me for strategic advice. Then I thought he was asking if I planned to join the Volunteers – which in fact I had considered, in a vague way which I was hoping would somehow make the actual necessity for choice or action recede. Did the Hong Kong government, or the colonial office, recruit soldiers one by one? Could this possibly be an efficient use of resources?

'Plans?'

'Ideas about what you might do. If there is a war.'

'Well, fight in it, I suppose.'

'Think we'll win?'

'I beg your pardon?'

'Think we'll win? If there's a war.'

'Well, yes, of course. Eventually.'

He smiled at that.

'Eventually – that's a good answer. But do you think Hong Kong is defensible? If the Japs come, could we keep them out?'

'I don't know enough to know, sir.'

'No one knows enough to be sure. But I know enough to make a decent guess, and the answer is that we can't. There aren't enough of us and there isn't enough water. If we can't hold the reservoirs, we lose the colony. If we defend the reservoirs, then we don't have enough manpower to defend the rest of the colony.

If we attempt to hold a line across the New Territories, which is what we'll try to do, we'll be stretched too thin. It's a simple problem; our reserves are limited and theirs aren't. If they want to commit enough men to taking Hong Kong, they can.'

I felt sick. I did not want to know or hear any of this. 'So what do we do? Run off to Singapore?'

'Does that idea tempt you?'

'Not particularly, no.'

'Just as well. Singapore has enough troubles of its own. No, we can't just run away and leave Hong Kong. Women and children will be evacuated, soon, and the rest of us will stay and fight.'

Wilson seemed with these words to have reached some sort of conclusion. He stopped in front of a tree with dark green foliage and drooping flame-red buds; a jacaranda, as I know now but didn't then.

'We'll win the war, in your words, eventually. The Americans haven't been doing anything to help, as you may be aware. They're jealous of the Empire in general, and Hong Kong, it seems, in particular. But sooner or later the Japanese will take them on and if they do that, sooner or later, they will lose. In the meantime, we'll have lost Hong Kong and most of us will be dead or in prison.'

I felt a wave of bitter regret. What was I thinking when I set out to fulfil my childish ambition to 'go to China'? I had wasted my life. I was going to die or swelter in jail. Wilson stood still looking at his jacaranda. He did not seem disturbed by his own vision of the future. For a long moment neither of us spoke. My mind gradually began working again. I said:

'What do you mean, most of us?'

After that, Wilson turned and looked at me, hard, as if for the first time.

'Know anything about sums, maths, keeping the books, that sort of thing?'

'A little, yes.'

'Enough to learn a bit more, and a bit more still?'

'Yes.'

'Kept up the Cantonese?'

We hadn't mentioned my Cantonese before this.

'Yes.'

'Fluent?'

'It's difficult for a European. But I'm not bad.'

'Kept up the walking?'

'Well, yes.'

He nodded. 'Walter Marlowe told me he bumped into you.' Seeing my expression he added: 'Major Marlowe of the Hong Kong Volunteers. He said you nearly broke his sergeant's leg.'

'His sergeant nearly broke my neck.'

'Said your map reading wasn't up to much.'

'It was pitch-dark. Sir.'

'He also said you were, and I quote, "an independent-minded little bugger".'

I didn't know what to say. I watched the men doing their t'ai chi, all three making waving motions with their arms while they swayed from side to side. It was impossible to describe without making it sound comic, but the sight itself was never comic. The participants always looked serious and dignified and calm. Wilson paused and then went on:

'Fancy doing something a bit more interesting than rotting in prison?'

Chapter Six

The start of the war was a shock but it was not a surprise. In the preceding weeks, Japanese attempts at provocation, including raids over Hong Kong's border with China, plane overflights, and incursions into our territorial waters, had increased. It was clear that they would invade. The official line was that Hong Kong would fight to the death. I'm glad I never believed that.

The first Japanese bombs dropped on the colony on the same day that we heard the news about Pearl Harbour. I was in 'my' office at the Hong Kong and Shanghai Bank when I heard a distant noise like that of a series of paper bags bursting. But the noise had a deeper reverberative note and hung in the air in a new way. I could hear the noise of aeroplane engines at high revs. I stood and went to the window. Looking north-east I could see three columns of smoke. Without my noticing it, Cooper had crossed the room and was standing beside me.

'Fucking hell,' he said. 'It's started. Kai Tak. They're bombing the airport.'

Another series of explosions came from somewhere out of sight. I didn't know it until some time afterwards, but that first series of Japanese bomber attacks destroyed all of Hong Kong's RAF planes and anti-aircraft batteries – all its air defences.

Cooper and I looked at each other. For the last couple of months I had been spending spare mornings in this room in the Bank's HQ at Queen's Road Central, learning to bluff my way through the rudiments of banking. This was Wilson's plan.

'The Japanese will need to run the colony. They can't just let it all collapse. There are a few things they must do. Utilities is one. But they can bring in their own people for that. And they'll try to steal everything that isn't nailed down. Policing will be a problem for them. And they'll need to keep the economy running. Which means they'll need to keep the banks running. Which means they'll need some bankers. And that's where you come in.'

The idea was that I would be inserted into a list of key Bank personnel. (Bank in this context, as in most Hong Kong contexts, meant Hong Kong and Shanghai Bank.) I would appear on the payroll and on staff registers as something fancy like deputy chief accountant. I would acquire a bluffer's knowledge of how the Bank worked. Then when we were under Japanese occupation, I would use my Cantonese to help with whatever it was I was asked to help with. Roughly six people knew about this.

'Remember: don't call us, we'll call you,' Wilson told me.

'Isn't it better if I know a bit more?'

It would be untrue to say I blush at the memory of asking that question. But it was one of the stupidest things I ever said.

'No, it's better if you know a bit less,' said Wilson, gentle as ever.

Cooper, who had been swallowed whole by the life of the Bank and whom I had seen at irregular intervals since we'd arrived in Hong Kong, was my instructor. He had spent the intervening six years in a sequence of not-quite-love not-quite-affairs, usually with the daughters of Bank and colonial bigwigs. He was currently pursuing a Miss Farrington, whose father was something in government. Women and children had, by order of the government, been evacuated from the colony in mid-1940, but people with connections, or nursing qualifications, were able to wangle their way into staying. Miss Farrington had done that. Cooper described her evasions and withholdings in a way which made it clear she hadn't the slightest intention of reciprocating any of his feelings.

'What do you say, old boy? Sound promising?' he asked me.

'Only the bold deserve the fair,' I said, borrowing a Masterson line. He used it whenever a couple were visibly mismatched, usually a hideous middle-aged man escorting some, to use the then-current word, 'popsy'.

'Good advice,' said Cooper uncertainly. His inability to keep his mind off his private life was both an irritation and a comfort. It was combined with a striking ability at his job. He had absolutely no interest whatsoever in his work – less, I would say, than anyone I ever met, since even the most bored and resentful kitchen porter will acknowledge his job by complaining about it. Cooper never even did that. He simply chugged through his paperwork as imperturbably and remorselessly as a tugboat through heavy seas, light seas, harbours, channels, anything. His feelings were elsewhere. It made him a very effective administrator.

The office I was sharing with him, for the purposes of my indoctrination as, and impersonation of, a member of the Bank's staff, was twelve feet square, with – a sign of Cooper's relative eminence – a view out towards the harbour. He had decorated it with a single bad Chinese painting and a temperamental African violet over which he fussed, shifting it from location to location, and experimenting with different levels of watering, all unsuccessfully. He would have done better, I thought, if he treated it less like one of his love objects and more like part of his job. Our office was on the third floor, above the level of the main banking hall, 'the largest air-conditioned space in the world, when it opened', according to Cooper. The roof of that main hall was decorated with an extraordinary socialist-realist painting of Chinese labourers, dockworkers, factory workers, farmhands, all nobly engaged in collective toil. 'It'll come in handy if the Communists win the war,' was Masterson's joke about it. I often tried out this line on Bank employees, and none of them ever laughed.

I liked the feeling of being inside the Bank, behind the public façade, in the smell of paper and business. As a trade, with its emphasis on maintaining appearances, separating morality from practical judgement, and keeping the customer intimidated, it had many similarities with hotel-keeping.

I had privately wondered whether the war would bring out the shaky romantic Cooper or the unflappable administrator. This was a way of not asking myself about myself. Wilson's offer, by giving me the prospect of something to do, had also helped insulate me from the reality of the imminent invasion. I was repaid for this, when the first bombs dropped, with a wave of pure terror unlike anything I had ever felt. I began to pant as I stood at the window. I didn't think it was possible for my heart to beat so quickly and I was possessed by a realisation that I was going to drop dead there and then – dead of fear, pure and simple.

Cooper was looking at me. 'Steady on, Tommy,' he said.

I thought, nobody apart from my brother calls me Tommy. I felt a chink of reason shine through on my panic, and then felt the fear begin to ease. Cooper saw that.

'Fucking hell,' he said again, with a sigh.

For the rest of the day people kept coming in and out of our office, bringing news and rumours. Many Bank staff were in the Hong Kong Volunteers, so the Bank was only half manned, and the mood could have been mistaken for festive. A fortnight before, two battalions of Canadian infantry had arrived in the colony, bringing the fighting strength to six battalions. This was taken as an optimistic sign that the colony was to be held until reinforcements could be sent. The Canadians featured in much of the gossip and speculation, with the truth – that they were recruits straight out of training camp – not getting much of a look-in. The Japs were dropping a couple of bombs before turning their back on the colony. The Japs had no stomach for a proper scrap. Hong Kong would be impregnable, like Singapore. The Japs had frightened themselves off with their reconnaissance over the border. The Japs knew they could never get past the Gin-drinkers' line. (That was the defensive chain of bunkers and dugouts in the New Territories.) The Japs couldn't bomb, the Japs couldn't fly, the Japs couldn't react to unexpected situations, the Japs couldn't see in the dark.

Wilson's instructions had been that, if at all possible, I should be found at my desk when the Japanese arrived. 'That will give us a flying start,' he said. So I stayed where I was and spent the day breathing the fear and nonsense and watching the window for planes overhead.

After work I crossed the road and queued for a North Point tram in Des Voeux Road. I had decided to go and see Maria, either at the mission in Wanchai or in Happy Valley where she taught. The streets were strange. Normally Hong Kong was all noise and movement and colour. On that day the movement and colour were as usual but there was almost no noise. People rushed on their errands, grim and intent and frightened. It did not make me feel any stronger.

The tram was packed but quiet. I stood squeezed between a Chinese woman carrying five huge string bags of food – decapitated chickens, not-quite-fresh fruit, and green vegetables tied in bundles, evidently the end-of-day market bargains – and an office worker apparently on his way home, chewing already very thoroughly chewed nails while he read a folded-up Chinese news-sheet. We leaned against each other as the tram rattled from side to side. At Wanchai I fought my way to the doors. Happy Valley Road and Des Voeux Road were both busy, and I scrambled across in defiance of traffic. It crossed my mind that it would be a bad day to be run over by a tram.

The alley that led up to the mission building was between two furniture shops specialising in camphor-wood chests. One of them was closed and shuttered, as if its proprietor and family had already fled. The owner and chief artisan of the other shop was taking the other approach. He sat cross-legged on a stool in the front of his premises, glasses on his nose, executing a carving on the untinted wood before him. Behind him I could see stacked furniture and a small shrine to the goddess of compassion.

I went up the hill. Excitement, haste, and anxiety made me short of breath as I strode between the two open gutters. When I got to the mission I knocked at the double doors, waited, knocked louder, waited, and then pushed my way in. The hallway, which I had never seen empty, was now silent. On the walls were exhortatory posters and notices of church events. The classroom was just off the hallway: it was empty, and that was the strangest thing I saw that day, since I had never seen it without teachers or pupils, or nativity-play rehearsals, or small discussion groups, or solitary readers, or one-on-one duos engaged in remedial tuition. I went back into the hall and called up the stairs:

'Father Ignatius? Sister Maria? Anyone?'

Only the echo. Then I went up the stairs and explored the private rooms of the mission building. The first doorway across the landing was exactly above the hall downstairs. I opened it and saw a dormitory, home to several Chinese families. Curtains separated the space into separate living and sleeping areas, some with bedding on the floor, others with folding chairs arranged in little groups, everywhere full of clothes and trinkets and shoes and lanterns and things. There were old cooking smells, and the feeling of a room occupied by many bodies in close proximity. I stood in the doorway for a few moments. At that time I had never been invited into a Chinese home. I wondered where everyone had gone. I left the mission and on a hunch pushed further up the hill before starting back towards the middle of town. In about a quarter of an hour, I came to St Joseph's, the main Catholic church on the island. It didn't sound as if there was a service in progress but I went in anyway.

The church was not just full, there was scarcely room to stand. A priest I had never seen before was standing facing the altar, leading the congregation in silent prayer. No one turned and looked as the door closed behind me. I tried to spot Maria, but it was impossible to identify a single person from behind in a congregation of several hundred. I decided to stand and wait for the end of the service.

'May we also remember in prayer our brethren elsewhere in Asia,' said the priest, who had turned to face the congregation. From his accent I realised he was Portuguese. 'In India, in the Philippines, in Siam, in Burma, in China, in Japan also. May we remember them in our tribulations. Our Lord who sees into all men's hearts . . .'

I stopped listening. There were more prayers and another period of silence before the service ended and the congregation began slowly to break up. There were more Chinese than I had expected – some of them, I supposed, recent refugees. Many of them would have a very vivid picture of what the Japanese were likely to do. I looked for Ho-Yan more out of hope than expectation, but he wasn't there. None of the passing faces was familiar. Then I found myself standing opposite the compact, soutaned figure of Father Ignatius in the crush outside.

'Father – I came looking for Sister Maria. I wanted to be sure she was all right.'

When I heard myself say it, it sounded odd. I was grateful to him for taking my worry entirely without surprise or side.

'I'm worried too, Mr Stewart,' he said in his quick, clever County Cork voice. 'She went up to the mission school in the New Territories on Friday and we were expecting her back last night. I'm sure Our Lady is taking good care of her but it would still be comforting to have some news.'

His saying this made me suddenly remember. The play – I was an idiot. Maria had told me that the community out near Fanling was performing a nativity play and she had promised to help.

'In any case, with the bombing, she's probably safer there,' he added.

'When she gets back tell her I was asking for her,' I said.

'I'll do that.' Father Ignatius shook my hand and gave me a man-to-man, or priest-to-man, straight look. I made my way up through the crowd outside the church, who seemed reluctant to leave its precincts. They were scruffier and more racially varied than an Anglican congregation. I remember thinking that the churches would be busy that night.

It was by now early evening. I couldn't face the thought of going home and sitting on my own, waiting for whatever would happen to happen, so I set off back downhill to the Empire, telling myself that I was going to check on things and see how Masterson was.

The hotel was eerie, with all the public rooms empty apart from staff. I found Masterson sitting in his office over a pile of papers with his head in his hands, not despairingly, but concentrating on his work. There was a cigarette in his left hand, in some danger of setting his hair on fire, and a glass of whisky beside the desk lamp.

'There's good news and there's bad news,' he said. 'You'll want the bad first.'

'Very well.'

'The Japanese have come over the border. They're fighting through the New Territories.'

I didn't know what to say.

'The good news is that the Japanese have attacked Hawaii and sunk most of the American fleet. They're at war with America too.' I don't remember what I said. He bent down to a drawer of his desk and took out the whisky bottle and another glass.

'It won't be Nanking,' Masterson said. 'It'll be bad, but it won't be Nanking.'

The next day I woke up in a room at the Empire finding that something had rearranged itself inside me during the night. I had to go and find Maria. I wrote a note to Cooper and asked one of the staff to deliver it to the Bank when he had a spare moment.

Empire Hotel

Dear Cooper,

I find myself called away at short notice. Back in a day or two. Keep my abacus warm for me.

Yours,
Stewart

Then I packed my rucksack and went down to the Star Ferry. The harbour was a strange sight. The plan was to conduct a fighting retreat from the Gin-drinkers' line back into Kowloon, and then to evacuate to the island. In accordance with that plan, every boat, sampan, junk, ferry, and dinghy which was crossing from Kowloon side was dangerously full of men and *matériel*, ammunition, little old ladies, nurses who were called to duty at St Matilda's or St Stephen's, every kind of food and supplies, livestock and sundries and fleeing relatives. But they weren't the only boats in the harbour. All British ships had headed off for Singapore at the weekend, but there were plenty of Chinese boats, the usual family groups about their usual activities on deck, cooking and cleaning and smiling and generally pottering about. If they had been trying to send a message that this war was none of their business, they couldn't have done it better.

Air-raid sirens were going off at regular intervals. Often a Japanese plane – the bombers now unaccompanied by fighters: no need – would pass overhead, either before or after dropping a stick of bombs somewhere on the mainland. It would be the island's turn next.

I took an almost entirely empty ferry over to Kowloon and as I did so began to wonder how I was going to get to Fanling. When I woke that morning my resolution had been that I would walk there if I had to. In daylight and full consciousness, that began to seem a less good idea. I could hardly order a taxi to take me north of the main defensive line. I was unlikely to be able to hitch a lift with the army.

But that was what I did. From the ferry terminal I walked past the heaving, milling ruck of people wanting to cross to the island, past where the taxis and rickshaws would normally have been, towards the railway terminal. A number of lorries, some of them in army canvas and some commandeered, were surrounded by a large group of mainly Indian soldiers. I took a deep breath and walked up to the back of the man with the biggest pips on his shoulders. I cleared my throat and he turned around. I have always had a good memory for faces. It was the silent artillery officer who had sailed out to Calcutta with us.

'Tom Stewart,' I said. 'From the *Darjeeling*. The chap who was learning Cantonese?'

'I remember. Roger Falk. Bloody funny way to meet again.'

'Bloody funny. I – I thought you were a Gunner,' I said, feeling a mad need to make small talk.

'On secondment to the Rajputs,' he said, making an explanatory gesture towards the troops around him. 'Bit of a cock-up really, they don't have any artillery yet. We're going to the New Territories.'

I said: 'I don't suppose you could do me a teensy favour?'

In the cab of the lorry, squeezed into the long front seat along with Falk, his Indian CSM, and the driver, we drove past Kowloon, past Boundary Street and into the New Territories, past a relentless flow of people heading in the opposite direction. People seemed to be carrying or pushing as many of their possessions as they physically could, on every kind of improvised trolley, cart, adapted rickshaw, bicycle with towing rack behind, anything. Women carried four or five bulging slings, bending forwards against the weight so that the black cotton sacks looked like multiple humpbacks. I think I expected panic, people fleeing in screaming terror, running for all they were worth. But it wasn't like that. The refugees showed no emotion I could recognise and moved at their own pace.

'Once we get up to Golden Hill you'll be on your own. We're going off to the right. The Punjabs are over that way, too. The Royal Jocks are on the left. A few patrols are up further north to give them something to think about and to slow the Japs down.'

Falk, with considerable delicacy, had not asked me why I needed to get to Fanling, and had not attempted to dissuade me. Perhaps, as a professional soldier, he knew that the defence of Hong Kong was a pointless gesture; so why interfere with anyone else's irrational, dangerous, self-imposed errand? When I think back to that time I don't know whether to feel more pity for the soldiers who knew what was going to happen, and knew that their lives were being expended in vain; or for the ignorant and deluded, who were at least able to tell themselves stories with a component of hope. (A popular fantasy involved a non-existent relief column being sent from the north by the Chinese army.) I suppose on reflection I feel sorriest for those soldiers who knew what was being asked of them. To give your life is one thing; to do it for a gesture is another; but to do it for a gesture you know is meaningless is a desolate trick of fate.

Before long, the lorry stopped. The three vehicles behind us came to a halt also. The road was passing through a defile in the row of hills where the main defence was supposed to take place. The Gin-drinkers' line was supposed to be held by at least 20,000 men, and was being defended by perhaps a third of that number. I could see a pillbox emplacement halfway up the hill on my right. I must have passed it dozens of times before without noticing. The CSM jumped down from the cab and banged on the side of the lorry. In the wing mirror I could see the soldiers beginning to debus. The NCOs were shouting in a language I did not recognise. A woman in black pyjamas on the other side of the road, who was pulling a kind of sled stacked with crates, stopped to take a breather and to watch.

'Well, this is us,' said Falk, who had stayed behind in the cab to bid me a private farewell. I think that although he did not know what was on my mind he was giving me a chance to change it. 'It's a fair step still to Fanling,' he said.

'Ten miles or so,' I said. 'I've done it before.'

'Keep your head down,' he said as he got out of the cab.

The walk, which I hoped to do in three hours, took me all the rest of the day. I began by keeping to the road, still moving in the opposite direction to the main stream of people, which was thinner than it had been nearer Kowloon, but still steady. Once or twice somebody crossed over to try and sell me something – cigarettes, a flagon of water, half a chicken. Three or four times a Japanese reconnaissance plane flew overhead, and a stir would go through the refugees. Some of them looked up, some moved to the side of the road in an act that seemed less a practical attempt to avoid harm than a form of superstition, like touching wood.

I had been walking for about an hour when a woman, stooped from the weight of the slings on her back, stopped in front of me.

'Go no further!' she said in Cantonese. 'Soldiers!'

'Where?'

'Ten minutes.'

She rejoined her family group, who were looking after her with disapproval. Ten minutes; half a mile at best. On the right of the road about a hundred yards ahead of me a scruffy track led to a hamlet. I slid down the bank by the side of the road and into the dry gully which ran alongside it. Bent over, I scampered along beside the track and then turned right to the little village, bending as low to the ground as I could while I ran. The village smelt of fermented fish and seemed to be deserted. There were no people and no livestock. If the Japanese came they would go into the bigger houses first. I went through a bamboo curtain into a hut-sized house with an enclosure for pigs at the back.

A very old Chinese man was sitting in a rocking chair facing the entrance. He looked at me without surprise.

'I need to hide. The Japanese are coming,' I said.

'My family all left. I told them I'm too old to run away,' he said. 'Get into the pig-feed locker. It's by the back door. They won't look in it, it stinks.'

I took the old man's advice. The back door – another bamboo curtain – led to the pig yard. There was a wooden locker, six foot by three by three, against the rear of the house. It did smell bad. I opened it, fearing the worst, but Cantonese frugality was such that it had been cleared out. I climbed in and pulled the lid after me.

'Comfortable?' I heard the old man call.

I couldn't see my watch so I don't know how long it was before the Japanese soldiers arrived. It was probably under half an hour. There were clanking metallic sounds and then, soon after, raised voices. They must have searched for only a few minutes, seeing the village empty and undefended. Then I heard voices in the hut. Two people and then a third, harsher voice, all in Japanese, apparently talking to the old man. The harsh voice repeated itself three or four times.

'Go fuck your grandmother's corpse in the arse,' said the old man in Cantonese.

There was a brief silence and then a noise like an axe hitting wood, followed by a crashing and rolling. Then the Japanese voices resumed, at a conversational pitch, and faded as the patrol walked away.

I waited in the pig-food locker for a long, long time. When I tried to get up both my legs had gone dead.

The bottom of the old man's rocking chair was lying against the bamboo curtain; he had fallen backwards and sideways. I stepped over the chair. He was still in it. The sword had removed his head from his body, apart from a flap of skin at the back of his neck. His head was rolled back at ninety degrees, so that the top of his hair was on the ground. The floor of the hut had turned muddy with blood. His eyes were open. I closed them, filled my water canteen and left the village.

I was more careful after that. Whenever I could I kept to the gully by the side of the road. There were fewer refugees now. Anyone who went southwards from here would be heading for trouble, towards the Japanese soldiers advancing into Kowloon. Whenever I heard anything metallic, anything which could have been a gun or a sword or a canteen, I crouched over in the gully and hid. I thought of a proverb Maria had laughingly told me: 'Of the thirty-six alternatives, running away is the best.'

At one point, towards dusk, I heard gunfire not far away, and shouting in what sounded like Japanese – I couldn't tell. A short distance in front of me was an overturned cart which had spilled a consignment of rice over the road, and whose main body now hung over the dyke. I crept up to the cart and slid underneath. I thought I could hear the Japanese approaching; I thought I could hear booted feet, whispered orders, preparations for opening fire. I would think I was imagining things; then I was sure I wasn't. The underside of the cart was humid and smelled of rice. I stayed there for an hour until it was dark. When I came out nobody was there.

I jogged the last mile or so into Fanling. My timidity had cost me the chance of finding Maria until next morning, if there was going to be a next morning. I was convinced that if a Japanese soldier saw me he would shoot me, but with nightfall I felt I now didn't care.

There had been fighting in and around Fanling. When the moon came out of the clouds I saw that buildings had been hit by shells and gunfire, and one or two houses were still smouldering. A dead soldier in a uniform I did not recognise lay against the wall of a low outbuilding, his intestines spilled open into his lap and gleaming black in the moonlight. There was a single bullet wound in the middle of his forehead with a thin line of encrusted blood around it. His eyes were open.

I realised I had lost my bearings. The dark made all village houses look like one another. I knew I should find somewhere to lie down and wait for daylight. I went to the nearest building and saw that it was the side entrance of the school. I had been at right angles to where I thought I might be. I tried the door; it was open but something was blocking it on the other side. I shoved hard and it gave way. I squeezed through the doorway and found that I was standing over a dead soldier. The rest of the room was pitch-black. I took out a box of Empire Hotel matches and lit one. At first I could not make out what was wrong with the room; its floor seemed to be undulating and irregular. Then I knew: it was covered in bodies. Twenty or thirty British and Indian soldiers were lying on the floor, all of them – I don't know how I knew this, but I did – dead. Another group of bodies, dressed apparently in white, was in the corner of the room, many of them half propped up against the wall. The match burned me and went out.

I heard a noise. It was an animal sound, a whimper. I struck another match and saw in the corner of the room a crouched Chinese woman in black pyjamas. She was crying. I stepped towards her, put my foot on a corpse, and fell forward over it onto another corpse. I tried to stand up but couldn't find my footing. I had to step on a body to reach a patch of clear floor.

I crossed the room. The woman looked up. It was Maria. I took her in my arms. She was shaking and trembling.

'They were using it as a hospital. Then some soldiers came and began shooting from here. Then the Japanese came and –'

Now she started to cry properly, gulpingly, as if she was going to break in half.

'Don't talk,' I said.

Maria and I were cut off behind the Japanese advance. Neither of us could face the thought of sharing a mortuary with the dead soldiers so we crossed the school compound to a one-room building, a kind of storage hut, and made a bed there on the floor. We woke up in the morning to an eerie quiet. I could be certain that Kowloon and Hong Kong were being bombed and shelled, but on the other side of the mountains, we couldn't hear a thing. Only the absence of ordinary village sounds was unusual. There were no dogs, no cooking fires. We spent that day burying the dead soldiers.

We spent the next two weeks there in Fanling. After the burials, I did not go out again. Although the overwhelming bulk of the Japanese soldiers were involved with the occupation of Kowloon and the battle for Hong Kong Island, a smattering of troops was stationed near the village. They were dividing their energies between shooting looters and doing looting of their own. Even more dangerously, there were Chinese fifth columnists who would report my presence to the Japanese. Their presence was part of what had made the Japanese attack so effective. Now that the Japanese were so obviously winning, the fifth columnists were more and more confident. The risk was that if they found me they would kill me out of hand.

Maria went out for supplies every day. Sometimes she went as far as one of the fishing villages. I waited for her return in the most acute anxiety I have ever known, imagining her being found by a patrol of soldiers and questioned, or beaten, or raped, or shot, or betrayed by a villager, or followed back to our hiding place. One of my fears was that she would be recognised and asked for some favour which she felt she could not refuse and which would lead to her exposure. I could imagine that very easily. But none of these things happened. She always came back, always with some food. We cooked it over a tiny wood-burning stove we found in one of the school outbuildings. I would feel, when I heard her approach, light-footed and quick-moving in her black trousered mufti, a moment of pure happiness. It was like a gust of wind blowing from some very far-off place. Then I would remember where we were.

Maria wanted me to come with her into China.

'You cannot go into captivity of your own free will,' she said. 'It is immoral. It would be like suicide. You would be throwing away an opportunity given to you by the Lord. You would be defying your own chances of life and freedom.'

'I don't have a choice. I promised.'

'The circumstances are different now.'

'If I don't go back, then my coming here to find you was a form of running away. Don't you see that? If I go back it makes it into that.'

That made her angry. 'This is metaphysics. It is' – she made an upwards and outwards gesture with both hands – 'froth.

Freedom is real. China is real. You are exchanging a known good for an unknown evil. That is mad.'

'I made a promise. You must surely understand that – I gave my word. It's the only time I've ever done anything like this. I was asked if I would do it and I said yes. I'm not doing this for myself, I'm doing it because I was asked to do it for something bigger than me.'

'Death is bigger than you, and it is that you are choosing.'

I have to admit I felt sick when I heard that. If I had not been so tempted to do what Maria said I wouldn't have been so disturbed by her attempts to persuade me. I also had a fear, or a secret, that I could scarcely admit to myself: the unknown future in China, on the run in a country I did not know, permanently identifiable to anybody at a glance as a European and therefore always at risk, seemed as frightening as returning to Hong Kong. At least in captivity I would know where I was. I am ashamed to admit that I did what might seem the braver thing partly out of cowardice. Maria and I had this argument at least once a day.

Every time she returned, Maria brought back reports of the fighting. Chinese rumours proved to be much more accurate than their British equivalents. The bamboo telegraph traced the progress of the battle: Kowloon had been evacuated of military personnel. The Japanese had set up their HQ in the Peninsula Hotel. The Japanese were shelling the island. The Japanese had invaded the island across the Lei Mun Channel. The Japanese had fought their way up into the Wong Nei Chong Gap and divided the island in two. And then, on the day it happened, Christmas Day, Maria came back empty-handed and told me that the British had surrendered.

'You have to choose today. All the British will be put in camps. Anyone they catch outside will be shot. Come to China with me or give yourself up.'

'I'm sorry, Maria,' I said. The next day I gave her my grandmother's gold necklace and made her promise that if she needed to, she would sell it and use the proceeds to escape from China. Then I made a white flag out of a towel and went out to find a Japanese officer. The soldiers subjected me to certain indignities.

Chapter Seven

In addition to his property at 124 Nathan Road, the one Masterson had looked over and decided not to buy, Mr Luk owned a brothel in Wanchai. It was a tenement building which had been a European brothel, switched to being a Chinese brothel when European brothels were made illegal, and then stayed in business when Chinese brothels were banned. The only concession to the appearance of legality was a seamstress's business installed in the ground-floor shopfront. Prospective customers had to go into the seamstress's and ask for a Mrs Wong.

After the surrender of Hong Kong, this is where the Japanese put the bankers. If the Japanese occupation forces had gone in for jokes, this might have been one. Most civilians were rounded up and sent to Stanley internment camp; soldiers were sent to the military prison in Sham Shui Po. A few people escaped; a few, such as us bankers and some hospital staff, were made to stay at work. Wilson was right, they needed bankers to run the colony.

The Japanese had taken three days to overrun the Gindrinkers' line and fight their way through to Kowloon. At this point they sent a barge with a white flag over to the island to offer terms for unconditional surrender. The offer was refused. They then invaded the island. There was a feeling of inevitability about every stage of the battle. The Japanese advanced to Wong Nei Chong Gap, where the bitterest fighting took place, and split the island's defences. The Governor, who had arrived in the colony only on 7 December, and General Maltby offered their unconditional surrender on Christmas Day. All the deaths in defence of the island, between the first invitation to surrender and the eventual capitulation, were in vain. They included Falk the Gunner, who died in the fighting for Wong Nei Chong Gap. Potter, the second of the Hong Kong Bank men from the *Darjeeling*, was a Volunteer; he was killed by an artillery shell in the battle for Stanley. There were a number of atrocities, including the rape of nurses, the bayonetings of doctors, and the killing of wounded soldiers at St Stephen's hospital on the island. Some people thought an early surrender would have meant that the Japanese would have been in less of a frenzy than they turned out to be. Years later I read of a Dr Li Shu-Fan, who reckoned that he personally treated ten thousand victims of rape.

About ten thousand soldiers died in the fighting. There is no accurate figure for the number of Chinese dead.

I had expected the business of passing myself off as a banker would be much harder than it actually was. But the Japanese seemed, apart from a quick glance at the payroll for confirmation, more or less to take my word for it. It was as if winning the battle for Hong Kong was so exclusively the focus of their thinking that they had given no thought to what would happen afterwards. They had a name for it – the Greater East Asia Co-Prosperity Sphere – but no real plan.

As an ironic result, I was extraordinarily busy in my impostor's role as a banker. Because all the other people spared from captivity were genuinely senior Bank staff I was the only person who could be easily spared for the most mundane tasks. In practice that meant supervising the destruction of the existing currency, double-checking the quantification of the Bank's liquid assets, and supervising the counting of the new money being issued by the Japanese. This was Greater East Asia Co-Prosperity Sphere currency bearing the name of a bank in Yokohama. It was not intellectually demanding work but it required constant attention and vigilance.

There was no real need to count the destroyed currency, it was merely the Bank's habitual and, I found, rather engaging belt-and-braces caution. A roomful of Chinese clerks and I, in the airless basement of the Bank building, counted notes and weighed coins all day for weeks. Every day for us bankers was the same: getting up just after dawn – we woke ourselves, rather than let the guards turn us out of bed – a bowl of congee, and then a march in a shambolic attempt at formation along the mile from Wanchai to the Bank's head offices in Queen's Road. Evidence of the bombardment was everywhere. The city had a half-deserted, half-ruined feeling. The trams weren't running; hardly anyone was going to work; some shops had been looted. Japanese

130

soldiers were everywhere but they brought no sense of ordered subjugation; the atmosphere of the colony was violent and chaotic. Occasionally a passer-by would jeer, more, one felt to ingratiate himself with our guards than out of real hostility. Most people passed by without looking at us. I was grateful for that. My whole day would then be spent in the Bank's basement, where I would at some point be given a ladle of rice and sometimes meat with the clerks. Because most of the clerks would get other, albeit meagre, food at home, they often topped up my portion with their own when the guards weren't looking. At about seven, one of the Taiwanese guards, or, more rarely, one of the Japanese soldiers, would come downstairs and tell us to pack up. We would march to Wanchai in the dark. The days were a mix of fear and uncertainty and routine.

This went on for several months. Then one day the guards stepped back from a cauldron in which a bowl of wet rice soup – a sloppy, loose congee, entirely without any meat or vegetables, the seventh or eighth such meal I had eaten in a row – had been brought down to the basement. It was carried by two coolies, sweating from the heat of the bowl and the exertion. The guards moved ten or fifteen feet away and began smoking looted American cigarettes. As I went up to take my portion one of the coolies looked up at me. He was angry, or so it seemed; people who are frightened often look angry. He had a flat northern-Chinese face and when he spoke he had the twang of a an accent.

'Night-time go to roof in Wanchai house,' he said in a tight hiss. The pitch and accent made the words hard to hear and I took a few seconds to work out what he had said. I fought a mad impulse to loudly ask him to repeat his message. I realised I was standing still at the front of the queue, got a grip of myself, and moved away to eat my slop.

Is this it? I wondered for the rest of the day. I had no idea what Wilson's plan might consist of, though I suspected there would be an approach of some kind. I was frightened, but at the same time this was why I had stayed in the colony. Coming halfway around the world to lose a war when we were doing a perfectly good job of losing one back at home was enough of a joke as it was. To spend the whole of the war counting banknotes would have felt like too big a joke even for my mood in 1942.

News about what had happened around the fall was sketchy and enlivened by rumour, but there were stories that some people had escaped into China. So this might well be the first moment of contact with the outside. But it could just as easily be a trap – say, an attempt at pleasing the Japanese by uncovering or inventing a British plot.

'So what do you think?' I asked Cooper. I had taken him into my confidence. I was under no illusions about what would happen to me if I was captured – I would be tortured. I was also under no illusions about what I would do if that happened – I would give them names. I thought that I might as well get the benefit of Cooper's advice, since if tortured I would betray him to the Japanese anyway. I don't know if he knew what my logic was because we never discussed it.

'I don't think you have a choice,' he said. We were sitting on our beds in the ex-brothel; the Japanese, for reasons of their own, had us sleeping four to a room. His calm, such a surprise to find in a man with such muddle in so much of his personal life, was always helpful – it was a force on which he always seemed able to draw, except when he needed it for himself. Miss Farrington, the girl he had been wasting his time dreaming about, was in Stanley internment camp with her father. Cooper would occasionally wonder out loud about how she was, pretending that his real concern was about her falling in love with some, as he put it, 'opportunistic toad' while in the camp. I tried to ease his mind on that score.

'Yes, all right,' I said. It was true. It would make no sense to have accepted the risk in theory and then reject it at the first opportunity in practice.

There were two ways up to the roof. Just outside our window a fire escape was not so much attached to the building as hanging off it. It was a rickety structure which looked as if it would only just bear a man's weight. (Mr Luk had not seemed the type to worry unduly about fire precautions, but as Cooper explained, 'it's not there for the girls, it's there for the customers' peace of mind'.) The adjacent tenement was only a few feet away across a narrow, warren-like Wanchai alleyway; a very brave, very athletic man might even have risked the jump. There was a smell of rotting things from the alley below. If I went up the fire escape I would have a good chance of not being seen by the guards, though if I were seen, I would have no easily believable story of why my actions were innocent. The other way to the roof was straight up the main stairwell, which circled around an open space, at the bottom of which at least two guards sat, smoking and gossiping. They generally let us move freely among our three floors; the two floors above were empty, and then a half-flight of stairs led to a door, which in turn led straight out onto the roof. The main staircase was in sight of the guards, but for that very reason seemed less furtive. If spotted, I could act ignorant, or as if I were just going for some air.

After looking hard at Cooper and taking a deep breath, I opened the door and walked as slowly and quietly and unhesitatingly as I could up the stairwell. The Japanese, as usual, were talking loudly at their seated posts. It wasn't apparent whether they'd be able to hear me, though they could see me through the banisters if they looked up. They didn't. I got to the top and, praying hard, tried the doorknob. It opened easily and noiselessly. Much later – years later, as I thought back – I realised it must have been oiled. To the right of the shed-like door structure a wooden ladder had been laid to the next-door tenement, and standing at the other end of it, presumably ready to kick it away and run if the first person out of the door was Japanese, was the last man I expected to see: Ho-Yan's brother, Wo Man-Lee.

When he saw me, he flicked the cigarette he'd been smoking out and down into the alley between the tenements. He stepped forward onto the ladder, very gingerly, and then picked his way across, looking forwards but not down. I got the impression there was a question of physical dignity. At the end of the ladder he hopped down and straightened his sleeves. He was dressed in a dark suit and a white shirt with its collar out over his lapels.

'Wo,' I said.

'Mr Stewart.'

'I did not expect you.'

I thought this was a statement of some interest, but he treated it as mere small talk.

'I bring messages from Mr Wilson. He says, give me Japanese

money to pass to him. He says, tell the others to stand by for more requests. He says you must think about how to get parts for a radio. He says, next time he will send written instructions. It's not safe this time. You have a message for him?'

I couldn't think of a thing. I shook my head. 'Uh . . . it's good to hear from him.'

Wo nodded, turned, and tiptoed back across the ladder. Then he pulled it after him and bent to hide it under the parapet. He nodded at me again, more amiably, and went down through a trapdoor. I took a few lungfuls of tainted Wanchai air and went back down the staircase. I could only have been gone from my room for two minutes but felt a decade older. When I sat down on the bed, I saw that I was shaking.

It turned out that the other Hong Kong Bank people were ahead of me. They had already been thinking about the question of a radio. Receivers were, obviously, easier to find than transmitters, and two of them were already hidden in people's desks at Queen's Road Central; there were transmitters there too, in the locked part of the building near what had been the chief accountant's office. That was how it began.

The first practical thing I did was hand a bundle of Yokohama banknotes to a clerk who said, or rather hissed, 'Wo sent me.' A few days later Mitchell, one of the Bank's most senior staff, came into my room at the old brothel.

'We've sorted out the radio,' he said.

That was the first thing we smuggled into Stanley internment camp, via Wo and his associates. The radio transmitter went through in several dozen parts. The great worry was that the Japanese would find one of the parts as we carried it, or the cannibalised radio itself, which was hidden in a false compartment behind a janitor's cupboard.

I also passed on messages, sometimes written, more usually not, from Wilson and others in the camp, and passed messages back. The main subject was how things were to be smuggled into the camp. The organisation we were working for was the BAAG, British Army Aid Group, which was scattered throughout southern China in areas not effectively controlled by the Japanese. The BAAG looked after escapees and passed news in both directions.

I had no overview of what was happening, and by now I knew that I didn't want one.

Some months later, in early 1943, we were moved from Wanchai to quarters closer to head office. We worked longer hours but the surveillance was less strict. The Japanese had convinced themselves that there was nowhere we could go. We were now guarded by Taiwanese soldiers; they were not as strict or as quick to violence. We could move around more freely inside the Bank building; smuggling became easier. Our new quarters were more comfortable.

'No normal banker would put up with these hours,' said Cooper. 'As soon as the war is over I'm putting in the most phenomenal claim for overtime.'

One day I sat down on my bed and felt something lumpy beside me. I pulled back the blanket, a torn green British army-issue item, and saw two oranges, one of which had been peeled and fanned out into the shape of a flower. This was one of Ah Wang's tricks. I had no idea how he did it, but from then on, once every ten days or so, I found small gifts of food under or in the bed – packets of pak choi and other Chinese greens, cooked fish wrapped in a lotus leaf, slow-cooked pork. The food was always cold and there was never very much of it, especially after I'd shared it with my roommates, but it felt as if it was keeping me alive. I was both moved and frightened to think of Ah Wang, no one's idea of a born hero, running these risks on our behalf.

The colony was not thriving as part of the Greater East Asia Co-Prosperity Sphere. There were far fewer people about; the second half of the proverb 'trouble in Hong Kong, go to China' was having its effect. Power and water supplies were erratic. Schools ceased to function and so, more or less, did medical services. It was a great surprise quite how bad the Japanese were at running things. Although our part of Victoria was not affected, because there were so many soldiers about, in other parts of the colony looting and petty crime were rampant. There were sketchily obeyed curfews and random shootings. The Japanese shot people more or less indiscriminately, and – almost as bad – went around from dawn to dusk slapping faces. They had to enlist the help of gangs to try to keep the peace. Wilson had again been right; without the help of the police, who had fled, been locked up or killed in the fighting, law and order was a big problem. The fifth columnists who had helped the Japanese saw it as their right to take what they wanted.

During the war, there was a great temptation to wonder what was happening elsewhere. That was one reason the long hours at the Bank were always so welcome. When I came round the corner and could see the stone lions at the foot of 1 Queen's Road Central and knew that before long I would be breathing the cool air of the Bank's high-vaulted ceiling, my heart always felt easier. Otherwise I would be worrying and daydreaming. What was happening to David and my grandmother? Just how badly was the war going in Europe? (The Japanese published an English-language newspaper, the *Hong Kong Daily News*, which fed us a steady diet of Allied defeats.) What was happening in China? Where was Maria? Was she still alive? Would we be sent to internment camp? (There were always rumours about that.) If we were, would there be enough food? What would happen if the Japanese caught us? And then the question which I couldn't stop myself asking, which was why: why me, why us, why here, why Maria, why were any of us doing what we were doing in the place where we were doing it? Why had we been abandoned?

Perhaps it is appropriate that the only time I had anything resembling a real conversation with Wo Man-Lee was also the only time I asked him a question about his motives. I was working on the floor of the Bank, in the main pool, a tiresomely unde-manding job which consisted largely of strolling around with my hands behind my back looking as if I knew what I was doing, and waiting to be asked to step in and solve small disagreements with dissatisfied customers. It was one of the parts of banking that was most like working in hotel management. We weren't very busy; the part of the Bank which dealt with the public never was. I was promenading up and down when I heard a raised voice, looked across, and saw to my utter amazement Wo argu-ing with one of the tellers. It was the first time I'd seen him in a non-clandestine context, and I thought for a moment I was going to faint with the shock. The teller caught my eye and wordlessly implored me to come over.

'Can I help?' I said in English.

'Gentleman have problem,' said the alarmed teller, also in English.

'Perhaps I can be of some assistance,' I said, again in English, pointing to a desk and two chairs in the corner beside the counters, just out of earshot of the tellers. Wo followed me over. He seemed to be enjoying himself. At the same time there was a ferocity in him. He walked across the Bank's main lobby as if he were thinking about buying the building. I pulled a chair out for him. He liked that. We sat down.

'This is madness,' I said.

'Something has gone wrong.'

'What?'

'I'm going away for a little while.'

'The Japanese . . .'

He shrugged. I was one of the few people who could betray him, since I was one of the only people who knew the identity of our main Chinese point of contact. I understand now, thinking back, that he must have considered threatening me, or killing me, and rejected those alternatives on purely practical grounds. He could hardly threaten me with anything worse than what the Japanese might do. And he couldn't know which of my colleagues I might have told about him, so killing me would not guarantee his safety. Only disappearing from view could do that. Of the thirty-six alternatives, running away is the best.

I was sitting there without speaking. We can't possibly have looked much like a senior banker in discussion with a client. There were certainly informers among the staff. I said, loudly:

'Well, if there's nothing else I can help you with . . .'

He straightened his jacket and stood up. I did too; our faces were close. Without planning to, I found myself asking:

'Why? Why are you doing this?'

Wo shot his cuffs while looking at me. He might have been amused, or angry, or neither.

'Maybe you win,' he said. He walked away.

The Kempetai, the Japanese military police, raided our quarters at dawn the next day. I was woken up by being kicked in the back. Half a dozen shouting soldiers, under the command of two or three members of the Kempetai, were standing in the room I shared with Cooper and two others. They overturned the mattresses we slept on and tore our clothes into shreds. One of them repeatedly screamed what I took to be a Japanese phrase. I remember thinking, that's odd, he must be swearing – but I've been told there's no swearing in Japanese, isn't that interesting? Then I realised he was saying, 'Where radio? Where radio?'

We had nothing clandestine in our room. I no longer knew where the radio was hidden. I had told Mitchell, our radio expert, about Man-Lee's warning when we returned to quarters the night before. He had merely nodded.

Before long the soldiers stopped searching the room and began beating us instead. They took turns kicking us on the ground and hitting us with the butt end of their rifles. The Kempetai men supervised this. The first blows to my head and lower back were excruciating, but after that I felt nothing. As someone said, being beaten is like eating very hot food, in that after the first few bites you don't feel anything.

The shouting and beating went on for some time. When they were kicking the others one prayed for it to go on.

Then we were, one at a time, dragged to our feet. They tied our hands behind our backs with twine, and forced us down the stairs. Cooper, who was immediately in front of me, fell. He slid down the half-flight in front of him and smacked into the wall at the bottom. Two of the guards kicked him once or twice, a little half-heartedly. They were breathing hard from the exertion; that was something I always noticed about beatings, what hard work they seemed to be for the men inflicting them. The soldiers pulled Cooper to his feet. At bayonet point, we clambered into the back of a lorry. Several Bank people were already in it, staring at the floor under the rifles of several very excited Japanese soldiers. The most senior Bank people were not there. The flap of the lorry was pulled down behind us and the interior of the vehicle was a strange hot green twilight. The lorry started and drove up the hill to a building I did not recognise. We were turned out, punched and kicked some more, and thrown into two windowless rooms whose former purpose was hard to decipher. The doors clanged shut, and we were left in the dark.

'Another fine mess you've gotten me into,' Cooper said to the room at large.

We did not speak of anything consequential, acutely aware as we all were that the guards might be listening. Since we had not been caught in the act, it was not difficult to work out that we must have been betrayed by an informer. It was a comfort not to be alone – and a mistake on the part of the Kempetai. We were left for perhaps half a day, enough time to discover that there was a bucket in the corner of the room.

They took Walker, the oldest of us, first. Four guards burst into the room and dragged him out. It wasn't clear whether he was chosen at random. Nobody spoke while he was gone; it must have been about an hour. Then the door opened and they threw him onto the floor. He was unconscious and in the daylight which came in when they opened the door – already, after that brief time in total dark, the light was head-splitting – I could see that he was bleeding heavily from his scalp. The guards then grabbed Cooper and took him away.

They worked through all of us in sequence. I was the last to be taken – I was also the youngest – so by then Walker had come around. They had not asked him any questions, merely beaten him. It felt strange to hope that they would do the same to me. I will not describe what happened in detail, other than to say we were subjected to three sessions each, over about three days. The favourite means of the Kempetai involved covering the face with a towel and then pouring water over it. The victim feels that he is drowning. They did not ask questions; not of me, anyway. Perhaps once a day the guards brought a bowl of rice into the room and exchanged an empty plastic lavatory bucket for our full one.

The third of my sessions with the guards was, I later learned, the longest. It took me some time fully to come round from it. The experience was like waking from an anaesthetic. Dreams blurred into reality; faces and voices came and went. I saw my parents, Masterson, my brother, my grandmother, Maria, all talking both over and at me. I was aware of feeling pain and at the same time feeling disconnected from it. I was back home in Faversham for much of this time, lying in bed on a Sunday morning listening to sounds coming through the window and voices from downstairs. It was comforting and strange to know that my parents were waiting there for me while at the same time I was aware that they were dead.

Chapter Eight

When I came properly around I was lying on a camp bed. I felt great generalised pain, which it took a few moments to interpret: my head had a blinding, throbbing, localised pulse above my temples; my ribs ached when I breathed; something had wrenched my lower back over my kidneys; my knees and feet were on fire; my knuckles were black and so were my remaining fingernails. I could smell cigarette smoke. I turned my head. That hurt a great deal. Masterson was sitting on a folding chair beside the bed with his legs crossed, smoking a roll-up. He had never been fat, and was now twenty pounds lighter. He had aged by thirty years.

'Where am I?'

'Not in Kent, I'm afraid, Tom. You're back with us now, aren't you? We're in Stanley. This is the camp hospital.'

For the first time since the outbreak of war I found myself crying. That hurt. Masterson put a hand lightly on top of my shoulder, and that also was painful. But I was very glad not to be dead.

Curiously, since I had no recollection of anything having been done to my legs, it was those injuries which kept me in bed for two weeks. There were no painkillers in camp. We had helped smuggle some in, but they were finished long since. I found the passivity of just lying there waiting to get better very hard to take.

Cooper was up and about before me, using an impromptu pair of crutches made out of old brooms. He told me that the others were all right, though a few had been beaten so badly they were in the prison hospital. We were mere internees; the people in the prison were regarded by the Japanese as criminals, and were treated much worse.

Cooper was in a subdued but strangely good mood; his stock with Miss Farrington was unrecognisably high. One day he even brought her to see me. She was a sweet, mild-mannered, slightly mousy brown-haired colonial daughter who bore not the slightest resemblance to the tormenting, elusive phantom of his bachelor longings.

The camp doctor came in daily. There wasn't much he could do now that the drugs had run out, but he checked that my bones were setting correctly. The only actual breaks were in my ribs and fingers. I received a check-up visit from the dentist who told me I had a bruised jaw but that my teeth were intact. Masterson visited me every day, chatting and – one of the favourite internment camp activities – gossiping.

'They're putting on a Coward play in a few weeks' time,' Masterson told me. 'First play while we've been in here. Not sure that it's appropriate really but then I don't much like Coward. Too poofy.'

After two weeks, on my first day out of bed, I moved across to a folding chair and sat beside the window. It was then that I found out what had happened. Cooper came in and sat on the bed.

'Your last day in here, then,' he said. I had been warned that once I was up and about – though the ability to sit in a chair stretched that definition, I felt – I would be assigned somewhere to live.

'Good,' I said. Cooper gave me a thin smile which made it clear he had something else on his mind.

'Tommy,' he said, and as soon as I heard that I knew that something had gone wrong. My first thought was: Maria. So when he told what had happened my initial momentary reaction was one of relief. 'There's some bad news. We were betrayed, you know that. We've been keeping it from you until you were stronger. The thing is, they got both ends of the operation. The people in camp with the radio, as well as us. Fourteen of them. All BAAG people. I'm afraid Wilson was one of them. They were tortured and then executed on the beach.'

He moved his own head, perhaps involuntarily, to watch the window. Part of the camp had a view of Stanley Beach.

'Why didn't you tell me earlier?' I said, more for something to say than for any real reason. It wouldn't have made any difference. Cooper didn't have anything to add, and nor did I. We sat in silence for some time. I couldn't think of anything I wanted to know or say. A day or two later we heard over the bamboo telegraph that Ah Wang the cook had been executed. That's all we knew – no more than that. For me, that was the worst moment of the war. A few more Bank people were moved from the camp to the prison. But they never came for me.

Stanley camp was a compound, consisting of a block of flats and a number of bungalows and impromptu structures in the grounds of what had been St Stephen's College. About two thousand civilians were interned there. There were roughly an equal number of men and women, and a few hundred children whose parents had ignored the order to evacuate, or who had been born after it. Stanley prison was immediately adjacent to the camp, but the Japanese had given us orders to avert our gaze from it. Occasionally groups of prisoners were led from the prison down to one of the beaches, where they were executed. The preferred method was beheading.

Prisoners of war were kept some distance away, in Sham Shui Po on Kowloon side. In many cases, men who had joined the Volunteers were kept in Kowloon as POWs while their wives were locked up in the Stanley. They weren't allowed to communicate but they were allowed to send each other money, so they would send Bank of Yokohama bills to the value of five yen as a way of saying they were still alive. Then the spouse would send it back. Some of those banknotes kept going back and forwards to the end of the war.

After the crackdown, most of the bank people – other banks as well as the Bank – had been moved to Stanley. Some were still in the hands of the Kempetai, and others were in the prison hospital. Mitchell died there. Many others did too. I was one of the lucky ones. I gave up speaking Cantonese or admitting that I could. My escape from the Kempetai had been too close. I felt I had used up all my luck. It helped that the Taiwanese guards spoke a different dialect. I couldn't stop thinking about the fact of our betrayal, and the fate of Wilson and Ah Wang.

But it was a relief to be in Stanley. The camp was less claustrophobic than life in quarters and at the Bank had been. The air and sunshine were the best thing. Compared to the internees, we bankers were pale as maggots. The setting, in a bay surrounded by hills, was incongruously lovely. Some people, more finely grained than I, felt the physical beauty of the location kept them live. The worst things about Stanley were the overcrowding, the absence of privacy, and the food. I was assigned a room in the main barracks which I shared with three other people: one of them, inevitably, was Cooper.

The camp was for the most part self-organising. The Japanese left the internees to run it – they didn't have the resources to do it themselves. There was an extraordinarily complete structure of committees and block representatives, organising everything from cooking to laundry to medical care to lectures. It was often irritating and petty, but there was something impressive about it too. Civilian hierarchies were duplicated inside the camp with a numbing completeness.

The whole day was structured around food. In Chinese the word for food is the same as the word for rice, and that's what it was like in camp: rice soup – congee – for breakfast; congee for lunch, sometimes with a few fragments of vegetable. Dinner was the big culinary event of the day. It consisted of rice with any-thing that the cooks could find to make it more interesting – a tiny piece of fish, or once, late in the war, some tired old buffalo from the New Territories, or, again late in the war, the occasional sup-ply of luncheon meat from a Red Cross parcel. I grew to like the burnt, stuck-together rice one sometimes found at the bottom of the saucepan. Its charredness gave it the illusion of flavour. It's a taste I still have to this day.

After breakfast the rest of the morning was spent doing chores and allotted tasks – in my own case, gardening and maintenance duties. One did things as slowly as possible, to conserve energy. There was a rest period after lunch and then – after the sunshine, the best thing about camp – lectures. This made a big difference. I did some work on my schoolboy French thanks to the camp doctor, who had spent some years in Paris as a young man. Professor Cobb – the only man in camp, according to those who knew him, who did not appear to have lost any weight during internment, because he was already skeletal – gave lectures on Chinese literature. Those were my favourite. We learnt later that people in the prison were made to sit on a bench in solitary con-finement and stare at a blank wall all day, 'meditating on their crimes'. Some men's minds broke. I am sure that mine would have.

The diet induced feelings of lethargy that were close to over-powering. Many internees had already died. The rations were only just enough to live on, and the emaciated camp inmates could be killed by what should have been small setbacks – a cough, an upset stomach. The thing which kept people alive was a belief that the war would end and we would be released. When people let go of that hope they did not last long.

After I had got my strength back, or as much of it as I was going to get back on a diet of rice gruel, I did the rounds of people I'd known outside. Morale was surprisingly high, not least because when it dropped, people tended to die. All the ex-Bank people preferred being in camp to being outside. Everyone was paralysed with anxiety about what was happening to our colleagues in the hands of the Kempetai; but we also knew there was nothing to do, nothing we could do. The great nagging worry was that the Kempetai would find out more about BAAG and arrest and execute more people; but that had been the worry before, too.

I was walking back to the barracks one day for a lie-down after doing some slow-motion weeding in the vegetable patch when saw a figure I knew I knew but couldn't quite place. That was a familiar sensation in camp, when people were so physically changed. This woman was coming out of the door in front of me She was wearing a clean flower-print dress which had apparently been taken in to compensate for lost weight. Something about the purposeful angle of her head and her walk was familiar. She was carrying a bucket in the crook of her arm as if it were a hand bag.

'Mrs Marler?' I said. She turned. I hope I kept my face straight it was Mrs Marler, mahogany brown, and so thin that her face was a crowded field not of lines but crevasses. Her mouth was set firmly downwards. She had no idea who I was. 'Tom Stewart from the *Darjeeling*. The chap who learnt Cantonese for a bet?'

'Ah!' Mrs Marler was smiling now, her teeth yellow and because of receding gums, very long. 'The nuns' chum! Yes, of course!'

She told me she was a 'blockhead': camp terminology for leader of one of the inmates' committees. I asked after her husband and her face changed again.

'Bert's not . . . he's a bit down in the dumps. I don't . . . Perhaps you might come and see us? It might cheer him up.' And then, becoming firm again: 'Come round after lectures tomorrow. And call me Beryl.'

The next day, after hearing Professor Cobb on the subject of Tang Dynasty poetry – especially his favourite, Wang Wei – I went to see the Marlers. They had what looked like a former boiler room in a bungalow inhabited by about two dozen people. There was space in it for a camp bed, which they folded away during the day. Beryl had somehow got hot water and so there was tea.

Marler was sitting on the floor. He was looking down as I walked in. I could see that something had gone wrong; not just physically but in his spirit. It was as if the air had been let out of him.

'Mr Marler! How nice to see you!'

He looked up. He may have thought he was smiling. She was fussing with cups.

'Stewart.'

'You look well,' I said in Cantonese, cheerfully, to show I was making a joke. At first he didn't react. Then, very slowly, he said: 'You kept it up, then.'

'Oh yes – best thing I ever did. I'm in your debt, Mr Marler. I can't tell you how useful it's been. One of things I miss most about being in camp is not being able to keep it up – I'm worried I'll forget before the war is over.' That didn't come out quite right. 'I mean, my memory's like a sieve, I'll have forgotten all the Chinese I know in no time.'

'I'm sure we'll be out long before that happens,' said Beryl, brightly. Her husband didn't say anything. 'Have you noticed in the *Hong Kong Daily News* how the sites of the terrible defeats the Allies are suffering keep getting closer to Japan? Terribly encouraging. It won't be long now, it really won't.'

As if speaking from the bottom of a well, Marler said:

'They'll execute all internees before they lose. None of us is leaving Stanley.'

His despair was so raw it was like a social gaffe. One felt fear when people began to talk like that: in our hearts, all internees knew that despair was contagious. Neither Beryl nor I knew where to look. She and I talked about nothing for ten minutes and then I left. A week later Marler was dead. When it happened, it could happen very quickly.

'We should open a hotel somewhere else,' said Masterson one day, a few months after Marler died. We were on duty in the kitchen, washing vegetables. This was important because of the use of night soil – human excrement – as a fertiliser. In Masterson's top pocket I could see a rolled cigarette, a special treat waiting for when he stopped work. He had been known to swap food for tobacco, a fact which led to one of the few real arguments we ever had.

Cooper, who had been in the middle of a disquisition on some aspect of Miss Farrington's many virtues, looked a little non-plussed. Then, recovering, he began:

'Mary says –'

'Kowloon, you mean? Like the time with Mr Luk? Going into competition with the Peninsular, only less snooty?'

Masterson shook his head. 'Somewhere else altogether. Out in the country. On Lantao, or one of the islands, or even Stanley.'

'No, not Stanley.'

'Well, Big Wave Bay then, or Repulse Bay, or somewhere. Where people can go for a break or for weekends.'

'No adulterers, though, Hong Kong's not big enough.'

Masterson had often spoke of the importance of adultery to the hotel business. It was one of the things he said was tricky about Hong Kong from the professional hotelier's point of view.

'That's right. Lots of other business, mind you. Weekends. Wedding receptions. Somewhere to go.'

'Mary says that when the war's over she wants to buy a boat and go sailing every single weekend.'

For a moment I could almost feel the movement of the boat under my feet. Sitting on deck with a beer after a swim; fishing; diving; finding unoccupied island beaches. At times the thought of freedom could be too sharp, too painful. Hope and despair were alike in the way that opposites often are, and the extreme form of one could become the other very easily. You had to keep your balance.

The need to do so was more acute because it began to seem that we were going to win the war. We could see it in the way our

146

Taiwanese guards behaved: they would whisper items of news, rumours of Japanese defeats and Allied progress. A coolie bringing fuel for the incinerator (where blankets ruined by dysentery were burnt) told Professor Cobb about the Normandy landings. As Beryl pointed out, even the *Hong Kong Daily News* couldn't conceal the trend of the war, since its chronicle of Allied defeats moved ever closer to Berlin and Tokyo. Allied planes began to appear overhead. Some of them dropped bombs; an American bomb killed fourteen people in one bungalow. Canadian internees were repatriated. The idea of our eventual release made camp life harder to bear. There were rumours that we would be exchanged for Japanese civilians whom the Australians had interned. It was life day by day; I stuck to the near horizons

In early August 1945, we heard that the Russians had declared war on Japan. That was the first sign that the war was ending. On the evening of Thursday 16th August I went down to the kitchen to see if there was any hot water left after dinner.

'They're saying something's happened in Japan,' Beryl Marler said. She was sitting at one of the tables checking a duty rota. 'Someone heard it from the Chinese. Something about a bomb.'

We had all become experts at attempting to sense the texture of rumours – what felt possible, what was clearly nonsense; the difference between wishful thinking and informed speculation and genuine bamboo-telegraph information. Perhaps it is only with hindsight that I can remember feeling that this time it might be real. I said:

'I hope it was a really big one.'

The next day we were given a special allocation of cigarettes and, for the first and last time in the whole war, a roll of toilet paper. That is when I knew it was finished. I gave my cigarettes to Masterson.

'I do hope you're right,' he said. 'I'm going to smoke all of these straightaway, so if the bloody war isn't over I'll never forgive you.'

The next day the *Hong Kong Daily News* announced that the Emperor loved his people so much he had decided to allow the war to end. We were advised to stay in camp until the situation had clarified and to refrain from excessive celebration.

Chapter Nine

The Plough,
Faversham
1 September 1945

Dear Tom,

I was so happy to get your telegram. We had been so worried and it was difficult to believe that no news was good news. Anne and I look forward to seeing you very much. She says it is funny to think she has a brother-in-law she's never met! The boys also want to meet their 'nuncle'.

I'm sorry to say that in with the joy of hearing you are alive is some sadness also. Grandma, whose health had not been well for some years, had a stroke in summer of last year and passed away after a short illness. She had been in good spirits all through the war, even when it was difficult, and had a good innings as she used to say herself. I hope you will let this be a comfort to you in with the sad news.

I will not write any more so I leave something over to tell you when you come here!

Your brother,
David

Saint Francis Xavier's Mission,
Chung King
Szechuan
19 September 1945

Dear Tom,

I cannot say what a relief it was to learn you are alive and well. *Deo Gratia*. The hardest thing was not hearing anything other than rumours. You have been in my mind and I have often asked the community to remember you in their prayers.

As you can see from the head of this letter, I am at our mission in Szechuan. I have been here for three years. Before that I was mainly in Hunan. There have been shortages of food and the people are tired of war but we here are all well.

Father Peter Wu, whom you have not met, is going to Canton and then probably on to Hong Kong so he will either deliver this letter himself or ask a member of the mission to do it for him if he is detained. I will be in Chung King for the forseeable future, owing to the demands of our mission.

I give thanks for your survival.

Yours in the love of Christ,

Sister Maria

Masterson and I sailed back to England on the SS *Abergavenny*. We were lucky in that it had been a passenger ship; troop ships were less comfortable. We shared a cabin. I took the upper bunk. The cabin was the same size as mine had been on the *Darjeeling*. When I asked if anyone had tidings of the *Darjeeling* I was told that it had been sunk in action in the North Atlantic with the loss of all hands.

I spent as much of the days as I could walking around the deck in the open air. At first this was no more than a couple of circuits. Before long I could walk for an hour at a time. I began to realise that I would get better. That was not a foregone conclusion. Many internees never recovered their health.

Masterson spent the whole voyage sitting in a chair on deck, reading. The ship's library had a selection of nineteenth-century fiction, especially Dickens and Trollope. Masterson would wrap himself in a jacket, coat, and sometimes even a blanket as we crossed the Indian Ocean, Red Sea, and made our way through the Suez Canal, so absorbed in his book that I would have to address him two or three times if I wanted him to look up.

By the time we reached the Mediterranean I was, if not back to my state of health before the war, at least much better. I could exercise until I was out of breath without causing my heart and lungs to feel hysterical with the effort. My digestion was working well, as long as I avoided fatty foods and cheese. My gums had stopped bleeding. Other ex-internees were starting to look better also, putting on weight. You could, on the metal decks of the ship, hear the difference. This in turn made it clear that Masterson was not thriving; not getting any stronger. He needed help to climb stairs, and would stand aside to let people overtake him if they came up behind him in the corridors and gangways. He was perfectly calm and stoical about this.

'The thing about us old buffers . . .' he would say. Once or twice he had a headache which made him look pale and grey beneath his tan. His face would become tight around the eyes. Then he would ask me to read from whichever book he had on the go. I tried to give the characters different voices, until he begged me to stop.

We arrived at Tilbury just after dawn. I had been up on deck for more than an hour, my bag already packed. It was drizzling and the sky was clouded over in a dense English way. It was as if greyness had leaked out of the sky and contaminated everything visible. I had thought that I would go straight to Faversham, but by the time I had disembarked and gone through customs with my temporary papers and single canvas bag I found that I could not. So I took a bus into London instead.

I have sometimes wondered what would have happened if that had been a bright blue autumn day, and a girl in a thin dress had sat down beside me on the bus and started a conversation. I had not been sure, on my way to England, whether I was ever going to return to Hong Kong. I felt that my experiment or adventure might have ended in Stanley. But that first morning, perhaps even that first glimpse, made me feel sure that I could not go back to England. The country seemed drab, flat, and lifeless. English voices seemed straining to be reasonable and apologetic, so unlike the frank contention of the Cantonese. There was no colour anywhere. It was not warm, and at the age of thirty-two I could feel a numb ache where my fingers had been broken. There was bomb damage everywhere. Parts of London looked as if they had been trodden flat. It did not look like the capital city of a victorious empire.

The bus dropped me at Waterloo station. My plan had been to wander around the centre of the city, see Trafalgar Square and Piccadilly again; but I was tired and shaky and my bag felt suddenly much heavier. I found a café underneath the station and sat with a disgustingly strong and over-milked cup of tea.

There was a train down to Faversham in the late afternoon. I took it, using a pass I had been issued in Hong Kong. It was some years since I had last been on a train, so the trip was a great delight. Once we got outside London, the eye had some relief in the golds and reds of the autumn foliage. I smoked so many cigarettes I felt like Masterson. At Faversham station I set out on foot for the Plough. The town was more or less intact: it had been far enough from the docks to escape the bombing. I saw one or two faces I knew but nobody recognised me.

When I got to the Plough I went round to the yard at the back to get my breath before going in. As I put my bag down and straightened up I became aware that my brother David was looking at me. Or at least, it would have been my brother David if he had been a five-year-old child standing with his hands on his hips and a suspicious expression.

'You must be Martin,' I said. The look of suspicion darkened. Then he said: 'Uncle!'

'That's right. I'm your Uncle Tom.'

We shook hands very formally. Then he turned and ran inside, shouting, 'He's here!'

I had been dreading it, but it was fine. David, stocky and bluff and shrewd as ever, could not hide how pleased he was to see me, nor I him. His wife Annie was much prettier than I had expected, tall (at least David's height, or an inch more) and gentle and quick-witted. He was slightly careful with her, as if he could not quite believe his luck; it was sweet and funny to see. Martin was exactly, in every detail, like David had been like a child. Tom, the youngest, was shyer and better-looking, and barely spoke.

Martin was particularly interested that I had been in a camp. He interrogated me at dinner, a roast leg of lamb which Anne must have gone to some trouble to obtain, and which I could barely eat. For Tom the novelty of my arrival had worn off, and he was struggling to stay awake. There was thickly cut bread and freshly churned butter.

'Did you have tents?' asked Martin.

David and Anne exchanged a glance. I gave them a look to show it was all right.

'No, not really.'

'Did you climb trees?'

'No.'
'Did you go fishing?'
'No.'
Some people at Stanley had sometimes tried to catch fish from the beach on the infrequent occasions when internees were allowed to walk there. But the expenditure of effort involved was so great that it left the fisherman gasping with exertion and ravenously, dangerously hungry. For the same reason, although the water looked beautifully tempting, nobody ever swam. All this was too much trouble to explain.

'Did you have sing-songs?'
'No – well, once or twice.'
He didn't try to conceal his disappointment.
'He's mad about the Cubs,' said David.
'We made a boat out of a barrel,' explained Martin.
'I hope you'll take me out on it,' I said. All four of them said:
'It sank.'
'I was frighted,' Tom added, quietly but firmly.

Over the next few days I saw people I knew. Most of the boys I was at school with had been in the war, and a good few of them weren't yet home. Some – not an enormous number, but not a tiny one either – had been killed. The worst single incident had come when a bomb had a direct hit on a rickety shelter and killed a group of dockworkers, four of whom came from Faversham. Many of the women had been working in the fields and looked amazing: they were healthy and fit and golden, not the deep leather suntan of the tropics but with skin the tint of ripe wheat. There was cider and beer and plenty to eat. (After the end of rationing, my brother never ate rabbit again.) I settled down a little. Here out in the country everything did not seem grey. In the afternoons I would go for walks out of town, taking footpaths I hadn't been on since I was at school. The walks all seemed much shorter than I remembered, but on the other hand I was weaker, so it evened out.

I was due to go back to Hong Kong after three months. Halfway through that time I began helping David at the Plough, pulling pints in the evenings, stacking barrels as I got stronger, and doing paperwork. I could see in the ledgers and files that there was a period when my grandmother had done the books. Her tiny, rhythmical handwriting was present in several sets of them: when she had been a young married woman; then again after my parents' death, until we could afford help, and before I began to do the books myself; then again at the end of her life, during the war. It was good that she had kept her faculties right until the stroke that killed her.

Two weeks before I was due to leave for Hong Kong, David joined me on a walk. Without discussing it we went out back, across the hop fields and down to the orchard. The wall was still there and still crumbling. We climbed up onto it and sat with our legs dangling over the side. In ten years not much about the location or the view had changed.

'So?' said David.

'I'm going back.'

He exhaled, or sighed. He shook his head.

'That's what Annie said you would do. You know it's your pub too. As much as it's mine.'

Perhaps it wasn't until that moment that I was really truly sure. But the idea of sharing the pub made it clear.

'No, I'm for Hong Kong. It's good of you, but . . .'

'Unfinished business,' he said. He always was the shrewd one. Then he reached in his jacket pocket and took out a brown envelope. 'The sixth of the profits till Gran died, and then a half from then till now. I still don't have enough to buy out your share, but when I do, I will.'

'David –'

'It's what we agreed.'

I took the envelope. Later that evening I counted what was in it: more than five hundred pounds, the most money I had ever had in my life.

Two days before I sailed back to Hong Kong I saw Masterson for lunch in London. I was staying at a hotel for the last couple of nights, to get a taste of the city. We met in the grill-room of the Café Royal – his choice. The walls and ceiling were covered in paintings of naked women. He had not taken his coat off and sat swaddled at a corner table in several layers of clothes. He was reading a book as I approached the table: *Brideshead Revisited*. He was of course smoking. As I got to the table he looked up and smiled. He did not look any worse, nor any better.

'Makes a change from our own beloved Bank,' he said, by way of greeting, looking up at the paintings. 'Perhaps we should copy it for our dining room.'

His laugh had a cough in it. We made small talk while we ate. It was heavy going, which Masterson normally never was. When they cleared our main courses away, he said:

'Tom – I have news. I'm not coming back.'

It took me a moment to realise what he had said. I don't know why I was so taken by surprise. In retrospect his decision seems perfectly obvious. It may be that to me Masterson was Hong Kong, and the idea that it could exist without him, or vice versa, did not seem possible.

'Alan, I . . . I don't know what to say.'

'I'm not well. As you know. I have liked staying with Catherine' – his sister – 'and,' he smiled, 'I love her girls. I'm not getting any younger. You'll run the hotel better than I did anyway, and I'll live in *rentier* luxury in Surrey, spending the fruits of your labours.'

'But –'

'It's settled in my mind,' he said, flatly and seriously. 'I know it's not an easy thing to face, out of the blue. I know you can do the job, so if you want to do it, it's yours.' Then he paused and said: 'It's all up to you, now.'

What could I say? I agreed, feeling that something fundamental about my life had just changed. The talk went more easily after that. At 3 o'clock, I felt someone approach our table from behind and stop there. Masterson smiled.

'Catherine.'

I turned. His sister was tall and fair and elegant, and she looked a good twenty years younger than him.

'You must be Mr Stewart,' she said. 'I hope he's managed to talk you into running the hotel. He says you're brilliant.'

I didn't even bother pretending to resist her charm.

Chapter Ten

Hong Kong, when I arrived back there in the spring of 1946, was beginning to recover. The water and power supplies worked, buses and trams ran, streets were clean, shops and schools were open, and people had returned from China, which had gone back to civil war.

Chung King
21 vi 1946

Dear Tom,

Just a brief note to let you know that all is well here. It has not been the easiest time in China as I am sure you know but the work of our mission has been prospering despite that. People are more receptive to the Church's message when times are hard. Perhaps I have made that observation to you before.

I am glad that your work at the Empire Hotel is going well. I look forward to visiting you there when my order allows me to come to Hong Kong, though I do not at this moment know when that will be. Sister Benedicta passed through last month on her way north and asked me to send you her regards.

Yours,
Sister Maria

Those were the busiest years of my life. Hong Kong was recovering, business was picking up, the hotel was getting back on its feet. I seemed to be working all day every day, and yet when I think back I can also remember spending weekends walking on Lantao; staying at friends' houses there and on Cheung Chau and in the New Territories; boat trips; visits to Macao; a fairly energetic social life. I was also going to a study group led by Professor Cobb, who had spent a year in England recuperating and then returned to take up his place at Hong Kong University. The subject was classical Chinese literature, and involved me learning written Chinese. I carried flash cards around with me in my jacket pockets and in spare moments would look at them and memorise characters; I remember doing this on the Peak Tram, the Star Ferry, before meetings, in the loo at dinner parties. I loved the way you could carry the language around with you in your pocket. I suppose the cards were what would later have been called a security blanket. Before very long I knew two thousand characters and had a reasonable reading knowledge of basic Chinese.

I also began seeing a girl. Her name was Amanda Howarth, and she had come out to work for Jardines. She was staying with her aunt and uncle; he was a bigwig at the Hong. We met in late 1947 on somebody's Sunday boat trip out to Clear Water Bay. She had very fair skin, always wore a hat and often carried a parasol, but liked the heat. The first time I saw her, she was sitting in a circle at the rear end of the boat, under the awning. She was being urged, partly teasingly, to tell everyone the story of a secret admirer at her office, who left her flowers and little presents and eerily infallible horse-racing tips in a red New Year's envelope. She was laughing, and everyone else was laughing too. She was pretty but the most attractive thing about her was her evident talent for happiness. We bumped into each other a few times more at dinners and dances and things took their course. I took her to a tea house to test her flexibility, and she ordered a dish of tripe and jellyfish. The waiter sided with me, and tried to warn her off.

'Too stinky,' he said. 'Not for English people.'

Amanda insisted, the dish came, and was indeed very difficult to eat, not because it was stinky – it had almost no smell – but because of its slithery texture.

'He must have learned stinky as a useful all-purpose word for putting off Europeans,' I said. We had eaten about a third of the dish and I had hidden the rest in a handkerchief to save face. We both began giggling.

'Thank you,' Amanda said when the waiter came to take away our plates. 'That was execrable.' He gave me a suspicious look. 'Too stinky' became our code phrase.

'She seems like a nice girl,' Beryl said, the first time they met. I could hear unspoken things in her voice and ignored them. Beryl

Marler was my new friend. She had been on the *Abergavenny* on the way back to England; I had barely seen her then, and when I did she was subdued, more so than she had been in camp. But she was also on the boat back out to Hong Kong, the *Pride of Wessex*, and in much more energetic form. She was going out to take over the business, for a while anyway.

'It's what Albert would have wanted,' she told me in the bar. I had not noticed – it had been concealed by her husband's noisier and more visible presence – but she was a tremendous gin drinker, the sort who keeps up a steady rate of imbibition without any visible effect apart from a slight improvement in mood. I gradually learnt to pace myself by having one drink for every two of hers.

'I thought about going home and just sitting around being a widow but it wouldn't have suited me. That's the trouble about the East, it spoils you for the parish council. Bert couldn't have borne the thought of having his businesses just fall apart into nothing. So I'm going to sit on the board and boss them about and generally keep an eye on things.'

I have to admit that it sounded like a bad idea to me: I thought she would be out of her depth, and that Marler's business associates would eat her alive. I kept that prognosis to myself, though, and we became friends through a process which seemed about acknowledging shared history as much as anything. We were both working very hard, as was everyone in the colony; it was as if there was a general agreement to seek amnesia through absorbed effort. Kipling, when he visited Hong Kong in the early years of the century, was impressed by the fact that he never saw a Chinese asleep in the daytime.

1949 was the decisive year in the history of Hong Kong, the time everything changed. Mao and the Communists won the civil war. The Kuomintang packed up and fled to Taiwan. A long time afterwards, Cooper, by now one of the most important people in the Bank, told me that when he came back to the colony in 1953, he could not believe the change.

'There was something different in the air. That's the only way I can put it. For starters the place was a lot busier, more crowded. That was the point at which it became much more crowded every time you went away and came back or took the trouble to notice. Noisier, more hectic, less sense that one knew what was really going on. More crime, obviously, and more of it hidden. Triads. All the Shanghainese lot pouring in, taking on the local chaps who'd been quietly minding their own business. Kuomintang. Secret CP members everywhere. More fun. Not for a respectable married man like me of course, but more fun in general.'

Cooper had married Miss Farrington, now Mrs Cooper, in 1946, while on leave in England. They had two daughters.

'Remember that business about opium?' he went on. He was referring to the criminalisation of opium in 1949. This was a splendid joke, since Hong Kong owed its existence as a colony to the enforced sale of opium to the Chinese. There were rumours that those Triads which had helped the British, Wo and his associates prominent among them, had called in favours and lobbied for the banning of the drug – which of course sent the price rocketing upwards.

'I remember.'

'I once asked one of the bigwigs at Government House about it. Old friend of my father-in-law. You've never seen anyone get so cross so quickly. Chap literally was puce. Said it was the sort of question which only succeeded in casting imputations on the person who raised it. I must say I rather took that as a "yes".'

Hong Kong underwent a deep change. People began pouring over the border on a scale which made the influx during the thirties look trivial. Many of them were people who had good reasons for fleeing the Communists. Some of them had good good reasons and some had bad good reasons. Shanty towns sprang up all over the island and Kowloon. We called the occupants squatters, which made their presence sound more temporary than it was. Businesses which had concerns in Shanghai transferred as much of their operation to Hong Kong as they could. A smattering of import–exporters, spies, former internees, Bank people, and other Europeans came down from Shanghai and, as Cooper said, made life more interesting. A Frenchman and a Russian from Shanghai joined Professor Cobb's reading group. They were Prévot, an untidy French left-winger, and Zhukovsky, a neat White Russian, and they often argued – something hitherto not in the atmosphere of the occasion. One began to hear talk about the Triads.

Not that this was entirely new; but where people had once spoken of the Triads as something half-comic, they now became more real. They were no less real for being, to Westerners, largely invisible. Beryl Marler was a self-appointed expert on the subject. This was thanks to her company's interests in construction. She had ignored advice and sold off most parts of Marler Ltd's business interests. Her father had been a surveyor and she felt, correctly as it turned out, that she understood the rudiments of how the building industry worked. Rapid population growth meant more business and more cheap labour, both of which were good news for Beryl, who took on a large number of Shanghainese workers (she had several Shanghainese foremen). Some of them may have been Triads; or not; but in any case they brought with them stories and rumours about the gangs, which she collected, partly for sheer interest and partly for the pleasure of curdling her listeners' blood.

'People think it's all mysterious initiation ceremonies, all that stuff about "overthrow the Qing and restore the Ming". It's not a bit like that underneath. These chaps ran China. Sun Yat-Sen was a Triad. Chiang Kai-Shek is a Triad. It's not some picturesque thing from the past, devoted to secrecy for its own sake. It's more like a cross between the Mafia and the masons and the Hongs all mixed up.'

'Yes, Beryl, very good, we'll all be murdered in our beds.'

One day in November 1949, shortly after the Communist victory, Beryl and I had lunch at the Empire. Our new Shanghainese chef, Ah Ng – who preferred to be known by his English name, Peter – was settling in well. We had onion soup followed by grouper *à la meunière*. Afterwards we walked a little way west towards Kennedy Town, Beryl for the exercise and me to clear my head after three half-pints of gin and tonic. It was not a warm day. Food carts and street vendors were busy. As we headed east past Central Market the streets narrowed and the buildings crowded together. We were arm in arm. There was a smell of fish oil in the alley, and laundry hanging overhead. A single sheet of newspaper, very cheaply printed, was caught by the breeze and blew against my leg. With some difficulty, after several attempts, I managed to kick it off.

'Bloody nuisance,' I said.

'Now that's a Triad thing,' said Beryl, not in her blood-curdling mode but matter-of-factly. 'A sort of gambling called numbers. Like in Damon Runyon. People buy these numbers in a lottery and then these papers are published to tell everyone the results. It's not a real paper, just an excuse for the numbers printed on it.'

'Beryl!' I said. 'How very Agatha Christie-ish of you to know that.'

'It's a big business,' she said, quietly, pleased. We turned and headed back into Central.

A week later, after Cobb's Monday-evening reading group, I got back to the Empire at about 9 o'clock. Ah Lo, the barman (a find of Masterson's and, in the opinion of regular customers, maker of the best martini east of Venice), saw me come in and raised his eyebrows. I went across to speak to him.

'Missy come see you, Master,' he said. Like most of the staff he usually addressed me in English and let me switch to Cantonese if I wanted to.

'When? Which Missy?'

'I think she still here,' he said and went back to tactfully polishing the inside of his cocktail shaker with a tea towel. Sitting at the bar across from him was Chief Inspector Watts of the Royal Hong Kong Police. We exchanged nods. He was in uniform, sitting with a pink gin and a copy of the *South China Morning Post*. Masterson had advised that a hotel should always have a tame policeman or two. His man, Superintendent Putnam, was a clever alcoholic who had been an important figure in Stanley – the police were in the civilian camp – and had retired shortly afterwards. Watts had come out to Hong Kong after the war. He was a teak-coloured, teak-tempered man, a classic colonial policeman type. I never liked him.

I went into my office and there was Amanda, obviously not long recovered from a big fit of weeping. She was sitting in my chair behind my desk. For a moment I thought this was to do with us – we had last seen each other at a dance and had parted on a note somewhere between an argument and a misunderstanding after a mix-up about when we would be partnering each other in a waltz. But she was too upset for that. Her nose was red at the tip, as if she had a cold.

'Amanda, my dear –'

'I'm sorry,' she said. 'I'm sorry, I'm sorry. I couldn't . . . I don't know why it . . . I'm sorry.'

'What is it? What can I do?'

'I –' she broke down again. I gave her my handkerchief and went to collect two large sherries. She went to the bathroom and straightened her make-up. Then she told me the story.

'The secret admirer. Remember, I told you about him, the flowers and perfumes and so on. It was a joke at first. I'd get these little gifts on Monday morning. And then sometimes tips for horse races, a card left on my desk with a horse marked in a particular race at Happy Valley. Never more than one. At first I thought it was a joke. Then after the third or fourth time I began to check the results. The horse had won. I checked a couple more times and it won again both times. Also the presents were a little bigger – a pair of jade earrings once. I had started by telling people, like that day on the boat, and also Mr Grafton,' her boss. 'But by now I was far too embarrassed. I didn't know what people would think. Thing was, the presents weren't always consistent. Sometimes they'd be there and sometimes they wouldn't. No pattern. That was part of what was so confusing. I felt that someone was watching me and I couldn't work out why.'

I thought about paying her a compliment here, something along the lines of, I can think of a reason why someone would want to watch you, Amanda. I managed not to say it.

'So this went on for a while. One day I got a copy of the *South China Morning Post* with a line drawn under the name of a horse on that weekend's card at Happy Valley. I thought, the hell with it,' blushing slightly as she said that, 'I'll have a bet. But I didn't know what to do so I got Sally', her friend, 'to ask Tony', Sally's boyfriend, 'to put ten dollars on for me. The horse was called Starboard View and it won at 8–1. Tony was impressed and I was speechless. Two weeks later, Fever Heat, 12–1, same thing. And then again, and again, but always at irregular intervals. By now I was beginning to feel I was going mad. I couldn't tell anybody. It had got too serious.

'Then last week I had a tip, the first for a few weeks. Underlined in black ink. Helpful Secretary and 9–1. I put twenty dollars on, and in my mind I'd already spent it on that tea chest we saw, do you remember the one? Saturday came, I listen out for the results and it not only hasn't won, it's come last by ten lengths. Bye bye twenty dollars.

'Well, I thought it was funny, but I also thought it was bizarre. Couldn't work it out. Then I came into the office today and there's a copy of the paper sitting on top of the filing cabinet. Then I remember the horse's name. That's when I realised . . .'

She was beginning to choke again. I reached for her hand. 'It was the filing cabinet. Mr Grafton's files. Obviously some of them are quite important. Company secrets, that sort of thing. And I should always lock the cabinet, but I don't always bother, especially during the week, because it's a sort of complicated double lock, and there's another lock on the door, and . . . anyway, that's it, I'd get the presents when I left the cabinet unlocked. I suppose the size of the gifts was to do with how useful the secrets were. They realised I hadn't worked it out, and so they decided to teach me. And now I'm sick of Jardines and sick of Hong Kong, and I . . .'

I took her other hand. I said:

'Welcome to Hong Kong.'

That came out wrong. I meant it to be wise, comforting, consoling, mature; but it sounded pompous and smug. Amanda now burst into tears. I tried to comfort her. By the end of the conversation we were engaged.

I had more or less given up expecting it, but that same year, a week before Christmas, Maria arrived back in Hong Kong. The first I knew of it was when she simply turned up at my office, my secretary Ah Wing knocking and then opening the door with an odd expression on his face. I had a small mountain of papers on my desk to do with staff wages and was grumblingly making my way through them. I looked up and behind Ah Wing saw Maria, looking at first glance wholly, frighteningly identical to the last time I'd seen her, eight years before.

'Thank you, Ah Wing,' I said. The ability to disguise curiosity was not one of his virtues but he left us anyway. I came round the desk. It was somehow clear we were not going to touch, but Maria was smiling broadly, and as if despite herself.

'Well, well, well.'

At close range there were fine lines at the corners of her mouth and at the ends of her eyes: not deep cracks, but tracework. She might have been five pounds lighter. Someone who did not know her would have been able to tell that she had known some difficult times. That was new. She was again wearing some kind of modified habit, like a nurse's uniform.

'You are older, Tom. But you look in good health.'

'Virtuous living, wholesome thoughts. You look more or less the same. That's a compliment.'

'It is not necessary to compliment a sister on her appearance,' she said, still smiling as she sat down. For a brief moment I thought: she's turning into Sister Benedicta.

There was a knock at the door. Ah Wing, without waiting to be asked, had brought tea. I was both irritated and grateful to regroup.

'Sister Maria is an old friend from before the war,' I said to him. 'She taught me Cantonese.'

That did the job of letting everyone in the Empire know. Ah Wing left, and I poured the tea.

'So what are you going to do now?' I asked Maria. 'Prospects in China must be pretty bad.'

'It is more complicated than that. The Communists are in some ways more easy to deal with than the nationalists were. Less unpredictable and less corrupt. This is already evident in many areas. So we are not pessimistic about the years ahead. At the same time the change of regime coincided with work which needed to be done here. And the order felt my presence in Hong Kong was advisable.'

'You've been away for quite some time,' I said, trying and failing to keep an edge of bitterness out of my voice.

'Under the circumstances, not all that long,' Maria said. 'A world war both preceded and followed by a civil war, in conjunction with the demands placed by total obedience to a religious order, make this gap of eight years not a very surprising one.'

'It's obviously very stupid of me to expect anything else.'

'It is not a question of stupidity. Our perspectives are merely different,' she said, more gently. And then, more gently still, 'Eight years is a long time.'

I said: 'I'm engaged.'

'Ah. May I know the name of your . . . your fiancée?'

'She's Amanda Howarth. Works at Jardines. Lives with her aunt and uncle on the Peak. Bowen Road. Nice view when it's not foggy. Been out here two and a bit years. We met on a boat. She's . . . she's a very nice girl.'

Maria sat perfectly silent and still through this, and then for a moment or two afterwards. 'Well, it has been a pleasure to see you and renew our acquaintance,' she said as she got up to go, and then did, leaving me feeling that something I had been depending on had gone badly wrong.

St Francis Xavier's Mission
Wan Chai
19 December

Dear Tom,

I felt after our meeting that I had not acted with good grace over the news of your engagement. Please excuse my lapse of manners and accept my heartfelt congratulations.

The mission here is giving a Christmas concert on 23 December. Father Ignatius has arranged it. If you and Miss Howarth could come as my guests I would be delighted. There will be refreshments afterwards.

It is strange to be back in Hong Kong. I cannot pretend that it is not something of a relief after the privations of wartime China.

Your friend,
Sister Maria OABV

'You think of here as being home, now, don't you?' said Amanda, on our way to the nativity concert.

'I hadn't thought about it. I suppose so.'

'I don't think I'd ever feel entirely at home here. It's too –' She looked around and made an outward sweeping gesture with her palm. I took it to mean something like too Chinese, too foreign, too far away, too subtropical.

'Too stinky,' she said. I laughed.

'I know what you mean,' I told Amanda. She put her arm through mine.

We arrived at the mission hall. It was the same building I came to when frantically looking for Maria on the day the war broke out, and for a moment I felt a kind of vertigo at being back there. That seemed to have happened ten minutes ago; yet when I added up everything which had subsequently taken place, it felt like a hundred years had elapsed. The feeling eased when we entered the hallway. It had been decorated with two huge Christmas trees made of felt, with tinsel stars and hand-painted fairies strewn through the branches. There was something Chinese about the trees; they were perhaps modelled on Chinese firs rather than European ones. I could see the hall beyond was crowded with people sitting on folded chairs facing the stage. Father Ignatius, who was greeting guests at the hall door, recognised me.

'A happier occasion than our last meeting, Mr Stewart.' That was at a funeral he had conducted in camp.

'It certainly is, Father. You're looking well.' Which was true. He had filled out, and had the fleshy look which often belongs to priests in mid-career. He was holding my hand in a double clasp and gave it an additional sincere squeeze.

'Please go through and take your seats. Maria reserved them for you at the front,' he said.

We did as we were told. Father Ignatius, or the Catholics in general, certainly could turn out a crowd. A surprising number of Hong Kong's great and good were in the hall. I recognised the Lancastrian head of the electricity utility, an Irish-born judge, a French businessman. In the front row, one of the Governor's senior economic advisers was looking at his watch. There was a smattering of Portuguese, Macaunese, and Mr Yamashita, a Nagasaki Catholic who had emigrated to America in the twenties and spent the war in an internment camp in Arizona. Always on the lookout for a friendly face, Mr Yamashita caught my eye and nodded as we made our way to our seats. He had been sent to Hong Kong with supreme tactlessness by his employer, an oil firm, and was at this point the only Japanese civilian in the colony. I liked him and he was a good customer; he needed to do a considerable amount of entertaining for his work, and the Hong Kong Club still had a race bar. He could not go to our competitor, the Hong Kong Hotel, because its pre-war barber had turned out to be a Commander in Japanese naval intelligence.

A sheet of paper on each of the chairs announced that we would be treated to some singing, some magic tricks, and then a Christmas play. A note scribbled on my sheet said, 'See you afterwards!' in Maria's handwriting.

A peculiarity of these evenings of Father Ignatius's – over the years, I was to go to many of them – was how variable the performances were. One might have thought he would regularly achieve a certain standard, or lack of it, but on the contrary; some productions could have been translated without amendment to the professional stage, while others were so poor that the audience could not be confident as to whether it was listening to *Oklahoma!* in English or Cantonese. Happily, I suspect, my memory spares me most of the details of that evening's performance. I remember a Chinese Mary, radiantly beautiful, and genuinely pregnant, attracting all the attention in the play, and a deeply embarrassed Amanda being asked onto the stage to pick a card from the Great Miraclo, a Brazilian Jesuit, real name Father Augustine, who did card and coin tricks at children's parties. His pièce de résistance involved tearing up the *South China Morning Post* and magically putting it back together as the *Macao Gazette*.

'Well, that was something,' I said to Maria afterwards, backstage, in the converted classroom and storeroom where people were standing around loudly drinking and talking. She seemed pleased by how it had gone. Amanda was smiling hard and saying little.

'Yes, the performance went well, I think, we had all been rather nervous.'

'It must have been strange, doing it in the open in Hong Kong, after those years when . . . when it was more difficult,' said Amanda, beginning confidently and then running out of steam.

'What do you mean by more difficult?' said Maria. Before I could intervene, Amanda said:

'Oh, you know, China, and the war, and the Japanese, and . . . you know.'

'As it happens I do not know.'

'Maria –' I began.

'No, I'm just saying it can't have been easy, and Hong Kong isn't perfect, but it must be easier, that's all.'

'China has been through a period of great turmoil encompassing invasion and defeat at the hands of a foreign power as well as a civil war,' said Maria. 'Many people have died. Christ's passion is being enacted in many places over the world in our lifetime and China is one of them. I do not understand where the idea of ease is relevant. We are missionaries.'

'Oh, come off it, Maria, it was a perfectly reasonable –'

'As for the supposed superiority of Hong Kong, I must tell you that to many of us it combines the least attractive aspects of China, specifically the corruption and factional fighting, under a superficial veneer of legality and procedure and obsession with appearance which manages to imitate and surpass the Chinese at one of their very worst vices. At the same time its denial of dignity to non-European inhabitants, the attitude embodied in the "no dogs or Chinamen" sign of Shanghai, and the fundamental self-interestedness of the British colonial power, make it a unique combination of criminality, hypocrisy, and the death throes of two different empires.'

'Maria, that is the biggest –'

'So why don't you go back?' said Amanda. 'If it's so awful here.'

I saw a glint in Maria's eye. She said: 'Do you desire to see people die? Innocent people?'

'Innocent of what?' said Amanda. I have to admit I was impressed.

'We both know what we mean. Hong Kong is in many ways a corrupt and corrupting place but it is physically much safer than China and it is in this respect that our duty to our mission brings us here.'

'So it isn't all bad here, then?'

'As I said, in this respect –'

'It sounds rather like what I said about it being easier.'

'I repeat that that it is not a term which I find relevant in relation to our mission's work.'

'Ladies, ladies,' I said.

'Perhaps I may ask you to excuse me,' said Maria. 'Señor Pesquera looks as if he is stranded.' She crossed the room to talk to a man who was drinking punch and looking at his feet.

'Well,' said Amanda. 'So that was your friend.'

'I, uh, yes,' I said. 'I'm sorry, she can be a bit . . .'

'A bit?'

' . . . difficult I suppose is the word.'

She smiled and squeezed my arm.

'I liked her. Let's get to the buffet before everybody's scoffed it all.'

I felt a real warmth for her that evening. I also realised that I was in no state to be engaged to anyone. The longer I kept the attachment going, the more harm I would be doing her. So I broke off the engagement. It is a conversation I prefer not to recall. For three months I heard reports of how broken-hearted she was. Then she took a boat home to England, without my seeing her again. On the voyage she met a young Grenadier Guards officer going home from a secondment to the Australian army. They were married a couple of months later. Her Jardines uncle stopped coming to the Empire. He had been a good customer and we missed the business.

Chapter Eleven

In 1953, I was forty. My birthday fell on a Sunday. I was woken by a waiter with a tray of tea and a telegram:

MANY HAPPY RETURNS STOP GOT MY SHARE
PLOUGH MONEY ABOUT TWO THOUSAND DO YOU
WANT IT STOP ALL WELL HERE LOVE DAVID

I had been due to go out on a boat trip to Silvermine Bay, followed by a walk and picnic on Lantao, but many of the party had come down with flu in the previous week and the trip was cancelled on Friday. I put the telegram in my pocket and decided to take a whole day to walk over Hong Kong Island, something I had not done for a while. I had the kitchen make me up some sandwiches and put them in a rucksack along with a canteen of boiled-and-cooled water and a few tomatoes. I had had a particular craving for these in camp, and now I ate them whenever I could. For some reason the Chinese don't like tomatoes.

First I walked all the way straight up Old Peak Road. It is almost vertical and I had to take frequent stops to ease my shouting leg muscles and racing heart. At the stops I would catch my breath and the view would settle. The Hong Kong Bank building, a dozen or so storeys high, still dominated the middle of town. The harbour was as busy as it had been before the war; more so. There was a good view of Government House and its peculiar Japanese tower.

The Peak Tram terminal is over a thousand feet up the mountain and it took me more than an hour to get there. There was a sprinkling of Sunday walkers, people who either lived on the Peak or who had taken the tram up for a constitutional. The proximity of St John's church to the lower tram station meant a few of them had come straight from services in their suits and frocks and hats, with their well-scrubbed children, amah-less for the only time in the week. In shirtsleeves and shorts and boots, dressed for serious walking, I felt conspicuous and physically virtuous.

I set out down the far side of the hill, on the track that led down to Pok Fu Lam reservoir. Where the path led off from the circular road around the Peak, a couple were comforting a boy who had run on ahead of them, fallen over, and cut his knee so that the blood ran down into his white socks. I stopped at the reservoir for a ham sandwich and a couple of tomatoes and then pushed on down towards Aberdeen. It was hectic, and very many people were out and about, but I still didn't feel as tired as I wanted to so I kept walking, along the side of the road that ran up and down and eventually to Deep Water Bay, where, properly footsore, I thought I could have a beer at the golf club and call a taxi to take me home.

Then, as I started down into the bay proper, I saw it: a big new house, about three-quarters built, with a number of Chinese workmen moving around in front of it. The building had a wide view over the bay. Its long veranda had open French windows. Although it was a mere fifty yards or so above the beach there was a swimming pool, a rarity in Hong Kong then. The style of the building was European rather than British colonial.

'What's the matter?' I asked the oldest and glummest looking of the workmen, standing in a singlet with his hands on his hips.

'American man build house, today we hear he's gone broke,' he said in Cantonese worse even than mine. 'We don't know if we're going to get paid.'

'That's bad luck,' I said. 'Does the American man live in Hong Kong?'

'Singapore. Or America.'

'Can I look?'

He turned to the other men and shrugged. I came through the gate and walked up the short circular drive to the front door. The view out over Deep Water Bay – about a minute or so's walk away – was perfect. Inside, the house was much bigger than it looked from outside, stretching out backwards and up the slope. It was so big it was hard to imagine what use the owner would have had in mind for it. I later found out he had been turned down for membership by the Royal Hong Kong Yacht Club some years before and, in a mixture of pique and revenge and self-celebration, decided to create a sort of private yacht club for himself and his friends – which was why every room had a sea view

*

Beryl appointed herself chief sceptic. Leaning on the walking stick she had begun using, as much, I suspected, as a stage prop as a necessity, she said:

'The point isn't, is it a nice spot, which it obviously is; the point is, will anybody come?'

'People love to have somewhere else to go. It's like Lantao or Fanling or something only much more convenient. You can come here for a drink after work.'

'This isn't India,' Beryl said. I said:

'Beryl, I have no idea what you think you mean.'

We were standing outside the gates of the house at Deep Water Bay on the Tuesday evening after I had found it. A beautifully fresh breeze was blowing in off the sea.

'It's like a cross between the Mediterranean and Scotland,' she said, softening a bit.

'Thank you.'

I had made enquiries. The owner, Jackie Lee, was an American businessman who had made and lost a fortune in oil speculation in China during the thirties. He returned to America, did well out of the war, then went back to Shanghai and lost all his money, essentially because he bet his assets on Chiang Kai-Shek winning the civil war. This house had been planned to be his Hong Kong retreat and in its three-quarters-finished state it was, although not cheap, the closest thing to a bargain one could find in Hong Kong.

'Good feng shui,' said Maria. I had been due to meet her for tea; when I called her to say I had to cancel because of this business, she asked to come too. It wasn't at all clear to me that she had ever stayed in a hotel; though with Maria that would not be a bar to her having strong views on the subject. She seemed to be enjoying the spectacle of Beryl – with whom she got on well – and me.

'You're a Catholic nun, Maria. You're not supposed to believe in feng shui,' I said, irritated by her amusement.

'There is a distinction between superstition and belief. Many a devout Western Father touches wood and refuses to walk under ladders.'

'It's not at all –' I began.

'What about transport?' asked Beryl. We talked a little more about all that. The quick subtropical sunset came and went and lights came on here and there around the bay. We got into the hotel car I had ordered and went back to the Empire. Ah Ng had made crab salad and shepherd's pie, the daily specials (an old idea of Masterson's: 'People love a clubby feel'). I had divided the main dining room into two so that there was now a European room, decorated with wood panels and dark curtains, and a Chinese one, with gold-leaf dragons painted on black lacquer and clever use of mirrors – like a tart's boudoir. We were in the European room.

There was a question I had been meaning to ask Maria. For whatever reason, it was one that made me feel nervous. I waited until we had started in on the shepherd's pie and she had drunk one of her infrequent glasses of red wine.

'Maria, do you ever hear news of Ho-Yan?'

She put down her knife and fork.

'Wo Ho-Yan. He was someone I sent to Thomas from the mission in Canton,' she said to Beryl. 'He is still working for his brother. I knew them both from childhood.'

'Bloody hell,' said Beryl. 'Wo Ho-Yan? Wo Man-Lee's brother? Biggest hoods in the whole colony.'

'He is a gangster,' said Maria. 'What has happened is exactly the thing I most feared since I first met Ho-Yan in Canton many years ago. But perhaps I was trying above myself. You can help people, but without God's grace you cannot transform them, and if people refuse that grace, then there is nothing you can do.' She turned and looked straight at me and went on: 'I know you did everything you could to help Ho-Yan, Thomas. There is nothing more you could have done.'

'Ho-Yan was a nice boy and I don't think his brother is rotten all the way through,' I said. 'Wo did things for us during the war anyway, and we were grateful enough for it at the time.'

'He only ever does things for himself,' said Maria. 'You do not know of what you speak.'

'Well I must say, that's a facer,' said Beryl. 'You kept quiet about that one, Tom. I bet you did not know Wo Man-Lee owns more newspapers than anyone else in the colony. All Chinese, obviously. Doesn't take sides – he's too clever for that. Some of them pro-British, some wildly anti-. It all grew out of those numbers rackets. Remember those newspapers we saw that day, the ones used in the numbers racket? That was him. Lots of other things too. First they gave the papers away to communicate the numbers, then they started to put ads in, then they realised they got better ads if they had real articles, then they gradually turned them into proper newspapers. If that's not a contradiction in terms. All Triad up to their eyeballs, goes without saying. Don't expect the papers make nearly as much money as the drugs and the girls but it's still not a bad source of cash flow. Ho-Yan is the front man for the legitimate side of the business. He does the building stuff and the paper stuff. We've bid against them a couple of times and needless to say we lost. Hard to compete over a tender when the chap doing the buying is worried about waking up minus a couple of limbs. All the people at the heart of the shop are from the same place. Fukien toughies. Wo Man-Lee only really trusts people from the same village. If they let him down, he takes revenge on all the relatives. Very clever, very nasty. I say, the pie's damn good today.'

I tried to imagine Wo Man-Lee presiding over a stable of newspapers and other ramifying subdivisions of a criminal empire. It was not difficult. Ho-Yan I had a little more trouble with – but only when I saw it in the abstract, as the idea of Ho-Yan the criminal. When I thought of it as a family affiliation, a form of loyalty, it made perfect sense.

These were the years when one began to hear the word 'Triad' used often, usually with a lip-smacking relish or enjoyable shudder, and always in connection with hoodlum outrages. It helped that a favourite instrument of retribution amongst small-time, street-level Triads was the meat cleaver. Chief Inspector Watts was a particularly good source of stories about choppings. He would stand at the bar and describe these atrocities to a steadily expanding circle of appalled, enthralled listeners. I remember one about his going into a restaurant in response to an emergency call and being greeted on the threshold with a small mound of severed arms. That was the way people liked to think of criminal culture in Hong Kong. It was to do with lurid stories about meat cleavers and initiation rites. But most of the infrastructure of Hong Kong was built by the levy on legal gambling. If illegal gambling was as extensive and as lucrative, where was all that money going? And then there were the drugs and the girls and the Triads' 'legitimate' businesses. Nobody wanted to think about it.

'Golly,' said Beryl. 'Let's not dwell on it. Tom: so tell me what you're expecting your occupancy rate to be, and what you'll need it to be to break even?'

We got on with talking about money while we ate our shepherd's pie.

Chapter Twelve

In the event, I bought the house from Jackie Lee's bankruptcy receivers. I renamed it the Deep Water Bay Hotel. It took two years to get through the legalities and overcome a series of obstacles too tiresome to enumerate, each of which seemed certain to derail the whole arrangement. As for the money, I used my share of the Plough cash from David, borrowed more from the Bank, brought Beryl in as a sleeping partner, and wrote a difficult letter to Masterson. I said what I intended to do, offered him a sleeping partner's share in the new business, and added that I wanted to keep running the Empire – after all, a vastly bigger hotel – while setting up Deep Water Bay. Ah Wing would be the manager under me. I thought it was fifty–fifty that Masterson would accept. About a month after I wrote with the proposal, I had this letter:

> The Elms
> Godalming
> 12-2-56
>
> Dear Tom,
>
> I had mixed emotions on receiving your letter, as Pygmalion must have had when his creation first did something he did not expect. I cannot pretend that I – or rather we, the Mastersonian family 'we' – would not prefer to have the benefit of your continuing undivided attention in running the Empire. But we have had that exclusive benefit for over a decade, to our great profit, and should not be graceless about acknowledging the fact that life, and people, and protegés move forwards. We would be delighted to accept your offer to continue running the Empire in conjunction with a 20 per cent stake in your new venture, along the lines of the terms you propose.
>
> English winters do not, I find, become any easier. Come and see us soon.
>
> Love,
> Alan

The actual building work was surprisingly quick. Beryl's firm took on the contract to complete the project. I asked her to retain the workmen who had been employed on the house to date. She was sceptical – 'I have workmen of my own to employ, you know' – but she saw the force of my argument about fairness and about their knowledge of the building. She insisted however that the site foreman – the man in the singlet – be answerable to her foreman, who in turn would report to her.

'We can't insist on that. He'll lose face.'

'Does he speak English?'

'Don't know. Not much, I shouldn't think.'

'Then we'll say it's because we need the overall foreman to speak English. All his boys will still report only to him. It'll be fine.'

On site, seeing Beryl give orders to the two crew chiefs, I understood why she had been a success at the head of Marler's. As a woman in authority she was instantly recognisable as a figure to these men – she was a Dragon Lady, tough, autocratic, formidable, her authority unquestioned. This was a role and a status she would not have had in this kind of work back in England. The men hung on her words in a way that no English workmen would have. It was strange and in a way terrible, the extent to which Marler's death had liberated her and given her a new life.

After Deep Water Bay had been up and running for some time, I went back to England for the first time in fifteen years. I felt that I could afford to. The hotel was going better than I had expected, and the restaurant much better. At this rate I would pay off my debts in two to three years and begin making a profit within four.

There were differences about this trip to England. Last time I had described it to myself as going home. This time I was going back. Also this time I flew. It was my first time in an aeroplane; that seemed a somehow embarrassing fact, and I made a point of not telling anyone. The plane was a BOAC Boeing 707, much bigger than I had imagined, and the flight took a day, with stops in Singapore, Delhi, Bahrain, and Rome. At Delhi, in the middle of the night, I bought two Indian-made watches as presents for David's boys. The proprietor of the shop, the only one open, was a Sikh, and the sight of his turban bending over the display case as he fished out the watches gave me a twinge of nostalgia for Hong Kong. I stretched my legs at each of the airports, which were less undifferentiated than they have since become. Pilots and crew changed regularly but the passengers did not. That made the trip seem even more exhausting than it was.

David came to meet me at Heathrow. We sent each other pictures now and then, so I was braced for changes. The reality was still a shock. This middle-aged man, as broad as he was tall, his hair now grey, with a chubby caricature of my brother's face – that was David? The giant who stood beside him seemed also to be taking a mysterious amount of interest in my arrival. Then I realised it was Martin. David's letters had said something about the boy 'shooting up'. David saw my look.

'Anne's brothers are both over six foot,' he said as we embraced. He was so broad my arms did not meet around his back, and he felt not so much heavier as denser, stronger.

'Well, at least you're no taller,' I said. Martin picked up my bag. He was lanky; one might have thought he was my son rather than David's. He was quiet, with lively eyes. David and I squeezed into the Morris Minor as Martin got behind the wheel.

'Dad's a terrible driver,' explained Martin. 'Much too impatient.' From the back seat, David gave an amused grunt. As a father, he was much less of a disciplinarian and patriarch than I would have expected.

Travelling around the outskirts of London and down to Kent, England seemed huge, spacious, provincial. We drove for hours – a novel sensation. We left the city behind. Martin asked me questions about the flight and about the East while I looked out of the window at all the various greens.

Anne was waiting for us when we got to the Plough. She wiped her hands on her apron before taking mine. David's a nicer man because of you, I thought. She still seemed clever and pretty and not worn down.

'It's been much too long,' she said, tears in her eyes.

The Plough was exactly as it had been only busier, shinier, cleaner, and therefore somehow newer. Business was very good. Tom was involved in running the pub, while Martin worked in an estate agent's in Faversham and, I gathered, chased girls. I spent two weeks at the Plough with them and then two weeks travelling in France. It felt like the first proper holiday I had ever had. I didn't think I had much to learn from the hotels but I loved the food and the trains and the pace of life. I went down to the south and pottered around the Mediterranean coast for a few days. I spent a night in Marseilles, visiting it for the first time since my trip out on the *Darjeeling*; since the day I met Maria.

I liked the Med. In some small ways it reminded me of Macau. My schoolboy French came out more readily than I had thought possible. The papers, which I read with the aid of a dictionary, were full of France's difficulties with Algeria.

The day before I was to fly back home I took the train down to Godalming to see Masterson. Again there was that sense of greenness and space. His sister had given me directions from the station: it was a ten-minute walk uphill to a house he had more than once described to me as 'classic stockbrokers' Tudor'. I found it easily: The Elms. (There were no elms.) There was a short curved gravel driveway and a wide double-fronted building with white paint and black beams. I felt nervous as I went to the door.

One of Masterson's nieces answered my ring. She was pretty and businesslike, and was dressed for tennis.

'Uncle Alan's in the sitting room,' she said and led me out of the hallway, which had an elephant's-foot umbrella stand. We went into the sitting room. From here one could see the lawn, much bigger than I would have predicted, with large clumps of colourful shrubs – pink and blue – at the far end, and a tennis court to one side, behind a hedge, where I could hear but not see a match taking place. Masterson was sitting in an armchair with the sunlight behind him. He took a moment or two to stand up. Because he was backlit it took me a few seconds to register his appearance. Perhaps that was deliberate on his part – no sudden shock. It's the kind of thing he thought of. He was almost unrecognisably older, and the history of a painful failure to recover from Stanley was imprinted on him. Since the war he had never been the same again. One could read that at a glance.

'Tom,' he said. His voice, too, had become an old man's, with a scratch in it. The effect was querulous, which he himself never was, or rather never had been. 'Darling, how would look in the paper if our guest was to perish of thirst?'

178

'I'm so sorry, Mr Stewart,' she briskly said. 'Can I bring you something?'

'I'm fine, thank you.'

'She's too keen to get out on the court, which your dividends paid for,' Masterson said. To her credit, the niece simply giggled and skipped out.

'Lunch at one,' she called over her shoulder.

The general effect of the day was close to that of visiting someone in hospital. There was the same difficulty in finding things to say, the same sense that the other party's energies were being conserved for the real, important work of his health. Masterson was in a painful way very insistent on reminding everyone – his sister, his two nieces, and their two bland young male friends – of my work in Hong Kong, and how their prosperity was sustained by it. He made a pointed reference to the subject every five or ten minutes. I was, before long, feeling obliged to make apologetic glances around the table every time he did so. He spoke at length about how much he disliked England and its climate, unfriendliness, inefficiency, endemic sloth, punitive taxation, hypocrisy, narrow-mindedness, and 'grey-mindedness' – there was a touch of the old Masterson in that last phrase. His sister, I could see behind her tight smile, took all this personally, as perhaps she was intended to. As soon as they decently could – not all that soon, after a meal progressing from smoked salmon to coffee – the women and their guests excused themselves, and clearing-up noises from the kitchen were succeeded by happy sounds from the tennis court.

Masterson and I moved to the sitting room. Every now and then Catherine or one of her daughters would look in and see if we 'needed anything'. At four-fifteen I announced that it was time for my train. Masterson got to his feet.

'Well, you know how I feel about you and what you're doing,' he said. 'I hope they didn't seem too ungrateful.' I suddenly understood: he was talking about himself, about his feeling that his English family had no idea what he had done, who he had been. Here he was somebody else, and his past didn't matter. It was the reason for leaving home put into reverse. People left England so that it wouldn't matter who they had been; but if they returned home, it also didn't matter who they had been when they were away. Nothing would be more draining for a man like Masterson than to be in other people's debt, to constantly feel an obligation to be grateful.

'I hope you'll come back out and see us soon,' I said.

'Yes,' he said. 'Goodbye.' Once I was out of sight at the end of the driveway I broke into a run, to make sure I caught the train.

The Cold War was good for the hotel business in Hong Kong. It corresponded with the years of the boom in all sorts of ways – the population exploding, the economy taking off, the shanties going down and the blocks of flats going up. Before very long Hong Kong had the largest proportion of publicly owned housing in the world, much of it paid for by the state's monopoly on legal gambling. I should also mention that the Chinese regard living on welfare as a shamefully important loss of face, which helps to keep government costs down. I am told that this circumstance is different elsewhere.

But in addition to all that, the Cold War itself was good for us. It kept Hong Kong the centre of operations for anyone in the West with an interest in China. This guaranteed a stream of customers in the form of soldiers, spies, soldier–spies, businessmen, compradors, would-be compradors, aspiring Hong founders, thieves, buccaneers, refugees, journalists, salesmen and wheeler-dealers and opportunists of every description. Both the Empire and the Deep Water Bay Hotels thrived. Americans did not find it tremendously easy to gain admission to the Hong Kong Club, for the predictable reasons and also because President Roosevelt had wanted Hong Kong to be handed over to China at the end of the war. But there were a lot of Americans around – it was where many of them came for R & R from Vietnam, in addition to all the other Cold War reasons – and they liked to have somewhere to go, and we made them very welcome at the Empire. One of our best customers, Cleveland Weston, was a CIA man who came to the hotel when he wanted to be seen doing things in public. That was good for business too. So was the Hong Kong Club's continuing race bar. Chef Ng went from strength to strength. In my view he never quite scaled the summits known to poor Ah Wang, but feelings of other sorts were perhaps at work in my thinking that. I more or less lived at Deep Water Bay and either drove in to work – still possible, without losing one's mind, in the Hong Kong of the early sixties – or had one of either hotel's drivers take me. Once a week I would spend a night in one of the rooms at the Empire, taking whichever one happened to be free; a Masterson trick to test for flaws in the plumbing, the air conditioning, or the mattresses.

Professor Cobb's reading group slowed down during these years. Our French intellectual, Prévot, now had two small children and as he himself claimed, 'these days I read only Babar.' A former Miss Simmons, now Madame Prévot, had made concerted attempts to tidy him up, with only partial success. He was usually wearing perhaps one cleaned and pressed garment, cancelled out by two dirty, crumpled ones. On one of his last visits to Cobb's room he wore a crisp white shirt set off with a tie which appeared to have had an entire egg yolk decanted over it. He seemed happy and spoke often about moving back to Paris.

Cobb had become increasingly absorbed with a Chinese work he was translating called *The Lives of the Emperors*. In place of the dignified, official narratives and myths it substituted a cavalcade of murders, adulteries, drunkenness, vengeful plotting, assassinations, infatuations, an extraordinary love of cruelty for its own sake – and a sense that Imperial China's past was a suppurating sewer of open secrets. Cobb explained that he felt it was his mission to make this scabrous alternative vision of Chinese history known to a wider public. 'Not that anyone will want to publish it,' he said. 'Even the Communists are touchy about this stuff, in case people start to see parallels with Mao. That's the thing about China. *Plus ça change . . .*'

One day he let slip that he had begun going to church again, for the first time since his early twenties.

'I'm not absolutely sure why,' he said. We were sitting in his office after one of the final meetings of the reading group. He had told us that we had 'learned all he had to teach' – which was manifestly untrue. It seemed to me that he was more bent on conserving his resources. He must have been in his late sixties by now, and *The Lives of the Emperors* would be his last big project.

'I don't in fact much like St John's,' he went on. 'Doesn't quite come off . . . or not for me, anyway . . . But it's good to keep aesthetics in its place . . . Jane thinks it's very eccentric of me, to go back to religion. She won't come. But she oftens joins me for dim sum afterwards, so if you felt inclined, one of these Sundays . . .'

We made a date. I was curious about Jane, whom I had met only once or twice. Cobb was, in his quiet way, a ruthless compartmentaliser. She was ten years younger, brisk and outdoorsy. She had obeyed the evacuation order for women and children in June 1940, and so had missed Stanley internment camp. That seemed often to cause strains in a marriage, but it hadn't in this case. In a small way, Jane was quite well known in Hong Kong, because she gave a weekly radio talk about gardening. The invitation to meet them *à deux* felt like the significant crossing of a line in our friendship.

I arranged to meet Cobb at church, on the grounds that it was more polite to join in rather than just to turn up at lunch. I must also admit to a lowlier motive, in that I was curious about the sight of him kneeling at prayer; I found it difficult to imagine.

I arrived early, before Cobb, and stood outside the porch for a few moments while the congregation trickled in. Among the crowd of familiar and half-familiar faces I saw one that I knew in a different way, a man with a deeply lined scowling face who was striding towards the building in an unkempt suit with flapping, schoolboy-like trousers. He was smoking a final pre-service cigarette. Something about him seemed forty years younger than his actual age. That thought made me remember: the poet Wilfred Austen.

'Mr Austen?' I said as he was going past me. He stopped and the scowl momentarily deepened. 'You won't remember me. My name is Tom Stewart and I showed you and Mr Ingleby round some temples and what-not in 1938 when you were on your way to the war.'

His face cleared. There was great charm and mildness in his slow smile.

'Why of course. You're the Taoist chap. From the hotel. Jolly good. If I'd thought you were still here I'd have looked you up. I'm on one of these British Council thingies. Calcutta, Hong Kong, Tokyo. All a bit different from the last time I was here and largely for the better, so far at least. One of the noticeable things about the disintegration of empires is –'

At this point Cobb arrived from behind me, wearing a Sunday best Panama hat. He stood blinking expectantly.

'Mr Austen, excuse me for interrupting, this is Professor Raymond Cobb from the University of Hong Kong. Professor Cobb, this is Wilfred Austen.'

'When shards of time shall pass
As diamonds do, in larger space
And all our aches, our dreams,
Become, is one enormous grace,'

said Cobb, looking pleased, embarrassed, resolute. 'Excuse me,' he added. 'I don't think I've ever before had an opportunity to quote an author's lines to his face.'

'I am doubly privileged. As I was saying to Mr Stewart, the thing about the disintegration of empires is –'

Inside St John's, the organ struck up. We wordlessly agreed among ourselves to go into the service. Austen led the way.

'The thing about ancestor worship', Austen said, about four and a half hours later, 'is that it's such a rational, liberating religion. Christ was quite wrong about all this. "Let the dead bury the dead." No, no. Frightful rot. If people worship their ancestors, they're freed from the normal human impulse to worship the past, because they carry the past with them. It sets them free to think about the future. The future is more important than the past. It's the task of religion –'

'One of them,' said Cobb. He was counterpunching splendidly. Austen acknowledged the point with a nod.

'– one of them, to orient people towards the future. Look at this – picnicking on their grandparents' graves, thinking about tomorrow. Splendid, splendid.'

We were sitting on a hillside in the New Territories. Austen was holding a roast-beef sandwich in his right hand, taking large mouthfuls from it at irregular intervals while continuing to talk non-stop. He seemed to eat, drink, smoke, and talk almost all the time; we had finished lunch about three hours before. In the course of the meal conversation had turned to ancestor worship and the habit of visiting graves, and Austen had become galvanised with a desire to see the practice in action. I had called the Empire and arranged for a car to meet us at the Star Ferry terminal on Kowloon side, and we had driven out to the New Territories. Now we were all sitting on the ground at a discreet distance from a group of graves where one or two families were happily enjoying their Sunday outing. A brightly clothed and wrapped baby, solemn as an emperor, sat at the centre of each party.

'Yes, well, no, it's not always true, though,' said Cobb. 'One can't see Roman cults of the family as being especially forward-looking or especially successful at inculcating the virtues the empire was attempting to stress. The whole idea of the Lares and Penates –'

'Yes, but imperial circumstances are different,' said Austen. 'They need to emphasise virtue because they are all slowly going mad. They're poisoning themselves with power. The Romans, the Dutch, the British, the Americans next. This thing in Vietnam, this is all becoming perfectly clear. The question of course is whether the world *needs* an imperial power. Actually, on balance, it probably does. Perhaps *needs* is too strong. Say, is better off with. And imperial powers are always obsessed with the past. Not like these people.' He took another bite of roast beef and then gestured with the remains of the sandwich.

Lunch had been one those social successes which at the start looks like a disaster. Jane Cobb, waiting for us at Yuen Kee Tea House, had been visibly nonplussed at the unannounced arrival of our eminent guest. If Austen noticed he did not show it; he simply monologued away harder than before. We ordered a range of dishes and he ate them with the ravenous hunger of a young man after a long walk, rather than a poet in late middle age who had just been to church. As he had grown older, he had become even more dogmatic, a better talker and worse listener. Still, he had his charm, and so here we were in a Chinese cemetery, where one of the fathers was gently wrestling a thermos out of the grip of his fat little baby, against strong protests.

'Well, we're due an Asian century,' Austen said, after finishing his sandwich. A tiny fleck of horseradish lurked at the corner of his lips like a beauty spot. 'I hope they do better by us than we did by them. And that it doesn't blow up too badly round here, when it does.'

Nobody asked him what he meant. We headed back to the car and back to the Star Ferry. I parted with Austen at the taxi rank

The Cobbs set off for the Peak Tram – they had a flat on Bowen Road – after the professor had shaken our hands and said 'most enjoyable, most enjoyable'. Later, he several times referred to the day and how memorable it had been, but I never got to know Jane any better, and our friendship did not move past the point it had already reached. It was as if the very unusualness of the day had helped to derail the potential friendship; that instance of meeting them as a couple was the only time I saw them together. I had drinks with Austen in the bar of the Empire the next day, before he left for Kai Tak and took a plane to Tokyo.

Chapter Thirteen

Masterson died not long after that. He had an aneurysm in his sleep; in that sense, his death was sudden. In another, he had been dying for twenty years, ever since Stanley. His sister let me know in a touching and affectionate letter. She got the point of her brother; I was glad to know that. She wrote about his 'dry, wild humour and permanent air of politely suppressed amazement at the human comedy'. That letter was written the day after he died. A week later I received another, stiffer letter from her, saying Masterson had left me some money and some voting shares in the hotel – though not enough to outvote the family's share, which was put in a trust jointly administered by lawyers in London and Hong Kong. I knew Rathbone, the Hong Kong end of the operation, an exquisitely dressed fat man with a soft voice and legendary knowledge of UK tax avoidance. I did not anticipate difficulties.

At that time I had other things on my mind. There was, as Inspector Watts put it over the rim of his usual large pink gin, trouble brewing.

'It's a look in the eye. Or the fact that they won't catch yours. A surliness. Seen it a thousand times. Palestine. Malaya. You can always tell. One minute some chap's glowering at his mother-in-law, next thing he's chopped his neighbour into roasting joints with his parang. Amok. Then he tops himself, or we come along and shoot him. Afterwards his chums always say they'd seen it coming. Of course, in a country where everyone's wandering around with bloody great machetes, you have to expect a bit of trouble every now and then. For sheer brooding nastiness, Indonesia. One day I'm on duty, bloke comes in, his bearer pulled a knife on the cook. Very definitely not handbags at ten paces. Chap separates them. Goes to the station, makes everybody give a statement, thanks the bearer for his long service, sacks him, pays him off and gives him a severance bonus, writes out a good reference, all above board, right in front of us. Bearer goes off, all smiles. Two days later, the boiler blows up and takes the back half of the house with it. Right up in the air. Miracle no one's killed. Bearer's put paraffin in the boiler instead of petrol. Never seen again. That's Indonesia, the most dangerous place I've ever been in,' Watts took a theatrical sip of his pink gin, 'until I was in Mongkok last night.'

The audience – half a dozen regulars – gave a collective shudder. Watts's act was done for effect; but there was something in it. China was going insane. Everyone was frightened that the Cultural Revolution would spill over into the colony. In Macao, there were already signs of that. Portuguese soldiers had fired shots at Red Guards. I began to believe I could feel the atmosphere myself. Before a typhoon there is a day or two of entirely clear skies and perfect stillness. The weather seems calm but is in actuality violent. This is what that time was like. There were troop movements and mini-skirmishes along the border. Allegations about corruption and predictions of imminent doom were filling the Chinese newspapers.

One weekday evening I went to Mongkok to meet Maria. An English adult-education class of hers had an exam coming up and I was to give the students some dictation and comprehension practice. Her regular native English speaker, Father Ignatius, had appendicitis. The plan was that we would meet at the Catholic school in Mongkok. I took a bus there from the Star Ferry on a clammy summer evening. A small crowd of pickets and strikers was gathered around the terminals at either end of the ferry crossing. There had been a series of heated protests about a rise in prices on the ferry – all rather bizarre, since the rise only affected first-class fares.

The bus went north on Nathan Road, as crowded and streaming as ever. Every time one saw it there were new businesses: Taiwoo Sewing Machine Emporium, with a huge pink neon Singer sign. Lotus Garden Dim Sum. Wishful Cottage Tea Shop. Cheng Kee Electronics. Sam's Tailors. Auspicious Festival Men's Tailoring. A huge branch of China Arts and Crafts, the company which sold goods from Communist China. Prosperous Future Watch Repairs: Cheaper Faster Better. The pavements were full of charging pedestrians. The only time I had ever seen Nathan Road anything other than seething with people was the day after the Japanese invasion.

I walked the last few hundred yards to the school. The build ings were as tightly packed as anywhere in the colony, with tha feeling one sometimes had that the balconies were converging overhead. I was jostled once or twice. Many men were standing or squatting in the street. The Empire Hotel felt quite some way away.

Maria, with an uncharacteristic look of worry or preoccupa tion, was waiting for me outside the school gates.

'Everything all right?' I asked.

'Oh yes. All fine. I hoped you weren't caught up in demonstra tions or anything like that.'

'Of course not. Just a bit of arm waving. People waving their lit tle red books. Looks oddly like a bank deposit book, doesn't it?'

She gently, reproachfully, tapped me on the arm with a folded up devotional pamphlet. We went through to the schoolroom which was already full. The lesson went on for an hour and a half I was out of practice. The room was airless, the evening wa. warm and humid, and the occasion was something of a struggle At the end of the class, Maria had to stay behind to have a wor with a pupil. I had promised to wait. We were going back t Hong Kong island together via the bus and ferry. The pupil' business, whatever it was, took some time.

'Excuse me,' Maria said to me at last. 'That was more involve than I expected.'

It was dark when we left. Immediately I felt that somethin was not right. There were far more men in the street than ther had been before, and an atmosphere of expectancy as they stoo and jostled and smoked and looked around them. It was hard t squeeze past the barging groups and resist the temptation t walk unnaturally fast. In a tight spot, never run. That was th standard advice.

We had covered perhaps a third of the way down the cross streets to Nathan Road when a noise came from farther down th alleys. It was not like a human sound so much as a natural phe nomenon: a gale, or the groaning noise made by an earthquake People turned in one direction, away from us, and then ran th way we had come, at first in ones or twos, like men who had sud denly remembered an urgent errand, and then not as individual but as a single mass. We turned and began to run also. There wa no choice or volition involved; if we had not joined the crowd we would there and then have died under its feet. Some of the men were swearing and some were crying for their mothers. Their faces were blanched and tight with fear. Someone pushed hard against my back and I almost lost my footing, but Maria caught my arm and with astonishing strength gave me a pull which helped me regain my balance. At the end of that first alley we managed to squeeze our way into a side passage. Overhead, linked awnings were tied together so that no light from above penetrated to the street. A small group of men were here, many of them gasping, their hands on their knees. One, in a white short-sleeved shirt with pens clipped to his top pocket, was being sick just in front of me. No one spoke. The roaring in the alleyway behind us was thinning and fading as the stampede moved away. We waited for a few minutes. The man finished vomiting and leant with both his arms against the wall, quietly saying 'fuck fuck fuck fuck fuck' to himself.

'Are you all right?' Maria asked him. The man waved her away. She looked hot and ruffled but not, I was amazed to see, fundamentally discomposed.

'Which way do we go now?' I asked. My feeling was that once we got back to one of the main roads, out from the crowded warren of flats, we would be safe.

'Keep on?' Maria replied. I shrugged and agreed. A few of the men who had taken refuge with us had already melted away, but some followed us. I looked around the corner into the alley we'd come out of. It was empty – not sparsely peopled, but completely empty. There was no noise. In the most crowded place on earth, that was frightening. We turned the corner and the others scattered, running off in the opposite direction while we headed towards Nathan Road. We walked as quickly as we could. I was conscious of being observed from the flats above us. After a couple of hundred yards the alley bent to the right, and suddenly there was an explosion of sound. A crowd of people about fifty yards ahead were running back and forth across a small open space where four alleys intersected. At first I could detect no pattern in what they were doing; then I saw that their arms were loaded, and they were carrying all sorts of goods – boxes, crates of bottles – and I thought they must be evacuating a building.

Then I realised that they were looting. The individuality of those men's faces was visible – a pair of buck teeth here, a bald patch there – but at the same time, all particularity was lost in the mad urgency of the crowd.

'Better go on back,' Maria said. 'We must get to Nathan Road.'

So we turned around, again trying not to run. I could feel people looking at our backs. One man, his hands holding a crate of dead, unplucked poultry, his eyes empty, looked for a moment as if he was going to stand in front of us and block our way, but he saw me seeing him decide what to do, and in that second's pause Maria and I were past him. The alley went around another slight bend, and then another, and opened out a little so that the buildings no longer seemed to close together over our heads, and just as it opened we could hear the same roaring noise from not far away, and then three or four youths, their faces rigid with fear, came sprinting past, falling and shouting and picking themselves up like tumblers. They might have been trying to be funny if it had not been for the terror in their faces.

Just to our right there was a furniture shop, its front fortuitously or presciently boarded up. But the rioters' attention had already been drawn to it and the door, smashed open at the lock, was swinging open on its hinges.

'In here,' I said, and took Maria's arm. We went in. I pushed the door closed. I had expected devastation, but inside there was only mild disarray and an overpowering smell of camphor wood. Chests of drawers and office furniture had been pushed about, but not smashed. A desk at the end of the room, which was half sales and display area, half workshop, had all its drawers opened. They had gone for the money.

The noise outside grew louder. Through chinks in the boarded-up window we could see a shouting, swearing crowd run past. Without warning somebody kicked hard against the door, much too hard, so that it rebounded in the face of whoever was trying to break in. Then it was finally kicked off its hinges and fell into the shop. Five or six men came into the room. They were panting, furious, maddened. One had a badge with a picture of Chairman Mao, the only such sign I saw that day. They clearly did not know what they wanted to do. But violence was a part of it. There was cacophony outside the room while silence stretched inside it.

Maria, who had been standing about a pace behind me, stepped forward, and gave the men a second to take her in fully. They might not have been able to tell at a glance that she was a nun, but they could probably sense something official about her; just enough of a whiff of magic. She reached out a hand behind her to the ransacked desk and said in an absolutely calm voice:

'There's no money left. If you want to take some furniture, though, just help yourselves.'

The man in front, the one with the Mao badge, did not smile, but gave a sort of grunt. Some colour came back into his face. All the men, I suddenly saw, looked relieved. Whatever they had been about to do they hadn't wanted to do any more than we had wanted them to do it. The man with the Mao badge looked around the chaotic workshop, turned, pushed through the others, stepped over the door, and went out. The others followed him. There was perhaps a faint tinge of sheepishness. I realised I had been holding my breath.

'Jesus,' I said.

'Don't blaspheme,' said Maria. We waited there for a half-hour and then headed to Nathan Road without further incident.

This episode was the start of what became known as the Riots. It was by far the closest encounter I had with them. There were comparable incidents, and many bombings, and not a few deaths. Many people panicked. I didn't, because if the Chinese wanted to take back Hong Kong, all they needed to do was to shut off the water supply; the world wasn't going to be turned upside-down by a few Red Guards shouting and waving copies of the Little Red Book. Eventually, the Gurkhas were sent to Hong Kong, and things quietened down. For my part, I started renting a cottage on Cheung Chau, the same one where I live today. It occurred to me that Masterson would have described what I was doing as 'sitting out the Riots'. The public inquiry into the Riots blamed people who had made public allegations of corruption in the colony and accused them of fomenting trouble.

Chapter Fourteen

Cooper, my old chum from the *Darjeeling*, the war, and Stanley internment camp, was by now an extremely senior big shot at the Bank. He had done stints in the US and the UK, and by the late sixties was back in the colony for his last few years before retirement. He and Mrs Cooper, the former Miss Farrington, would occasionally come out to visit me on Cheung Chau at weekends. He had lost almost all his hair but otherwise seemed trim and fit, as intelligent and as uninterested in his job as ever. She seemed much more in love with him than she had when they were younger. Their two daughters, both now in their teens, were at boarding school in England. It was always touching to see how much happier he was during school holidays.

One Sunday afternoon I was expecting the Coopers, their daughters, and some friends to drop in for tea. I spent the morning doing chores and tidying up, and then set off down to the village to buy some odds and ends – I had promised to serve moon cake. My way down into the village was blocked by Ming Tsin-Ho, my closest neighbour. He was sitting on the porch of his house. This seating area was a small but potent irritant, since he would sometimes listen to loud Cantonese music there, especially at weekends. He greeted me as I went past, by no means a standard occurrence.

'Mr Stewart,' he said. 'Extraordinary news!'

'Oh?' The Riots were not long past. I assumed it would be some recrudescence of fighting or bombing, or a mob outside Government House. I didn't much care what it was.

'Wo Man-Lee has been arrested! Big scandal!'

I felt my heart begin to beat quickly and threadily.

'Arrested?'

'Murder – drug dealing – conspiracy – extortion. Big big scandal!'

His grin was dividing his face into two. I struggled to work out why. Later I found out that the Wos had a controlling interest in the film studio which made most of his brother's movies. Hence his delight. Anything that was bad news for his sibling was an occasion for festival.

The people from the Bank boat arrived in mid-afternoon, puffing a little from the climb. Most of the adults were Bank people and their wives. They were the usual mix of bluff happy ones and clever malcontents. Everyone smelt of suncream and alcohol and salt water. Cooper's daughters and their friends – it was hard to count them, I mainly had an impression of brown limbs and bathing jackets – went straight to the front of the house.

'They're trying to hypnotise each other,' said Mrs Cooper. 'They've been at it all day.'

Ming was right about the arrest being a big scandal. My guests could speak of nothing else. Their talk had the usual Triad note of horrified excitement.

'It's directly linked to the Riots,' someone said. 'They had to have a clean-up. There'll be a big fuss and drama and some high-profile arrests and then it'll go back to business as usual.'

'Surely it's no different from home, from the Kray twins or something,' said another of the visitors. Cooper shifted round slightly in his seat and said, a little reluctantly:

'There's a bit more to the Triads than that. They aren't just people waving choppers about. It starts off like that, small, but money always wants to turn legit. Has a mind of its own, almost. Chaps like Wo are very old-fashioned now. They're an embarrassment to the new chaps. Why make risky criminal money in drugs or gambling when you can make safe legal money in property? Of course the drugs and girls and gambling and all that are good cash-flow businesses, but the future lies in looking as respectable as possible. No different from Jardines and all that lot, if you take a long enough view. Wo sent his son to Harvard. That'll show you.' Cooper looked at me, inviting me to tell my I-knew-Wo-when story. I silently declined.

'Well, the trial should be quite something,' one of the men said. 'I do wonder what evidence they've got. I thought the whole point was that nobody ever spoke about anything.'

I remember thinking that was a good question. Conversation moved on to golf, and gossip about the Governor's wife.

The case was all over the news the next day, covered in that unique Hong Kong style in which the most significant information is present in the gaps, omissions, and implications. The Wos were described as 'prominent local businessmen', a designation which, when juxtaposed with the charges – to do with drugs – positively screamed Triad. Wo Man-Lee had applied for bail and judgement on whether it would be granted had been reserved. Wo Ho-Yan had not been charged with anything. Presumably, as the legitimate front of the business, he would now be running the shop.

'Interesting,' said Beryl, who was entertaining business contacts at the Empire that day. 'They must have lost their protection. Or have they? We'll see. All sorts of stuff going on behind the scenes, no doubt. I've never seen my boys so surprised by anything, ever.'

'What do they think will happen?'

'Well –' Beryl made a face. It was an expression she sometimes adopted to indicate philosophical resignation at the mysteries of the East. 'They don't think Wo Man-Lee will end up in jail. Let's put it like that. Ah, this is me.' She downed the remains of her first gin and tonic and pulled herself to her feet to greet a small middle-aged man, advancing towards the table with his hand outstretched.

A couple of times that week I found myself walking into a room at the hotel and having the assembled company suddenly go silent. I did not enjoy the sensation. The fact that I had known Ho-Yan was of course no secret, and there were still a few employees at the Empire who remembered him – who may still have known him, for all I knew. I took my traditional refuge in working hard and did not think any more than I had to about what had become of the Wo brothers. I twice called Maria and twice left messages at the mission but she didn't call back. I thought her way of coping would be to keep her nose down.

Looking back at those days I can see how I was in many ways scaling down my life, retreating from contact with people. Without knowing it, I was generally withdrawing. This was not apparent to me at the time. That weekend I again went out to Cheung Chau, on my own, with no plans to see anyone. I took some books and records and a bag of groceries and drank my usual bottle of beer at the rail of the ferry. I was looking forward to being quietly, pleasantly lonely for a couple of days. I was also planning on fixing the stove, which had kept cutting out at inconvenient moments; I was going to take it apart and put it back together, armed with the manufacturer's schematic diagram.

On Saturday morning before the first weekenders' junks and powerboats arrived, I was sitting out on the balcony looking down at the bay, drinking coffee and reading the *South China Morning Post*. I had already been down into the village and back. It was hot and clear and still, not quite pre-typhoon weather but not far off. There was a ring at the doorbell followed without pause by a loud, rapping, confident knock. I thought that it could conceivably be a telegram – but no postman knocks like that. I went through, put the door on its chain and opened it. The face on the other side of the door was so unexpected that it took me a moment longer than it should have to recognise Chief Inspector Watts. He was wearing shorts and long white socks and a crisp short-sleeved shirt, a sort of semi-mufti which left it unclear whether he was on duty. He was holding a panama hat, half crumpled, in his left hand, which he tapped against his leg as I opened the door. His face was an impressive baked colonial red-brown. There was a rigidity in him which in a different man would have been embarrassment.

'Hello there, just let me get this,' I said as I undid the chain. He stood there looming and unapologetic as he said:

'Well, hello to you as well. I hope you don't mind, I came out here for a ramble and a swim. Doctor's orders, to keep the consti tution up. I know I don't have to tell you, being a great walker and all that. Thought I'd invite myself in for a cup of coffee. Know I should have called.'

'Of course not, it's a great pleasure, and well timed. I've just got the percolator on.'

'No servants out here? Good for you.'

He came in, his hands now behind his back, openly giving the place a look-over. More than any other trade, policemen never quite manage to stop being policemen. A man who acquires the habits of suspicion and distrust will find that life never gives him an adequate reason to shed them. Watts went over to look at a carriage clock Beryl had given me for Christmas a decade before.

'Made a bit of a study of these. They're mostly from Paris, as you know. The Mandarins went mad about them in the eighteenth century. I always think that if I was a bit more clever, I'd be able to tell something original about the Chinese mind from that. This one isn't bad. I could get it valued for you if you like. There's a chap in Tsim Sha Tsui I know. Count your fillings after you shake his hand, but he's straight with me.'

The message went something like this: I may not be clever, but I have other things at my disposal which mean I don't need to be. Watts straightened up from the clock and continued looking at other bits and pieces while I went for the coffee. When I got back to the sitting room, he wasn't there. He had gone out onto the balcony and was sitting in one of the rattan chairs, flicking through my *South China Morning Post*. He was smoking and letting the ash fall onto the veranda floor. I doubled back into the kitchen and retrieved an ashtray.

'Nice place you've got here. I can see why you like it. Bit of fresh air, get the Hong Kong out of your lungs.'

'Thank you.'

'We used to have a place in Malaya, up in the hills. It was like Scotland. In fact there were so many Jocks there it almost was Scotland. Lovely air. Cheap. Much less humid, that was the thing. Didn't get there as much as we'd have liked, and of course it was never all that safe . . . Good country though. Funny, although the place was going through civil war, in lots of ways it was more straightforward than Hong Kong. You'd know where you were most of the time. Not really like that here, is it?'

This was the most abstract I had ever heard Watts being. He had the manner which close-mouthed men sometimes adopt when they are feeling their way towards making a confidence.

He seemed to be waiting for a reply.

'No, it's all about layers here,' I said.

'Layers. That's a good word for it. Layers.' He got up and went over to the low wall at the far end of the balcony. Below it a patch of garden sloped away fifty feet or so to where the hill dropped more sharply downwards. I had a *fah wong* come in during the week to do some watering and general upkeep, but aside from that, the garden was mine.

'You like it here, don't you?' he said. 'You properly like it. Lots of people like the pay or the taxes or the girls or the being away from home or the East in general, but you actually specifically like it here, in Hong Kong. For itself. Unusual.'

'You get past a certain point in life and you've accumulated a history in a place, and so that's where you're from. Most of my memories and all of my friends are here.'

'Yes, you've got a lot of friends here. That party . . .' Watts smiled. He had been to the do I had thrown for the opening of Deep Water Bay. 'A good night. I don't think I'd ever got pissed on champagne before. Didn't half feel it the next day . . .'

He trailed off and kept looking across the garden towards Hong Kong.

'Friends from different walks of life, like that professor, and Mrs Marler, and your friend the nun. Sister Maria.'

'Well, the last two are from the same place, really, since I met both of them on the boat out. The *Darjeeling*. Sister Maria taught me Cantonese on that trip. That's how we got to know each other. Beryl and I were in camp together afterwards.'

'I didn't know that,' he said. 'But it's funny you should mention Sister Maria. There's been something on my mind about her. On my conscience. I haven't known what to do. It's difficult. Not clear where my duty lies, as a friend as well as a policeman.'

He sat back down.

'This is the thing: Sister Maria has been giving us a bit of help. Not me directly but some of my colleagues. They've been having a spot of trouble with some translation. We've got some tapes. The tapes are all in some sort of dialect. A type of Fukienese. You know how it is in China, move a couple of hundred yards down the road and they speak a whole different language. The trouble is, no one will help us translate what's on the tapes. Most people don't speak the dialect and no one who does is going to help us. That's because the person we've arrested is important. Very, very important. And very, very frightening, especially to anyone with any sort of living family or relatives back in the old country. It's been a famous case, all over the papers.'

'Wo Man-Lee,' I said. He nodded.

'So we have all this evidence and no way of using it. Frustrating. But then some bright spark finds out that there has been a missionary involvement in that part of China and asks a few questions and comes to meet a person known to you, who speaks the dialect and, what's much more to the point, is willing to help us with it. To considerable effect.'

I felt myself go cold.

'Maria has been helping you.'

'The target of our investigation, when discussing business matters with trusted subordinates, communicates entirely in village dialect. The structure of the criminal organisation is completely integrated with that of the old village. Everyone is known to everyone else. Highly secretive. No way in. We've been extremely lucky to find a person with the relevant linguistic skills and willingness to help. It's a break no one was counting on. The thing is – well, the thing is, to be frank, it's whether the person who is helping us is quite as lucky as we are.'

'I'm not sure I understand.'

'This is one tough Johnny. It's no accident he's not been arrested before. No one will talk about him. That's not because he's universally loved, but because everyone around him is scared shitless. If you talk about him you're odds-on to wake up dead. Your friend is doing more than talk about him, she's indispensable to the process of putting him in chokey for the rest of his life. That is an extremely high-risk thing to do.'

'And you want me to . . . tell her that?'

'I have a conscience. It's not always the most useful thing in police work but there we are. We're using her. She's risking her life. I don't know if she knows that. I'm not sure if that's been made clear.'

'I see.'

I thought for a moment.

'On whose behalf are you here?' I asked.

'I beg your pardon?'

'Who sent you here? What's the message you're supposed to convey?'

I felt as if I had been short-sighted all my life and had suddenly put on a pair of spectacles.

'What are you implying?' Watts was turning red and getting to his feet.

'You were sent here to give me a message. To convey a threat, disguised as a concern.'

'I'm not going to listen to this.'

'Good. Get out.'

I went to the front door and opened it. He stopped as he went through and turned to me. His expression was strange. It was contorted, but not with anger; it was as if he was wrestling with an emotion that was close to grief. He was at the same time bitter. He said:

'You've been here too long.'

I closed the door in his face.

The first thing I did after Watts left was sit at the table in the drawing room and write down as full and verbatim an account of the conversation as I could remember. I found that I was breathing quickly and shallowly; the action of recollection and writing calmed me and I began to try and work out what I should do. I felt that passing on Watts's message, on behalf of whoever his masters were, would be a kind of betrayal – I would be doing the bidding of bad men. At the same time I didn't feel it would be right to leave Maria unaware of the warning. In the way I had been put in the position of being forced to do someone else's mischief I could feel a malign cleverness at work.

I decided to give myself the weekend to think about it. But every time I stopped doing something physical, working in the garden or fiddling with the stove, the threat came back. In the late afternoon, I went down to the village and out to the beach and swam its width over and over again, until I was as physically tired as I could ever remember being, and my arms and legs were pricking with premonitions of cramp. Then I walked back to the bungalow and fell on the bed. But when I closed my eyes I couldn't stop replaying the conversation with Watts. I got up and put a Louis Armstrong record on and had a whisky. Then I went into the kitchen and fiddled a little more with the stove. Then I lay down on the bed and tried to read. Then I turned out the light and tried to sleep. That was how the weekend passed.

On Monday I went to see Beryl. Her offices had moved out to North Point, where her company was involved in a complicated, multiply contracted housing development. To show willing, as she put it, she had moved her offices into the first phase of the project to have been finished. When I went into her corner room, she was in conversation with Leung, one of her praetorian guard of young besuited Cantonese men. He had a large set of papers, covered with numbers, spread over the table between them. She liked having men doing tasks about her.

'Ah Chan, if you could excuse us for a moment,' said Beryl. Leung smiled and left. I pulled a chair up close to the desk, told her the Watts story, and asked what she thought I should do. Beryl puffed out her cheeks, an old gesture of hers which now looked odd; she had had a small stroke the year before and it had reduced mobility on the left side of her face.

'Chief Inspector Watts, eh? I don't think one could have been expected to guess that. Watts. It's the ones who've worked in drugs who you always tend to assume are a bit fishy. The old colonial types, well you know they cut corners and all that, without really wanting to imagine the details, but still . . . Bert, mind you, always used to say he'd never met a copper who wasn't to some degree bent.'

Once Beryl had mentioned her husband it always took a moment or two for the conversation to get back on track. I waited.

'Well, that's Hong Kong,' she now said, briskly. 'I suppose the idea is you can pass on the threat without acting as if you know it's a threat. It gives you an out. You can just say you had this funny conversation with a policeman, and tell yourself that's all you're passing on. As long she gets the message it doesn't matter what you think. Sort of saves face for you. Clever.'

They had left me room to lie to myself. I could see that. I said: 'But what if something happens?'

'Bert,' said Beryl, and then cleared her throat. 'Albert would have certainly told Watts to bugger off and refused to do his dirty work for him. I can hear him saying it. Then he would have gnawed himself to pieces worrying about it, without ever saying a word.'

'Well, yes.'

'If you choose to pretend that Watts was telling the truth, and the main thing he's worried about is that Maria doesn't understand the risk she's taking, then what he's said is a load of rubbish. Of course she understands perfectly well. She's known these people her whole life.'

'You may say that, but there's an innocent side to Maria. That sounds stupid – she is a bloody nun – but you know what I mean. She might think it was, you know, all talk.'

Beryl was shaking her head.

'No, she wouldn't think that.'

'In which case she knows she's risking her life.'

'In which case there's no point in telling her. And there's also perhaps no harm in telling her.'

I sat back. We looked at each other.

'I know you'll say no,' Beryl said, 'but I could tell her for you.'

My turn to shake my head.

'Sorry,' said Beryl, by way of farewell.

For the next forty-eight hours I was unable to decide whether Maria was in mortal danger, or whether I had simply over-interpreted, or misinterpreted, a half-friendly warning from a half-honest policeman. I stayed away from Maria and spent as much time as possible rushing at work. I went from Deep Water Bay to the Empire at least twice a day. I had a long, gruelling meeting with Rathbone, in his capacity as the Mastersons' family trustee. He must have thought I was insane; I needed everything said to me at least three times.

Late on Wednesday morning I was sitting at the bar keeping an eye on things and looking over a deeply corrupt new restaurant guide to Hong Kong. It had a large advertisement for both the hotels, and lavish reviews of both establishments. Jim Connor, a star reporter with the *South China Morning Post*, an alcoholic Irishman and fellow sufferer at Father Ignatius's first nights, came into the bar, not running so much as shuffling at high speed. He was carrying a hat, a notebook, and a copy of his own newspaper.

'Large Powers and water please, Arthur,' he called. Arthur was the English name of Ah Lo the barman. The drink arrived. Connor downed it in one, made a signing motion to Ah Lo to put it on his tab, nodded at me, and got up off his stool to go.

'That certainly redefines the meaning of a quick one,' I said. 'What's up this clammy subtropical morning?'

It was Connor's habit to speak in a humorously inflated way. This was, when you were talking to him, catching. He continued to shuffle towards the door while he breathlessly addressed me, the whiskey fresh on his breath.

'Wo Man-Lee's just been given bail. Biggest story since the Crucifixion' – that being a standard phrase of Connor's. 'Blind luck I was there – only went to the hearing on the off-chance. How conscientious can a bugger be? Mortimer Troy appeared for Wo, so smooth you couldn't use him to shovel shit if you wanted to. Fucker's suit costs more than my flat. All the usual tricks. Upstanding member of the this. Established citizen of the other. Benefactors of the doo-dah and contributors to the diddly-pom. Deep roots in the community. Thinness of Government's case. Absolute lack of physical evidence. Reputations to uphold, businesses to run. Wo's son sitting there in the front row like he was posing for a graduation photo. Government lawyer makes a very poor fist of it. Bingo. Fishiest thing you've ever heard, eh?'

I could not move or think. It was as if my mind and body had entirely seized up. What might this mean? Good news or bad? It might be that the government wasn't taking Wo Man-Lee seriously enough and had been legally overmatched. But that was difficult to believe. More likely that Wo had been able to pull strings and call in favours and arrange for visits of the sort that had been paid to me. That could only be very bad news. But I still felt I shouldn't tell Maria about Watts's visit. Nothing substantial had changed – beyond the fact that it looked possible that Wo might get off.

Or so it seemed. The next big piece of news came the next evening. Beryl rang me in my office. She disliked the telephone so I knew as soon as I heard her that something consequential had happened.

'Beryl – what is it?' There was a very faint slurring to her voice since the stroke, which one could hear over the phone but not in person.

'Tom. I've just heard something my boys have picked up on the bamboo telegraph. Wo Man-Lee has flown the coop.' For a moment I thought she must be referring to the news about bail. Then I realised that couldn't be the new news.

'What – left Hong Kong?'

'Nobody knows where but it would be a shock if it wasn't Taiwan. For all the obvious reasons. He's put out a statement regretting the necessity of the action but expressing a lack of confidence in colonial justice.'

Taiwan. Run by the Kuomintang; no extradition; a comfortable life, guaranteed free of any legal unpleasantness.

'My God. So what does that imply for   for our friend?' We both listened to the crackling of the telephone.

'I think it might be an idea if you and she had a chat,' said Beryl.

I took her advice. Both the hotel cars were busy so I queue-jumped at the Empire's taxi rank – a terrible piece of hotel-keeping, Masterson would be spinning in his grave – and went down to the mission in Wanchai. Central had been quiet but here the alleys were packed and busy, and all the shops were open. A jeweller's had opened at the street corner beside the mission hall and a splendidly ferocious Sikh stood outside with his shotgun and turban and jet-black beard, glowering at anyone who dared to walk past. I couldn't shake off memories of the other time I had dashed, stomach revolving, to the same place to try and find Maria, in the sick panic at the outbreak of war. I told myself that this couldn't be as bad as that.

Needless to say, Maria was out. 'Sister somewhere else,' explained, very patiently and slowly, the man who worked as a sort of concierge in the downstairs hall. He was wearing pyjama bottoms and a vest, smoking, and sitting in front of an upturned crate with a Chinese chess set on it.

'What time will she be back?'

'So sorry.'

'Damn,' I said, in English, at which he giggled politely. Maria could, and would, be anywhere: visiting pupils, or one of the drug addicts with whom the mission was increasingly concern-ing itself; with Father Ignatius; at the mission's new outpost in Kowloon walled city; in the New Territories; anywhere. I settled down to wait. There was a folding chair on the other side of the hall, so I opened it and sat. The concierge did not try to disguise his curiosity. Before too long the appeal of his game mastered him however, and he went back to playing himself at Chinese chess. From upstairs I could hear family hubbub and the noise of televisions. Occasionally people came in or went out, always giv-ing me a frank stare as they did so. One or two even asked, 'Who's he?', which the concierge pretended not to hear. I think he may have regarded me as a deranged suitor.

I had arrived at the mission at half past seven. I resolved that I would leave by midnight, on the grounds that if Maria wasn't home by then she must be staying the night somewhere else. The concierge had evidently decided to stay up and wait until she arrived or I left. He was on his umpteenth game of chess when Maria came in at five minutes to midnight, walking so quickly and quietly she had almost gone past me to the stairs. The self-appointed guardian of her virtue and I both stood up.

'Maria.'

She looked at me, startled, abstracted and distant at the same time.

'Tom,' she said, perfectly amiably, but as if it had taken a few seconds to remember my name. She did not ask what I was doing there.

'We should have a word,' I said. It sounded, even to me, even at the time, a grotesquely English thing to say.

'Let's go up. Goodnight, Ah Tung,' she said, firmly, to the concierge. He smiled at her and frowned at me.

We went upstairs. I had not been in the living quarters at the mission since the outbreak of World War Two. There were the smells of cooking and disinfectant, and of communal bathrooms. The corridors were quiet by now, though one or two lights were still on. A few rooms down the corridor Maria pushed open a door. The room was startlingly empty. There was a bed with a copy of the *De Imitatio Cristi* on the pillow. It looked as if someone had returned the volume by dropping it there. The only furniture was a table and chair, a crucifix on the wall, a narrow shelf of language textbooks. The room was lit by a bare bulb overhead.

Maria sat on the bed and pointed at the chair. Something about the heaviness of her movements made me realise she was exhausted.

'Maria, I need to tell you about something which happened a few days ago,' I began. I told her about Chief Inspector Watts. She listened without commenting or changing her expression.

'It must have put you in a difficult position,' she said politely, formally, when I finished.

'That's hardly the point, Maria,' I said. 'The thing is, what are you going to do? First he gets bail, which shows just how much power he's got, or just how unwilling the government is to do anything, or both, then he skips out, which means he's out of reach, and he can do anything he likes. You're in an exposed position here. He can't be seen to lose face, and if it looks as if someone could help the police against him and get away with it that makes him look weak. He won't allow that. You've got to do something which gives him face, which makes it look as if you're frightened of him. Get the Order to post you somewhere. Go to Rome and learn another language or something. Go to the Philippines and teach orphans. Go on a long retreat. I don't know, anything – but get out of Hong Kong, you have to. Please.'

'As you are well aware, the reasons you are giving why I, as you put it, "have to" leave Hong Kong are the precise reasons why I cannot. It's very simple. I have no choice.'

'This is sheer pride, Maria. It's like suicide to stay here. Pure wilfulness. You've already done the courageous thing. To stay here would be a form of weakness, and, I say again, of pride.'

'You feel free to accuse me of what we're taught is the greatest deadly sin, merely because I am not doing what you tell me to do.'

'Even the way you say that reeks of pride. Get down off your high horse and do the obvious bloody thing for once.'

'You simply do not understand what is involved in this matter. You are speaking much too freely of matters about which you know nothing.'

'I know you, and that's the main thing. And thanks to you, as you are perfectly well aware, I also know Wo Man-Lee, and what he's capable of doing. Maria, by staying in Hong Kong, you are leaving him with no choice. It'll be open season on him, and people like him, if they can be betrayed which is how, in their terms, they see it – and have nothing happen to the betrayer. It just doesn't work like that.'

We were more or less shouting at each other, but at hissing level, as one does in a bitter private argument. My anger and my desire not to be overheard were soaring and parallel.

'You forget who I am and whom I represent,' Maria said. 'Even if I wanted to I would not run away from Hong Kong as if it were I who was the criminal. I will not walk in the shadows for any-body. My Lord does not permit it.'

I had known in advance that if Maria mentioned God the chances of getting her to agree with me would be non-existent. But I kept going.

'Don't blame God for your own bloody-mindedness. This has nothing to do with Him. He created me as well as you, which is something you seem to forget. I think as far as God is concerned He'd much rather you stayed alive doing your work than point-lessly sticking your head through the bars of a lion's cage and daring him to eat you.'

Maria sighed and shook her head but said nothing. I could feel my anger curdling, or settling, and turning into sadness, and per-haps she did also.

'What about your parishioners, the community?' I asked, more calmly. Without a second's pause, but without any heat, she said:

'And I serve their interests better by absenting myself, by run-ning away?'

'If something . . . happens to you, nobody's interests are served apart from Wo Man-Lee's. Surely you can see that. If you stay put you give him an opportunity to make his point. You're behaving like the hero of a Western, and there's no good reason for it.'

'And when you stayed on in Hong Kong and went to Stanley, there was a good reason for that?' Her voice had completely changed. It was as if these words had been forced out of her by some great pressure. She sounded bitter – something I could never have imagined from her; as if this was something which had happened the previous day, and not more than a quarter of a century before. I was at a loss.

'That was different,' I eventually managed to say. 'Everything about the time, the circumstances, was different. For Christ's sake, Maria, it was a world war. I had made a promise. You know all these things. And besides, if I had come with you I might very well have ended up dead. Plenty of people lost their lives in occupied China. I can't believe you're bringing this up like that.'

'Perhaps you would believe it more easily if you had a real con-ception of what those times had been like for me. If you had known that, I do not think you could have left.'

This was such an utterly outrageous thing to say that I couldn't think of a reply. There was no point in taking this any further. We sat in silence for a while.

'There's going to be a judicial inquiry,' Maria said, still sound-ing bitter, or at least sarcastic, but mercifully not directing the feeling at me. 'It has already been announced.'

'That's something.'

'Is it? I suspect not. There will be the usual cloud of words and determination to conceal unpleasant realities with a fog of British noble intentions and hypocrisy.'

'But all sorts of things will surely come out.' She shook her head. I made a last try:

'You must see reason about this, Maria. It doesn't make sense to stay. Look at it this way: Wo has left the territory and will never be able to come back, not with this hanging over him and having jumped bail. You leave the territory too. You're quits, except he's lost more than you, and you're still alive.'

'Or I could take my own life,' she said, the bitterness back in her voice. 'That also would be doing what they wanted.'

There might have been something more to say, but if there was, I couldn't think of it.

'Do you remember Fanling?' Maria asked, much more softly.

'Of course I do. I think of it all the time.'

She smiled. 'Me too. I'm glad. And now you must go.'

This time I did leave.

Maria disappeared two days later. She left the mission in the morning, on her way to the Sisters' drug-rehabilitation clinic in the Walled City. One of the other nuns, Sister Euphemia, was supposed to go with her but had an upset stomach and begged off at the last minute. A few people saw Maria on the Star Ferry, travelling second class, but she didn't arrive at the clinic, and the police could not find anyone who saw her on Kowloon's side. It was as though she had simply vanished.

I learned she was missing that night. Father Ignatius called and told me. I could hear in his voice that he knew not just the immediate news but the story which lay behind it. He told me that the police were doing everything they could and that there was nothing for me to do.

Maria's disappearance was a big story for a few days, a story for a few weeks, and a memory of something scandalous for a while after that. Rumours almost immediately started to circulate about her and the Triads; not about Wo, but about her having crossed local bosses who sold drugs at street level, through her work with addicts. For about a month after she went missing I felt as if I encountered her picture on posters everywhere I looked.

It was the closest imaginable thing to being haunted. Then her face began to be posted over by more recent disappearances, until one no longer saw it anywhere.

When did I accept that she had gone missing for ever? Part of me knew as soon as I first heard that she would never be seen again. The part of me which expected the news was also able to accept it. Another part of me never accepted or understood or even believed what had happened, and still doesn't. I still very clearly see her going around a corner in Central Market, or on the upper deck of a moving tram, or in a photograph as the page is turned in somebody else's newspaper. But the face I see is always Maria as she was a long time ago, years even before she vanished.

As for the specifics of what happened, for a long time I tried not to think about them. I had nightmares, I woke up in tears, I would have times when the work of trying not to think about Maria seemed to be the only thing I was doing. So I decided to face the question and try to work out what had happened, as well as I could. This is the conclusion I reached. Because Maria would certainly have struggled and screamed, they had to silence her quickly and immediately, so I think they drugged her, with chloroform or an injection, and bundled her into a car. All this probably took place near the Kowloon Star Ferry terminal, perhaps while a diversion was staged somewhere nearby. Then they drove somewhere, probably in the New Territories, killed her and disposed of the body. It would all have been done with a minimum of fuss.

The inquest was held three months after she disappeared. I tried to submit the notes of my conversation with Chief Inspector Watts, but the coroner decided they were not relevant. The inquest returned an open verdict. The general opinion was that Maria had fallen foul of one of the drug addicts with whom her work brought her into such frequent contact.

Chapter Fifteen

Grief is the hardest emotion to describe because so much of it is numbness; it is also passive, something one undergoes rather than something one undertakes. It becomes difficult to locate oneself. When Maria went missing a part of me did too. My capacity for love, which had always seemed elusive and equivocal even to me, was bound up in my relationship with Maria. I discovered that after her death. I had not known it before. It is a familiar story. There is nothing original about pain.

Hatred is of course a comfort. Wo was said to dislike Taiwan greatly, and to yearn for a return to his adopted homeland. The newspapers controlled by the Wos began to run little pieces about the thinness of the case which would have been brought against Wo, and hinted about anonymous, corrupt enemies in the police force. There were occasional implications that he might return to face trial. I knew that that would never happen; the scandal of his flight had been barely containable, but that around his return would destroy the colonial administration. I liked to think of him festering in his villa outside Taipei. I hoped that he would die soon.

Beryl took a firm line with me. She was utterly furious about what had happened, saw it clearly, and talked about it with nobody but the most trusted and senior of her boys and me. At the same time she insisted on seeing what had happened as a victory.

'She destroyed Wo. Wherever she is now she's looking down on us and laughing at him. If she'd just pottered quietly off to Singapore and run an opium clinic or a leper colony or something he'd have sweated in Taiwan for a few years and then been able to come back when his brother had done enough whingeing and greased enough palms. As it is, he's going to rot there until the day he dies.'

'The inquest didn't see it that way. There wasn't a word to incriminate the Wos.'

'Don't talk rot, Tom, you know that's not the way Hong Kong works. Everyone knows what happened. She forced them to go too far. She knew what she was doing.' Then Beryl's manner became less gung-ho. She thought for a moment. 'I suppose, in a way, that makes it harder to bear.'

'She was so stubborn, so bloody stubborn.'

From about a week after Maria's disappearance I had been forcing myself to use the past tense about her.

'She wouldn't have wanted to go quietly,' said Beryl.

When the mission had a service of thanksgiving for Maria, six months after she had gone missing and a few months after she had been declared legally dead, Beryl came with me. Father Ignatius had taken the lead in arranging both the legalities and the memorial. He was good at the practical, administrative side of things.

I picked Beryl up in one of the hotel cars. She was still living in the same flat she had in mid-levels, an area now being compressed by buildings spreading up the hill from Central. Her amah let me in, and I found Beryl in the sitting room adjusting her hat in front of the mirror with a gin and tonic on the mantelpiece.

'I'm rather dreading this,' I said by way of a greeting. Beryl shook her head to indicate that this was not how I should think. She offered her arm and we went out to the car.

The church was packed. It was the first service I had been to since the day with Austen and Cobb, and the first time I had ever been to a Catholic mass. I remember almost nothing about it except a constant wondering at who all these people were – which made me feel that the section of Maria's life I had seen was only a tiny fragment of her whole being.

The other thing I remember is Father Ignatius's eulogy, which was, to my amazement, at least at the start, very funny. 'There is an English saying,' he said in his quick Cork voice. 'I often, in dealing with Sister Maria, and especially when an issue of principle was involved, or perceived to be involved' – he smiled after the 'perceived', which got a chuckle – 'I often thought it guided her conduct. The saying is: "Why be difficult, when with a little extra effort, you can be impossible?"'

He then spoke about the various aspects of her work. Much of it was news to me.

After the service there was a mêlée outside, curiously happy in its emotional texture. It was all much more of a celebration than I had braced myself for. I had offered the use of the Empire to Father Ignatius for a reception, but he had politely declined, so there were tiny sandwiches and dim sum at the main mission hall instead. As I was leaving, a tiny old European nun, bent over at thirty degrees from the vertical, came towards me on the arm of a younger Chinese sister. The younger nun was beaming. I realised that the older woman was blind.

'Mr Stewart,' she said.

'Yes, Sister.' ,

'You do not recognise me.' Her accent was French.

'Good God – Sister Benedicta, of course I recognise you.'

'It is a sad day.'

'Yes.'

'She was stubborn.'

'Yes.'

'You had that in common.'

'There are lots of ways in which I was Maria's inferior, and that was one of them.'

She smiled. 'Are you sure?' Then she shook her head. 'I feel too old. No one should have to outlive their children.'

Longevity can be a form of spite. It was from around now that I began looking forward to news of Wo Man-Lee's death. The slim intent youth I had known was now an incessant smoker known to have heart trouble. He did not want to die in Taiwan.

His brother Ho-Yan did not last long. The strain of running the family business was too much for him. He died of a stroke, and Wo Man-Lee's son, Tung-Ko, took over. He was a serious, unsmiling, charmless young man who spoke impeccable American-accented English thanks to his time at Harvard. It quickly became clear that he was a brilliant businessman. He ingested a chain of competing Chinese newspapers, and was said to have bought, through a subsidiary, controlling shares in one of the local television stations. He now owned outlets across all media and all political views. At the same time the family's property assets rocketed in value. He floated some of the business on the stock market, after setting up a system of nested public and private ownership through holding companies which left all control in his hands. The umbrella company was called Po Lam Holdings. From being very wealthy, the Wos now became billionaires. There was talk of Tung-Ko's standing for Legco, the undemocratic advisory council which had a role in government. I hated him.

Work had helped me through difficult times in the past. As I got older I found that to be less true. My mind wandered off more, and the ability of things such as inventories, staff problems, restaurant margins, furnishing replacements, supplier price rises, and bed occupancy rates to occupy all my attention, in the way that the area under a spotlight absorbs all the light, had lessened. I missed it; as one gets older, one begins to miss one's former appetites. Chef Ng asked if he could move from the Empire to Deep Water Bay, saying he wanted a slower pace of life and a smaller kitchen to run (though, it should go without saying, no less money). Once that would have seemed a fully fledged drama, requiring extensive deployment of tact and negotiating skills to explain to the other shareholders in the Empire that I was not effectively poaching my own staff. Now it seemed like a not especially big practical problem, solved by a couple of emollient letters. Part of me missed the drama.

One should always be careful what one wishes for. That at least does not change with age. Rathbone, the plump trustee lawyer with whom I had always had excellent working relations, asked me to come to his office one morning, for what I thought would be a routine meeting about the hotel's accounts. In retrospect, a note of more than usual formality in the letter, and the unusual venue, his territory rather than mine, should have tipped me off, as it perhaps – to give the clever, affable man his credit – was meant to do. Rathbone's secretary let me into his office, on a high floor of a block in Des Voeux Road with a lovely view of the harbour. The air conditioning was turned up high enough for him to be wearing a charcoal-coloured three-piece pinstripe suit with a watch chain.

The hotel business trains one to smell money. This is not always to do with people who have enormous amounts of it, so much as with people who move in money, theirs or others'; who

212

have money as their natural element. It was a smell one encountered more and more often in Hong Kong, and the lawyer gave off a particularly sharp whiff of it. He padded softly across the office towards me, his hand extended.

'Tom,' he said. 'So good of you to come.'

We sat down on chairs in front of his desk and went briskly through the figures. All was, as I had known it would be, well. The Masterson family's share of the profits was accruing nicely in a Hong Kong-based holding company, safe from the insatiable maw of the UK tax system.

'Good,' said Rathbone, closing the folder on the papers. 'And now, I have something to convey which may prove less welcome. There is no euphemistic way of imparting this news, so I will not attempt to minimise its surprise. The Mastersons have been made a direct offer for the ownership of the hotel, based not on its profitability as a going concern, which I may say is, thanks to your efforts, formidable, but on its value as a property, specifically, on its potential value for demolition and redevelopment. It is a very considerable offer and, not to beat about the bush, the Mastersons have told me to use their controlling interest to accept it.'

I'm not sure if I had anything quite as discreet and identifiable as a first thought. Several notions seized me at the same time. One of them was that the prospective buyer must have found out who the family were, established that they had a controlling interest, and approached them directly without letting me know, and that couldn't have been done by accident. Company papers did not name the Masterson family as owners – their share of the Empire Hotel belonged to the trustees. With that thought, instantly, came the realisation that Rathbone had to have been involved. I'm not sure how I was so certain; but I was. It might even have been him who set the deal up. But that was fair enough, in a way; he was supposed to look after the family's interests, and this was without doubt an offer worth considering, even if he had generated it himself in the first place. He would be taking a cut from the buyers as well as his trustees' fee. That would make sense too. It was cynical, clever, lucrative, and as long as I was happy to sell out, it left everyone ahead on the deal.

A part of my brain was running over these thoughts. Another felt at the same time a complete lack of surprise. One would have had to be unusually stupid not to realise that the land the Empire stood on was worth a very great deal of money. Hong Kong was shooting up, buildings were being torn down and replaced with skyscrapers all the time. Because space was strictly finite, property values were only going to continue to rise, which meant that investment was rocketing. Beryl's company, by her own account, had made more money in the last five years than in the previous thirty. Cooper had once asked me, 'How long do you think you'll hold out?' I shrugged and said, 'As long as the family wants me to.' And now they didn't want me to any more . . . There was a twinge of rejection in the thought. And then, mixed in with all this, an idea which was like nausea came over me. I could not keep it out of my mind. What if the buyers were the Wo family? The son was known to have a business-school interest in 'diversifying' the family empire. Property was a one-way bet in Hong Kong, as well as a notoriously good business in which to launder money. A bid for the Empire by the Wos would make perfect sense. It would also make me want to kill somebody. I would be the punchline of somebody else's joke.

I realised that I must have been silent for about five minutes. In the context of a meeting in Rathbone's office it was an extremely long time. I made an effort to control my voice.

'Might I ask the identity of the buyers?'

'They would prefer that to remain confidential, for the time being,' Rathbone murmured. But as Chief Inspector Watts pointed out, I had lived in Hong Kong for too long.

'It would be misleading of me if I gave the impression that this idea had never been mooted before,' I said. 'One has had numerous expressions of interest in the Empire on precisely this basis. Mere feelers, obviously. I usually deflect inquiries with the words "if the hotel is ever up for sale, I'll let you know." Of course, a situation in which competitive bidding was involved would be of considerable interest to your clients.' Rathbone blinked. 'The Mastersons, I mean, of course. I'm sure they'd regard an open auction for the property as an exciting development.'

He knew I knew. He knew I knew he knew I knew.

'I have reasons for wanting to know who the buyers are not,' said, man to man, 'much more than I need to know who they are.

I'm not sure how much of it he got, but he got enough. His fac

214

cleared. He moved his fountain pen on the leather desktop, which held an unmarked sheet of blotting paper.

'The financial entities involved are European interests with an extremely optimistic medium-term view of the Hong Kong economy in particular and the south-east Asia sphere in general. They are using the expertise of one of the local Hongs but the overwhelming bulk of the capital is western European. To put it another way,' he went on, delicately, 'it's no one you know.'

I could feel myself unclench. He saw that. 'It should go without saying that the special nature of your contribution to the Empire will not go unacknowledged,' he said. Rathbone was now enjoying this; he loved to please; a good deal was one from which everyone walked away richer, happier, and freshly stroked. 'My clients know that the debt they owe you is greater than is reflected in your share of the enterprise as it currently stands, and intend to make a settlement when the hotel is sold which I think you will find reflects that esteem.'

I had a vision of Masterson's Surrey nieces, each with a well-fed husband and a tennis court. I said: 'How much?'

He told me.

Those years were brightened for me by the activities of a new, very deeply flawed institution, the ICAC: Independent Commission Against Corruption. The Riots and subsequent scandals had brought this subject as close to the surface as it had ever been; and a huge scandal involving a corrupt British police inspector – as opposed, of course, to the other sort of British police inspector – meant that something had to be done. That something was the ICAC, a body with powers to arrest and interrogate anyone it wanted on almost any pretext. A broad swathe of the police retired, fled, or was forced out of the service. Best of all, Chief Inspector Watts was arrested and died of a heart attack while in custody.

I went to see Connor from the *South China Morning Post*. I asked him to choose a place where there would be no journalists, and no one who recognised me. We had a drink in a Wanchai bar. In one corner a group of British sailors had gone past the louder stages of intoxication and were now quietly, slurringly incapable. Connor looked around the room fondly.

'Haven't been here in ages,' he said. 'Had a reputation for being a bit lively at one time. American navy used to come here too. One night there's a British ship and an American ship in harbour at the same time. You're more or less guaranteed trouble. There's about fifty Yanks and about fifty limeys, all bombed out of their minds. The Yanks' ships are dry, don't forget, so they go even more mental than our lot do. They're sizing each other up all evening. Finally the biggest and ugliest American goes over to the biggest and ugliest Brit. Complete silence. The Yank says, "So how come you limey bastards aren't fighting in Vietnam?" The Brit gets up and says, "'O Chi Minh ain't asked us yet." Jesus fuck. All hell lets loose. Takes a couple of hundred military police to break the fight up and the whole place is completely demolished by the end. Wrote it up for the paper, page one.'

'The landlord must have been pleased.'

'Well yeah he was, actually. It was insured for double its value and he cleaned up. Bought a place in the New Territories.'

Connor took a long gulp of his San Miguel. He had, as he explained, switched from whiskey to beer to 'take it easy for a bit'. Even in the dark bar he did not look well.

'So what can I do for you?' he asked.

'It may be more the other way around,' I said. I slid across the table a manilla envelope with a copy of the notes I had taken after Watts's visit. Connor raised his eyebrows. 'I won't spoil it for you,' I said, and left a hundred-dollar bill for the drinks.

It took a couple of weeks before I saw my act bear fruit. Connor did not tell the story about Maria directly – I had not expected him to – but he wrote a front-page article saying the *Post* now had 'strong evidence' linking the late Chief Inspector Watts with Triad boss M. L. Wo, currently in exile in Taipei. Watts's reputation was posthumously destroyed. It did not bring Maria back but it did make me feel slightly better.

I did not exactly retire after the sale of the Empire, but I began taking life more slowly. I had in fact considered approaching some backers and making a counterbid to buy out the old hotel, but then decided that I was simply not able to summon up the energy. The thought of the large cash lump, versus a vigorous business–political battle followed by years spent squeezing every available drop of cash out of the business – well, that choice was not too difficult to see clearly. I spent the weeks at Deep Water Bay and the weekends on Cheung Chau. My life was more simple and more limited than it had ever been. I cannot claim that I was happier than before, but my circumstances had fewer moving parts, and there was less to go wrong.

The early eighties brought one public event which attracted a great deal of attention in the wider world. Mrs Thatcher went to Beijing, overexcited by her recent victory in the Falklands, and struck attitudes the Chinese found so obnoxious that the question of Hong Kong's sovereignty was publically reopened. There could of course be only one conclusion, once the issue had been raised. For the previous several decades the subject of the 1997 handover had never been brought up except by visitors. Now it became impossible to leave one's room without having a conversation about it. The topic was discussed at great length, from every angle, with wild oscillations in both private and public mood not just weekly or daily but in the course of a single conversation. I found it easy not to join in; it is easy to be stoical about something when one doesn't care. The received wisdom in the colony changed. Previously it had always focused on the fact that the Communists did not recognise the unequal treaties which had ceded Hong Kong: 'All rubbish, old boy. The Commies don't want the place back, it's full of Triads and Kuomintang, and they don't recognise the treaties anyway. They've got a standing army of two million soldiers – what are we going to do, say boo and make them run away?' Then it became: 'The Chinese don't need to take Hong Kong over, they're buying it up. Look at the ownership of –' (fill in the blank with name of any large new Hong Kong company). 'All Peking money. They need the foreign revenue, old boy. Why rock the boat? By 1997 they'll own most of the place anyway. It's not in their interest to make it go wrong.' Now it became: 'All bets are off. We're moving our corporate offices to the Bahamas.'

To me it had been perfectly obvious for years that the Chinese would take Hong Kong over in 1997. Why on earth wouldn't they? I thought that if I was still alive – I would be eighty-four – it would be then that I would consider moving back to England. But I would first see which way the wind was blowing. My will, which left everything to David and his children, had long since been settled. With any luck, Wo Man-Lee would be dead by then and I wouldn't much care what I did. But things did not work ou like that.

Professor Cobb, professor emeritus as he then was, died earl in 1983. After his retirement in 1975 he'd stayed in the colony though his research trips and fellowships meant he was ofter away. When he came back he would always give me a remark ably Cobbish view of wherever he had just been, saying, fo instance, after spending three months in Berkeley, 'rather dam climate'. He added, 'Not at all benign for the preservation o manuscripts.' After a comparable period at the Sorbonne, he saic nothing about the temptations, bright lights, cultural life, or cui sine of Paris, but merely: 'Some of the people there are . . . ver sound.' He spoke about *The Lives of the Emperors* in the same dis tant, amused, embarrassed way, as if it were a guilty pleasure, o an indiscretion he couldn't quite bring himself to regret. Jan Cobb, who made no secret of the fact that she would rather hav retired back to the UK, took great comfort in all the travelling. Sh would buy one outrageously expensive item of clothing wherev er they went, then have it copied in different sizes to give t women friends at Christmas.

To the best of my knowledge, Cobb had never had a singl day's illness. He was one of those men who look more or less th same age all their lives; his extreme thinness meant he had bee deeply lined for as long as I had known him. So although he wa eighty, his death, of a sudden massive cerebral haemorrhage, wa a complete surprise. It happened in the middle of the night, with out his waking Jane. That terrible shock was reserved for th morning.

The Lives of the Emperors was left unfinished. Jane asked me if would help her to put it together, even in uncompleted form, fo publication.

'I'd like it to be you,' she said. She looked shy, as if she kne that what she was about to say would make it impossible for m to refuse. 'He thought of you as his best friend. He asked me t say that if anything happened to him . . .'

So I said yes. I was pleased and surprised and a bit daunted The manuscript was still in his office at the university: not the fu professorial office he had once occupied but a small moder corner room, still with its good scroll painting and wooden Buddha. The papers were in three cardboard boxes, and they looked more chaotic than they actually were once I realised that several chapters had been typed in different versions, marked out with numbers written on the top right hand of the page. Cobb's office had to be emptied to make way for a keen young Chinese literature professor, who would occasionally stand in the doorway, embarrassed but eager, and offer to give Jane and me a hand with the packing. Jane asked me to read the book first, because she couldn't face it. When she said that, her face looked pinched and red and lonely and English. I took the manuscript to Deep Water Bay, promising to report back as soon as I was able.

Over the years I had turned my rooms at the hotel into a kind of office-cum-bedroom. I had a room full of books and papers and then off it an archway leading to an L-shaped bedroom, which in turn led out to a balcony with a view across the bay. The austerity was supposed to be a way of reminding myself that if I had time off I should be spending it at Cheung Chau. In theory, of course, I could use the public rooms of the hotel – but there is something offputting about a hotel proprietor too obviously lurking in his own establishment. My armchair for reading was in the bedroom, but I would sometimes take a book out onto the balcony, unless or until the light began to attract mosquitoes. That's where I sat with the first box of Cobb's typed pages. I read all night. It was like watching a parade go past: not a benign triumphal parade but a phantasmagoria, a vision of what people could be at their worst. Every variety of hatred, murder, lust, treachery, ruthlessness, violence, envy, and rage was on display. Cobb had spoken of Chinese literature as the world's largest body of writing that valued tradition, continuity, allusion, calm, distance – 'the greatest echo chamber there is,' he said on one occasion, 'the most civilised conversation there has ever been'. ('Conversation' was his word for a body of writing or learning.) This was the shadow side of that. The First Emperor of Ch'in, the emperor who built the Great Wall and gave the order to burn all the books, was the presiding spirit of *The Lives*.

I stayed up all night and called Jane in the morning.

'I think it's remarkable. It's . . . well, rather horrifying. But remarkable. What do you want me to do?'

'I've no idea. I think, if it is publishable, Raymond would have wanted me to publish it but beyond that . . .'

'Well, I've had an idea,' I said.

> Deep Water Bay Hotel
> Hong Kong
> 17 May 1983

Dear Mr Austen,

Please excuse this impertinent and unsolicited approach from the most distant of acquaintances. My name is Tom Stewart. I am the hotel manager who met you first in 1938 when you were en route to the Chinese civil war and then again when you passed through the colony during a British Council tour of the East.

I do not know whether you will remember that latter occasion. We met at St John's Cathedral, or rather, St John's Church as it then was. I was in the company of my friend Raymond Cobb, a professor at Hong Kong University. We had lunch and then went out to the New Territories together to witness the Chinese custom of visiting ancestors' graves.

It is in connection with that day that I am writing to you. I am sorry to say that Professor Cobb has died: the sad suddenness of his death is qualified by the fact that he was eighty. For the last third of his life he had been working on a translation of a book called *The Lives of the Emperors*, a history of China through the biography of its leaders. He described the book as a Chinese Suetonius. There is no other translation extant. Cobb's work was not finished but the last version of the manuscript is about a hundred and twenty thousand words long.

The book seems to me to be extraordinary. I am writing – and I expect your heart is already sinking – to ask if you would have a look at Cobb's work and suggest what should be done about publishing it. Although Cobb often discussed the project with me my knowledge of how the publishing world works is minimal and I would be grateful for any advice.

I quite understand if you for any reason at all cannot help; I know how busy you must be.

I often think of your visits to Hong Kong, and wish there had been more of them.

Yours sincerely,
Tom Stewart

I sent the letter via his London publisher. A week later there came a two-word telegram: 'DELIGHTED AUSTEN'. I had the last version of the manuscript photocopied, and then sent it to the same address. I told Jane what I had done over dinner and as far as I could tell, through her thick carapace of grief, she was pleased.

I didn't hear back from Austen for many weeks, as indeed I hadn't been expecting to – though I still looked much more eagerly than usual through the mail every morning, in search of unfamiliar handwriting and a UK postmark. My experience has been that an awaited response always comes at exactly the moment one is not expecting it. One sits beside the front door waiting for a glimpse of the postman; and then returns from making a cup of coffee to find the letter on the doormat. I was beginning to be genuinely impatient at the lack of a reply from Austen – the slight but definite unreasonableness of my initial request making me more, rather than less, irritable – when Ah Wing knocked on my door on a muggy summer morning of low cloud and high humidity and handed me a letter, saying,

'Mixed up with my post, Mr Stewart, so sorry.'

I recognised the letter immediately; or rather, I recognised that I didn't recognise it, and therefore knew what it must be. I opened it with a memory of the long, long distant experience of facing examination results.

Church House
Ottery St Mary
1 August

Dear Mr Stewart,

I should warn you at the start that this letter gives a much more equivocal response than the one you have a right to expect.

I remember Professor Cobb with great vividness and was keen to read his manuscript, despite the fact that I know nothing about Chinese culture. It seemed unlikely that it would be uninteresting, and indeed it was not. The cavalcade of darkness it describes is so extraordinary that it reminded me of something entirely frivolous, a remark of Kafka's quoted in a contemporary's memoir, that the conversation of a mutual acquaintance 'was like having world literature parade past one's table in its underpants'.

I am, however, as I have said, no authority on anything to do with the East, and thought I must seek a verdict from someone who knew the, to me, wholly unfamiliar source material. I dropped a line to an old friend, Donald Shuttleworth, who taught Chinese for many years at the University of London, and who indeed translated some Tang poetry himself. You may have heard of him. I described the work and said I was not asking for a detailed reading, merely an inspection which would give me some indication as to the overall level of the translation – like boring a sample to find if there's oil at a drilling site. He agreed in a letter which had a degree of amused curiosity that I found surprising; I hope you won't take it amiss if I say one's first response to unsolicited requests for reading a manuscript tends not to be overwhelmingly positive. I sent Shuttleworth the manuscript and think the best thing would perhaps be if I enclose a copy of his letter, as he has given me permission to do.

I wish I could suggest with confidence what you might do next. I think the book is worth publishing and would be happy to be quoted as saying so.

I have recently been reading a great deal of an extraordinary French writer called Simone Weil. One of her memoirists recalled that at their last encounter he said, 'Let us hope we meet again in the next world.' She replied, 'In the next world there will be no meeting again.' Let us hope she was wrong.

Yours,
Wilfred Austen

This was Shuttleworth's letter:

47 Old Church St
Chelsea
27 July

Dear Wilfred,

I was intrigued by your letter, as you may have sensed in my earlier reply. I know of Professor Cobb's work on the *yuë-fu* lyric form, which was his only publication in my field of interest. I was not aware until your letter that he had ceased to publish any scholarly work in favour of his efforts on this project. But the point which chiefly piqued my interest was the fact that to the very best of my knowledge no such text as *The Lives of the Emperors* exists in Chinese. I wondered if the work was a recension of other biographical material, or a far-fetched title for something one might already know – there is a considerable body of historical writing in the Classical tradition to which the title would not be entirely inappropriate. The former supposition is the more accurate. The work in question does not correspond to any Chinese original. It is a kind of anthology of biographical material of the Chinese emperors, edited together to read as a single narrative. As such it is of considerable interest.

Cobb went to a great deal of trouble to do two things. First, the style of the work is modelled on that of Classical Chinese; to use an imprecise term, it 'feels' like a translation. This is something a number of translators have sought to capture, among them Arthur Waley and myself, and I am not perhaps indulging in self-flattery when I say the influence of these attempts is apparent in Cobb's work. It is to do with a limpidity of the verbal surface and a seeming flatness in affect which in fact conceals great intensities of feeling. There is no precise equivalent in English.

The second point on which Cobb has expended effort is on the stitching together of his tapestry. The effect is of very great interest to me, a scholar in Classical Chinese. Whether it will be able to find a publisher and a wider interested audience I have to admit I do not know.

Yours ever,
Don

'I'll find a publisher, Jane,' I told her. 'Leave it to me.' That's what I promised – but if I had known what I was saying, I wouldn't have.

I found a list of publishers in a reference book, and did some research by looking at their books in the university library. I started at the top of the list and began to work down the names. Each cycle of submission-to-rejection, as they became, took weeks or even months. Each rejection entailed my opening a letter telling me, usually politely, sometimes interestedly, sometimes with what appeared to be genuine regret, that the book could not be accepted for publication. Often the letters gave a reason, to do with its length, or its .Chinese-ness, or its erudition, or reconditeness, or difficulty, or the condition of the market, or the special problems presented by the fact that its author was dead, or its being a cross between a narrative and an anthology, or its simply being – this was especially popular – 'not quite right for us'. Of all these letters, the ones which gave a reason were the most irritating. After each rejection I ticked the company in question off the list, filed the letter, and started again. Parts of the manuscript would be filthy not just with fingerprints, but also tea stains, ketchup marks, water smudges, and once even children's drawings. When I got back the rejected work I would get out my list of publishers, make a fresh copy of the original manuscript, write another submission letter, wrap up a parcel, and travel to the General Post Office in Central to send it by recorded delivery.

The great boon of the *Lives* affair for me was that I began to correspond with Austen. He wrote to me a couple of weeks after his initial letter, saying that he expected by now the shock would have worn off, and asking me what I was intending to do. I wrote back, and before long we were in regular touch. The sight of his cramped, uneven, rather mad handwriting on an envelope never failed to give me a lift. In a curious way, I think I represented a choice he felt he had not made. 'I stayed in England and became a member of the establishment, despite myself, something which would not have been possible had I left,' he wrote. 'It's nice being able to tell people my story about the time I met the Queen, but I've often wondered, now that it's too late to usefully wonder, what sort of price I may have paid for that in my work.' I could sense in him a loneliness. Perhaps that was something else we recognised about each other.

Chapter Sixteen

Wo Man-Lee died of lung cancer in the winter of 1983. I read the news in the *South China Morning Post*, in a story headlined 'Fugitive Dies'. I was surprised to notice that I did not feel anything other than a sense of relief. I was not conscious of having anything left in life to look forward to.

One day in February of the new year, after one of my trips to the Post Office with a parcel, I decided I needed some air and exercise. I couldn't do anything too strenuous since I had to be back in Deep Water Bay by late afternoon to supervise the arrangements for a do. Beryl had come clean: it was her eightieth birthday. Her 'boys' were giving her a private dinner and were touchingly solicitous about everything being just so. Leung, her right-hand man, had made a point of asking me personally to oversee the arrangements and I had of course agreed. I assured him that Chef Ng would cook the meal himself. That pleased him.

But the party was a few hours away. My plan was to take a tram up to the Peak, walk the circuit around the hill, and then take a cab from the end of the walk back to Deep Water Bay. It was a nice day, the clear winter weather which is Hong Kong's closest equivalent to a spring day in a temperate climate. Once or twice in the walk from the GPO to the lower station of the Peak Tram – a few hundred yards up the hill, during which I felt the effect of all the exercise that I had not been taking – I had a curious sensation of being watched: that instinctive human awareness which no science has explained. But there was no reason for the feeling, as far as I could tell – and in Hong Kong one is in a sense watched all the time anyway. It must be a challenging place to be a spy; perhaps that's why they seem to like it so much.

There was a queue for the tram, much of it consisting of schoolchildren on an excursion. I had to wait for the second tram and took a seat at the front. As always, the steepest section of the ride was a few degrees closer to the vertical than one had remembered. I could hear the children's giggling excitement behind me, and their teacher pointing out the sights to them in Cantonese. As usual in the middle of the day, hardly anyone got on or off at the intermediate stops on the way to the top.

As I get older I find I have developed a faint trace of vertigo. Or it may be that as the buildings in Central have grown taller, seeming to reach almost all the way up to the Peak, one has become increasingly conscious of the height; either way, I don't take quite the same relish in the view on the way up that I once did. I was glad to get to the Peak Tram terminal and get out on Mount Austin Road, the first half of the path running around the hill. An hour's stroll would be about right.

There were more people than I had expected: European tourists, as well as the schoolchildren going up to the old Governor's house at the top – a ruin and a garden since it was destroyed by the Japanese. I took the walk easily, enjoying the views out towards Cheung Chau and the thought of spending the weekend there with a book and a bottle of wine, after Beryl's party. The dinner would be an odd combination of her work friends, her nephew by marriage who was visiting from London, and me. I had made solemn assurances to her boys that the parts of the event for which I was responsible would be a success, but I could give no guarantee that the evening would work as a whole. It would be an odd mix.

Once or twice again as I walked I had the sensation of being kept under surveillance. I put it down to a mild anticipatory anxiety about Beryl's do.

When I turned the corner into Lugard Road there were eagles circling in the currents a hundred feet or so below the top of the Peak. The visibility was beautifully, freakishly good, and the hills around Kowloon stood out like papier mâché models of themselves. The last stretch of Lugard Road is uphill, and I was puffing by the time I got back to the tram terminus. I saw with a sinking heart that there was a queue at the taxi rank: I had been caught out by the mid-afternoon shift change. Ten people were silently and gloomily waiting in front of me. A taxi came and dropped three American tourists off; then the driver covered his flag with a red cloth to indicate he was off duty and drove away.

I had nothing to read. I thought about taking the tram down-town and setting out from there instead; but the Peak Tram was busy and there was bound to be a taxi queue at the bottom termi-nus also. At last a taxi arrived and, as it did so, from nowhere appeared a group of five British tourists, all of them noisy young men. They made no attempt to defer to the queue but merely got straight into the cab, squeezing in, laughing and joking. The peo-ple in the queue in front of me, all of them Chinese, looked at them, appalled but, it has to be said, not particularly surprised. I stepped over the metal rail which kept the queue in order and moved to the cab while the last two youths were still getting into it. I put my hand on the arm of one of the young men. He was large and short-haired and smelled of beer. He had an earring.

'Excuse me, but this is a queue, and these people have been waiting for some time.'

He stopped and turned.

'What the fuck's that got to do with me, shithead?' he said.

'You've jumped the queue. Perhaps you weren't aware. You should get out of the taxi and let these people have it.'

He raised his hands up to my chest. We were about the same height but he must have been three stone heavier. He spread his fingers, put them at the top of my chest, and pushed. I stepped backwards two or three feet. One and then another and then the last of the youths got out of the taxi and came around to me. He pushed me again.

'You going to make me, old fart? Come on then, you going to make me?'

Every time he pushed I gave ground. I did not say anything more. He was visibly becoming more and more angry; working himself up to something. It was strangely like the self-induced, self-incited fury I had seen among Japanese soldiers during the war. I was sure he was about to hit me.

A young Chinese, not one of those who had been waiting in the queue, approached from beside and behind me. He was neatly dressed, wiry, and looked about eighteen. He said, as if reciting a textbook phrase, in English:

'Can I help you?'

'Fuck off, Chinky,' said one of the other youths, who hadn't spoken before. He too smelled of alcohol. The large youth pushing me looked at the Chinese boy for a moment and then turned back to me, his face very close. His eyeballs were bloodshot. He raised his arms to my chest and was about to push me again when the Chinese youth, moving incomparably more quickly than it takes to describe, stepped forward and made a pulling-and-chopping movement at his outstretched arms. There seemed to be no transition between the man moving to push me and his kneeling on the ground screaming, both arms hanging loosely in front of him. A second Briton took a step backward, then a step forward, and lifted up his right hand to throw a punch. The Chinese, again moving at an entirely different speed, stepped forward and hit him very hard on the bridge of his nose with the heel of his hand. A tremendous amount of blood started pouring out of his nose and he dropped to the ground.

'Fucking hell, it's one of them kung fu chinkies,' said one of the other youths. They did not run, but simply turned and walked briskly away back towards the terminus, leaving their two friends behind. The Chinese youth took my arm and led me into the taxicab.

'Excuse us,' he said to the queue. I don't think I've ever seen such a collection of openly gawping faces. He said something I did not hear to the driver – who looked a little reluctant, but was not about to say no to this particular passenger. It was a few moments before I could collect myself to speak.

'Thank you. But who are you?' I asked.

Speaking carefully, in schoolroom English, as if these were words he had often practised, he said:

'I am your grandson.'

PART THREE

Sister Maria

Zhen Lu
Hunan
10 October 1942

Dear Tom,

It is strange to be writing this letter to you while I do not know if you are alive or dead. Even if you are alive I do not know your whereabouts any more than you know mine. And if it ever finds you I may no longer be alive. There is an old Chinese story called the Song of Lasting Pain, in which the emperor goes into the land of the dead to find the soul of his beloved consort. They took a vow to love each other in their future lives throughout eternity. It is a famous sad story. This too is something out of an old Chinese story, since you may be dead as I write this, or I may be dead as you read it, and both of us are for now lost to each other.

I have given birth to our child. If this letter has been delivered to you then you know that. I gave him the name Zhu-Lee. It was my father's name.

Zhu-Lee was born two weeks ago. Tomorrow I give him to a member of our community, Sister Gabriel, who will travel with him and a wet nurse to Shen Lo, a village on the coast in Fukien near where I was born. There is a family there called Ho. They are a husband and wife who lost their only child two years ago and can have no more children of their own. They will raise him as theirs. The Hos will not know about my shame. They will believe that I was your lover in Hong Kong, that I fled to save my life while you stayed behind to fight, and that I died in childbirth.

It is said that a man telling a lie should include as much of the truth in it as he can. So it is with my falsehoods. I was your lover. You did stay behind to fight. Part of me did die in childbirth. So these are clever lies.

I will not give great details of what occurred after we parted. It was difficult to get as far as Canton but once I was there I made contact with the community and they helped me. I came to our mission in Szechuan, where the Japanese occupation is not present. There I realised I was pregnant. Sister Benedicta helped me. She sent me here, to a family she knows, and arranged for Sister Gabriel to come and see me through the birth. Sister Gabriel is a midwife. Thus only two members of our community know what has happened. Father Luke, my confessor, knows also. But he is bound by the confessional. I can rejoin the rest of the order without any shame except what is in my heart.

Our son has been lying on my breast all day. He is tiny and beautiful. He has many wrinkles. You are wondering how I can give him up. The answer is that I do not know but I know that I must. I have betrayed my vocation but it is still real. That call is one I cannot deny. This is something of which I am sure but cannot explain. I fear you will not understand this so I ask you to accept it as a fact. If this makes you wonder whether I have any love for our son, any real love, all that I can say is that what I feel for him is so great that I do not regret what has happened, with all the consequences.

I have asked myself many times why I did what I did. Why we did what we did. For a time I tried to convince myself that I had consented because I wished to make it impossible for you to leave me. I believed it my duty to stop you going back into Hong Kong. It is true that I did feel that. But that was not the reason for my actions. The answer is that I did what I wanted to. It is necessary for you to know that.

I am leaving this letter for our son when he grows up, to give to you if he ever decides to come and find you. If this letter comes to you, I leave it to you to decide what to tell him.

I dread tomorrow as much as, more than, I dreaded parting with you. God is love. But sometimes love can be terrible.

Love,

Zhang Sha-Mun

whom you know as Sister Maria

PART FOUR

Matthew Ho

Chapter One

'A good rabbit has three burrows,' my father-in-law said. It is one of his favourite sayings. It was 1996, a year before handover. We were visiting a house in the Sydney suburb of Mosman.

'It is a good neighbourhood,' my wife said. 'Five minutes' walk from the ferry. A view of water. Good feng shui. Plenty of Chinese people in the area so good food shops and restaurants. Good schools. Safe. A subtropical climate not dissimilar to Hong Kong but with more blue-sky days. Also the Australian dollar is very weak and this is an excellent time to make a purchase.'

'Once the property has been bought, however, a significant proportion of our assets will be denominated in this weak currency,' said my mother-in-law. 'The Hong Kong dollar is tied to the US dollar. It is strong. The Australian dollar is not. It is weak. Their economy is based on commodities. Our capital investment may decline in value,' she concluded. Before their retirement my wife's parents were both mathematics teachers.

'But this is a very attractive city,' I said. 'Hong Kong's future is uncertain; Sydney's is not. Property here will not decline in value. It is a big house and there is plenty of room for all of us. Think how little we could buy for five million dollars in Hong Kong. Here we will have much more space. Father-in-law will have a garden. He can do his t'ai chi. Mother-in-law will have good opportunities for social activity. Mei-Lin will have excellent schooling. Living costs are lower than in Hong Kong. If we decide after a time that we do not like it, and there has been no significant change in Hong Kong – very well. We go back.'

My wife and I had agreed that we would not go back, but that we would present the option to her parents.

'The air is good here,' said my father-in-law, sniffing. We both knew that he would be easier to convince.

'You do not have to surrender the lease in Sha Tin,' my wife reminded her parents.

'None of the arguments about leaving Hong Kong has changed,' I said.

'Mei-Lin already says she likes it here,' added my wife. This was true. My daughter already had a small zoo of toy koalas and kangaroos.

'What is the alternative, other than to stay put in Hong Kong?' I asked.

'Your grandfather is staying put,' my mother-in-law said. When she counter-attacked like that I smiled inside because it meant she was going to agree.

'It is different for him,' I said.

My mother-in-law walked over to the porch of the house. Down in the bay, two Australians were studying the mast of a yacht while a third, balancing a long way up, adjusted some ropes. There were no clouds. We could hear children two houses away play a skipping game. My mother, who had come to see the house the first time my wife and I looked at it, had not spoken until now.

She said, 'It is a long way from China.'

'A million Australian dollars is a good price,' my wife said.

'We'll be safe here,' I said.

My father-in-law looked around him and nodded.

'A good rabbit has three burrows,' he said.

Chapter Two

I was born and grew up until the age of eight in Shen Lo, a village in coastal Fujian. Shen Lo had been my family's home village. My grandmother had left Fujian as a girl to be educated by missionaries. She had gone to live in Hong Kong, where she met my grandfather and fell in love. When the war came, he stayed behind to fight the Japanese and she left for safety in China at his insistence. He gave her a gold necklace to sell if she needed money to keep her safe during the war. Although they did not know it at the time, she was carrying his child. Her son, my father, was born in September 1942. My grandmother died shortly after childbirth, although not before knowing that her son was healthy. My father inherited the necklace. There was also a letter my grandmother wrote to give to my grandfather if her son ever met him.

After my grandmother's death, my father was sent to Shen Lo, where a married couple called Ho brought him up as their own. My father's adoptive father had been a schoolteacher but times were so hard that he had to work as a fisherman to keep the family. Then, after the Communists won the war, things gradually began to improve and he went back to teaching. My father was a clever but sickly child, very gifted at his studies. In time, he went to university in Beijing and studied mathematics. There he met my mother, a local girl whose parents were Party cadres and who was at the university also, studying medicine. They fell in love and were married despite the opposition of her parents. Because of their attitude, my parents left Beijing after my father had finished his degree but before my mother had completed her qualifications. Although he could have found a job teaching at university level, at this moment in China there was a great emphasis on the value of peasant life, so my parents chose to go to Shen Lo and work as a village schoolteacher and a nurse. The coastal climate was less severe than that of Beijing and it suited my father. My parents were happy in Shen Lo.

I was born in the village in 1966. My first memories are of the communal garden at the back of our house where my father was growing broccoli. Everywhere in the village you could smell the sea. My father was a tall, thin man with glasses who told old Chinese stories and made shadows with his hands and the light from a lantern. People would sometimes give my parents gifts of fish or pig meat in thanks for services they had performed. But when the Cultural Revolution came, my father was anonymously denounced to the Red Guards. He was forced to abase himself in front of his pupils and was then sent to a re-education camp in Hunan. The climate there did not suit his lungs and the physical labour was extremely hard. He was bullied and picked on because his physical appearance was not entirely Chinese. He had been away for six months when my mother heard the news that he had died. This was in 1969 when I was three years old. My mother inherited the necklace and the letter.

My mother had to work so I spent many days with my great-aunt. There was no schooling. The Red Guards had destroyed the education system. My great-aunt taught me to read and write, and one or two of the other village children came to the house also. But she would not teach more than a small number and only the children of people she knew very well, because of the risk of being denounced. The Red Guards often had meetings with all the children of the village. There was much chanting and shouting and everyone was encouraged to attack counter-revolutionary elements. When they shouted, their faces seemed to shrink and their eyes to grow bigger. One, called Chen, used to pick on me and stand in front of me as he chanted slogans. He said my father had tried to destroy the revolution and that meant I would try to destroy the revolution also, and that I must make a gesture to show my loyalty. All of the Guards said that the revolution must be permanent, that it must go on without ceasing. People believed them and cooperated at first but gradually lost their faith and stopped joining in. Or they joined in with their bodies but not their hearts. The Red Guards could tell this and it made them more frenzied.

'What do you want to do when you are a big man?' my mother asked one day when she came back from visiting patients. She was washing vegetables as we talked. I did not know it, but several people had died in the previous days, of diphtheria. I was eight years old. I could see she was very tired.

'A tractor driver or fisherman.'

'Don't you want to be a doctor or an engineer?'

'They are sent to the farms. It is better to be on your own farm.'

She turned away to the sink.

Two or three days later my mother told me to put into her bag one object I wanted to take with me because we were going on a journey to visit relatives in Guangzhou. I said I did not know we had relatives in Guangzhou and she said, there are many things you do not know. I took a laisee packet my father had given me for Chinese New Year. It held in it a red star badge that I had won from a friend in a race. My mother spent all that night packing.

Very early the next morning, before it was light, she shook me awake, dressed me in new clothes that I had not seen before, gave me a bowl of soup, and told me that we must go and that it would be a long day. We walked a great distance out beyond the village, further than I had ever been through the fields, where the first people were starting their day's work in the paddies, until we reached beside a road and stopped to wait. Just as the day was breaking, a bus came. It was noisy and it rattled so much I thought I could feel my teeth loosening. I was excited but my mother was quiet. She gave some money to the driver and we sat beside an old woman with many gold teeth carrying a chicken on her lap. I sat on my mother's lap also and the woman asked my mother if she wanted to swap her little chicken for the woman's little chicken. My mother smiled at her but I was frightened.

We rode on the bus for a long time. Some of the time we travelled through fields, and then we were back along the coast. More and more people got on board. It grew hot and I was hungry. My mother gave me some rice wrapped in a leaf. The old woman looked at me and I could tell she wanted me to offer her some rice but I did not. The journey seemed to go on and on. We came to a town bigger than anywhere I had ever been before. In the course of an hour I saw more people than I had in the whole of my life until that day. We walked some distance and then we were in a railway station. There was great noise and confusion, with people running and shouting. I was frightened again, but my mother seemed to know what to do, and that calmed me.

We waited in the big main hall under the roof of the tallest building I had ever seen, and then we got on a train. It was even more crowded than the bus. I sat on my mother's lap again. But people were more friendly than they had been on the bus, especially when the train began to move. When people asked my mother where we were going, she would squeeze my arm and say in a calm voice that we were visiting relatives. She would ask them questions about their own families and they would talk. At one stop, some policemen got on the train and the train did not move. The policemen had Red Guards with them. The Red Guards did not speak. The policemen asked people for their papers and then asked them questions. They did not stop in front of everybody but they stopped in front of my mother.

'Give me your papers,' said one of the policemen. He looked at my mother's documents. Then he bent his head down to me. He was a tall man, a Northerner, and his breath smelled of rice wine.

'Where are you going, little Emperor?'

'We have relatives in Guangzhou,' I said.

'What do they do?'

'Nobody told me that.'

He and the other policemen smiled. He straightened up and gave the papers back to my mother, his eyes already looking for the next person to question. My mother squeezed both my arms. I could feel her heart beating. No one spoke until the policemen and the Red Guards left the carriage. Then the train began to make more noise and finally it gave a big jolt and started moving out of the station. My mother gave a long slow breath. People began to talk with each other and to share food. It was becoming dark. I tried to move along the train but it was too crowded. People scowled at me and told me off as I tried to squeeze past. A boy my own age told me that if we were at his village he would fight me. His mother only laughed.

We travelled all that night and some of the next day and by the time we arrived in Guangzhou we had eaten all our food. My mother had never been to Guangzhou before and even I could tell she was not confident. We tried to find a map of the city but there was no map in the station. Eventually we approached a woman who had put her heavy bags down for a rest. My mother showed her an address on a scrap of paper. She spoke to my

240

mother in a dialect that I did not recognise while pointing and talking. We set off on foot. All I remember of the walk was how much I wanted to be able to fly. I imagined taking off into the air and shooting to anywhere we wanted to go, carrying my mother with me. At last we came to a set of buildings which looked like some of the new developments in our village, only a hundred times bigger. They were all very ugly. My mother took out the address and made me sit on a bench where she could see me while she looked around the buildings. A man spat and just missed us. The building was the furthest one away. She beckoned me over and we went up the stairs. The cooking smells made me very hungry. I had never climbed so many stairs. Then my mother knocked on the door. She seemed shy. A woman opened the door and looked at my mother. She looked as if she was about to laugh but sad as well.

'It's you, Ah Chan,' she said.

'It's me,' said my mother. 'This is Ah Man,' she said, holding up my hand. The woman crouched down.

'I'm your new Aunt Wen,' she said. 'Your mother and I used to be closer than sisters.' Then she looked at my mother. 'Come in,' she said.

Aunt Wen lived in a room with her husband and her baby who was nine months old. Sometimes her mother stayed with them but at the moment she was not there and her husband was out also. I sat and drank sugared water while the two women talked in quiet voices beside the sink. The baby was fat and smiled at me. The women's eyes shone. My mother looked younger. When there were footsteps outside Aunt Wen got up and went to the door and slipped through it. Then a few minutes later she came back in with a man who was her husband. He was wearing a cap with a red star on the front. It was the last thing I remember before I fell asleep.

When I woke up it was morning and he had already gone back to work. The baby was sitting on the floor and Aunt Wen was cooking rice.

'We didn't think you'd ever wake,' she said. 'Your mother went out to see someone, she'll be back soon.'

'Are you from Beijing?' I asked. I knew that my mother was from Beijing. She smiled.

'No, I'm from here, but I went to university in Beijing. I met your mother and father there.'

'My father is dead now.'

'He was a good man. If you are like him when you grow up, you will be a good man too.'

'Yes, I know.'

I tried to teach the baby some fishing songs from Fujian but he was too small so I just sang to him. My mother came back in the afternoon. She looked at me and said:

'I hope you haven't eaten all of your poor Aunt's rice.'

'He needed it,' said Aunt Wen. I had had six bowls of rice and some vegetables. 'Did you find what you were looking for?'

My mother said, 'I think so.'

We stayed in Guangzhou for two more days. I did not go out very much because we did not want to make the neighbours curious. On the third night we said goodbye to Aunt Wen and her baby. I could tell that her husband was pleased to see us leave. We went downstairs and met a man I had not seen before. He had only three or four teeth, all black. I did not like him. He led us on a walk of about an hour to a garage where there were lorries parked. There was a padlock on the gate but it had not been clicked shut and the man opened it with a piece of metal. We went in. He lifted up a flap of tarpaulin at the back of a lorry and gestured for me to climb in. I did not want to but my mother said it was all right so I went up. It was very dark under the tarpaulin but I could tell there was some sort of machinery in boxes. Then my mother climbed up and then the man. My mother asked him how long it would be and he said, we go when we go. It was the most he had spoken and to my surprise he had a Fujianese accent. I thought it would be a long wait but in a short time we heard someone walk along past the side of the lorry and hawk and spit and then get into the cab. The engine turned on and the lorry shook loudly and we moved off.

At first it was noisy and cramped but also more comfortable than the train. That was when we were near Guangzhou and the roads were better. As we drove further the roads became more bumpy and difficult and the boxes began to move about. My mother braced a leg against the boards at the end of the vehicle and pressed her back to the nearest boxes, holding them in place so they did not slip on top of us. She and Aunt Wen had made some food for the journey and after a time she took out some rice parcels and a leg of chicken and gave them to me. The man drank spirit from a bottle he carried on a pouch over his shoulder.

The journey went on for several hours. My mother smiled at me and I saw her teeth in the dark. Then the lorry stopped. I heard the door open and the driver get out and walk away. The man with us moved to the flap at the back and crouched beside the tarpaulin. After a minute he pulled up the cloth and looked out. He got down and gestured for us to follow. When I tried to move I could not. My legs had gone dead. The man swore and got back into the lorry and lifted me onto my feet until the blood was moving again. It hurt. Then we got out. We were in the middle of paddy fields with a little shack like a bus shelter about fifty metres away. That must have been where the driver went. The man bent over and set off on a raised track across the fields, half running. I went behind him and my mother after me. The fields were on slightly different levels with earth walls between them and once we had got two fields away we were no longer in sight of the lorry. The man slowed down and caught his breath. He was gasping. Then we set off across more fields. There was a quarter moon so it was not pitch-black except when clouds covered it. Once or twice we had to stop because of the darkness. We went along like this for some time. Then the man stopped so suddenly that I bumped into him.

'We are here,' he said. 'Now you do what I told you.'

'I remember,' said my mother. But she seemed distrustful.

'This is the place,' the man insisted. My mother waited for a moment and then reached inside her tunic. She felt around and took out what I thought was a piece of string. Then I realised it was the gold necklace. She put it in the man's hand. He seemed to relax.

'No PLA here,' he said. 'Guaranteed. Wire cut. Leave the boards where I told you. Easy route. Remember, Boundary Street. But watch out for the monkeys.' Then he was gone. He did not say goodbye.

'What are the monkeys?' I asked.

'Never mind. He was joking. We must go on now, it will soon be light,' said my mother. She knelt down and squeezed me. She

243

was trembling. She stood up and set off in the direction we had been heading.

We crossed many fields. Sometimes the path would go sideways a little while before returning to the straight direction we had been heading. Once we walked three sides around the square of a paddy. Then there were marshes. We were already very wet so it made no difference. My mother picked her way more slowly. There was a fence, low and made of wire with sharp points all over it, but my mother felt along it and found a place where it had been cut. She held the gap open and I slipped through. I waited as she came after me. She cut herself on the leg but not badly. The water was deeper here but there was a small tree and tied to it my mother found a set of wooden boards nailed together. She helped me climb on to the boards and then walked out into the water. The moon had gone behind the clouds and it was very dark. In a moment she was swimming, kicking hard with her legs as the current took us sideways. She gasped and coughed as some of the water got into her mouth. The river was much colder than I had expected.

'You're a good swimmer, mother,' I said out loud even though she had told me to be quiet. She kicked and coughed. Then she put her feet down for a moment. She could touch the bottom. She rested and then she made a small cry as she began to push again.

'Weeds. I thought I was stuck,' she said. We were at the other bank of the river. I walked up to the low reeds on the far side, while my mother pushed the raft of boards into the reeds and followed me. She crouched. Her chest was going up and down and she was coughing. When she was able to talk she whispered:

'Now we must be very very careful. Until we get beyond the paddies. If I stop you must stop still and not move until I do. If I press my head down, you must lie down and not move or make any sound until I tell you.'

'Is this because of the monkeys?' I asked. I knew it was.

'You must do as I tell you,' she said.

We set out to cross these new fields. There was even less cover than there had been on the other side of the river. Ahead of me there were hills. I felt we could easily be observed from their height. But it was still very dark. Once or twice I lost my footing and my mother put her hand on me to make me lie still as the sound of splashing died away. It was so loud. I could not believe we would not be heard for miles. Then my mother did the same thing and fell flat on her face. She lay still and I thought she had hurt herself. I wanted to come up to her but she made a gesture with her hands for me to stay where I was. So I knew she was all right. She lay there for minutes. Then she slowly straightened up and began to move forward again. A bird took off from a clump of reeds not far in front of us and she stopped. A man stepped out from behind the reeds. He was only feet away. He was a type of man I had not seen before. His face was broad. His arms were long. He wore a kind of cap on his head and carried a gun. He had a long knife in his belt. Without thinking I reached forward and put my hand in my mother's. He did not look like a monkey. He looked like a fighting man. He only stood and stared at us. By now the moon had again come out. The man kept staring at us. I did not know that any person could be so immobile. Then he turned and went away. He made no noise.

We made it to Boundary Street by the middle of the day.

Years later, when I told my grandfather the story of how we came across the border, he said, 'I always did have a soft spot for the Gurkhas.'

Chapter Three

When we first arrived in Hong Kong my mother and I went to stay with her relatives in Mongkok. Their father, a first cousin of my mother, had fled to Hong Kong in 1949. He had been a local official in the Kuomintang. He had a bullet wound to the side of his abdomen where he would sometimes let me put my finger. Later, when I had a scar from a smallpox vaccination, I pretended that too was a bullet wound.

We all lived in one room. The apartment was on the eighth floor of a block. It was very difficult but I was too young to understand. Before long my mother got a job working in a pharmacy and, not long after that, we were given a room of our own. I don't know how we jumped the queue. But my mother's cousin was a big man in the electricians' union and had his old Kuomintang connections and also was on the Residents' Committee. I began to go to school properly at St Mary's. I was very good at mathematics because of my great-aunt's teaching but my Cantonese was not good and people laughed at my accent. So my mother's cousin began to teach me Wing Chun fighting and I got into some fights, which I won. The Fujianese had a reputation of being very tough. At one point I was loosely attached to a group of other Fujianese and things might have become difficult. My mother did not know. But I got a scholarship to senior school and left them behind. The scholarship made my mother very happy.

Because of the Cultural Revolution, I had had no real experience of school. Once I began to win fights, I found that I liked school very much. The teachers were strict but they were consistent and I found that reassuring. My mother was much happier than she had been in Shen Lo. She told me once that when she got to Hong Kong she realised that she had been frightened every moment of her life for the previous five years. I missed living on the sea. I missed the air and the fishing boats. But in every other respect Hong Kong was better. A big family who had two apartments on our floor, the Yips, most of whom had come from

246

Guangzhou ten years before, adopted us and made us feel part of their big family. Yip Xu was a week older than I was and we played together all the time. I helped him with his schoolwork and he let me ride his bicycle. My mother rose in her work until she was managing a branch of her pharmacy in Tsim Sha Tsui. Once she had learned good Cantonese, she began to take English lessons three nights a week.

Two days after Chinese New Year in 1984, my mother came and interrupted me while I was studying. I remember the moment well because I had just bought a Casio pocket calculator with my laisee money for that Chinese New Year. It was the first calculator I had bought with an LCD display. I would be eighteen that year and was preparing for my examinations. My intention was to study electrical engineering at the Chinese University near Sha Tin.

'Ah Man, can I speak with you,' my mother said. I knew this formula: it meant an important subject of general significance rather than a minor discussion or rebuke. I switched the calculator off. 'Do you remember the stories we used to tell you about your grandfather – your father's father?'

'Of course.'

I had grown up hearing about the great love affair, and how he had stayed behind to fight the invading Japanese.

'There is something I have not told you. When you were a child I did not know it. I became aware of it after we had moved to Hong Kong. I could not decide when to tell you so I decided to wait until you were eighteen. I will not say what you should do. But I think it is time for you to know. It is this: your grandfather is still alive. He still lives in Hong Kong.'

'I thought he died fighting the Japanese.'

'That is what the story was, but it is not true.'

She handed me a piece of paper. It said: Tom Stewart, Deep Water Bay Hotel, Deep Water Bay Road, Hong Kong.

'How . . . why . . .?'

'My cousin knew the story. Someone he knew did repair work at this hotel, and mentioned someone, and he recognised the name. It is the same man. He was in prison during the war with the Japanese.'

I did not know what to do. My first thought was that I could

247

never speak to the man. He was nothing to do with me. I felt anger: as if he were to blame for something. But in a few minutes that passed. He had not done anything to me. Then I thought that if I went to see him he would simply refuse to believe I was who I said I was. Anyone from my grandmother's village could tell the same story. I could be an impostor. I could be in search of an inheritance. I would go and see him and he would walk away refusing to acknowledge me. I lay in bed and imagined that. When I woke up in the morning there was an envelope propped up beside my bed. I recognised it. It was the letter my grandmother had written to my grandfather during the war, when she was in China and he was in Hong Kong, and neither of them knew if the other was alive.

I went on the bus to Deep Water Bay to look at the hotel. It was a long low building above the road. I walked up the driveway. A Chinese man in a white uniform was polishing a car. I had no plan and did not know what to do so I turned around. I waited at the bus stop while two buses went past. Then I saw a European man come down the drive and head towards me. He was going in the direction of the beach. He was an old man but still straight. He had white hair and a big nose. He walked quickly and swung his arms. We looked at each other as he walked past. I knew it must be him.

Two weeks later I went back and waited outside the hotel again. I wanted to watch my grandfather and to understand what kind of man he was. But I did not see him. The next day I went back, this time borrowing Xu's new motorcycle. A taxi pulled up at the hotel. My grandfather came out of the hotel and got into it. I followed him to Central where he went to the post office. Then he walked to the Peak Tram and went up the Peak. I left the motorcycle chained up and followed him. I stood at the back of the tram. When he got out he set off to walk around the road at the top of the hill. I started to follow but realised I was much too conspicuous. There was only one way he could go in any case. So I waited by the terminus for him to appear at the other end of the circular walk. I waited for an hour. He went to get a taxi. There was a queue and some Europeans began to cause trouble. They were going to beat my grandfather. I had a fight with them and went away with him in a taxi. Then I told him who I was. What

emember most is that he did not for a second doubt or suspect
ne. He knew it was true. He looked very pale. He kept saying:
'I had no idea.'

My grandfather paid for all my education from the time we met.
He asked us to move in with him, but my mother and I thought it
would be too strange to move from Mongkok to the Deep Water
ay Hotel. Instead he began subsidising our living costs. At first
my mother wanted to resist but he was very firm and asked if she
ould let him do so as a gift to him. He understands face. Then
then I got into the university to study electrical engineering, he
elped with fees, and when my mother was sick for a year and
ad a series of operations, he paid for all that too.

I liked university. I liked the fact that it was out in the New
erritories. I liked the feeling that people could think and talk
out anything they wanted. By now I thought of myself as a
ong Konger, and I was proud of Hong Kong. There was more
olitics than I had expected. There was a club where I kept up my
'ing Chung. There were many girls.

In the first week of the electrical engineering course, I met my
ture business partner, Lee Wong-Ho. We sat beside each other
a lecture. Afterwards we began to talk. He was more definite
an other people our age. He was very confident. His parents
ad fled from Guangzhou in the fifties. We kept talking after the
cture and on the MTR home. He lived not far away from me in
ongkok. We were excited by the fact that we got on so well. As
e parted on the street he said:

'Let's go into business together and make a hundred million
3 dollars.'

'Okay,' I said.

Ah Wong had many friends. He had more friends than I did
en though I was more sociable. People were drawn to his cer-
nty. One of them was a girl called Sha Lin-Xu who was study-
g dentistry. Her English name was Lily. After a few meetings in
oups, I asked her to go and see a film with me. She refused and
e did not speak properly for almost three years.

'I thought you were stupid,' my wife told me later. 'Always
aking jokes in your Fujianese accent, so proud of yourself for
ways being in the top three of your class.'

'You thought I was stupid because I used to come top in the class?'

She made a dismissive face and a gesture of sweeping something away with both hands. I did not pursue the question.

Wong and I had an understanding that after university we would go into business together. But first we would need to spend time working to make money and to see what opportunities there were. I went for interviews before my final term and got a job as an engineer with a company that made industrial boilers. It was a family firm and chances for promotion were limited but it was an opportunity to learn. This was in summer 1989. Wong got a job working for an architect who specialised in converting and fitting out restaurants.

The day after he told me he had the job we heard the news of the Tiananmen massacre. Everyone was shocked and angry. The atmosphere of Hong Kong changed. We went on a protest. We marched through Central. There were banners accusing the Communist Party leaders of murder. There were rumours about how many hundreds of people had been killed. Most of the victims were students our own age. Some of the people in the square were distantly known as friends of friends or relatives. Sha Li Xu came with us. She was crying and chanting slogans at the same time. I was so caught up in the feelings about Tiananmen that I forgot to try to impress her. In the demonstration we were separated from the rest of our group and I went home on the MTR with her. There were other demonstrations in the next few days and we met several more times.

'She likes you,' Wong told me one night after the three of us had been to see a film together.

'She doesn't seem to,' I said, though I hoped I was wrong.

'I've known her since she was three years old and I can tell.'

So the next day I called her up and asked her on our first proper date, just the two of us, not even a demonstration to go to. She said yes. We went to see a Jackie Chan film. We were married six months later.

I know that my grandfather read my grandmother's letter because I asked him and he told me. But he never told me what it said.

Chapter Four

We bought the house in Mosman and moved to Sydney in 1996, four years ago. I felt that with the handover to China coming I should do something about my family's security. Australia has a program of accelerated immigration for prospective citizens with sufficiently high net capital. To qualify for Australian citizenship it is necessary to spend two years in the country: seven hundred and thirty days. It is not necessary for these days to be consecutive. My mother, wife, daughter, father-in-law and mother-in-law all qualified within seven hundred and thirty days of their arrival in Sydney and are now all Australian citizens. I had so far accumulated a hundred and eighty-four days towards the necessary total. It was a source of contention with my wife.

'By the time you have spent two years here you will be three hundred years old,' she said.

'My work will not always make these demands on me,' I said.

'You are a spaceman. Live on aeroplanes. Always breathing that bad air.'

'If I travelled by boat and train, I would be away for much longer.' The argument went on from there.

But my wife was right. I spent too much time travelling. The headquarters of our company were in Hong Kong, where I had an office in Tsim Sha Tsui. There was a small room there, once a cupboard, where I had a bed I sometimes used. When I had more time, and the ferries were convenient, I went to stay with grandfather on Cheung Chau. I worked on my computer on the ferry, and I had a three-band mobile phone which works everywhere I go. My partner also had one. Sometimes he rang me when I was on the ferry and he was at our factory in Ho Chi Minh City. Sometimes he rang me when he was in the office and I was in Shanghai or Sydney. Once I was on the toilet in a hotel in Chengdu in Szechaun province.

Our company was called AP Enterprises. My Chinese name is Lo Man-Wei; my English name is Matthew. My partner, Lee

Wong-Ho, has the English name John. Our company manufac
tures and sells air conditioners. We specialise in industrial-size
solutions for buildings and industrial plants. This is a big growth
area in China, which is the principal focus of our business. W
own a franchise of a German company called Weigen AG. Ou
business plan in the medium term is to concentrate on the indus
trial aspects of air conditioning. Then as China becomes mor
prosperous, we aim to move into the market for personal an
domestic air conditioning. This is an undeveloped area of eno
mous potential. At the time I am describing, our head office wa
in Kowloon, and we had subsidiary factories where the machine
were constructed in Guangzhou, Shanghai, and Ho Chi Min
City. Hong Kong was extremely important to our business as th
legally incorporated basis for our company. There is no compan
law in mainland China so it can be a difficult place to transac
business.

Unfortunately there was a problem with our plan and with ou
company. We were running out of money. In the aftermath of th
Asian crash in 1997 we took the opportunity to expand aggres
sively, confident that the downturn was a temporary one. W
borrowed heavily from banks. We bet the company on rapi
expansion. But expansion was not rapid. The region recovere
more slowly than we expected. In addition, we had problems
our factories in Guangzhou and Ho Chi Minh City. I was facin
the prospect of losing everything which I had worked to buil
up since arriving in Hong Kong as a refugee. It was the mo
difficult time in my life. At night I would have dreams abou
being back in Shen Lo during the Cultural Revolution, with m
mother and wife and daughter, in front of a crowd shoutir
slogans at us.

Chapter Five

'I have to be honest, I don't think Ah Li's lobster is as good as it used to be,' Grandfather said as we walked up the hill to his house on Cheung Chau. We had met in the village and had dinner at the tea house.

'Sometimes it's good, sometimes less good,' I said. 'That was always true.'

'The noodles were good.'

'His noodles are always good.'

Food is one of the interests we have in common.

Grandfather was a little out of breath by the time we got to his house, but he walked up the hill without stopping. His walking has been very good for his health. Also he drinks a lot of tea and coffee, which helps keep him thin. He insists on living by himself even though he is now eighty-seven. He has a girl from the village who helps with the cleaning and cooking.

Grandfather was the first person I ever knew who had money. His way of living influenced me a great deal. His front garden has raked pebbles and a Japanese stone lantern. He keeps it in order himself. Inside the hall there is an umbrella stand. We have a similar one in Sydney and I also have one in the hall of our apartment in London. It rains more in Sydney than it does in London, but the weather in London is less predictable so I use the umbrella more when I am there.

The living space of Grandfather's house is a big room with a dining table at one end and comfortable chairs at the other. When he is on his own my grandfather uses the dining table as his desk. It was covered in a big pile of papers, which I recognised as the book written by a dead friend which he had been trying to have published for many years. One wall of the room is dominated by a window which looks out over the South China Sea. French windows open to a patch of garden at the back. The side wall is given to bookcases. The other two walls are covered in photographs of me and my wife and Mei-Lin and my mother and my wife's parents. A small door leads to the kitchen.

I ask about the manuscript approximately once a year. Any less would show I have no interest. Any more would be to touch too often on a painful subject.

'Any news?' I said.

My grandfather's face changed. He looked away from me as he put his wallet and keys down on a side table. There was a twist to his expression.

'Well, something a bit different. I've had an unsolicited expression of interest and a request to look at the book.'

'But Grandfather! This is excellent news!'

'There's a catch. I can't accept it.'

He was reluctant to talk more.

'I don't understand,' I said.

'It's a new outfit called Hong Kong Heritage. A press. It's part of the Wo empire. I won't have anything to do with it. An editor there heard of the book. It's not so surprising, everyone with half a mind in publishing has been sent the damn thing at least once. So I've been drafting a polite letter telling her to piss off.'

Grandfather will not have any contact with any part of the Wo family's business enterprises. He will not watch their TV station, listen to their radio station, go to films made by the studios they partly own, eat in any of the hotels or restaurants they own, visit shops situated on any of their properties, buy or read anything published by any of the book companies in which they have a stake, or travel on the airline in which they have a share. If the ferries were sold off and the Wos bought them, he would swim to Cheung Chau. Like many other Hong Kong tycoons the Wos gave enormous amounts of money to the British Conservative Party to fight the 1992 general election. I once asked my grandfather, as a joke, if that meant that the British government was another thing that the Wos owned, so that he wouldn't be able to go to Britain until a different government was in office. I thought that was not a bad joke. He walked out of the room. I have a business contact at the Wo company whom I have never been able to use for fear of upsetting my grandfather. The irony is that I don't even know what the source of his grievance with the Wos is, since he refuses to tell me.

'You have been seeking to have your friend's book published for a long time,' I said.

'Not at any price though,' he said. 'Look, this is all history – I don't want it to loom over your life. It's old business of mine. The future is more important than the past. Let's talk about something else. Is Mei-Lin showing any signs of becoming a Methodist yet?'

My daughter is at Mosman Methodist Girls School, so Grandfather jokes that she will grow up to be a Methodist. We talked about her until it was time to go to bed.

My partner called in the morning. I had just had a bowl of congee at a noodle shop. The Chinese say that the poor like congee because it gives them the taste of what it would be like to be rich and the rich like it because it reminds them of when they were poor. I was drinking coffee, a bad Western habit I learned from Grandfather. No one else had yet arrived at work.

'Ah Wong, good morning. You are well? Where are you?' I said.

'Ah Man, hello. I'm at Chek Lap Kok. I couldn't get on a Shanghai to Guangzhou flight, so I've had to take Dragonair here to pick up another flight to Guangzhou. Aeeyah! It leaves in three quarters of an hour. I hope I'm there in time for the meeting. Chan is not capable of measuring his own genitals without help.'

Chan was the son-in-law of a senior Communist Party official whose cooperation was important to our interests in Guangzhou. We had to give Chan a job for *guanxi* reasons. His nickname was Fat Fucking Fool.

'I'm going to Ho Chi Minh City,' I said. 'This afternoon or tomorrow depending on who I can talk to in Germany. Best to arrive with as many answers as possible.'

While we spoke, Min-Ho, the company secretary, came in, nodded, and began sorting through letters at her desk. My wife says Min-Ho is the most smartly dressed person she has ever seen, so much so that she frightens men off.

'They take one look at her and think no, she is too expensive,' my wife says. She once told Min-Ho this and Min-Ho said she didn't care. Her family works in the garment business and almost all her clothes are very high quality fakes. As well as being an efficient secretary, she is an excellent source of advice about shopping for clothes and presents.

At ten past ten, an hour after everybody else, Wilson Chi came in. Wilson is the younger brother of someone I was at technical college with.

He was wearing a baseball cap and dark glasses, even though there was no sun. He was carrying what looked like a Japanese comic book. When he took off his Walkman I could hear the noise of Cantopop. Wilson says his ambition is to earn so much money that he has to work only three months a year.

'You will damage your eyes and be unable to see,' said Min-Ho. Wilson took off his dark glasses.

Wilson's job was to set up a web site to enable the factories to order components directly, customers to check orders, and the Hong Kong office to supervise both sides of the process and manage the supply chain. The Germans are very keen on this idea.

'I was up working till four in the morning,' he said and then, seeing me standing over my desk and realising that meant I might have been there all night, added, 'at home of course.' He held up his laptop case as evidence.

'I need you to check the remote log-on for the server,' I said. 'I'm going to Vietnam and the last time I was there I had trouble getting my email. You said you were going to fix it.'

'If I remember correctly, I think I said the problem was likely to have been with the wiring in the hotel switchboard.'

'I had difficulties at the factory also.'

'There it is very primitive.'

'As long as we both agree that it doesn't work, and that it would be better if it did work, and that it is your job to make it work, we are in perfect harmony.'

Wilson sat at his desk and began unzipping his computer carry-case. I felt remorse at having delivered a too-public rebuke. I find it difficult to talk to Wilson. He is not a natural subordinate, which makes me conscious of not being a natural boss. My partner, by nature a more blunt man than I am, handles him better.

I spent the day dealing with the backlog of matters that had built up since my partner's departure two days before. My partner and I have a rule that whoever is in Hong Kong deals with all the outstanding difficulties, and since one or the other of us is usually travelling, this means that time in the office is usually spent solving problems. As the Americans say, 'Business is one damn thing after another.'

At 6 o'clock only Min-Ho and Wilson were left in the office. I said goodbye to them, took my bag out of the cupboard, and caught the train to Chek Lap Kok. At the Vietnam Airlines counter there was only a short queue.

'Could you tell me what type of plane it is, please?' I asked when it came to my turn.

'Airbus,' said the girl. I gave her my ticket and passport. Vietnam Airlines has some old Russian aeroplanes which often crash. When I went through to the departure lounge I called my grandfather. I explained that I had to go to Ho Chi Minh City.

'I'll call Lily and keep her up to date,' he said.

I almost began to say that I would speak to my wife myself. But the exchange of news was not the main reason my grandfather would call Sydney. He had acquired a family only late in his life and was still like a man with a new toy. After speaking to him I rang Sydney.

'Hello,' said my daughter. Mei-Lin speaks English with an Australian accent. She is six.

'How is my little flower?'

'I came top in a test of drawing and putting words with pictures and the teacher said my tiger was more frightening than a real tiger.'

'Very good. You must have been working very hard.'

'It took five minutes. Beth-Ann asked me to go swimming on the weekend at Avalon but Mummy said maybe and I have to ask you.'

'Of course you can go swimming, dearest. Can I speak to Mummy?'

'You should call from the office, not from the mobile phone,' said my wife when she came on the line. 'It is expensive.'

'I had to get away quickly. I did not want to miss the plane. Why is she still up?'

'She wanted to stay up until you called,' my wife said. 'I said she could.'

In the background I could hear the television.

'What are you watching?'

'Father and Mother are looking at one of their detective programmes. I was studying.'

My wife was a dentist before she had Mei-Lin. Now she was preparing for examinations so that she could qualify to work in Sydney. We wanted to have another baby but she refused to do so until I was at home more.

'Anyway, I am saving money,' I said, 'because if I was not talking to you I would be in the airport shops buying presents.'

'Then I should let you go now,' said my wife. We laughed and hung up. I wandered around Chek Lap Kok, walking quickly to get some exercise. Then my flight was called and I boarded the Airbus 320. It was full. The man next to me tapped figures into a laptop until the cabin doors closed. We took off three quarters of an hour late. I had a window seat and as we banked over the harbour Hong Kong was a black bowl of lights.

Chapter Six

Tan Son Nhat airport is unpleasant. The Vietnamese authorities are frightened of foreigners attempting to smuggle subversive literature and videotapes into their country so they subject all baggage to X-ray examination on arrival. It is a slow process which ensures long queues. On this occasion the man in front of me in the queue for customs was carrying videotapes. It was late before I got to the arrivals hall.

I went with the oldest of the taxi drivers who approached me. Vietnamese roads are dangerous and my theory is that the older a driver is, the more cautious he has been. I showed the driver the hotel's address in Vietnamese characters. He nodded and we set off.

'Business good?' I asked as we headed into Ho Chi Minh City.

'Better than 1998. Still bad,' he said.

At the hotel I gave them my name and they gave me forms to sign. In Vietnam there are always many forms. The room rate was listed as a hundred US dollars. I said:

'The price we were given was forty dollars.'

'This is our business concession rate,' said the girl. I took the confirmation fax from my bag and showed it to her. She typed out another form and gave it to me without a word. The price listed was now forty dollars. 'So sorry,' she said with a smile. She was very pretty. She rang a bell on the counter and a man came and carried my bag up to my room. I tipped him in dongs. It was too late to call Sydney so I went straight to bed.

My grandfather taught me to make coffee, and the coffee he and I make is the best in Asia. After that the second best is the coffee in Vietnam. It is one of the things I like about Ho Chi Minh City. The next morning I had coffee at the hotel and then I went to the factory in Cholon. The trip took half an hour and we almost had three accidents. There are more cyclists even than in China and none of them ever stops at an intersection. I made the taxi driver drop me in Hung Vuong Boulevard around the corner from our factory. One of the side doors was open. I stepped in and went up the stairs immediately to the left, leading up to Nguyen's office. From the stairs I could look down on most of the floor space. It was busy but not too busy.

I smiled at Nguyen's secretary, Mah, and went straight through to his office. I could see him through the glass. He was seated at his desk wearing a baseball cap with his head down over some papers. He looked up as I went in and for a moment there was a look of horror on his face. Then he made a big smile.

'The sun has risen twice today,' he said. That is a Chinese proverb on meeting a friend unexpectedly. He said it in English. He speaks excellent English, nearly as good as mine. 'How are you? And please: how is your family – is Lily well, and Mei-Lin?'

'Yes, thank you – and your son? His examinations are over now?'

'Top in his class,' said Nguyen, straightening slightly. He made a gesture over my head at Mah and she came into the room. 'I have forgotten my manners. Tea?'

'Thank you.'

His look at her, I thought, contained some other instruction. As she left he bent and began to take some folded papers out of a low desk drawer.

'Can I interest you in our latest operating figures?' he asked.

The reason for my being in Vietnam was as follows: we were losing money on our factory there, with costs considerably greater than revenue, and had begun to suspect that a fraud was taking place. The nature of the fraud was likely to involve the inclusion on the payroll of workers who did not exist. I had come to Ho Chi Minh City to assess the evidence about this. The difficulty was that our operation was a joint venture with former members of the Ho Chi Minh City government, who provided capital and also help with the legalities of permits and permissions. If there was fraud it was likely that they would be involved in it. The further difficulty was that the rule of law in Vietnam is not strong and it would be hard to prove fraud or to prosecute it. By now we were in what the Americans call a lose–lose situation. If there was fraud it would be a big problem but if our factory was losing money for other reasons it would also be a big problem.

It was not a fruitful day. I did not achieve my primary purpose. Nguyen kept me in his office and my only opportunity to look at the factory was when we went to lunch. I asked to take a walking tour around the floor. There did not to seem to be as many people engaged in machine assembly as I would expect. All I learnt was that the figures were indeed bad. The latest numbers were even worse than the data we had most recently seen in Hong Kong.

'Our quality is high but so are our prices,' said Nguyen. 'Western machines.' He gestured at the overhead air-conditioning unit above his desk. It was not one of our own models. For a second I thought: I must not say anything about labour costs. He will realise I am thinking about the size of the workforce and perhaps that I suspect fraud. Then I thought: no, it is too obvious. If I avoid the subject he will realise that I have suspicions. So I shrugged and said:

'But if you could make them more cheaply . . .'

He smiled and said:

'The owners of a business always think costs are too high.'

I smiled back:

'And the owners are always right.'

I snapped my folder shut and stood up. We were finished for the day. I went back to the hotel to tidy up before dinner. Nguyen had insisted on taking me out. I knew this would happen. He had called his cousin who owned a restaurant near the Continental Hotel. It was a good restaurant and the meal would be good.

I had a shower. The water was not quite warm enough. I changed back into my work suit and then thought that was too formal, so put on a short-sleeved shirt and trousers instead. This is a shirt that makes my wife giggle because of its bright pattern so I wear it only when I am away from home. Because I had half an hour to spare I walked to the restaurant. The streets were crowded and lively and colourful. I was glad to be going somewhere. I find that the end of the day when I am travelling is often lonely.

I was early, but Nguyen and his wife were already there. He was sitting at a round table, laid for six, in the middle of the room. They stood up and we greeted each other. The others arrived while we were still on our feet. Thieu was a senior figure in the bureaucracy of the city and Lau worked for the Ministry of the

Interior. They were both senior Party members. Thieu brought his wife, who was related to Nguyen's wife. They were both very beautiful and smartly dressed.

Nguyen spoke to his cousin and ordered the food. Everybody drank beer. The atmosphere was very friendly. We spoke English. I talked to Nguyen's wife about their son. We discussed the economy. I talked about Sydney and about astronaut syndrome and everyone pretended to have sympathy.

'People say the Internet this, the Internet that,' I said. 'It's going to change the face of business. No one will have to go anywhere, everything will be virtual, everything will be video conferencing. When? Always next year, next decade. Everything is always about the future: next week, sometime, never. Okay, it sounds good. No more flying for me. No more excellent food in Ho Chi Minh City – what excuse would I have to tell my wife? I get to live with my family and do business. But when?'

The waiter brought bowls of phô. It was a modern version, like the consommé my grandfather makes when he feels unwell. The bean sprouts and chillies and mint were served on a little white plate to the side. I always think Vietnamese food tastes clear and light. When the waiter went away Thieu lent forwards. I could feel discomfort behind his smile. His eyes were bright.

'I will tell you something. The Internet is not a friend of Vietnamese people.'

'Surely it is merely a tool, capable of good and bad use like any other instrument,' I said.

Nguyen said something in Vietnamese. He turned to me.

'I was explaining "instrument",' he said. Thieu spoke rapidly back to him in Vietnamese. 'He says, the Internet is full of lies. It is like a river, a torrent of lies. Many falsehoods about Vietnam. He says the Party has as much of a duty to protect the people from lies as it does to keep excrement out of people's drinking water.'

'Not very different from television, I think,' said Lau, older and calmer than his friend. 'It is what is broadcast that is important.'

'Television can be in our control,' said Thieu. 'Internet very difficult to control.'

A year or two before, the government had closed all the cybercafés in the country and confiscated all their computer equipment. I argued with Thieu about this for a while, until the waiter arrived to take our plates. Mrs Thieu asked a question about what presents I was going to take my wife and daughter, and the conversation changed. The rest of the evening was calm. I drank more beer than I had intended to.

After dinner, I walked back to the hotel. It was much cooler but no less humid and only a little less busy. There were still many people on bicycles. A small group of Western backpackers stood around one of them who was vomiting into a gutter. I could smell the alcohol as I walked past them. A prostitute accosted me in Putonghua. I said, no thank you. The walk made me feel a little drunk.

When I got back to the hotel I checked my email. There was a one-word message from my partner.

'Well?'

I typed back:

'Don't know yet. Plan B.'

In the morning Nguyen and I walked to the factory together. Several competing noodle carts across the street were already busy. The smell made my mouth fill with saliva. We worked over papers and orders while his secretary brought many cups of tea.

'Where would you like to go for lunch?' Nguyen asked at 1 o'clock. I pushed my chair back from the desk and stretched.

'I'm not so hungry,' I said. 'But I'm feeling a little sleepy and thick in the head from the jet lag and the beer last night. I think the best thing is if I go for a walk. Then maybe when I come back I will be able to keep up with you.'

'Well, I don't like to miss a meal if I can help it,' he said, making a joke of cupping his stomach in both hands. It was true, he had begun to put on some weight. But he was still handsome. I did some more stretching and yawning as I headed for the door.

When I got out of the factory I walked around two corners, looked left and right, and stopped a passing cyclo.

'Thien Hau Pagoda, please,' I said.

The driver was young and fit and we got there quickly. There was a crowd of incense sellers and pilgrims outside the temple gates. I went in and looked around. Then I saw him: a Chinese man in his sixties standing beside one of the giant urns in the main pagoda. He was wearing thick glasses. He nodded at me. I approached him and we shook hands. We walked slowly around the courtyard together.

'Ah Fu,' I said. 'It is good to see you again.'

'I like to come here to thank Thien Hau,' he said. 'I came with my brother the night before he left Vietnam.'

Thien Hau is the goddess of the sea. In Hong Kong there is a big festival for her. Many of the boat people came to this temple to pray before they left Vietnam.

'Thien Hau looked after him well,' I said. Fu turned to me. His glasses made his eyes look bigger. His eyes were rimmed with red.

'I was scared to leave,' he said. 'I should have been scared to stay behind.'

Fu's brother had left after the North won the civil war. He was a businessman who had good contacts with the government of the South. Because of that and because of being Chinese he was in a vulnerable position. Fu himself had been a university teacher and he had stayed. He lost his post soon afterwards and had lived on menial work ever since. His brother got to Hong Kong, where he spent three years in a refugee camp. When he was released he found work in a hardware business and eventually came to know my partner's father. They played mah-jong together. My partner's father said Fu's brother had the best memory for mah-jong of anyone he had ever met.

'Shall we go outside?' Fu said.

There were many people outside. We stood beside the temple wall. Fu took out a spiral-bound notebook covered in beautiful tiny Chinese characters, a real scholar's handwriting.

'It is obviously difficult to give exact figures. There is much different business, men come and go, there are deliveries. But I observed the traffic in and out of the factory during working hours for more than two weeks and I would put the likely range of employees present during that period – which obviously does not allow for longer illnesses or vacations, both of which I suspect are unlikely but that is your consideration – I would put the likely range as being between seventy-five and eighty-five with an absolute upper limit of ninety. That is the figure for everyone going into the building on non-delivery work, including temporary workers and the like.'

He held out the notebook, offering documentary proof. I handed him an envelope from my jacket pocket. Five hundred US dollars was objectively too great a payment. But Fu both needed and deserved it. He took the money as if it was an insult.

'Thank you, that is excellent. How . . .?' I asked.

Fu was too proud to smile. 'Noodle cart,' he said.

I hailed another cyclo outside the pagoda and headed back to the factory.

That evening I wrote an email to my partner:

'It is as we feared but worse. The real number of workers is at best ninety, more likely eighty. Payroll as you know is 135. When one of us goes there, Nguyen must use temporary employees. The eighty he has must work very hard to achieve the levels of productivity that they do. But that is not relevant. We have a big, big problem.'

Chapter Seven

The next day I flew back to Chek Lap Kok and caught a connection to Baiyun airport in Guangzhou. The flight was very bumpy. Then I took a taxi to an apartment belonging to a cousin of Ah Wong's called Lai, as I often did. He knew I was coming. It was restful to use his apartment because he was almost always out. I let myself in. In the hallway he had two posters, one of Bill Gates and one of Mao Zedong.

A girl was sitting at the table in Lai 's kitchen. When she saw it was me she looked disappointed.

'I'm Man. I'm his cousin Wong's business partner.'

'I'm Jade,' she said. 'I'm supposed to be his girlfriend.'

'You must be a model or an actress. I can tell from just looking at you.'

She gave a little pout. She was pleased.

'I have done some modelling.'

We sat down to watch television together. There was a historical soap opera about the Opium Wars. I had bought Lai a bottle of Chivas from the duty free at Chek Lap Kok. We drank some of it. At half past eleven, just as I was going to bed, Lai arrived. Lai is an engineer who worked for one of the big factories pirating Microsoft software. The factory specialised in Windows NT and 2000, which they customised and supported for individual businesses. It was a brilliant idea. Lai often said their support was better than Microsoft's. The business was owned by the People's Liberation Army.

'So sorry, so sorry,' he said to Jade. 'Big crisis at work. I called but your mobile was switched off. I didn't know where you'd be.' He tried to be cheerful but I could see he knew he was in trouble. Jade took her telephone out of her tiny expensive-looking hand bag. It was on and working. I said goodnight and immediately went to bed. For about half an hour, I could hear them arguing and then the door slammed as she went out.

I never sleep well in Guangzhou. The city feels too busy. I wok early and lay in bed. I could hear Lai moving about. He sleeps only at weekends. I tried to stay in bed longer but I couldn't, so I got up. Lai was eating congee. He was depressed.

'I spent a hundred yuan last night. Perfume. Dinner. Nightclub. A hundred fucking yuan. Do I get inside her pants? No. Do I lose the girlfriend I already have? Yes. Fuck. What's the matter with me? You tell me, Spaceman.'

That is Lai's nickname for me. I suspect, behind my back, some of the others in the office also use it.

'Maybe you are too ugly.'

He tilted his head from side to side and looked at his reflection in the window. Across the compound was another new apartment block with laundry hanging from many of the windows.

'No, it can't be that.'

'Too poor?'

'Definitely not that.'

'Too stupid?'

'No, and in any case women don't mind.'

'Maybe she's the kept mistress of a rich businessman in Hong Kong and was too ashamed to tell you.'

He clicked his fingers and spun round from the window where he had still been looking at his reflection.

'I knew you'd work it out.'

He sat on a stool beside the kitchen counter and sighed.

'Aeeyah. Maybe she'll have me back. It's all so tiring. Maybe I should get married. How's the family?'

'All fine.'

'Going to see the Fat Fucking Fool?'

'No, I am in Guangzhou for pleasure, because I enjoy the company of its polite, calm, philosophically minded inhabitants, temperate climate, slow pace of movement, and healthy lifestyle.'

We left for work. Lai gave me a lift on the back of his motorbike. It is a BMW. When Wong and I set up AP Enterprises we tried to hire Lai to come and work for us but he said that although we would pay him more than he earned in China, his standard of living would be much higher in Guangzhou. We used his version of Windows NT at our office. We paid him cash, in US dollars.

*

Chan's father-in-law was the second most powerful man in the Party in Guangzhou. The whole company might already have gone under if it were not for the contract we had won with his help. It was a contract to supply air conditioners to a new office block being built for a mixture of Party functionaries and city officials down near the riverfront. The deal was worth a million US dollars and we had paid about two hundred thousand in sweeteners to win it. That was cheap. We needed Chan's father-in-law. Unfortunately, this meant we needed Chan also.

I spent as much of the day as possible touring the factory. The deputy foreman took me around. He was a fifty-year-old Cantonese man who was missing the little finger on his left hand from an industrial accident. The factory worked well because he and the foreman ran it.

I did not eat all day because I knew we would be having dinner. Some contact of Chan's in the local Party or city administration would come out with us. This always happened. Because it was not his money Chan would order much too much food. The kitchen staff had the leftovers and he got credit at the restaurant for subsequent meals. It was the system.

At 6 o'clock, rubbing his hands, Chan came into the small office where I was working. He took a bottle of brandy and two glasses out of a cupboard.

'Very good, very good,' he said. 'A good day's work. Time for some refreshment.'

I accepted the drink but did not take any of it. Chan drinks more than most Cantonese. It would be a long night. I felt homesick.

'Wan Guo has a new Mercedes,' Chan said. I had no idea who he was talking about. 'Aeeyah! Sixty thousand American dollars! Probably the same again for the shipping and import licence! An SL. CD, air conditioning, every extra you can think of. He says the best thing about it is that it makes his girlfriend twice as active in bed because she is so worried about losing him to another woman! The man who sold it to him . . .'

Chan talked a lot more. I blocked my ears but kept him going with grunts and nods and by repeating the last words he had said in the form of a question.

'Went to Shanghai?' I asked.

'Aceyah, took two prostitutes and asked for a suite at the Hyatt. The man at the desk said . . .'

There was a slim chance Chan's father-in-law might be present at dinner. If so the evening might be worthwhile. I could feel him out on our prospects and ask about any large upcoming city contracts. If he wasn't there, the occasion would be pure *guanxi* maintenance.

'. . . which is why I'm so excited, I think he could be a very important contact for us,' Chan eventually concluded. He seemed to think he had been talking towards a conclusion. I tried to remember what he had been saying. Something about some spoilt little emperor, the only son of somebody or other.

'Remind me who his father is again?'

Chan was incredulous.

'Only the Party boss of the whole of Guangdong province and the Special Economic Zone!'

The chance that anything useful would come through contact with this man's son was zero. People are full of fantasies about how to do business in China. The key is that you must find people with power and deal directly with them and be clear about everything and be prepared to pay.

Chan drank brandy and talked for an hour and a half. Then we took a taxi to a restaurant. He had a new Toyota Jeep, which he described and praised at some length. Then he told me about the restaurant.

'The chef trained with Deng Xiaoping's chef. Szechuanese. Spicy food! But very good! Ingredients very fresh!'

The restaurant was in a new hotel, built with Japanese money but run by Chinese managers. We had a private room. There were mirrors on the walls and a revolving mirrored ball on the ceiling. The factory foreman was there, looking clean and scrubbed. I sat next to him. Friends of Chan's joined us. They were all princes and princesses, the children of people who had power. One wore dark glasses. There were two or three people from the local Party hierarchy. One of them, Xiang, I had met before. He was wearing a Party membership button on what looked like an expensive Western jacket. He had a small scar over one eyebrow.

There was a lot of food. It is difficult to get good Szechuanese cooking and I enjoyed the meal more than I thought I would. There was a delicious hot-and-sour soup thickened with chicken's blood.

'I was not sure about your Tung,' one of the Party members said. 'He has an unintelligent face. But he did well when he killed all the chickens.'

There was a scare in Hong Kong in 1997, after reunification, when a chicken virus crossed over to the human population. The Government killed every chicken in the territory and the disease went away.

'I haven't eaten half-done chicken since,' I said. That is chicken served bloody and half cooked.

'Ah, but it's good though,' said Chan, who was putting a bone down on the edge of his bowl with his fingers. His lips had a sheen of grease.

There were many courses. As a concession to Cantonese tastes the meal ended with a steamed fish, a grouper. The superstition is that the fish is not turned over, because if it is, a fisherman drowns. I could see Chan looking sadly at the uneaten portion of the grouper. All the others were so full they could hardly smoke.

Chan stood up. He rubbed his hands again.

'That's the hard part of the evening over,' he said. 'Now who wants some fun?'

About half of the group excused themselves. I said goodbye to the foreman.

'I don't think I'm going to eat again this week,' he said. He had the hiccups.

Most of the Party members went home but Xiang said he would come to the nightclub. Most of the princelings said they would come too. Taxis arrived and we got in. The man in dark glasses had still not taken them off.

The nightclub was called Shanghai Palace. The Chairman of the Communist Party, Jiang Zemin, is from Shanghai, so everything about the city is fashionable in China, even in the south. The nightclub had bright coloured lights inside.

'Fibre optics,' said Xiang. 'Expensive.'

Whenever I go to Guangzhou I think of my first visit there in 1974 on our way to Hong Kong. Then it seemed so colourless.

Now there are colours and bright lights everwhere. You can buy anything you want.

We sat at a table. Girls brought drinks. A band was playing Cantopop so loud that no one could talk. Chan looked flushed and sweaty from the meal. But he was content. Xiang had a faint smile that could have been a sneer. He had taken his jacket off and hung it on the back of the chair.

Two men began to argue at a table behind us, accusing each other of something. Their women tried to quieten them down. They only got angrier. Then one of them hit the other. But it was a bad punch and struck high on the temple. The man who had been punched dived over the table. He landed on top of his opponent. It was unscientific but effective because he had a big weight advantage. The table was made of glass, and it overturned and smashed. Three or four of the staff arrived and dragged the men apart before throwing them out. The women followed, trying to look defiant. The staff came back in and started to sweep up. The band kept on playing. By the time the song finished the mess was gone.

'Lucky there were no Public Security Bureau here,' I said.

'This nightclub is owned by the PSB,' said Xiang with his smile-sneer.

After two more songs, the band took a break. My ears were ringing. I would stay for one more set of songs and then I could go. The others began talking among themselves. Xiang turned to Chan.

'So how is your wife's father enjoying his retirement?' he asked.

I froze. Chan, nodding and smoking, said.

'Classical literature. Fishing. Gardening. He loves it.'

'He is a cultured gentleman,' Xiang said. He glanced at me. It would be a big loss of face to admit I did not know about this. But I had no choice. I said to Chan:

'Your father-in-law has retired?'

The Fat Fucking Fool was looking beyond me, towards the bar.

'Tired of all the, you know, work. The politics. Factions. Spends most of his time with his grandchildren. He's much happier. It's great.'

Xiang said to me:

'There have been some changes in the Party in Guangzhou. You know how it is. Modernisation. Different people.'

I said: 'And might there be a way of getting to know these people?' I didn't even pretend to spare Chan's feelings.

'Of course. But they are very very busy. Difficult to get access to. You know how it is.'

We changed the subject. The band came back and played another set. When they finished I said my goodbyes and left. I made sure I took Xiang's card. Chan was drunk and happy.

'A good night!' he said. He had a girl sitting on his lap. No doubt she too would end up on the company's bill.

When I got back to Lai's flat, it was past midnight. He was still out. I called Wong on my mobile phone. He was out too, so I left a message.

'Partner,' I said, 'I have good reason to believe that we are fucked.'

Lai still wasn't there in the morning. Either he was doing a big push at work or he had got lucky with a girl.

It took me two days to get Xiang on the phone.

'Please excuse my elusive behaviour,' he told me. 'My boss has had me rushing around Guangzhou looking at building sites. I've barely had time to go to the bathroom. So sorry. And after such an enjoyable evening.'

I had not noticed previously because Xiang spoke perfect Cantonese, but over the telephone I could hear a faint Shanghai accent. That explained his nice manners. It explained other things too. We made an appointment to meet the following day. I offered to buy him dinner but he declined. He was polite.

Lai came home that evening. I was waiting for him.

'Chan's father-in-law is out. I found out two nights ago. It was a fucking ambush. How come you didn't tell me?'

He put his laptop on the table. He looked tired from work rather than from sex. He said:

'What?'

'Chan's father-in-law. Our man. He's out. Retired. Finished. Fucked. Who cares? Same thing. We're employing the Fat Fucking Fool for no reason. The joke's on us.'

Lai reached into the fridge and took out a Tsingtao. He opened it and drank.

'Well, they sure kept that quiet. So who's in? Who are the new people?'

'Not sure. I'm seeing someone. Someone called Xiang. Maybe Shanghainese.'

He made a face that said this was not good news. He said:

'Sounds expensive.'

'I hope you don't mind my excusing myself from your kind dinner invitation,' said Xiang. 'But so many dealings in the old-fashioned Chinese way happened over big, elaborate, costly meals. It slows everything down. And it makes us fat. It is a dissipation of money and energy. In the new China we need new ways of doing business. I trust it wasn't too much trouble to drag yourself all the way out here?'

We met at a building site on the west side of Guangzhou, over the bridge past Liwan Park. A steel-framed building was under construction, and the bamboo scaffolding was following it upwards. It was a grey, wet, humid Guangzhou afternoon. This time we were speaking Putonghua.

'Not at all. I agree. We must all take China forward. This will be the Chinese century, combining new energies and old strengths.'

None of this meant anything except that there was a change in faction in the city. I was simply showing that I was aware of it too. Much more important was the fact that Xiang had made me come to meet him here, to show that he had power. The foreman had been talking to him when I arrived. I could not overhear, but the man's attitude was very respectful.

We walked around the new building's patch of land while we talked. For a while we exchanged mentions of people we knew in the Party hierarchy in Guangzhou. It went badly. Many of my names were unknown to him or had recently retired. There had been what in the old days would have been a purge. Without making me lose face he made this plain. Then we talked about the general situation in Guangzhou, and about the atmosphere in the Special Economic Zones. Then he got to the point.

'There is a big competition coming. Shanghai wants to be the most important city in China again. As the adopted son of the South, I say in all honesty that this will be difficult to resist. The fight will be hard, very hard. We in Guangzhou must be as competitive, as ruthless as we can.'

'It's all part of the process by which Guangzhou is taking over the rest of China. Reverse takeover,' I said. This was supposed to be partly a joke.

'The old way of doing things had many virtues. Solidity, consistency. *Guanxi*. Slow and steady. Inefficient but reliable. "No stones turn into bread." That is a saying of Chairman Mao. But perhaps that is what we need to do in China. We need to turn stones into bread, to press ahead. The world is changing very quickly. One point two billion people are Chinese. Slow, gradual change will not work. We need a revolutionary transformation in all practices.'

'I agree, of course.'

'The Party here is – Guangzhou is an important city for the revolution. Many crucial things transpired here. Much happened here before anywhere else. A new world was born. Perhaps there would have been no revolution without Guangzhou. But things have become a little entrenched. People too. Some changes are needed. A spring cleaning. A fresh approach. New faces for a new era. You understand?'

'Fully.'

'In the process of becoming more competitive, a new city administration is requiring all existing contracts which have not advanced beyond a certain point to be resubmitted for tender. All part of the big anti-corruption, pro-efficiency drive. Start again with a clean blackboard. Open things up. Open up the hood and look at the engine. Fix things! This will of course have a disrupting effect on existing relationships. Some things that were tied together may become untied. Things that people believed were done may prove to be unfinished. Races that were finished will be run again. A new beginning all across the city.'

He gave me a moment. I felt horror. The future of our company depended on the contract to fit air conditioners in the new city-administration building. If it was resubmitted to tender we would probably lose. There are no real contracts in China, only relationships, and ours were now worthless. I said:

'It sounds like a recipe for chaos.'

Xiang smiled.

'Yes, that is what it could easily become. A step backward. A formula to freeze Guangzhou in place. In the circumstances, the new city authorities are prepared to exempt some especially important contracts from the process of resubmission and re-evaluation. In cases where the work is too important.'

'The city authority's own building must be one of those cases.'

'It would seem possible.'

'And the nature of the formalities to be undergone . . .'

'Similar to last time.'

'Last time was an arduous and expensive process.'

'And Guangzhou has grown so much more important since then. At least twice as important.'

I could not believe my ears. Double the bribe we paid last time.

'So important that news of activities here has been known to reach ears in Beijing.'

He shrugged. My threat had no force, and he knew it.

'The mountains are high, the Emperor is far away,' he said in his Shanghai-accented Cantonese.

The next morning I felt depressed. I said goodbye to Lai, went to the factory and worked. Then I took the train from Guangzhou to Kowloon. It takes three hours. Once you allow for time to travel to the airport, waiting time, the time they build in for delays, other formalities, it's about the same as flying. I could use the other half of my air ticket some other time.

One reason I sometimes take the train is because it covers the same journey I made with my mother when I was eight. She likes it for the same reason. The first time we went back together, in the mid-eighties, Shenzen was starting to shoot up exactly where we had struggled through the paddy fields. She held my hand and I could see in her reflection that there were tears in her eyes. Now Shenzen is a city. Many skyscrapers there are taller than buildings in Hong Kong. When something breaks or falls down, they blame shoddy builders from over the border. Also, many Hong Kong businessmen keep mistresses in Shenzen.

It was dark by the time we came within sight of the new city. It is impossible to say what it is like to see a whole city existing in a place where there used to be nothing.

All the way to Hong Kong I thought about what would happened if we lost the Guangzhou contract. AP Enterprises would collapse. We would go into receivership. I would lose all the money my grandfather had built up and would put my family's security into question. It would be like going back to where we started. No one would say anything reproachful, not even my wife. That would make it worse.

The railway station is about fifteen minutes' walk from our office. It was too late to take a ferry home and in any case I was too tired. I love my grandfather but he is always so pleased to see me that it demands effort on my part. I had a plate of noodles and wind-dried meats at the Xailung Noodle Bar. The proprietor, Yun, insisted that I have some special tea.

'You are too tired,' he said. He could see my bag on the floor and my laptop case on the stool beside me. 'This tea is cleansing and strengthening. Very good for you.'

I felt fat and unhealthy. Travelling often has that effect on me. I needed to do more walking and drink more tea. After the noodles I bought three newspapers. One of the Chinese papers was part of the Wo empire. Like all Wo's other papers, this had switched from being pro-British to pro-Beijing in the mid-nineties, and had stayed that way. The other was the *Apple Daily*. This would contain the opposite version of the same events. I also bought a copy of the *Herald Tribune*. My plan was to read myself to sleep with current affairs.

On the stairs up to our offices I noticed a light on inside. I put my ear to the door and at first it was silent. Then I thought I could hear low voices. Burglars come to steal our computer equipment was my first idea. Or industrial espionage. I took my mobile phone out of my pocket and punched 999 for the police. I put my finger on the button to transmit. Then I pushed the door open. Only one lamp was on but I could hear sounds from the far side of the office. I moved forward. They were a man's and a woman's voices, coming from the cupboard where I kept my bed. I pulled back the door. Min-Ho and Wilson were on my bed. It was only just big enough to accommodate them. When they saw me, they jerked apart. Min-Ho screamed and reached for the sheet. Wilson covered himself with his hands.

'You're supposed to be in Guangzhou! You're in Guangzhou!' said Min-Ho.

'So sorry, so sorry!' said Wilson.

I held up my arms.

'I can't cope with this,' I said. 'I'll see you in the morning.'

There is a hotel down the street from AP Enterprises. They gave me a room once before when the pipes in the office upstairs burst. The desk clerk remembered me. When I told him I needed a room because I had just found two employees together in my bed he gave me a special price.

Chapter Eight

C. K. Leung is the head of a company called Marler Enterprises.
met him at the funeral of his boss, Mrs Beryl Marler, who was an
old friend of Grandfather's. She was over ninety when she died
and was still going to work every day. Grandfather keeps a pho‐
tograph of her on the mantelpiece. C. K. Leung was one of what
my grandfather called 'Beryl's boys'. He was a young man from
Mongkok whom Beryl noticed and to whom she gave opportuni‐
ties. My grandfather always speaks of him as if he were an eager
young man but he is now a powerful figure who heads a large
construction concern with many projects. In my grandfather'
mind he is a hungry, polite twenty-five-year-old. In reality he is
heavy, difficult man in his middle fifties. My grandfather ha
always encouraged me to use him as a source of advice and
patronage, which has often been embarrassing but also useful.

We made an appointment to meet in the Captain's Bar of the
Mandarin Hotel. Leung is a well-groomed man who wear
expensive clothes and a Rolex and he likes to show he is at ease i
formal settings. It is one of the ways he conveys the distance he
has come from his origins. I feel he particularly likes to do thi
with me because of the connection with my grandfather.

I arrived on time and sat drinking water for thirty minutes
Leung came in walking slowly and stopped for a few words with
the Captain running the bar.

'Very busy at the office,' he told me, 'so sorry.' Without being
asked, a waiter had brought him a glass of what looked like
whisky and a small bottle of Perrier, half of which he poured into
it. Leung looked around the room to see who else was there. He
nodded at a man with rimless spectacles in the corner who was
reading the *Financial Times*.

'How's your grandfather?' he asked.

'He is very well. He asked me to send his best wishes to you
and to your wife and family. I hope they are well?'

Leung had three daughters and no sons, a fact about which he was known to be bitter. He made small talk. Eventually he said:

'So how can I help you?'

I could tell this was his favourite part of the conversation. He liked the feeling of power. I did not mind. I told him about the state of affairs in Guangzhou. He listened without asking questions. He finished his drink and signalled for another. This time I was included in the round as well. He automatically assumed I would be flattered to have the same thing he was having.

'Not good,' he said. 'I heard about changes in Guangzhou. I didn't know you had business there. This man Xiang, is he the real power, or is he connected to it?'

'Connected. He does practical work and he takes messages. A subtle man, a courtier. But not the real power, not yet anyway. He's my age or slightly younger. The real people are being careful. All part of the anti-corruption drive.'

'Those bastards from Shanghai, they'll stop at nothing,' he said. A look of reluctant admiration came over his face. 'You have to admit, it's good, even by mainland standards – being invited to bribe someone as part of an anti-corruption campaign.'

'If it had happened to someone else I would probably agree.'

'Know how much we lost in China last year?'

Marler Enterprises had been slow to invest in the mainland. It now had interests in Shanghai and the special economic zone. I shook my head.

'One hundred million Hong Kong. Easy to get money in, make a splash, feel you're being a big man. Try to get money out – different story. My advice is pay the bribe. It will be cheaper in the long run.'

'We don't have that kind of cash.'

Leung swallowed the last of his drink.

'Then, so sorry, you're fucked,' he said. 'Please give my best wishes to your grandfather.'

I had saved enough air miles for an upgrade on the flight to London. Min-Ho told me this without meeting my eyes. Wilson was being as well mannered as he was capable of being. It was a change for the better. Nobody said anything about what had happened.

I prefer long flights to short ones. It is the only time I have to watch films or read books. Sometimes if there is no one beside me or if the person is asleep I play computer games on my laptop. I like Donkey Kong because it reminds me of Mei-Lin. Or I use a flight simulator and pretend I am flying the aeroplane. On this flight, scheduled to leave at half past midnight, no one was in the seat beside me. I enjoyed that. We had to wait an hour before we took off because the flight time was shorter than usual and there were no slots at Heathrow so early in the morning.

Whenever I arrive at Heathrow I am grateful for the British passport I acquired through my grandfather. There is usually a queue of non-citizens, many of them being subjected to a humiliating interview. On this occasion I went through quickly and caught an underground train just as it was about to leave. The journey to Golders Green took an hour and a half. I like the feeling of arriving in one of our family's three burrows, the only one which exists primarily for my use. Unfortunately I remortgaged the apartment in 1998 so it had become one of the things we would lose if the company collapsed.

I took a shower and changed into some of the clothes I keep at the apartment. The place had a closed smell. The caretaker is supposed to air it once a week but I suspect sometimes does not. I opened a window and breathed the mix of greenery and diesel fumes. Then I called my wife. It was 9 o'clock in the morning in London and seven in the evening in Sydney.

'Wei?'

It was my father-in-law. There was no echo or delay on the line. I hate it when there is.

'How is the venerable t'ai chi master?'

'Son-in-law! How's London?'

'How did you know I am in London?'

'The girls keep your itinerary pinned up beside the telephone.'

I did not know that. I was touched. My daughter came on.

'Hello Father, we had netball today and I was easily the best even though some of the other girls are much taller. And I got the top score in my Pokémon and I am the only person in school who has. And I came top in maths. I've seen a giant koala I want for Christmas. Tracey offered to swap all her Ricky Martin posters but I said no. Will you bring me a minidisc when you come through the airport shop? When will you be home?'

'In a little while.' I wrote 'minidisc' on the pad beside the phone. 'How are your violin lessons?'

'Mrs Howard says I make a noise like a cat being strangled.'

My wife came on the phone. 'You must be tired.'

'I'm fine. I'm just going to the factory. Haggling over prices.'

'Ask for twopence, take a penny,' my wife said, quoting Grandfather. She thought his English phrases were very funny. We talked some more and then said goodbye. The telephone sometimes makes distances seem very great.

A minicab came at 9 o'clock and drove me to Hertfordshire. The arrangement for the Weigen business is complicated. Although the parent company is based near Düsseldorf, their overseas-business subsidiary is based in the UK because labour is relatively cheap, employment regulations are minimal, and English is a useful language for business. The head office is in Hertfordshire. Many of the people who work here, especially the senior managers, are German. The security guards are from the Caribbean and the secretaries are English. The taxi driver was Pakistani with a thick accent I found difficult to understand. The sticker on the underside of the passenger's sunshield said 'Free Kashmir'.

The drive took a little over an hour. All the way it was so green. We came onto the industrial estate and nearly collided with a truck pulling wide on the corner as it headed in the other direction. My driver wound down the window and screamed at the lorry in Urdu.

'Arsehole!' he concluded in English. I paid him and went into reception. The receptionist was reading a magazine while she spoke into a telephone mouthpiece attached to her head. It is always the same woman. I recognise her but she does not recognise me.

'Mr Ho to see Mr Vogel,' I said. She pressed three buttons and spoke into her mouthpiece. 'Mr Vogel's secretary will be down for you shortly,' she told me.

I waited for a few minutes. Beside the metal-and-leather chair was a stack of English magazines about the marital difficulties of famous people. When I sat still I could feel the movement of the aeroplane I had been on for twelve hours.

'Mr Ho!' said Mr Vogel's secretary. She is another English

woman. She has enormous breasts. It is difficult not to stare. Mr Vogel makes jokes about them when he is drunk. We went through a door with a buzzer and into a lift.

'Are you over here long?' she asked.

'A few days only.'

'You must miss your family.'

Today she was wearing a pen on a leather neck ribbon which dangled between her breasts. Vogel was waiting when the lift opened.

'Matthew, my friend! And you look great!'

He was wearing a red jacket. It is easy to tell the German managers from the English because of their clothes. He shook my hand very hard. He is proud of his English.

'Helena, bring us a couple of cups of coffee the way Mr Ho likes it, very strong.'

I like Vogel. He is intelligent and direct. He has worked for Weigen all his life. His wife hates England and is always asking when they will go home to Germany. Sometimes she goes away for a month or two and then he says he is lonelier but also happier. They have no children. When I come to England he makes a point of introducing me to everybody in his office. He did this again. Some of the people remembered me and made small talk. Then we settled down to discuss business.

'There's a coincidence, Tommy Cheung is about too. He's in another part of the office. He'll be here later to say hello. You know him of course?'

Tommy Cheung has the south-east Asia franchise for Weigen's other businesses, the ones which do not involve air conditioning. Their company headquarters are in Singapore. He is a third-generation Chinese–American, educated at Stanford. He wears expensive clothes. At this point, relations between us were cordial but distant.

I explained to Vogel about the discounts we were looking for. We bargained for a little bit. The truth was that they could let us go out of business without suffering too much since the franchise would still have value for them. But it might slow things down. Also it would be a loss of face. They were very proud of their emphasis on relationships. Eventually we got down to discussing figures.

'Five per cent,' said Vogel.

'Ten is the minimum we need.'

'Five is all I can offer. I will have to clear it with Düsseldorf.'

'We may not be in business to claim it in six months' time.'

'Five per cent dated to cover outstanding invoices.'

'Okay. Thank you.'

We shook hands. I wondered what the real maximum figure was and whether I should have held out for seven and a half. As Vogel led me out of his office, Tommy Cheung came in from the left. He looked surprised to see me. We said hello and shook hands. There was small talk.

'Matthew, have you transport arranged? You can share a ride, yes?' said Vogel. I saw a moment of hesitation in Cheung and then he said:

'Sure. I have a driver. I'll drop you.'

'I'm heading for Golders Green. It's near the A41 into central London.'

'Whatever.'

We all went down together in the lift. Cheung and I said good-bye to Vogel. Again he squeezed my hand too hard. Outside an Englishman wearing a tie opened the door of a Mercedes for us. I got in first. Cheung followed.

'Driver, can we please go via –' He gestured at me.

'Golders Green.'

'No problem, sir.'

As the car moved off, Cheung took out a Palm Vx and made a note before slipping it back into his jacket pocket. Then he yawned. He undid the top button of his shirt and sat back.

'When did you get in?' he asked.

'This morning.'

'I got in on Monday. The third day is often the worst, isn't it? I take melatonin but it doesn't seem to work as well as it used to.'

'My wife forbids me to take it. She's a dentist. She says it inter-feres with too many important chemical processes in the brain.'

Cheung looked interested.

'My Dad says the only known cure for jet lag is tiger-penis wine,' he said. 'My daughter said, did he have any idea how that is made? She's nine. He says, of course, they kill a male tiger and cut off his penis. She says, that's disgusting, you're disgusting, someone should cut *your* penis off. Then she slams the door and disappears. Nine! They push all this eco stuff down their throats in the States. It's like a religion. The old man pretended not to mind but he was really upset. What can you do?'

'My daughter is six. I hope she doesn't know what a penis is yet.'

I found it difficult to imagine Cheung as a father. He seemed too young and too smooth. But he looked happy as he talked. He took out a photograph of a buck-toothed girl with pigtails and glasses.

'She's very pretty,' I said. 'Strong character in her face. Lovely eyebrows.'

'She's been driving us crazy about contact lenses. We say, not until you're in your teens. Not until the oculist says it's okay. She has a tantrum. "You're the worst parents in the world. I'm going to run away and hide in the woods and get eaten by a bear and then everyone will know how horrible you are to me!" My father is Chinese, I'm Chinese–American. My daughter is American–Chinese. It's the way it goes. Again, what can you do?'

We talked about our families all the way back to London. When we were past the Underground station he said:

'Wait a minute. I know this place. There's a great Japanese restaurant here. Want to take some lunch?'

I had nothing to do until the next day. I was flattered. I said yes. The driver pulled up and let us out.

'I'll call you,' Cheung told the driver. 'About ninety minutes.'

We went into the restaurant. Two chefs shouted a welcome in Japanese. It was a narrow, crowded place like a noodle bar. But they had a table.

'London's okay for food, but good sushi is hard to get. You been to Japan much? The sushi there is unbelievable. Go to Kyoto, they say, no, don't bother with sushi here, it's too far from the sea. That means forty kilometres.'

I understood: Cheung was not quiet at all. He was shy. When he began talking he talked all the time.

'I feel funny eating raw food,' I said.

'Well, you're more Chinese than I am, I guess. I can't get enough of it.'

'Please order for both of us.'

284

This gave face. He was pleased. When the waiter came he spoke Japanese to her. When a man speaks to a woman in Japanese it always sounds as if he is giving orders.

'I'm impressed,' I said. He shrugged.

'I spent two years in Tokyo after Stanford. I speak it okay. My Chinese completely sucks. In fact my daughter speaks it better than I do. She talks to her grandfather in Putonghua. They do all this ethnic pride stuff in school now.'

The waitress brought us two beers and a plate of raw soybean pods. I was surprised. Cheung did not look or act like a drinker. He picked up his glass:

'Here's to a free afternoon.'

'*Yum chu*,' I said.

'I try to take at least one afternoon or morning completely off when I'm on the road. I don't always make it but I feel better when I do. Catch up on sleep, do some shopping, make family calls, do my email. Otherwise the walls start to close in. Everything gets out of balance.'

The waitress began to bring food. Cheung had ordered spider-crab rolls; maguro sushi; eel teriyaki; a dish of pork stir-fried with baby Japanese asparagus; a dish of tofu stuffed with sushi rice and deep fried. We switched from beer to cold sake. He had flushed bright pink. We talked about business. It was clear that his Weigen franchise was at the moment more lucrative than ours.

'But I think we're going to take a bath in China,' he said. 'The business grows and grows and we still don't make any real money out of it. Plus you never know when they're going to change the rules. It's like you run on the field dressed for basketball and expecting a basketball game and they come out dressed for base-ball and so you think, okay, it's baseball, and then one of them comes over carrying a bat and hits you on the head.' He giggled.

'We have the same problem,' I said. 'In Vietnam too. Good fac-tory, good prospects, growing economy. Everything looks great. Trouble is we're being stolen from and there's nothing we can do.'

'There's never *nothing* you can do,' said Cheung, holding up a sake flask in the direction of the waitress. We were by now the last customers.

'In principle I agree. But –' I explained the situation. Cheung nodded.

'No problem. Sell us the factory.'

'Good joke.'

'Not a joke. We're expanding so fast in Vietnam we're tripping over our own feet. We're looking for a new factory anyway. Cholon is perfect. All we have to do is retool. Weigen will kick in some help with that. We did it before in Singapore. We'll buy out your share for a fair price and give the crooked partners nothing. We'll use the threat of exposure. Hold a gun to their heads. It's perfect. Everybody wins.'

'If we thought it was that easy to expose them we'd do it ourselves.'

Cheung, flushed and drunk, composed himself.

'Look. You know the Americans have these stories. "What do you call a nine-hundred-pound gorilla with a machine gun?" "Sir". These jokes. Well, it's like that. How do you get the attention of a nine-hundred-pound gorilla? You turn up with a twelve-hundred-pound one.'

'I don't think gorillas get that big.'

'They do in Vietnam. We've got one. Our Vietnamese partner is a member of the President's family.'

'I see.'

'It's a good business rule for Asia. When in doubt, get a bigger gorilla.'

We swapped cards. I took the bill.

Chapter Nine

My grandfather will not allow any publication from the Wo empire in his house so I keep the magazine cutting in a plastic folder in the office. When I got back to Hong Kong I took it out.

Astronauts *by* Dawn Stone

You see them in planes all over Asia. For them flying is the same as bus travel, and shares its main defect: it takes too long. They're the people who've spent so much time flying that the last flicker of emotion about travelling at six hundred miles an hour in a pressurised metal tube has been expunged. They're the people who stay on their mobile phones until the last possible second. They're the people who never look up when the flight crew go through the security drill; in fact, they're the people who spend more time in the air than flight crew do themselves. They're the people who spend so much time in the sky that the Chinese have a new nickname for them: astronauts.

When you meet an astronaut, there's an easy way to tell whether they still work for somebody else, or whether they've founded their own companies: if they're spending their own money, you'll find them at the back of the plane, in Economy

Matthew Ho, a young businessman who is planning to make a mega-huge killing in industrial machinery, is one of them . . .

The piece went on to talk about the subject of astronaut syndrome, using me and a number of other young Chinese entrepreneurs as examples. Miss Stone and I had met in a plane, which is why I suppose she thought of me as a possible interviewee. As it happened we had met in business class, thanks to my air miles. But there were many other inaccuracies in the piece also. When it was published in *Asia* magazine I did not recognise a single remark attributed to me.

287

My partner was angry when he saw the article.

'Industrial machinery!' he said. 'What does that mean? Does she know nothing? It's no use as an advertisement for our business! A waste of time! You should send her a bill for the time she wasted! A thousand dollars an hour, minimum!'

Perhaps because he was so angry he had not remembered Dawn Stone's name. But I had. She was often mentioned in the business pages after she moved from journalism to an executive post in the Wo media company. She was much in the news at the time of the handover. Gossip about her said that she was having an affair with her superior, an Englishman called Oss. After the handover he moved to run Wo's entire overseas operations, and not long afterwards Miss Stone became the head of the Wo media company. Wo himself ran the Asian businesses. He was also supervising their expansion into China.

I had kept in touch with Miss Stone through the exchange of Christmas cards, this being one of the ways in which Westerners maintain *guanxi*. I had on one or two occasions been able to help her, when she was still a journalist, with factual information and once with an introduction to some contacts in Guangzhou. Relations between us were cordial, even though I had met Miss Stone in person only on three occasions. The first time was on the flight to Kai Tak from Heathrow. She had never been to Hong Kong before. She seemed young and eager, and she wanted not to seem innocent. At the same time she asked lots of questions. Also she listened to the answers. I liked the fact that she was not a typical expatriate. She was dressed well but not expensively. I could see she was nervous. I talked about my business. At Christmas we sent each other a card.

The next time I saw her was for the interview. It was half a year later. She was much more confident. She had many opinions. Her clothes were more expensive. Her eyes looked different. She behaved like an important person. She was more aware of questions of status and face. But I still got a Christmas card every year.

I next met her in 1998, at a drinks party she gave to celebrate her promotion to head of the media company. The party was in Felix, the restaurant at the top of the Peninsula hotel. The fact that she was able to take it over for an evening was a big sign of her status. There was no mistaking that she was a senior executive of a powerful company. She was wearing a red suit. Her hair looked very expensive. She was still friendly on the outside. But everything about her expressed an interest in power.

'Matthew,' she said when she met me. 'Whatever you do, don't leave without having a pee. Apparently in the gents you wee on a glass window, looking down on the whole of Hong Kong. If it doesn't make you feel like a Master of the Universe, you need to get your serotonin levels checked.'

She turned away to talk to someone else. I didn't know anyone at the party so I didn't stay for long.

The Sydney flight arrived at eight in the morning. At customs, the sniffer dogs stopped an old Chinese woman, a grandmother, who was trying to bring some sausages and wind-dried meats into the country, wrapped inside many plastic bags. She was arguing with the customs officers. She was not going to win the argument.

There was no queue for taxis, which there often is at Sydney airport. It was a beautiful day. I sat in the front of the car.

'Come from far, mate?' asked the driver.

'Hong Kong.'

'Visiting?'

'I live here.'

'Ever been to the sashimi auction at the fish market?'

'No.'

'You'd love it.'

The taxi driver dropped me at Circular Quay. I like to arrive home by ferry.

People were streaming past on their way to work. The fact that they were at the start of their day made me feel tired. I bought a ticket to Mosman and stood at the railings. The harbour has a smell nothing like that of Hong Kong. There were commuter ferries, container ships, private yachts. The ride was short, and we came into Mosman bay. Quite a few Australians got off and began walking in the same direction as me.

I stopped at the little shop beside the quay and bought some mineral water. It is an expensive way of drinking water but it was a way of reminding myself to rehydrate. I walked up the hill. I was glad I had only my hand luggage. Two Australians ran past me.

'. . . the teacher hates it if you are late,' one of them was saying. When I turned the corner and could see our house there were thirty or forty people in the front garden. All of them were standing with their arms in the air. My father-in-law was facing them. He was in the same position. It took me a moment to realise they were doing t'ai chi. I walked up the driveway. My father-in-law smiled and nodded at me but did not stop speaking.

'Now push away! Slow hands! Push away! Repulsing Monkey!'

I let myself in the front door. My wife came out of the kitchen wearing an apron and embraced me.

I said: 'There are many Australians in the front garden doing t'ai chi under the instruction of your father.'

'Yes. I was going to tell you. People observed him doing his exercises. They grew curious. One or two asked him to teach them. It developed from there. Australians are very fond of outdoor pursuits.'

I drank some mineral water. We went into the kitchen where my wife did some small tasks and I stood and watched her. Mei-Lin was at school. Our mothers had gone shopping together. Through the open window I could hear my father-in-law.

'Little baby – give him your finger. Try to take it away. Very difficult! Baby very strong! Baby have good *chi*! No blocks! Grown people many blocks! Weak! Bad *chi*! Must be like little baby! Good *chi*! Strong!'

I always try to stay awake during the day after I have been flying because it helps to adjust the body clock. But I did not want to be too tired when Mei-Lin came home from school so I lay down for an hour after lunch. When my wife woke me I felt as if I was rising up from deep under water. The Australians in the front garden had gone away. I went to collect Mei-Lin and arrived just in time. A flood of small girls was coming out of the gates and being met by their parents.

'Dad!' she said. She ran up to me and gave me a hug.

'You are taller.'

'I know.' Mei-Lin did a comic curtsey. A blonde girl carrying a recorder and holding her mother's hand walked past. The mother smiled at me. She was very elegant.

The girl said: 'See you tomorrow, Mi.'

'See you, Ali. Tell Deb I'm sorry she's feeling crook.'

A frowning Chinese woman walked past with her daughter without looking up. Both of them were wearing sunglasses. They got into a Mercedes. Mei-Lin made a face at the girl's back.

'Who's that?' I asked as we walked away.

'That's Michelle. She's jealous.'

'Because you're prettier?'

'And better at swimming.'

We walked home. That night my wife cooked a special meal. Mei-Lin stayed up late with us and her grandparents. After dinner my wife and I talked. I told her about the difficulties with the business and what it meant.

'So the conclusion is,' I said, 'we are going to go out of business, unless we secure the contract in Guangzhou.'

'And that means we lose all our money, and the house, and the apartment in London, and our citizenship status in Australia is possibly compromised also, because bankruptcy would imply that we did not tell the truth about our solvency.'

'We would lose everything.'

My wife shook her head.

'And you don't know what this whole Wo thing is about?'

'He won't tell me. He just says, "the future is more important than the past."'

She shook her head again. 'Then you had better go and talk to Miss Stone.'

Chapter Ten

I made an appointment to see Miss Stone through her secretary. I
wrote a letter and then called twice. I could tell that there were
layers of importance surrounding her now. Eventually I managed to set a time.

When the day came, I went to her office. The building was a
new block right on the harbour, in Admiralty. It was Wo's latest
development. The bottom five floors were a shopping mall. There
was a hotel in the building. One whole floor was given over to a
swimming pool, with glass walls. Miss Stone's office was on the
fifty-sixth floor. The lift travelled so fast that when its acceleration
slowed there was a brief moment of weightlessness.

Outside the lift a secretary sat at a big desk. There were offices
with glass walls on either side of her. People were working.
Beyond the offices were windows with views to the east and
west. I gave my name. The secretary asked me to wait. I sat on a
red sofa and looked at the magazines and newspapers. There
were many of them from many different countries and it took me
a moment to realise that every one was part of the Wo empire.
There were two television screens above and across from where I
sat. The sound was turned down but I could see they were showing footage from a recent Hollywood film made by the studio Wo
part-owned. The screens showed a car chase followed by explosions.

I waited for about half an hour. Another secretary came out of
the room behind the first one and said:

'Miss Stone will see you now.'

I went through. The first thing I saw was the view of the harbour I had been expecting. From so high up Kowloon looked very
close, as if I could take a big jump and cross the harbour in one
leap. Then I saw Miss Stone. She was talking on the telephone.
The secretary showed me to a leather seat opposite her desk.
There were black-and-white photographs on the walls of people
with bad teeth who looked like circus performers. On the desk

where people keep pictures of their family was a photograph of a car. It was a silver Mercedes SLK.

'I have to tell you I don't think this one's going to fly. Yeah, me too. We'll talk later.'

She put down the telephone and stood holding out her hand.

'Matthew. I'm so sorry. I didn't want to seem like the killer bimbo from planet Zorgon but they put that call through just as Janice went to get you and I had to take it. So good to see you, you're looking wonderfully well. Has anyone offered you a refreshing beverage? Don't have a coffee, I swear they make it with harbour water. How's the family? Janice, can you bring me a Perrier?'

'I like these photographs,' I said.

'Arbus. Weege. They add a note of freak chic. From the Hong Kong point of view, the main thing about them is that they're outlandishly expensive.'

'I like these chairs also.'

'They're from the Conran shop in London. Or rather one of them is. I had it knocked off. I've got a couple more at home. Now – I've read your business plan. It seems okay. So what can I do for you?'

I made a slow breath in and out. I could hear my father-in-law standing in the garden shouting at his t'ai chi students: 'Good breathing, good *chi*! Bad breathing, no *chi*! You die!'

'The thrust of our business is to expand energetically into China.'

'Sure. Like I said, I've read the plan.'

'We have encountered certain difficulties which are not described there.'

I explained the position.

'The figures in our plan are, I believe, exceptionally cautious. This could be an enormous business. However, we have some short-term difficulties. Specifically, an important contract, one that guarantees our company's future, has fallen through in Guangzhou. A change in local politics has caused a change in local rules. You will be familiar with the phenomenon. We need advice, support, and subsequently further investment, to help resolve the situation. We need more friends in Guangzhou, Beijing, and' – I roughed – 'Shanghai. In short we need a new partner.'

She listened in a different way from how she had listened when she was a journalist. More aggressively. When I finished she sat pressing her fingers together.

'So the bottom line is, you need a big brother in China. Someone to open doors, run interference. Someone with more juice than the people who are jamming you up.'

'A partner and ally.'

'A bigger gorilla.'

I jumped. She smiled. 'It's an expression people are using. And in return?'

'Equity. A share of our business. It will be a big business, even a very big business, one day. Even by Mr Wo's standards. We are sure of that.'

It was the first time either of us had used his name. I was raising the stakes.

'You know I don't work directly with Mr Wo. My boss is Philip Oss.'

'You have *guanxi*, I know that. You're an extremely important person in the organisation. I know that the introduction to Mr Wo is within your gift.'

She moved about in her chair. Then she said:

'Okay, you're on. As I said, I looked at your numbers and they seem pretty good. The thing is, there's a time factor. He's off to London tomorrow evening to buy a mobile-phone company. That's a secret, by the way. Then he'll be out of town for a couple of weeks more. So it's this afternoon or never. I've spoken to his secretary and got you a slot at three. That's in about' – she looked at her watch – 'oops, it's less than half an hour. At his office. You know where it is?'

Everybody in Hong Kong knew that. It was the top floor of this same building. I did not know what to say.

'How long should I allow for the meeting?'

'If it goes well, who knows. If it doesn't, you'll be back on the street in two minutes. And just so you know, I won't be there. This one's all on you. Good luck.'

'Thank you. I say again, I'm –'

'One last thing. Now this really is between us. When I was a journalist back in England, I once had an editor who was mad about electronic devices. We used to say about him, "If he can't fuck it or plug it into the mains, he isn't interested." Now, if you omit the bit about sex, and replace the mains with a modem, that's Mr Wo. At the moment, it's all the new economy with him. So come up with an angle.'

I went downstairs and walked around for fifteen minutes to try and calm my nerves. I called my partner but his mobile phone was only taking messages. Then I took the lift up to the sixty-second floor. It was a separate lift which went to that floor only and I had to wait while a guard in the lobby rang to confirm my appointment.

I was expecting the best view of the harbour I had ever seen. But when I came out on the sixty-second floor I was disappointed. There was no direct view to a window. There was no sense of where I was. The office could have been anywhere.

The first receptionist led me through, introduced me to a second receptionist, and sat me down to wait. Again there was a big selection of magazines published by Wo family companies. There were two large framed photographs of oil tankers on one wall, and on another an electronic map of the world with the countries in which the Wos had an investment picked out in red. Almost all of the map was red. It was tempting to work out what the investments were. I could think of most of them: property, shipping, media. For a moment I could not think why most of South America was red. Then I remembered that Wo had recently bought a big share in the main Spanish-language Internet portal.

My previous experience had led me to expect a significant wait. There seemed to be a correlation between a person's sense of their own importance and how late they were. But at exactly 3 o'clock the door opened and a young Chinese man came out.

'Good afternoon, Mr Ho. I am Quentin Hong, Mr Wo's assistant. May I invite you to follow me?'

I went into Wo's office. Again there was no view. The drapes were drawn. A man sat in an armchair at the far side of the room and got up as I entered. It was Wo. He looked much smaller and frailer than he did in photographs. He pointed to a chair across from him. He was wearing thick tinted glasses.

'Mr Ho, has anyone offered you a drink?'

'I have no need of one, thank you, Mr Wo.'

295

His assistant sat in a straight-backed chair to one side of and behind Wo. He took out a pen and notepad. Wo took off his glasses and rubbed his eyes. Then he looked at the paper he had in his lap. It was the covering letter from my business plan. I had time to look around the office. There was a beautiful ornate kimono hanging on one wall, and above it a pair of Japanese swords in a display case. Across from the desk, near the door where I had come in, was a Go set with a position from a game set out on it. The room was lit with soft overhead lights and two desklamps, one of them beside Wo's chair. He noticed me looking around.

'I am having some trouble with my eyes,' he said. 'Daylight hurts them. Hence this arrangement.'

He went back to reading. I had been expecting more force and energy from him, but Wo seemed to be a mild man. Any fire was hidden. He did not act like a tycoon or a multi-billionaire. I realised that was probably because he had no need to.

He put the letter down. 'Miss Stone spoke to me. Good figures,' he said. 'Can I believe them?'

'Yes sir, I think so. China is a source of enormous potential opportunities for our company. As you know, it is extremely hot all over the country in summer. Air conditioning is scarce. When it comes, it could make as much difference as it did, say, to the south of the United States.' I had used that line before. It was always effective. 'We make the best industrial air-conditioning units in the world. Further down the line, as China's economic growth continues at the current rate, the wealth of the country will double every six or seven years. That means in twelve years' time the average Chinese will be four times richer than he is today. There are currently 1.2 billion Chinese. Taking these facts together we have here, in my opinion, the most important business opportunity in the history of mankind. I believe that in the medium term we are well positioned to sell an almost inconceivably large number of units.'

'But if your Guangzhou deal falls through . . .'

'Then no, you can't believe the figures. Our company will collapse.'

He nodded. 'So perhaps I should invest in the company who will get the contract in your stead.'

'I am sure that whoever has your backing will prove success-ful,' I said.

'It would certainly make life a lot simpler if that was true,' he said, turning slightly to look at his assistant, who was smiling.

'But less interesting, perhaps,' I said.

He looked at me again. 'Where are you from?'

'Sir, I was brought up in Mongkok, but now my mother and wife and daughter –'

'I meant before that. You have an accent.'

'Sir, I was born in Fujian. I came here when I was eight, in 1974.'

'That can't have been easy,' he said in Fujianese. I had not spo-ken the language in more than twenty-five years. I said:

'No, sir, it was not.'

Wo smiled.

'Well, well, a country boy. My father was from Fujian too. He said they always made the best pirates and the best businessmen, but that the Cantonese made the best whores, the best cooks, and the worst mothers-in-law.'

'My mother-in-law lives in Australia.'

'It sounds as if you have things arranged correctly. Still drink much Oolong tea?'

'Yes sir. I bring it back when I go to China.'

'Too strong for me. Makes me pee all the time. My father used to love it. Said it keeps a man thin. You have that skinny look.'

'It's partly the tea, and partly worry about our business, sir.'

'Ah yes – business,' said Wo. He tapped the plan, in its plastic folder, on his knee twice. 'You know all the talk about the future, China this, China that. Also the Internet this, the Internet that. My companies have many areas of interest, but this is now my main concern, you understand? The future. Other people study the past. I concentrate my efforts on the future. This is a good busi-ness on this piece of paper, but I see many many ideas for good businesses. The ones which interest me are about the future. About a different world. So tell me how this fits your proposal.'

Wilson had given me a line about this, which I had used when we were raising money from banks.

'Sir, the new economy means lots of big computers. Mainframes. Especially in China where there are so few. Internet systems, relay switches. One thing they all produce is heat. A great deal of heat. The kind of heat that you have to make go away with an air conditioner. If China gets a new economy, it will need a lot of air conditioning. Why else do they keep running out of power in California, sir?'

It was interesting: as I got Wo's attention he seemed to slow down. He showed less reaction, not more.

'. . . so an Internet economy means very many air conditioners. Somebody will make them. If not us, somebody else. But I would like it to be us.' He did not react. He was looking down. I struggled hard not to keep talking into the silence. He thought for perhaps a minute and then said:

'I will vouch for your business plan to my friends in Guangzhou. If the deal goes ahead, we will be partners.'

His assistant stood up. I did too. This time, Wo did not.

'A Fujian boy, eh?' he said. 'Good for you.'

The assistant led me out. 'Congratulations,' he said. 'That's the first pitch I've heard him say yes to in a year.'

I said, 'I can't feel my legs.'

The lift was like free fall. I went out into the road and a taxi missed me by a few inches. I took the overhead walkway back into Central. I had my mobile phone in my briefcase but did not want to call anyone yet. I felt as if I had done enough talking.

It was a sunny day and not too humid. I took my jacket off. I walked past the old government offices, across the road, and went through the park where the cricket ground used to be. There were many people sitting and talking and listening to music. I walked past Legco and across Statue Square and into Princess Building to find a café. I was beginning to panic about what I would say to my grandfather. I went to a wine shop to buy him a present and then I walked to the ferry terminal and bought a ticket for Cheung Chau.

I called the office from the ferry. Ah Wong answered.

'Wei?'

'He said yes.'

Wong whooped. I could hear him call to the others. There was cheering. 'You are a big hero. Now what?'

I realised that I didn't know. 'His people are setting it up. They'll be in touch. Listen, I'm not coming back to the office today. I'll see you in the morning.'

298

'Don't forget,' Wong said. 'One hundred million US.'

'I thought you'd forgotten.'

'No you didn't.'

Then I called my wife.

'Hello?'

'He said yes.'

She let out a very long sigh. It was as if she had been holding her breath since the last time I saw her. 'So when are you coming home?' she said.

'Soon as I can. But first –'

'You've got to tell Grandfather.'

'Yes. I'm nervous.'

She let out a sigh almost as long as the first one. 'Good luck.'

The people who took the ferry were different at this time of day. It was something I had noticed before. After work and in the morning the traffic is all commuters. But this ferry was full of tourists and people who had jobs with irregular hours.

The harbour was rough, and one or two people looked as if they were feeling sick. I stood in the air for about twenty minutes, and then when I had filled my lungs with the breeze and the smell of the harbour I went back inside. In the cabin, three boys were crowded together trying to watch *The Matrix* on a portable DVD player. All three of them were wearing caps with the Nike swoosh.

We came in past the fish farms. Because it was only afternoon, the restaurants around the little harbour were quiet. The night fishermen had not gone out yet and the day fishermen had not returned. I bought a *South China Morning Post* and set off up the hill to give Grandfather my news.

I knew he would be upset. But I would tell him that I did it because I am a refugee. I had no choice. The future is more important than the past. I did it because I am a refugee.